Praise for *Even In Dark*[...]

This is a Holocaust story certain t[...] [...]f the quiet heroism of its characters [...] [...]n *in Darkness* is a stunning historical endeavor.

—Foreword Reviews

This beautifully written story gives the reader insight into a woman who followed an unusual path, and a different angle on post–World War II life.

—Jewish Book Council

Stark-Nemon writes with an intimate elegance, as if she herself had stood witness to the fracturing of her extended family to the far corners of the globe. . . . This is a story of hope.

—Daily North Shore

Throughout the book, [Stark-Nemon] demonstrates the beauty and the treasure inherent in good storytelling, both by the stories told by characters in the book and by her own skill at weaving events into a coherent story line that honors love in all its forms . . . and respects courage in the many manifestations called forth by the Holocaust.

—*Chicago Examiner*

Barbara Stark-Nemon's novel, *Even in Darkness*, is a journey into and out of the darkness of World War II Germany. Masterfully written, the story draws you into the life of protagonist Kläre Kohler. I felt like I had entered a lovingly crafted tapestry torn by the horrors of war but also filled with love and color and vibrant with life. Woven throughout are threads of brilliant description and pitch-perfect dialogue. A very satisfying read.

—Rita M. Gardner, author of *The Coconut Latitudes*

Barbara Stark-Nemon's debut novel is a stunning portrait of her real-life aunt, Kläre Kohler, as she negotiates impossible hardship. Kläre demonstrates survival with grace and dignity in this expertly crafted, engaging read, and teaches us that with faith and perseverance, survival can lead to reinvention and to a life filled with love and gratitude.

—Claudia Whitsitt, author of the Samantha Series, *Between the Lines*, and *The Wrong Guy*

Kläre Kohler is an unforgettable character whose daily acts of kindness and caring breathe light and air into the most horrific of times as she touches and lifts those who surround her. Beautifully and honestly written, well researched and carefully crafted, this is a book that lingers long in the mind.

—Carole Bumpus, author of *A Cup of Redemption* and *Recipes for Redemption*

Heartbreaking and uplifting, haunting and triumphant.

—Dorene O'Brien, author of *Voices of the Lost and Found*

I finished reading the book with a quiet sense of joy that is rare in this literary world of bleak endings and oversimple conclusions.

—Andi Cumbo-Floyd, author of *The Slaves Have Names*

It's hard to read a novel that centers on the Holocaust, but Stark-Nemon's story is so absorbing and delicately told that *Even in Darkness* is not a dark read. She cuts the dread we feel about what is to come with a nuanced view of the daily life of the protagonist, the small decisions and actions that will seal her fate. I found the love story one of the most compelling parts of the narrative, as well as the wonderful way the author gives us the texture of life in a part of the world unfamiliar to me. This is a book that will linger long after you put it down.

—Celine Keating, author of *Layla* and *Play for Me*

EVEN IN DARKNESS

EVEN IN DARKNESS

A Novel

BARBARA
STARK-NEMON

She Writes Press

Published 2015
Printed in the United States of America
ISBN: 978-1-63152-956-6
Library of Congress Control Number: 2014915884

For information, address:
She Writes Press
1563 Solano Ave #546
Berkeley, CA 94707

She Writes Press is a division of SparkPoint Studio, LLC.

In loving memory of Kläre and Ernst, who inspired this story, and to my husband and sons and their families, who give me my daily practice in love and devotion.

1 1913, Norderney

If I say yes to Jakob Kohler, I could make a nice home for him. Mutti and Papa like him . . . He is serious about me and wants to make a good life. The argument against the match lay pressed at the edge of a sigh that Kläre Ente struggled to hold back. Her thoughts focused with the steady rhythm of pedaling and the deep breaths she was able to take, having loosened her corset, untying the knot that lodged in her chest. A sweet scent of clover and raspberries floated on the breeze as Kläre cycled down to the North Sea village.

She conjured Jakob Kohler's deep brown eyes and the inscrutable expression on his large face. Tall and thin, he comported himself with little passion, but with the self-assurance of a man no longer a mere youth. Kläre wondered for the hundredth time how his large hands might feel if allowed past the strictures of propriety and his curious reticence. These thoughts no longer shocked her, but she experienced a pensive doubt as to how to weigh them in her decision.

In these unsettled times, her father, Jonah, had remained in Hörde to tend to the family livestock feed business, leaving the conduct of holidaymaking to Kläre, her mother, and her two sisters. Here, in this sleepy seaside village, they were removed from the insidious pressure of impending hostilities between Germany and England that plagued daily life at home in Hörde.

A woman from the village approached on a bicycle and Kläre automatically moved to the right of the path, still lost in thought. A moment later, however, she stopped, intent on the approaching figure. Only yesterday, near this very spot, two boys barely out of knee pants had ridden toward her. One of them had suddenly veered into her path, and reflexively, Kläre had steered away into the brambles of the hedgerow. She had not fallen, but her leg had become entangled in her skirts and the heavy steel of the bicycle had banged painfully against her thigh. The boys laughed as they raced on, and unmistakably, she had heard "Jew!" as their bicycles receded behind her.

When had the florid Christian neighbors pedaling their way to and from the shops lost their stolid place in the scenery and begun to etch menace into the landscape instead? Kläre filed away the need for this new wariness for later consideration. The approaching woman passed with an unsmiling nod, and Kläre rode on, returning to her thoughts.

Jakob Kohler's courtship had been brief. He'd met her father through a supplier. The Entes, who were good businessmen with a reputation for honesty and acumen, sought out the young attorney's counsel as it became more difficult to comply with the conflicting regulations of the Imperial government. Jonah Ente worried quietly to his family that the loosening of economic strictures on Jewish businesses, with their subsequent success in Hörde and elsewhere, would feed the anti-Semitism that he believed lay close to the surface of the German social order—an order to which the Entes eagerly adhered.

Kohler's mild, unassuming manner and meticulous knowledge of regulations assisted the Entes in maintaining their business. Kläre never knew when or by whom the decision was made to arrange her introduction to the young lawyer. An invitation was extended, and Jakob Kohler visited on a Sunday.

Kläre's sister Frieda and her husband Oskar had come from Dülken, where Oskar had his own feed business. Like her mother, Frieda was quiet, dutiful, and devoted to the skills of homemaking. Oskar was large, loud, and raucous and fit in well with the Ente men. His booming voice, boisterous laugh, and continuous banter filled the sitting room, leaving Kläre to study her prospective suitor. A faint smile lay uneasily on Jakob Kohler's face as he listened to the explosive Oskar and his ribald jokes. Kläre watched as Jakob glanced at Jonah Ente, perhaps for an indication of the patriarch's concern at the impropriety of such language and humor in the presence of women.

Finding no apparent objection from the head of the household, Kohler remained passive until Jonah and Oskar moved to the study to discuss shared business interests, and the youngest Ente daughter, Trude, was summoned by her mother to the kitchen. Left with Frieda and Kläre, Jakob politely began a conversation about Frieda's home in Dülken and Oskar's business. Never addressing Frieda's obvious pregnancy, he spoke briefly and quietly until Kläre finally asked, "Have you long been in the law?" Her steady gaze penetrated her guest's detachment.

"Since the death of my father three years ago, I have been the primary Rechtsanwalt in the firm, but for two years before that I was his assistant." Jakob's response was mild, but it answered the gentle challenge of her entry to the conversation.

"My brother studies the law in Munich," Kläre said, "but I fear, should we go to the war, he will fight before he has a chance to enter a practice. As it is, he spends much of his time with a saber." Kläre's eyes fell to her hands, which were resting on the perfectly pressed folds of last year's dress. She wondered briefly if this man had noticed that the dress should be shorter, the skirt slimmer, the bodice looser to be current in style, but she decided immediately that he had not noticed, would not notice.

"Naturally, if there is war, I must serve," Jakob said without warmth.

Raising her eyes once more, Kläre watched him stand as he caught sight of her mother. A tall lace collar and carefully pressed sleeves softened Johanna Ente's strong, intelligent face. Dark hair shot with steel grey was captured neatly in a bun at the back of her head.

Johanna stood in the doorway of the sitting room, glancing at Kläre, a trace of disapproval flickering across the space between them as Kläre reached up to tuck a wayward curl into its pin. Frieda began to rise awkwardly from her chair, but Kläre waved her sister back and stood quickly to assist her mother.

If there is war, I must serve. She mused over these words, so different from her brother's, who wrote as if fighting would be a more adventurous version of the saber duels of his Jewish fraternity. Kläre poured coffee, and felt her color rise as Jakob Kohler's eyes followed her. She handed him a cup and then a slice of her mother's scrumptious *apfelkuchen.*

The afternoon visit had nearly concluded when Jakob Kohler, beginning his formal leave-taking, turned to Kläre. "It was a pleasure to meet you today, Fräulein Ente. Perhaps I may again have the opportunity to see you." He extended his hand to hers and bowing slightly, searched her face for a moment.

"That would be nice, yes," she answered.

Moments later, he was gone.

Kläre cleared the dishes, noting her mother's studious avoidance of comment. Not for the first time, she wished that her mother, whom she loved and revered, was more approachable about affairs of the heart.

Frieda was still seated in the sitting room, eyes closed, with one hand on the side of her swelling belly in the age-old contact of a mother feeling, from inside and out, the quickening life of her child. She opened her eyes and patted the seat of the chair next to her.

"Klärchen, did you like him?" Frieda's brown eyes and dark hair contrasted utterly with her sister's fair coloring.

"He seems like a nice man." Kläre spoke slowly.

"Only nice?" Frieda leaned toward her sister. "You speak about the squirrels in the garden with more interest than that." She dropped backward into the chair with a short gasp and closed her eyes as she continued. "You will like to be married, Klärchen, but"—she once again looked directly at her sister—"to the right man, so get to know him a little. It's a long life you will spend together with a husband. He looks very serious, this Kohler. Do you feel any spark with him?"

"I don't know exactly," Kläre responded. "He's older. He has a profession already. I don't think he's looking for a silly girl with romantic dreams."

"Ya, but what are you looking for, Kläre?" The sisters stared at one another for a long moment before Kläre dropped her troubled gaze and fingered the pleats of her skirt.

There had been a number of further occasions: more Sunday coffees, a dinner, and a walk home from the Red Cross, where Kläre volunteered to learn first aid—her hedge against the helplessness she felt in the run up to war. During this time, Jakob worked frequently with her father and uncles and slowly got to know them in their business and occasionally in their homes.

For the most part, Jakob was formal and unobtrusive. He rarely began a conversation, particularly of a personal nature, but he always responded to the direct questions that Kläre found opportunities to ask him.

"Are you close to your family?"

"I have lost many family members and we are spread across several states. I care for my mother, but my sisters can do more of what she requires. I don't speak much to my brother. He is also an attorney." A mask of disappointment stole across Jakob's features. Kläre did not ask more, though it pained her to imagine such a separation.

"Do you enjoy the theater or the museum?"

"I cannot say that I choose often to go. Perhaps if I knew more, or had someone to go with . . ."

Kläre blushed. She was transported by a fine play or the well-done painting, and dreamed of a husband who would take her to Cologne and Berlin. While cultural offerings in Hörde were meager, her mother had always insisted on taking the children to Dortmund and even to Cologne to see the symphony, the opera, and ballet.

"Do you read?"

"I read quite regularly in the law."

"Do you go to the dances or to the beer garden with your friends?"

"I do what most men do. As you may have noticed, my conversation is not fascinating." Kläre gazed up at Jakob's profile as he walked solidly beside her and knew that this man would not glide effortlessly across a dance floor, holding her confidently in his arms, but perhaps—for her—he would learn . . .

On this occasion, Jakob took her elbow and guided her along the path in the public garden, staring straight ahead, seemingly unable to speak and attend to the physical contact between them at the same time. It was pleasant to be steered carefully toward her street, and Kläre felt a mild excitement at the idea that some threshold of familiarity had been crossed.

Other small things changed. Jonah Ente, having tried to engage Jakob in the banter he shared with his father, brothers, son, and son-in-law, recognized that it was not natural to the younger man, and—with some care, Kläre thought—adopted an inviting but more formal tone when he was present. Jakob, whose reserve suited Johanna, was now greeted with one of the matriarch's rare smiles when he visited. When asked to join the family for Passover dinner, Johanna explained, "Our observance is mostly in memory of our parents. We aren't strict."

"I haven't had much training myself," Jakob replied. "I find I haven't much use for it, though I believe in being Jewish." Johanna's approval beamed from her smile as she served Jakob a steaming plate of brisket, roast potatoes, and stewed fruit. Seated next to him, Kläre wondered what Jakob meant. *I believe in being Jewish.* To her, the practice of Judaism had belonged in the home of her grandparents, both now gone, and in the Sabbath mornings of her early childhood, when she'd gone to synagogue with her grandfather and uncles. Since then, religion had faded from the Entes' family life like a wistful dream—remembered, but overtaken by the waking demands of daily life, and the menace that associations with the word "Jew" increasingly brought. Still, Kläre felt the bond with other Jewish families—in their education, a certain brand of humor, recognition—even as the outward manifestations of observance fell away. Perhaps this is what Jakob meant.

And so it happened, without drama, and in the midst of rising fear and concern for the world outside their home, that the Entes found themselves regarding Jakob Kohler as more than an acquaintance, more than a business associate, and more than a casual suitor to Kläre. It came as no surprise to anyone other than Kläre when Jakob presented himself to her father with an offer of marriage to the eighteen-year-old girl. Given consent, Jakob quickly made arrangements to visit Kläre, and with more intensity than he had ever spoken to her, asked her to marry him.

Stunned, Kläre was silent, searching the unusually eager face before her, her hands wrapped in his warm ones. "I am so honored that you would ask me such a thing," she finally said softly. "Please, let me speak to my parents. We go next week for a holiday; you will have my answer when we return."

A flicker of hurt passed across Jakob's face, but he immediately restored his composure and pleasant demeanor, and said only, "I would very much like to have a marriage soon . . . There is much talk of war, and I don't know when I might need to join the army."

Kläre stood on her toes and brushed her lips to Jakob's smooth, shaven cheek. It was unseemly to be so forward, but Kläre wished now to act on the feelings that stirred within her. Jakob pressed his eyes closed for a moment—then, looking directly at her, and with a power she had not previously ascribed to him, he pulled her to him in a swift embrace.

"Thank you," he said, and let her go.

It was now but ten days later, and the Ente women were settled into the village of Norderney and the routine of a holiday framed by the daily deepening of charges, counter-charges, threats, and counter-threats between Germany and its neighboring countries. Many of the holiday regulars were absent this year, either out of concern for safety and mounting instability, or, more often, because of financial difficulties.

At eighteen years old, Kläre already longed for the simpler days of her childhood in Hörde, when school, helping with cooking and sewing at home, and especially the magical Friday Sabbath evenings at the elegant home of her grandparents had held a warm predictability. On those nights, all the cousins and their mothers would assemble, and no sooner had Kläre settled herself on the scratchy sofa in the large sitting room when the door would rattle and the hall fill with the sound of stamping and animated voices as the Ente men arrived.

The younger children would fly to the door with boisterous greetings for their fathers, uncles, and grandfather. Kläre would wait patiently for the reward of her father's strong arms lifting her and drawing her close to the damp, smoky wool of his suit. A long and delicious dinner would follow. Eventually, the grown sons and their father would move from prayer to discussion, then to stories, and then to laughter, jokes, and play. Kläre would find her way to her father's lap, and her brother Ernst would stand among his uncles, learning the arts of argument and storytelling.

Kläre felt the sheltering memories of those halcyon days drain away on a sigh as she steered her bicycle down the final hill, the sea sparkling in front of her. Carriages, perambulators, mothers, and children crowded the streets and Kläre found it easier to walk the bicycle the last 100 meters to the rented house near the end of the seashore lane. An unfamiliar carriage stood before the door. Kläre leaned her bicycle against the rail and was about to enter when the door opened and her brother Ernst appeared before her.

"Ernst! My God! What are you doing here? We didn't expect you." Her brother stiffly allowed her to throw her arms around his neck and then push him back. "What is this uniform? What has happened?"

"I've joined the army. We are forming a cavalry unit: Frisch, Rosenmann, and I."

"No, Ernst, but why? There is no war declared. Jakob says he will wait and then join. Can you not do this as well?"

Ernst's amusement at his sister's outburst overcame his momentary annoyance at her questions. He took Kläre's arm and strolled in the direction of the seaside path.

"Wait? Wait for what? We must have an army." He smiled wickedly at his sister and changed the subject. "What's all this I hear about Jakob Kohler? Jakob this, Kohler that: Suddenly all I hear is his name. What are you thinking, my little sister?"

Kläre looked at her brother, always filled with the importance of the moment, yet lovingly attached to her, his closest sister. The strong and stocky man before her had a vital air of assurance that anchored the very sunlight around him. Even so, she could still see the schoolboy, a knapsack strapped to his back, bursting into the house flushed and breathing hard, exuding the smell of fresh air, wool, and hurry, his hair standing wildly around his thin face as he reported some fight or transgression that would demand her worry, her mediation, in some way.

Surely, Ernst would not understand her distress. For him there was always a clear path, a right decision. His smile now told her that in her absence, someone had spoken to him about Jakob's proposal.

"I . . . I am thinking of marrying him," Kläre said quietly. She continued before Ernst had a chance to say a word, more urgently this time—"But really, Ernst, must you do this?"

"Klärchen, don't you understand?" he said, his face grave. "There will be war. Jews cannot sit and wait. We have to fight harder and more bravely than anyone to prove ourselves." Ernst's tone was sharp, but his look was by turns proud and pleading.

Meeting her brother's pale blue eyes, in this holiday town where there was no real holiday, Kläre understood only that he was leaving for war. Fear for his safety and the inexorable change that was upon them all sent a chill coursing through her. The air seemed to vanish from the sun-filled scene, throwing the sea wall and waves behind it into high relief. Kläre stared at her brother, at the colorful sash draping down across his broad barrel chest, at the buttons of his uniform, glinting in the sunlight—and in that moment, her girl's dreaming gave way to a woman's decision. This was no time for selfish notions of romantic love. *Kläre Kohler.* She would have to get used to the sound of it.

2 1923, Hörde

Kläre leaned back in the wrought iron chair, eyes closed, to let the autumn sun warm her face under her broad-brimmed hat. A gentle breeze lifted the curls from her neck, sending wisps of hair across her face. Amalie had not yet arrived, and the café had only a few scattered patrons. A piece of torte lay untouched on the plate before her, her coffee cooling, neither likely to alleviate the vague queasiness which was with her now constantly. Even a café as fine as Hunziger's had not returned to using pure butter, and eggs were scarce. Still so much was missing from the years before the war!

Her face brightened as, looking up, she saw Amalie pass through the heavy glass doors and scan the terrace. Kläre waved a gloved hand and stood. Amalie approached and, holding her friend at arm's length, studied her with the frank intimacy born of childhood friendship. Immediately a question formed in her raised eyebrows and tilted chin. Kläre reddened at the scrutiny.

"Yes, I have news," she said, smiling. "We were not certain, but my mother thinks it is already sure."

"Ach, Klärchen, how wonderful." Amalie's voice caught, a mixture of joy and pain passing across the features of her pleasant face. Kläre reached over the small table and squeezed her friend's arm gently. Neither woman spoke, each one absorbed in a long moment of remembering. Hans Hermann, Amalie's fiancé, had died a gruesome death in the trenches of Verdun during the war. Kläre shuddered at the memory of the days and nights she had spent at Amalie's side after the news came.

Her own life had been a kaleidoscope of activity during the war years. She had volunteered at the hospital while Jakob was in the army, keeping their small flat and making daily visits to her parents. Her sister Trude was still at home, spirited and thoughtless with youth. Frieda, already pregnant with a second child, had come back to Hörde to live with her little one, Martin, as Oskar was gone to the war as a supply man. Kläre's youngest cousin, Paul, had also joined the Ente household when his mother Anna died. By day, Kläre brought her healing touch as a massage therapist to the broken bodies of young soldiers whose suffering made her heart ache. By night, she cooked, cleaned, and helped her mother and sisters with the children, in solidarity with her family and their men at war.

She frequently saw Amalie, whose own childhood had been joyless, and who had found in Hans Hermann a true love and the hope of a stable and contented life. His intuition of Amalie's depth and sweetness came with the bursting optimism and hearty laugh of a man able and willing to create happiness for the woman he loved. Slowly but surely, Amalie had been won, not only by the man, but also by the belief that she could be happy—and make another happy. This Kläre had treasured for her friend. Hans had gone to the war, showering Amalie with promises that all would go well.

How different had been Jakob's reluctant, thoroughly considered entry to the officer's corps. He had used his status as an attorney and his age—thirty-six years old—as stepping-stones toward assignment as a lieutenant in the field office, with its relative safety. Kläre had been grateful, but troubled in a vague way that her husband had neither the passion nor the belief in the importance of the German effort that Ernst and Hans felt. She, in turn, felt Amalie's abject fear for Hans's safety, and her own for Ernst's, more keenly at times than her worry for Jakob. Her guilt was a rebuke for the distance that disparity in age and temperament contributed to her marriage.

One July day, in the war's first year, Amalie had shared with Kläre a letter that Hans had sent to his father. In contrast to the letters Hans sent Amalie directly, which were full of loving and optimistic messages, these descriptions of his experiences terrified her.

Dearest Father,

I beg your pardon that for so long you haven't heard from me, but I couldn't write because there was too much to do.

Since we came from Urlaub in April we have been busy making communications for the military transport. The whole region is laid deep in unbroken fire. I've had to run double wiring with many switches and of course there are breakdowns and special requests by the hour. The shooting is continuous, from both sides.

On 22 June the French attacked, and with success held their position. That was a crazy day. From early morning, there was fierce gunfire. Since our lines were down, we got a light signal from Louvematt. The French took the Fort, but later we recovered it. Then a grenade struck that smashed everything into confusion; the shrapnel fell through the roof and walls. Our men escaped through the shelter entranceway. We are glad that we are out of that hell . . .

This letter was like the ones Kläre had gotten from Ernst: full of incomprehensible excitement for the adventure, a young man's dismissal of personal danger laced with keen descriptions of tactical circumstances. Hans knew better than to write all this directly to Amalie, but to his father he wrote of it proudly.

Not a week later, the telegram had come. Amalie had found Kläre at her parents' home, in the kitchen with Johanna, attempting to create a meal with the meager wartime resources available to them. She had stood shaking in the hall as Kläre dried her hands and pulled her pale, stricken friend into the sitting room.

"He is dead," Amalie had gasped, her voice harsh and toneless, already beyond tears. "The news was brought to his mother." Kläre's hand had flown to her chest, shock robbing her of breath.

Hans's death, reported by a fellow soldier as brave but wretched, had stricken Kläre deeply. Now, four years later, Kläre read the continued grief in the summoning of composure to her friend's face—for the loss of her lover, for the children that would never come from the brief, precious time Amalie had been granted with him.

"Klärchen, it will be a spring baby," said Amalie. "Will you like it to be a boy or a girl?"

Normal chatter did not return as easily to Kläre, who already wondered at the wisdom of bringing a child into the world at all after the devastation of the war. Jakob had been insistent that a family was required at this time in his life. He had a legal practice to revitalize, and a family to show for his marriage. He had been ill for months from gas poisoning. Having a child represented a return to normalcy that he craved.

"Jakob, of course wishes a boy, and I think a boy would be fine." Kläre carefully subdued her response. "Do you enjoy your job?" she asked her friend, eager to change the topic.

"Ya, it is fine . . . Herr Baum works hard and is a very good boss. Do you remember the Grussmans? They had a daughter Frieda's age."

"Yes of course, she was a heavy one, but good on the piano, right?"

"Yes, exactly. Well, Herr Grussman came to the company last week to speak with Herr Baum. I was taking dictation at the time, and stayed while they spoke. Herr Grussman went on about this new party. They say all the troubles with the money and the war are because of the Jews." Amalie met Kläre's eyes, reading in them permission to continue. "He said the Jews were not real fighters in the war. Does your father speak about this?"

"That's impossible!" Kläre sat bolt upright. "Ernst has just gotten the Iron Cross first class for his fighting in the Cavalry." Ernst's photo in Cavalry uniform sat on the highly polished table in her mother's sitting room, his proud, fierce face distinguished by the saber scars across his forehead and cheek.

Kläre's indignation put an angry flash in her eyes. Suddenly, her draining nausea and the softness of her swelling body were forgotten.

"My father is on the town council. He has worked hard, and he gave feed and money from his business to the army." She sat back and looked at Amalie across the table. Dearest of her childhood friends, Amalie had spent many long afternoons at the Ente home and at their table, thirsty for the kindness and generosity she found there. How could she repeat this assertion, even as hearsay? Kläre was at a loss to understand the question, however innocent, in her friend's open face. She was suddenly exhausted.

Amalie moved on to speak more of her job as a stenographer. She had gone to work over the objection of her father and despite the general disapproval of a young woman of her class securing employment. The smallest of jealousies arose in Kläre as she listened to Amalie's animated chatter. This world of offices and coworkers and commerce, limited though it might be, provided precisely the kind of stimulation that Kläre lacked in the life that lay ahead of her. The time for her youth, for her own world of work, and her dream of a life enriched by the arts seemed to have vanished in the long years of war and the toil and deprivations of keeping a home. Jakob Kohler worked hard in his practice, but what little interest and willingness he'd had in the life of the mind outside his work, or for the conversation of clever people, seemed to have been poisoned out of his spirit just as the gas from the war had poisoned his body.

Kläre shook these thoughts impatiently from her head as she nodded and smiled at Amalie, and tried a morsel of the poor pastry on her plate.

"Tell me of your work at the hospital," Amalie said.

"Ach, it was so hard in the war years. Such terrible injuries we had; more than we knew what to do with, but the doctors taught us whatever they could, and I particularly learned to work with amputees." Kläre became animated. "The muscles and nerves were so disturbed. We learned effleurage and petrissage. It's like long strokes and a sort of gentle pinching. These new techniques they hope will help the nerves and muscles to reconnect and reduce the inflammation and perhaps also the pain." She leaned forward toward her friend.

"The boys had so much to learn just to move their bodies again. The shock and the poison—you know, sometimes I could just touch them and know what to do to make them feel better. Other times, nothing felt better. In fact, sometimes they couldn't bear to have me do anything at all. When that happened, we could only talk or sing, or read."

"And when Jakob came home?" Amalie's voice was gentle.

"It helped, this work, when he got back." Kläre continued. "At first, he was so sick and he wanted me there all the time. I couldn't do much else. He's better now, not completely well, but better." Kläre could not tell her friend that the formerly gentle but confident physical passion she'd shared with Jakob had also fallen victim to his injuries—that since the war, illness had become a focus of their lives, and their sexual activity had become utilitarian and infrequent. Instead, she said only, "I miss my work at the hospital."

"Ya, and now with the baby coming you'll be busy. Are you sick?"

"No . . . no, it's not so bad. Really, it's not."

Amalie's kind face shone, but a vague sense of unease remained with Kläre as they went on to talk of other things. When an hour had passed, she hugged her friend good-bye and walked the short distance to the Ente home. Her mother had telephoned, asking her to visit, and Kläre had heard something disturbing in her voice. She was reluctant to add the worrisome questions that Amalie had introduced to whatever her mother wished to speak to her about; she resolved to say nothing until she'd heard her mother out.

The entry hall was dark with the fading afternoon, but familiar fragrances of fresh baking and oiled walnut, tinged with a musty hint of cigar smoke, greeted Kläre with their comforting warmth. She hung her coat in the hall and walked back toward the kitchen, calling "Mutti?" as she pushed the swinging door open. She was surprised to find both her parents in the large kitchen.

Jonah smiled weakly at his daughter. "Good afternoon, Klärchen. How are you feeling?"

"I'm fine, thank you, Papa. But what are you doing home so early? Is everything all right?" Kläre looked with worry from one parent to the other.

"Ya, so here is a letter we got this morning. It's from your cousin Arne," her mother said, weariness softening her voice. She retrieved the stiff pages from the pocket of her apron and handed them to Kläre.

Kläre sat at the massive worktable and read.

17 May, 1923

Dearest Uncle Jonah,

It grieves me to write to you under these circumstances, especially after all you have done for my family: caring for my father in his last illness, and taking my brother Paul into your family as if he were your own.

If I were not desperate, I would never ask you to do more and risk your own safety as well. However, I have reached the end of what I can do for myself, and I face doom if I do nothing. I am sure by now you have heard of the riot in Dortmund two days ago. The Brownshirts attacked the Jewish shops, and this time they did not only break windows and pillage the goods. They went from house to house, and pulled men from their homes and beat them; they attacked women and children as well.

Our people were terrified, and most hid from or submitted to those animals. You will think I should have done the same, but I could not—cannot—give in to this outrage. All I could think is that it could have been my mother, G-d rest her soul, or one of my sisters.

There was a terrible fight when five of us resisted their entry to our apartment house. All but one of us escaped, but they will be looking everywhere for us. I must leave Dortmund and Germany immediately. I fear that I have put all who know me in peril, particularly if I stay.

Please understand, Uncle, that I haven't put you at risk for no reason. You once offered to help me make a new start in

America. I beg you now for that help. I have made the money for ship's passage, but have not a penny to buy food or other provisions for the journey. I can wait no longer to leave.

I will come Friday early to the cellar where, in happier times, I helped you shovel coal and load the root crops for the winter. If you can spare any money or provisions, I swear I will make it up to you one day. I don't dare call on Paul directly, but please tell him that I think of him always, and beg him to follow me soon to America, where I will take care of him and all of you when I am established.

With my highest regards to you, my Uncle, and to Tante Johanna, Ernst, Frieda, Kläre, and Trude.

Arne

Trouble no one needed was the special gift that Arne Ente had always brought to his struggling family. Closest to the mother who'd died and ill-equipped to lose himself in the care and responsibility for his five siblings, Arne was outspoken in his contempt for the German social order, prone to calling his countrymen law-obsessed Jew-haters.

"I don't understand this. What happened?" Kläre gripped the edge of the table and sought an answer in her father's eyes.

"There were gangs of demonstrators last week in Dortmund. The police lost control."

"Demonstrations against what? What did Arne have to do with it?"

"Against the Republic, against the Jews, against the Communists . . . It's happening more and more everywhere. They burned businesses in Dortmund, and Arne didn't hide like the other Jews. There is an order for him to report to the police." Jonah clenched and unclenched his fist. Johanna leaned over the large kitchen table, the weight of her fear seeming to bear down on her large hands. The three of them formed a pyramid over the well-worn table as if the air between them could protect what semblance remained of a safe and orderly life.

"Papa, you will of course help him." Kläre looked with alarm from her father to her mother and back. Johanna bowed her head into her broad shoulders, and Jonah slowly met his daughter's eyes.

He reached for the letter from his nephew and sighed deeply as he handed it to Johanna. "Yes, of course. I will go now to the bank."

"Where is Paul?" Kläre asked, turning to her mother.

"He will be home from school shortly," she replied. "Perhaps you will get him to help pack some food and a valise."

Kläre's face was a strained mask as she watched Paul read his brother's letter. She sighed deeply and tightened her hand on his shoulder—and when he turned to her, she took his face in her hands and spoke gently.

"You will help Tante Johanna and me to pack a bag for Arne, yes? He will be all right, Paulie; he is a strong and clever boy, just like you."

In due time the oilcloth bag was stuffed with sausage, rolls, a precious apple, and the end of the prior evening's roast, sandwiched between thick slices of bread.

"Kläre," Paul asked plaintively. "Why is this happening? Will I see Arne again? What happened to the Hanselmanns? The Krafts? All our neighbors?"

"My sweet, I cannot understand it myself," Kläre answered. "People blame others for their problems in these hard times, and Arne got into a fight. He would be in danger if he stayed. But you are safe here with us now, and you know your brother loves you, don't you, sweetheart? He will send for you when he can. Beyond this, I cannot explain it myself. But come with me upstairs and we'll get ready for bed."

As she turned to leave the kitchen, Kläre saw Johanna swiftly pull a handkerchief from her starched apron and wipe away tears before packing a small almond cake into the top of the bag. This was her specialty, and a favorite of Arne's.

Paul and Kläre threw the letter containing Arne's wretched story and desperate requests into the fire. As they made their way up the stairs, they heard Johanna's whisper:

"Arne, Arne. Thank God Anna did not live to see this day." Paul bent forward, and Kläre put her arm around his thin shoulder.

The next morning, just after the sun made its smooth way above the horizon, wakening the day with rose light and crystalline dew, Arne Ente stepped into his uncle's garden. Kläre and Paul watched from high above in the garret room. Leaving the shadow of the massive linden tree, Arne stole furtively to the rear of the ample house, reappearing a few minutes later with a small valise and the oilcloth satchel.

As Arne reentered the brightening light once more, he raised his eyes, and Paul waved in the window far above. For an instant, Arne's shoulders slumped as though his purposeful resolve had vanished, and Kläre imagined that he wished to be here with his brother, inseparable as the two had been in the years before their mother died and Paul had come to live with the Entes. It had been months since Arne had seen Paul, and now he was going to America—to the city of Philadelphia, where a friend had secured him the promise of a job in a hotel frequented by Europeans. But Arne's air of dejection did not last for long. With a final look and a quick nod up at the garret window, he turned and was gone.

Kläre stood beside Paul as he watched his brother slip from the back of the garden into the shade of the linden tree. She could feel the pounding wave of his loss—a force that drove the boy back to his narrow bed and the shelter of his feather quilt.

3 1928, Hörde

Ernst and Ditha had brought their baby, Margaret, from Berlin for a rare visit home. Ditha was kind and solicitous and elegant as always. It was easy to understand Ernst's adoration of this lovely woman, and the open affection between them. Ernst was never far from his wife—his hand on her chair or touching her shoulder, his eyes feeding on her beauty.

Kläre marveled that her brother had so thoroughly given up his wild bachelorhood for a settled family life. His law practice in Berlin was successful beyond all expectation, and the stories he shared of society in the capital city were the stuff of his dreams. Ernst Ente from Hörde, a wealthy and successful attorney in Berlin; who would have thought it? Kläre still remembered the boy of their childhood: short in stature and underachieving as a student, though boundlessly energetic and always ready to engage in a prank. He had strained against the limits of their small town.

Ernst had woven his stories long into the previous evening, telling of theater, opera, long dinners, and fine bottles of wine. Tales of baby Margaret, whose own keen personality had fully emerged in the year of her infancy, made her father's eyes dance. Jakob had smiled and listened with the rest, speaking little but with measured pride about his own growing legal practice. The evening at the Ente parents' had ended late, but Kläre's weariness was more of spirit than body. It took great effort to represent her life to her brother as fulfilling—to convince him, as she worked to convince herself, that her hard-working husband

and she, as homemaker and mother, were building a life of promise, of interest. Kläre dared not ask herself what might be missing, what fervor for the future was tethered within her—but the strain pulled at the muscles of her smiling face and robbed her of enthusiasm for further talk.

At home this morning, with the tasks of a new day before her, Kläre reflected with mixed pleasure and ruefulness on her brother's happiness. She had withstood the scrutiny of his questions about Jakob's work, their friends and social events, and most of all, her children. Erwin, now five years old, was in school in the first form, though not happily. He was nothing like his uncle, whose Hebrew name had been given to the child with such love and anticipation. Ernst the uncle was vibrant, daring, quick-witted, and brave, if not always wise. Erwin the child was serious, nearly plodding, and found little in which to delight.

Earlier that morning, Kläre had waved good-bye to Jakob and Erwin as they'd stepped into the cool morning together. Jakob's deliberate steps had faltered as he stumbled slightly on the pavement. Erwin had waited without reaction for his father to recover. Father and son each faced the world expecting neither joy nor opposition; rather, it was simply work they moved toward. While Kläre loved them both, deeply, their weight of spirit lay heavily on her heart.

She suddenly longed to strike out into the day on her own—to fill her lungs with fresh air, startle the small flock of brown birds from their feasting on dried berries in the hedge at the end of the garden. She needed a brisk walk. She returned to the kitchen, where Werner broke into raucous laughter as he banged his cup on the leg of the heavy table, his face looking up at her from where he sat on the floor.

"Ya, come, little one. We go now to see Onkel Ernst and Tante Ditha and your cousin Margaret, yes?"

The morning at her mother's was a quieter version of the evening before, with only the women raptly listening to Ernst's stories. He launched into an imitation of his law partner's antics at a dinner party. The man was a notorious womanizer and made an art of the amusing story, and Ernst played the incident out with every embellishment. Kläre hadn't the heart to hear any more and ventured into the kitchen to find the children.

Margaret was eighteen months old, nearly a year older than Werner. She was small but sharp and already chattering much of the time. The older child was fascinated with her cousin, the first baby with whom she had spent time at close hand. Her beautiful green eyes followed his every movement. Werner, in turn, reached to her with his long fingers, a smile of baby delight seizing his face. They played on the floor, pushing a wooden horse on wheels back and forth. Werner drew the toy to his mouth and then banged it on the floor and attempted to push it back to Margaret, toppling himself in the effort. Alarmed, Margaret pulled on her cousin's arm until he sat again, laughing. Satisfied that he was unharmed, she smiled at his antics.

Kläre marveled at these two children, their fascination in each other—first cautious, but now thorough and continuous. She decided to take them both to the park.

With Ditha's permission, Kläre bundled the two babies in Werner's pram and set off. Once at the park, she sat on a bench, enjoying the sunshine, relieved to be safely away from the regaling of a life she could not have. She tucked the blanket tightly around the children. Having exhausted themselves at play all morning, they had been lulled almost immediately by the gentle breeze and the bounce and roll of the pram into contented sleep. Like rocks nestled in the sand on a wind-swept beach, they lay side by side—head to neck, hip to waist, swaddled both in each other and the beautiful knitted blanket wrapped around them, so that only their sleeping faces were exposed to the September day. Autumn had just begun to crisp the air, and so far there were only the first suggestions of falling leaves and the rains that would come.

Dappled sunlight fell across the bench where Kläre sat. After a few rocking pushes of the buggy, she let it rest beside her. She leaned back and stretched her legs, ankles crossed in front of her, eyes closing to allow the sun to warm her face under the narrow brim of her hat. The days of skin meeting breeze were fleeting, and an autumn day with sun was a rare pleasure. The brisk walk had calmed her, infused her skin with the glow of exertion and fresh air, and softened the tension that gripped at her center like a corset.

She could only have been sitting thus for a few moments when a shadow passed before her—felt more than seen—and she opened her eyes to see a tall man sit at the far end of the bench. Kläre straightened quickly.

"Please, don't let me disturb you," the man said, a smile playing across his handsome face. "I don't imagine you get a moment to sit often." His head nodded slightly in the direction of the pram. His spoken greeting of more than an obligatory word or two was startling—and his reference to Kläre's motherhood and the presumption of her need for respite were an unheard-of familiarity, though somehow, coming from this stranger, they didn't offend. The man said nothing further, but neither did he look away.

Kläre studied him with the same open curiosity and interest with which he had spoken to her. He was fair-skinned, with medium brown hair that was neatly trimmed under his stylish hat. Intelligent grey eyes stared back at her, unabashed. His deep voice communicated casual but respectful confidence. He rested a large hand on the bench next to him, and wore his well-tailored suit and coat easily on his tall, muscular frame.

Kläre resisted the impulse to compose herself further, or to respond to him quickly, and for a long moment they simply studied each other in silence across the bench. Smiling at him with a mere arch of her brow, Kläre turned her face back to the sun, closed her eyes, and assumed the still pose of the observed. An alarming arousal rose from her groin to her breasts, causing her to breathe in deeply, and this she knew he noticed. Willing herself to calm, and again allowing a small smile to play across her mouth, she sighed silently as the gentlest of breezes caught her honey-colored hair and whispered past her ears.

She remained still, trance-like, until the man spoke once again: "I pass here often after dinner, before I return to work. Lovely, isn't it?"

Kläre turned to find a surprised look on the man's face, as if it were she who had spoken. What was it in each of them that had permitted this breach of etiquette, this presumption of personal access? If Kläre thought of Jakob at all in these moments, it did not show in the open interest on her face, or her relaxed posture on the bench. Her entire attention was focused on the comfortable engagement she felt with this man, and the vitality that coursed through her. There had been no other man in her life since Jakob, ever, and yet in a single moment this man had entered a place where only she lived. Effortlessly, he had offered—and she had accepted—an understanding.

"Pardon me," he said, and rose. He made as if to leave—then hesitated, gazing down thoughtfully first at the sleeping children in the pram and then at her, as if there were something more he wished to say.

"No pardon needed," Kläre said, at once grateful for his intrusion and his departure.

With a slight nod, the man turned and walked away across the park. Kläre watched him until he entered the Oberschlesierstrasse and disappeared.

4 1932, Hörde

"Mutti, may we have a *lebkuchen?*" Werner asked. Kläre suspected he was asking on behalf of his brother, who was still working on the model train in his room up the stairs. The wall clock had just chimed three times. She looked out the kitchen window at the weak December light. Jakob was hours away from his arrival for supper.

"Ya, you may each have one, but you must go to the garden to eat it." The boy raced up the back staircase and moments later reappeared to claim his small cake, still warm from the oven. Painfully thin after a month of fever and illness, Werner nonetheless brimmed with purposeful energy. The brightness had returned to his large brown eyes—his father's eyes, liquid and intelligent, except that Werner's contained a hint of humor that Jakob's lacked.

With a fond smile but firm resolve, Kläre plucked the *lebkuchen* from her son's fingers. "You must absolutely put on your jacket; it is a fine day, but the air is cold. You have only just recovered your health. Go!"

Werner scampered off to find the wool jacket and the warm cap his Tante Frieda had made for him. The door to the garden shut solidly behind him as he skipped to the great pine tree at the back where the swing hung. Settling into the seat and wrapping his jacketed arms around the long ropes that stretched down from the branch above, Werner kicked the cold earth under his feet and settled into the long arc of the swing, at one with its rhythm, happily savoring the spicy cookie. Kläre watched him with an intense love that bordered on pain, grateful for the moment of reprieve she could spend just observing her younger son.

It was Christmas season, and with all the world around her preparing for the holiday of Jesus' birth, Kläre reveled privately in the miracle of her own child, who had brought her the joy, the forgiveness, the rebirth that this Christian season represented. What she provided out of commitment and devotion to Jakob and Erwin, she gave with joy and effortless spontaneity to Werner.

Forcing herself back to her work in the kitchen, Kläre finished the last of her baking just as the girl Etta entered the back door, returned from her half-day off.

"Good afternoon, Etta, how was your morning?"

"Good afternoon, Frau Kohler. Thank you, it was a fine morning. We visited the shops in Dortmund. We are nearly prepared for the marriage now." Etta's skin glowed with the fresh air of the brisk afternoon and the anticipation of her wedding, now less than a month away. Kläre smiled as the younger woman finished tying her apron and smoothed the starched white front over her skirts.

"I am certain it will be a lovely wedding, Etta. Is Stefan's father recovered already?"

"Ya, he returned to the shop yesterday, but he says Stefan will mostly be in charge now anyway." Etta's pride in her future husband brought another smile to Kläre's lips. She liked the boy, who often had delivered items from the butcher shop to the back door over the years, always lingering to speak with Etta. Their young love had blossomed in this very kitchen.

"I'm happy to hear this," Kläre said. She turned to her *lebkuchen*, cooling on the broad wooden table, and began to place several of the perfect little cakes in a tin lined with oilcloth. "I will take the children to my mother's for coffee, Etta. Herr Kohler will be home for supper by seven. If you would prepare some potatoes for a salad, I will warm the soup and prepare the *schinken* and *brotchen* when I return."

"Yes, Frau Kohler."

"Thank you, Etta. Good afternoon."

With another glance at Werner, now kicking his football around the garden, Kläre entered the hall. She closed the kitchen door behind her and shivered for a moment in the sudden chill outside the oven-warmed kitchen. She climbed the broad staircase, running her hand over the burnished walnut balustrade, and, reaching the upper hall, crossed noiselessly to the first door on the left and pushed it open. She found Erwin intently running his small train around the track laid out over most of the bedroom floor, his tin soldiers set up in small brigades around the station.

"*Blut muss fliessen! Blut muss fliessen!*" Erwin's voice was gravelly as he muttered the jingle.

"Erwin! What are you saying? Blood must flow? That's terrible." Kläre tried to speak calmly, but she could hear the sharpness of her words.

At nine, Erwin had left behind the soft roundness of childhood. He remained somewhat heavy, though he was already nearly as tall as his mother. Brown hair lay across his large head with several irrepressible cowlicks sending tufts in different directions. "It's what the Brownshirts say, Mutti. 'Blood must flow. Blood must flow. Let's smash it up. The goddamned Jewish Republic.' They were yelling it yesterday when we came home from school. I had to walk around Winkel Strasse to get home."

"But that's terrible," Kläre repeated, clutching the door handle as she stared into her son's impassive face. "You mustn't repeat such things. Why didn't you tell us last night?"

Erwin was silent. He drew his head down into his shoulders and returned his attention to the train set. He had suffered a number of taunts in recent months; once he'd even arrived home with his jacket torn and his lip bloodied. He would say nothing to Kläre by way of explanation, and when Jakob spoke with him later in the evening he dug into the carpet with the toe of his shoe as he nervously reported that older boys had attacked him and a classmate, calling them "Christ killers." Erwin had been knocked to the ground.

"Stupid," Jakob had forcefully hissed. He had composed himself and continued, "You're a big boy, and I'm glad you did not fight them. I'm sorry this happened to you." Erwin's face opened in relief, but also appeared somehow unsatisfied as he looked from one of his parents to the other. Kläre reached to stroke the boy's arm from her chair where she sat mending, but he pulled away, went up the stairs to his room, and shut the door behind him.

Today, Erwin's silence brooked no interference.

"What an interesting setup you have," Kläre offered, working hard to keep her voice easy.

Erwin looked to her for a moment and then back to the trains. "Father said he would help me make a bridge later. Will he be home soon?"

"Unfortunately, he thinks not; he has much to finish at the office today." Kläre watched disappointment and sharp annoyance play across Erwin's face before dissolving into an absence of expression. "Come, dear, we will go to Oma's house for coffee, alright? Did Werner tell you that the *lebkuchen* are finished? You may have one."

Erwin rose heavily and tucked his school shirt into his ample pants—the new long pants that he was finally entitled to wear as a second-form student. Kläre reached to smooth his hair but he moved away, seeking the small mirror over his bureau and quickly pressing down on the top of his head with both hands.

"Five minutes, then, dear," Kläre said and crossed to her own room down the hall. She was shaken by this new evidence of the unrest that threatened from the outside world. Jakob said they only needed to keep quiet and work hard—that it would all blow over. But his practice was filled with Jews whose businesses were increasingly being battered by regulations, taxes, and insidious policies aimed at limiting their participation in the economy, not to mention the rampant inflation and the increasing unemployment among construction workers and even farmers. It was just politics, Jakob said, but now Erwin was seeing these dreadful things in the streets. Was her son frightened? Did he worry? He would not speak of such things and became angry if Kläre tried to engage him. She would speak to Jakob. He should instruct Erwin on how best to remain safe.

It had been a tiring day. The tall bed with its strong walnut posts and heavy comforter buttoned in a fresh linen cover looked inviting. Kläre seated herself instead on the low, cushioned stool before her dressing table. The triptych mirror with its beveled glass revealed repeated images of her slender, upright figure, the honey-colored hair pulled back in an unruly bun at the nape of her neck, and the worried look still on her face. Errant strands curled around her head in a soft halo of gentle disarray. Kläre patiently recaptured them with a large brush until her hair was once more tidy. She sighed, remembering this polished silver brush handle in the hands of her grandmother, who had also seated herself at this very dressing table. More than the death of her grandfather, the death of Karolina Ente had brought a sadness to Kläre's days that persisted still. She busied herself with the children and Jakob, and did what she could to comfort her father as well, but she experienced an emptiness borne of missing the life that she'd once had: the life of a large, vibrant, prosperous family.

Shaking such thoughts from her head, Kläre pinned a soft green hat to her hair and drew the stylish veil over her eyes. She changed into her afternoon shoes and returned downstairs to gather coats, the tin of *lebkuchen,* and her boys for the short walk to her parents' home.

"Leave the ball please, Werner," Kläre called as Werner dashed around the corner of the house, kicking the football ahead of him. The two boys started off down the broad new walkway, only just finished, that allowed the residents of Virschow Strasse to stay clear of the road, the tramways, and the increasing number of motorized cars.

When they reached the park, Kläre involuntarily looked toward the bench under the large linden tree. Immediately she turned her attention back to the boys in front of her—Erwin plodding slowly, Werner dancing around him and chasing a pigeon with outstretched hands. The bench was empty, and Kläre realized she had hoped to see Bernhardt Steinmann, whom she had encountered there with increasing frequency over the past few years. Kläre remembered the day they had first met with great clarity: the sun, the children sleeping in the pram, his bold stare and bemused formality, her equally bold acceptance of his attention.

Several months went by after that day before she saw him again. Then it was she who approached the bench, alone, to find him reading the newspaper on a winter afternoon not unlike this one. Rain and snow, chilling but not yet bitter, had given way to a brief appearance of the sun.

She was returning home from a shopping trip and had on the smart new suit and fox fur that had been her private reward for her body's return to slim shapeliness after her second pregnancy. She held the handles of several small parcels and paused in the weak sunshine, feeling its warmth on her back. Even from several meters' distance, she recognized the figure of the man on the bench with the memory distinct to secret pleasures. She ought to have walked on, but did not.

Momentarily, he looked up from his reading and, with a small raising of eyebrows and a flicker of a smile, he rose to his feet and gestured to the other side of the bench with a slight bow.

"Good afternoon. Would you like to sit down?"

Kläre's stockings were warm and her suit of good wool, and she determined that being seated for a few moments would not unduly chill her. She placed her parcels on the bench between them with care and sat down, angling herself toward her companion, who had already reseated himself comfortably.

"How nice to see you again." His voice was deep and warm, the intelligent light in his grey eyes familiar.

"Yes, thank you." There it was. Recognition and interest, offered and accepted. "Do you come here often, then?"

"Yes, quite often. My office is nearby. I enjoy fresh air whenever I can. It helps me think. And you?"

"I like to walk through here on my way from the shops. I bring the children as well sometimes."

"It is nice to have a reprieve from the rain, isn't it?" He cocked his head toward the sun and closed his eyes for a moment, leaving Kläre to stare at his large, handsome face. The attractive surprise of the man's unorthodox openness, his subtle managing of these snatches of public intimacy, fascinated her anew.

"I suppose you enjoy it more in the summer, with the green and the flowers," she offered.

"No, I quite like the cold and the winter as well." He was studying her again. Kläre flushed. What was it about this man that made her feel appreciated, vibrant?

"I also," she replied. "The challenge of cold brings me closer to the outdoors. I quite like it when it snows here." This was a man to whom one spoke without artifice. Kläre couldn't remember ever having met anyone quite like him.

The afternoon light was beginning to fade. Kläre rose and gathered her packages, threading the twine handles around her gloved hand.

"Good Afternoon, Herr . . . ?" She paused with the question hanging between them, her boldness now matching and exceeding his. She needed to put a name to the precious collection of feelings he'd inspired, which she already cherished.

"Steinmann, Bernhardt Steinmann."

"Kläre Kohler." Her free right hand in its soft brown glove reached toward him as he rose to grasp it.

"My pleasure." He bowed slightly as she turned onto the path, and she walked briskly, smiling with the unforeseen delight of this meeting.

This is how their encounters had happened: never planned, always brief, comfortable but electrifying in their measured intimacy. Now, Kläre thought of Bernhardt Steinmann often. She looked forward to the possibility of seeing him, safely bound by the demands of her children and household to the limits of a passing nod and smile, an occasional short chat. It wasn't only his good looks and easy grace that charmed her. It was the unorthodoxy of his directness, the incisive observations that he shared with her that somehow set her at ease. Unwittingly, Bernhardt Steinmann had woven a tapestry of understanding for Kläre that she now wore around her life like a gossamer veil, light but beautifully patterned. Her thoughts wandered to him when she needed a balance to the loneliness of her worries about Jakob, the children, and the changes threatening life around her. She imagined him with her in intimate moments: at rest in the bath, waiting for sleep to come at night, or pausing at the kitchen window. She had learned that he wasn't married, but she wondered who his women might be, and where he lived. Always her thoughts of him returned to just the two of them, and the exclusivity of the little world they'd created for themselves across the park bench. She replayed their conversations again and again; moments of satisfaction and fulfillment that buoyed her and replenished the crucible of her compassion and energy for caretaking.

Kläre reached her parents' street, the park behind her, the children waiting at the corner, Werner swinging around a wrought metal lamppost. Approaching her mother's home, Kläre saw a woman and a young boy coming toward them on the walkway. As they drew nearer, Kläre realized it was Amalie.

Amalie had married a year prior, her grief at the death of her fiancé in the war overcome if not forgotten. The man was a widower with five children, and had a small, successful business in Bielefeld. The wedding had been a modest, sad affair, the children still stunned at the loss of their mother and uncertain about this new one. Amalie had herself entered the marriage with reserve that bordered on resignation, while it seemed that her new husband was looking for nothing more than to return his life to a semblance of stability.

Still, Kläre had found pleasure in the simple vows that had promised the two hurt souls to each other, and provided the children with a mother once more. She had baked for days to provide a delicious reception. Amalie's father, long dead, had if nothing else provided adequately for his wife and daughter, and the home on Benninghofer Strasse had been an austere but lovely setting for the ceremony. Since Amalie's move to Beilefeld, however, Kläre's contact with her friend had been infrequent, more so because Amalie's sudden complicated entry to motherhood had been overwhelming to her.

"Amalie! Is that you?" Kläre called as they drew close. As Amalie looked up at her friend, Kläre was startled to see that she looked exhausted, her forehead lined with tension.

"Ya, Kläre, good day. I'm just coming to my mother. She has been quite ill again." Amalie's eyes filled and she squeezed them shut.

Standing close behind Amalie was a young boy, perhaps seven or eight years of age. He was tall and sturdy, his shoulders slightly rounded. Spectacles made his already enormous brown eyes look even larger. Long arms hung at his sides, and big hands emerged from the sleeves of his coat, which were not quite long enough. He dropped his gaze to his shoes, waiting.

"This must be your son," Kläre said.

As if only now remembering him, Amalie turned to the boy and, pushing him forward, quickly introduced him. "Ya, here is Ansel. Seven years. Say good afternoon to Frau Kohler."

"Good afternoon, Frau Kohler." The boy extended his hand to Kläre's, bowed with proper schoolboy form, and then stepped back.

"Good afternoon, Ansel, I'm happy to meet you. You're growing up into a fine young boy. Are you in school still?"

"Yes, ma'am, I am in the second form now at Kinderheim St. Stephen's." Kläre looked at the boy in confusion and then to Amalie. *A Kinderheim? What was the boy doing in an orphanage? He was neither an orphan, nor destitute . . .* Amalie offered no explanation, however, and Kläre felt immediately that this was not the time to ask.

"All right, well, my boys have gone already into my mother's—but please, come over tomorrow for coffee so Ansel can meet the children. I made a good *lebkuchen* today. Could he take one?"

The boy dropped his head again, and Kläre searched her friend's face for an answer.

"Ya, thank you. He will like to have a treat."

Kläre opened the tin and extended the box of fragrant cakes toward the boy, who now looked at her with simple gratitude.

"Go ahead, have one," Kläre offered.

"Thank you," he said, taking the cake in both hands. He closed his eyes almost as if in prayer, and then took a bite, hunching slightly as if to make himself invisible.

"Thank you very much," he said when he had savored and swallowed, and opened his eyes to find Kläre's.

"You are most welcome," she replied. "And do come by for coffee, please." She grasped Amalie's arm with a gentle squeeze and the two women exchanged looks that felt like a confirmation.

"Good-bye then," Kläre called as she moved toward the gate of her parents' house.

"Good-bye," Amalie and Ansel responded in unison.

The next morning dawned cool but brilliant. It was a school holiday—a fact that added to the festive air in the Kohler household. Kläre was relieved to be spared the increasingly onerous task of readying the children for school. Ever since Erwin had been attacked, over a month ago now, he had become an even more reluctant student and left home each school day as though shackled to an invisible chain of slaves.

Jakob finished his egg and *brotchen* and folded his napkin before carefully sliding it into its monogrammed silver ring and placing it next to his plate. He lifted his coffee to finish the last of it. Kläre saw that his hand was trembling, and was startled when he put the cup down so heavily that it crashed into the saucer. Her husband cursed under his breath and pushed his chair back from the table just as the clock chimed the half hour.

Kläre glided across the carpet from the kitchen door with a coffee pot. As she leaned over to put the pot on the table, her satin housecoat moved softly around her, and she saw a flicker of appreciation come and go in Jakob's brown eyes. She offered him a smile.

"Will the children have something special today without school?" Jakob asked. "I see they haven't come down to breakfast yet."

"I've just now woken them. We stayed quite late at my parents last night. I've let them sleep in a little. I am quite looking forward to coffee today with Amalie. She's come home to her mother—and she's got one of the boys with her, the older one, Ansel. Quite a serious boy, it seems, but sweet."

"Fine then. I ought to be home for dinner at one, unless of course this hearing goes later. Judge Hertz usually moves things along. In the evening I expect Krauss and I will go to the *stube*. We'll no doubt need a beer by then."

Krauss was Jakob's law partner, and the case they had before the court today was a continuation of the civil suit over damages done to a small cattle vendor in Steele. Jakob had carefully steered the case away from the presenting facts of the damage. A grieving farmer had ransacked the business, claiming that the Jews were responsible for the death of his son in a farm accident. The man had produced a copy of *Der Stürmer,* the Nuremberg weekly published by Julius Streicher, a notorious Jew-baiter. The business owner had sought only to have his remaining cattle returned to him, and chosen not to press charges against the farmer. The case had required great finesse, and carried no small risk for the law practice. Jakob and Krauss had negotiated quietly and carefully, Kläre knew.

"Will it be a difficult hearing, then?" Kläre studied her husband, concerned that he looked tired already, pale and drawn. "Jakob, do you feel alright? You seem tired." She looked into his eyes, searching, but he lowered his gaze deliberately and pushed his chair close to the dining table.

"Yes, yes, I must be a little tired." He stepped toward her and took her lightly into his arms, placing a gentle kiss on her forehead. Kläre heard him inhale her clean, perfumed scent. She held his arms, keeping him in the embrace a moment longer, a ripple of uncertain fear disturbing the stillness of the moment.

Jakob gently pushed her away and with the slightest tremor slid his hands down her arms, took her hands, and brought them up between them to his lips.

"*Madame*, a good day to you."

Kläre watched as he walked to the hall and donned his topcoat, gloves, and creased hat. When he opened the door and slipped out into the morning, she moved into the sitting room, cozy with rich tapestries and Persian rugs. She stood at the window. Jakob looked suddenly older as he made his way down the street, his height no longer commanding, his step less certain. She felt again a small chill.

The clatter of Werner's feet on the stair returned her to the moment. She knew he was ready for a large breakfast and an accounting of the day to come.

"Mutti! Mutti!" His voice was imperious, but also full of the energy she loved in him. "Mutti, will we have cakes with the boy?" Werner paused, the question spilling from his face to his lengthening body.

"Yes, we have a good cake for today. But I want you to eat breakfast first. Is Erwin awake?"

"Yes. He says we will build a bunker in the garden."

Kläre sighed. "That will be good fun, I know." It was ironic that Erwin had become fascinated with the strategy and the trappings of war, considering how much his father had hated every moment of his army time. But something about the power of the war and the humiliation of the loss had created in the boys of Erwin's age a compelling need to play at daring and bravery and cleverness in the role of soldiers. Erwin was slow and methodical, but he was observant, studied strategy, and had memorized a catalog's worth of weaponry—and though Werner was much younger, Erwin happily recruited him for the adventurous, daring parts of the intrigue and battles.

The morning passed quickly with baking and dinner preparations. It was nearly noon when the telephone rang. Its loud jangle in the hall still caused Kläre to jump, even all the way in the kitchen. She hadn't yet gotten used to the small machine.

"Good morning!" she nearly shouted into the receiver.

"Klärchen? Here is Trude."

"Ya Trude, how are you?" Her sister had rarely telephoned since she'd married and moved out to a home at the outskirts of Hörde with Rudi, her sour husband. Trude's years of reckless challenge to the strictures of living under her parents' influence had ended in a marriage of escape. Kläre did not like Rudi Stern and grieved for the distance he put between Trude and her family.

"I am here now at Mutti's. Papa has come home from the store. He's sick to his stomach and looks quite awful. Were you coming for coffee this afternoon?"

"No, Amalie Liebler is coming with one of her boys this afternoon. But do you need me?"

"No, no. I'm happy to stay and put my feet up here. I'm such a fat cow anyway."

Kläre laughed at the disgust in her sister's voice. Beautiful Trude could bear least of all the Ente women the ungainly bulk of pregnancy. She was already past the point of proper confinement for most women, but refused to stay home and out of the public eye. Instead she had designed and sewn stylish maternity dresses that she wore, defiant as always, as she went about her daily life. Kläre often wondered how Trude would take to the conscripted life of motherhood.

"Okay, fine. Tell Father I hope he feels better soon. I'll check on you later also."

"Good. I want to hear about Amalie, yes?" Trude had spent nearly as much childhood time with Amalie as had Kläre, though they hadn't been as close.

"Yes, of course. Good-bye now." Kläre rang off and replaced the mouthpiece in its cradle. Another worry. Her father hadn't looked well for the last month now. He never left the store early. It was too much to think of now: Jakob's health, her father's health. Kläre stiffened with resolve and finished her work in the kitchen. Etta had helped with dinner preparations while Kläre had prepared an extra *pflaum kuchen* for her parents. It was her father's favorite, especially with the rich whipped cream for which she had paid dearly yesterday. Now she climbed the stairs to change out of her housedress and into her afternoon suit—a good green wool from Düsseldorf. The moss color set off her reddish hair, which she tidied. Finally, she tied the laces of the fine alligator shoes that were old, but still in good shape. They shone with Etta's polishing handiwork, and Kläre was pleased with her ensemble.

"Etta, can you please call the boys in to dress for dinner? They must clean up properly," Kläre called as she moved toward the dining room and then to the sitting room, where the small table was already set for afternoon coffee.

Kläre's grandparents had chosen a beautiful coffee service as a wedding gift for her, and it gleamed now on the side table in the sitting room. It was not as ornate as Ditha and Ernst's set in Berlin, but it was still elegant and understated. It suited Kläre well, and she was pleased with the preparations that had been made to receive her old friend.

Shortly before one, Jakob's assistant telephoned that the case was still at court and Jakob would not be coming home for dinner, but would eat nearby and return to court in the afternoon. While Kläre worried that this did not bode well for the case, she was grateful to eat a small dinner with the boys and tidy the dining room.

Promptly at three o'clock, the doorbell rang.

Werner and Erwin stood behind their mother and properly shook the visitors' hands with slight bows and a crisp "Good afternoon."

"You go now and show Ansel your trains, and we'll call you when it's time for cakes, alright?" Kläre watched as Werner pulled Ansel behind him up the stairs, heedless of the two-year difference in their ages. Erwin lumbered up last, resigned to his role of watcher. Werner would chatter and try different variations in the train setup, become distracted momentarily and return, while Erwin would keep to a careful plan, building slowly and always with familiar configurations. Kläre guessed Ansel would fall to play with a comfort known to small boys with an understood project.

Kläre and Amalie chatted in the sitting room. Before Kläre knew it, an hour had passed and Etta was calling the boys down to take turns washing their hands in the icy water at the corner sink in the hall water closet. She then shepherded them to the kitchen where the large wooden table was set with plum cakes, precious whipped cream, and warmed chocolate.

In the thin light of the fading winter afternoon, Kläre burst into laughter, leaning toward her friend and clutching her elbow: "Where is? Do you have? Give me. It's a complete vocabulary for the married man isn't it?" Kläre said, sending herself and Amalie into another flood of giggles. She gasped as tears danced down her cheeks. After the long and serious conversation of the last hour, she was reasserting her old skill at mimicry and delight in entertaining Amalie. Lately, the new vulnerability she'd been sensing in Jakob had led her to keep her normally teasing wit in check around him, even as he had become increasingly impatient with even small disruptions to their daily lives. It felt good to laugh hard, to make.someone else laugh.

"Ah, Klärchen. This was such a good idea you had. Thank you so much." Amalie smiled as she dabbed at her eyes with her handkerchief.

"Ya, it's good to see each other, isn't it? You've had quite a huge change. You mustn't rush to judgment, Amalie. It will all feel more comfortable with the children after a time. They do really need you, after all."

"Ya, it was Georg who wanted Ansel to go to the Kinderheim; his sister cares for the children there. He thinks it's much easier with only one boy and the three girls."

Kläre fixed her gaze on her hands. "Do they take boys who have a home so young there for school?"

Amalie straightened in her chair, a young-looking figure still attractive in her modest but well-tailored suit. A sigh escaped her as she smoothed her skirt. "Ya, I don't know, really. It has been between Georg and his sister, mostly. It's what he wants. The boy on his own is no trouble. No trouble at all, really."

The phone in the hall rang and the two women looked at each other, startled for a moment. Kläre rose quickly and met Etta in the hall, also heading for the machine.

"Good afternoon!" Kläre waved Etta back to the kitchen and was surprised to hear Hilda, her mother's maid.

"Ya, Frau Kohler, here is Hilda. Frau Kohler, please can you come to your mother? It's your father. He has collapsed. We've sent for the doctor, but she asked me to telephone for you."

"Yes of course. Is he all right?" Kläre kept her voice calm, so low it was barely above a whisper.

"Oh, Frau Kohler, please. You must come right now." The older woman's choked voice over the static connection brought cold fear like a knife into Kläre's chest, and for a moment she could neither breathe nor move.

"I will come directly," she finally whispered into the mouthpiece. In the instant of replacing the telephone, she knew her father was gone. The dizziness of panic swept over her with the deep resonation of thunder before an impending storm.

"Ach, Papa!" She was already moving to the closet for her coat.

5 March 1933, Dortmund

Bernhardt Steinmann stared vacantly at the letter on his desk. In fact, he had now read it through twice and was working to control his racing mind and maintain composure until he could legitimately leave the office and walk—walk and think. The typists, copy editors, and editorial assistants continued to work diligently around him, but the clack of type machines, scratching of pens, and low murmur offered no routine comfort today. The announcement was quite simple: *On 1 April, 1933, all Party members and associated agencies or services will boycott Jewish stores, doctors, and lawyers.*

The directive, sent to his attention at his publishing house, Berendt Verlag, confused Bernhardt—and worried him. Already the editorial department had been under pressure to cancel publication of Jewish authors' works. Elsewhere, Lion Feuchtwanger's novel *The Oppermanns* had created a scandal among the country's publishers and nearly closed down Aufbau Verlag before an American publisher picked up the book and the translation rights and made it a cause célèbre for anti-Nazism. Theodor Lessing, the noted Jewish philosopher, had left the country for Marienbad in Czechoslovakia, where he continued to publish despite the increasingly strident warnings of Hitler's regime, which had recently overturned the government and seized power. Hoheneichen Verlag was publishing Alfred Rosenberg's *Myth of the Twentieth Century,* defining ever more clearly the position of Aryan supremacy as the creator of values and culture, and the Jewish race as destroyers of the same. So far, Bernhardt, who headed tiny Berendt Verlag, had managed to keep his publication decisions independent and out of the arena of politics. His was a fine house, with a vibrant mix of literary work and scholarly academic publications. Jews were liberally represented in the authors' list.

Bernhardt arranged his files neatly in the drawer of his massive walnut desk and glanced through the inner window of his gracious office to those working in the editing room. His gaze rested on Aaronson, a slight man, who was bending over a sheaf of papers on the desk in front of him. Surely it was the Selig manuscript he worked on. Aaronson was a Jew, Selig a Jew also. Neither was a doctor or lawyer, nor this a Jewish store. On the surface, then, no obvious need for worry on April 1. Bernhardt drew in a breath and, exhaling sharply, rose to take his coat. After glancing once more at his tidy desk, he left his office and, stopping briefly to speak to his secretary, strode to the wide staircase leading to the hall below and the heavy brass doors that opened onto the street.

Berendt Verlag was situated in the Heiliger Weg in one of the more fashionable business sections of Dortmund, at the edge of the city where it merged with Hörde. Here the crowded old city with its curving streets of imposing stone gave way to broad avenues and fine buildings surrounded with shade trees. The publishing house had belonged to Bernhardt's uncle on his mother's side and he'd chosen to join the company despite his parents' wishes that he follow his father into medicine.

He settled into a brisk walk. The early March cold was no longer the dull cold of established winter, and without wind there was the promise, the scent, of impending spring. Walking and breathing deeply allowed Bernhardt to think. *No one knows. No one need know.* His mother's stricken face crept into his mind's eye before he banished the thought of her and her pronouncement. He glanced at passersby as if they could see her, hear her.

It had been only three months since his father's death and the somber funeral. His family was small and had arranged a simple burial at the Lutheran church where the infrequent christenings, marriages, and deaths of the Steinmann family had been marked. Christmas had been subdued, though a comfort, as Bernhardt's sister had come to their mother's home with her three small children and solid husband to make the *lebkuchen* and place the candles on the tree.

Oscar Steinmann had provided well for his wife, and the stroke that killed him had been swift and merciful. Bernhardt had stayed with his mother and sister for an extra day to go through his father's well-ordered papers and see to his wishes. The practice would continue with the able young doctor who had joined Oscar Steinmann five years ago. Rosa Steinmann would continue to receive an income from the practice and her many activities would serve to ease the pain that sat across her wide, pale forehead and lovely blue eyes.

Late that second afternoon, while Bernhardt sat behind his father's massive mahogany desk, covered in green leather and surrounded with the glass cases full of books and medical equipment, his mother had come into the study.

"Bernhardt, darling, I must speak with you a moment."

He rolled back in the creaky cushioned desk chair and rose to take his mother's hands as they moved to the sofa by the window. She sat and smoothed the rosy velvet under her hand.

"What is happening here in Germany cannot continue like this, can it? How is it possible that this Hitler now has become *Reichskanzler* and von Hindenburg gets rid of the Communists and suddenly no one can write what he wants?" Rosa's voice tightened to a strangled whisper. "I am afraid for you, Bernhardt, afraid for us."

"Mama, you are upset from losing Father. Why are you worrying now about these things? Liselotte and I are here. We will care for you, I promise." Bernhardt took hold of his mother, a tall, strong woman who suddenly seemed frailer and was now shaking with fear.

"Bernhardt, I must tell you something terrible. I have never talked about it before, but now I am so scared, and without your father I don't know any more what to do! You remember, I have always told you that my family is from Galicia and that your Opa and Oma died young, yes?"

"Yes of course, Mama." Bernhardt watched his mother's serene face crumple in pain and increasing fear.

"They died in pogroms in Krakow, Bernhardt. The Russians chased them to Poland and then they died there because . . . because . . ." She searched his eyes for something he did not know how to put into his worried expression. ". . . because they were *Jews,* Bernhardt. My parents were *Jews!*" She was clutching his arms now, the tears that for days she had held in streaming down her face, her chest heaving under the elegant lace of her high-necked bodice. "Please, don't be angry with me. I would never say anything to hurt you, but I am so afraid now. I don't want to tell Liselotte. I heard Alex talk to your father about leaving for America. It's crazy, but perhaps you should all go."

By now Rosa Steinmann was speaking in small gasps, her entire body shivering. Bernhardt took his mother into his arms and whispered, "Mutti, Mutti, hush now. It's too much. Don't speak any more now."

Her trembling continued and a deep chill penetrated to Bernhardt's core. Everywhere, the Jews. It was all he saw in the newspapers with these Nazis. The Jews who worked for him, the Jews whom he published, all were wriggling, jumpy, like tadpoles in a pond. *I? I should now worry like a Jew? My position at the firm? My sister? My mother? Oh God, my mother.*

"Mutti." He held her gently but firmly away from his chest. "Who knows this?"

Without loosening her grip on his coat sleeves she answered, suddenly fierce, the graceful sweep of steel-grey hair framing her intense blue eyes: "No one knows. No one need know."

Indeed. No one need know. Bernhardt continued down the broad avenue. In the months since that day, he had tried to understand how to navigate the increasingly intrusive restrictions on publications in a house that had long been known for its wide-ranging intelligence and promotion of diverse thought. Doctors, philosophers, novelists, poets, essayists, all came to Berendt Verlag. The quality of scholarship, writing, and excellence in genre had always been the basis for editorial decisions. The growing number of articles, directives, and ordinances were striking fear into the heart of the intellectual community, and threatened every independent publisher's existence. All this had weighed heavily on Bernhardt Steinmann, but the unthinkable tidings he'd learned from his mother had confounded his every attempt to make sense of his work or his life.

As a dedicated patron of the arts, Bernhardt had been sickened to learn that Max Liebermann had been ousted from the Berlin Academy of Art and his paintings removed from all German museums. A Liebermann hung in the Steinmann dining room. Bruno Walter, conductor extraordinaire in Leipzig and Berlin, had left the country. Albert Einstein had resigned his post at the Royal Prussian Academy of Sciences and was now in America. These were losses to be endured, railed against, but they had not been personal.

In his life, Bernhardt Steinmann had never experienced fear for his own survival. Too young to fight in the last war, too privileged to have suffered in the aftermath, he had only known opportunity and the courage born of a good education and the shelter of family. *No one need know.*

Bernhardt was still deep in thought when he arrived at the park, where he often came to stroll and think. Today he walked quickly to the outer walkway and began to circumnavigate the large, well-planned urban retreat. Hands clasped behind him, eyes sightless for thinking, he narrowly avoided plowing into a well-dressed woman, stopping abruptly and swinging to the side of the walk just in time.

"Herr Steinmann, good afternoon," Kläre greeted him, registering surprise at his near collision with her—surprise that was quickly supplanted by concern at his obvious distress.

"Oh excuse me. Ach, Frau Kohler, I am so sorry. I . . . I didn't mean to be so clumsy." Bernhardt stared at her as though he'd asked a question and awaited her response.

"Oh, don't worry; I'm fine, but you must be in a great hurry. Good afternoon, then." Kläre turned to leave.

Without a word, Bernhardt reached out and touched his gloved hand gently to her elbow. "Pardon me. I'm sorry for being so forward, but . . . would you take a coffee with me? I've . . . I've just thought to go for a coffee." His natural charm came to the rescue. "It would be my pleasure if you have the time to join me."

They stood quiet in the winter afternoon, absorbing the possibilities inherent in this extension of their carefully circumscribed relationship.

"Yes," Kläre said. "I would quite like that. The children will be at school for a while yet."

The waiters wore the expressions of professional calm as they danced around each other and the crowded tables at Café Hintz. Slender glass table vases held single roses rather than the opulent bouquets of days past, but the café was busy.

Bernhardt held the heavy door open for Kläre. They were quickly shown to a table, but Bernhardt spoke quietly to the maître d' and the table changed to a corner, away from the expansive window and the prying eyes of other guests. The black-and-red waistcoats of several waiters appeared in rapid succession; soon hot, strong coffee steamed in front of them, and a fine pastry followed.

Bernhardt watched as Kläre surveyed the other diners, nodding to those who met her gaze. Her eyes paused on a short, solid woman in a deep purple dress and rounded, black-rimmed glasses that magnified her startling blue eyes—Melisande Durr, an art dealer from Düsseldorf. Bernhardt sent a smile of recognition in Durr's direction. She nodded back at him, the small black hat perched on her head bobbing with the motion.

"You are familiar with Melisande Durr?" Kläre asked, looking at him with surprise.

"Yes, yes I have worked with some of her artists and writers. We publish quite a few of them. I actually have a portrait of her by Becker, which I quite like. She looks a good bit more unusual in the painting than in person."

"I'm fascinated," Kläre said, leaning forward, studying him more closely now. "Isn't it a little dangerous to be publishing her people these days? I understand that she owns and runs a bakery café and champions artists who do portraits of dissenters."

"There are many dangers in our lives these days," Bernhardt said darkly. He absently drew the vase on the table toward himself to breathe in the scent of the rose.

"Yes, quite," Kläre responded. Bernhardt wondered if she felt the danger all around her as he did. The daily news of the government's instability and wildly gyrating economy were troubling not only for the difficulty they presented to the legal and business worlds, but because it was clear that the fragile order of their society was disintegrating.

"Do you go to the opera?" Kläre asked.

Bernhardt looked up. "Yes, I do. We have the season here and then we go sometimes to Hamburg or Berlin. And you?" He was bewildered by the change of subject, but too polite to say so.

"I love the opera. I've heard just now that Otto Klemperer has left Germany. There were riots, you know, and they cancelled his concerts in Berlin. It's terribly frightening, isn't it?"

There it was, just like that. Kläre's steady brown eyes held fast to his, and the fear rising from deep inside Bernhardt surely showed. Klemperer! How subtle. How did she know? Was this a test? Why did this woman want to know what he understood of the increasing exclusion of Jewish artists and musicians? Curiosity and alarm mixed within him in equal measure. What would she think his view of the Klemperer situation might be? The famous conductor was not only a master of the full traditional repertoire, but also a champion of the newer composers—the exciting modernism flourishing in Berlin and hated by the Nazis.

And, of course, Klemperer was a Jew. After months of trying to prove his loyalty to the cultural strength of Germany, he had recognized the impossibility of continuing to work in the hostile, reactionary atmosphere of the new Nazi government and had left the country for New York. Bernhardt weighed his next words carefully.

"I am very frightened," he said, extending his hand across the table as though to take hers. "Many of my clients are facing terrible restrictions on publication, exhibition, and performance of their work—wonderful work that deserves to be published." His voice was nearly pleading, he could hear it, but still he went on: "One hears that Jascha Horenstein in Düsseldorf will be next to go. Although perhaps the censorship of the music, the literature, the art isn't even the most frightening part." These last words he spoke with an expression of grief that brought a soft look into Kläre's eyes.

The subject of Jews had never, in the years of their odd meetings, been spoken of. Bernhardt had guessed that Kläre might be Jewish, but had never thought about what she might fear until now. Did she share his growing dread of the Brownshirts, of the continuing attacks on Jews and their businesses, of their increasing exclusion from the fabric of everyday life?

"I have recently learned that I have more to fear personally than I thought," Bernhardt continued. "It has been bad enough to worry for my country and the life I love. I find now that I must worry for my own safety as well." The smallest beads of perspiration formed across Bernhardt's wide, clear forehead as he spoke these words.

Frau Durr, Bernhardt saw, had been joined by a couple now deep in conversation with her—customers perhaps. He reached for his cup, and Kläre also sipped the strong, good coffee for which the cafe was famous.

"I am sorry," Kläre said, seeming to search for something more but not finding the words. Her quiet concern calmed Bernhardt.

"My father died recently," he said now in a rush as Kläre's hand reached to rest on his. "It was quite sudden and he did not suffer, but it was a shock to my mother, to all of us."

"I am so sorry. I have also just lost my father," Kläre nearly whispered.

"Ach, now it is I who am sorry. I didn't mean to sadden you further." Bernhardt touched her arm, the physical contact a bridge over the river of pain and uncertainty in which he'd been swimming. The jolt of passion as their skin met shocked him. She felt it too—he saw it in her face, in her quick intake of breath. "You were close to your father, yes?"

"Quite."

Bernhardt went on, his hand warm on Kläre's arm. "After my father's death, my mother revealed to me that she was born . . . a Jew. I never knew it, and now she is frightened for me and for my sister. When I saw you today, I suddenly wanted to tell you this. I've told no one else."

Kläre drew a deep breath and pressed her thin lips together as she worked to absorb this information. She composed herself quickly. "How very shocking." Then, instead of offering empty words of comfort, she asked, "What have been your thoughts?"

Bernhardt felt his old, sardonic smile make an appearance. "Nothing that I'm very proud of, I'm afraid."

She smiled back at him, and seemed to relax. "That I can imagine."

After that they talked more openly, speaking of their fathers, the deaths, their worries, their voices rising to eagerness in a shared understanding and softening when pain overcame them.

"I can hardly conceive of doing so, but I have been thinking that we should leave," Kläre ventured. "My brother in Berlin thinks the Nazis will be thrown out in the election, but I am not so sure."

"Where would you go?" Bernhardt quite clearly recoiled from the thought.

"Perhaps . . ." Kläre paused and seemed to decide not to mention something. "Perhaps we could go to Belgium. I have a sister there, in Brussels."

"Could your husband practice the law?"

"Not right away, certainly. And he is . . . He has an illness. The doctors think it is the shaking palsy. He was very ill in the war from nerve gas. It's very upsetting. But I'm quite sure he could take the bar eventually and perhaps in the meantime . . . I can find work."

Bernhardt's eyebrows rose slightly and he tilted his head. "What is the work that would interest you?"

"I am hoping now to take a massage course. It would be a continuation of the work I did during the war. I volunteered at a hospital, and I learned to work with wounded soldiers"—Kläre tapped her finger against her cup—"or perhaps my sister and I can make a guest house together. It is so much to think about—but if it goes well in the election then we will have no need of such thoughts, will we?" She smiled.

"May God hear you," Bernhardt replied.

When nearly an hour had passed in conversation, Bernhardt cleared his throat and fixed Kläre's gaze with his own.

"Frau Kohler."

"Kläre, please."

"Kläre, then. I know it's quite forward of me, and perhaps not . . . convenient for you, but it would mean a great deal to me to be able to speak to you again. I haven't anyone that I can safely speak to now. As you said, these are frightening times. Would it be all right? May I telephone you?"

"Yes," Kläre said immediately.

Bernhardt smiled with relief. He knew he would phone, and now he knew she wanted him to. "Thank you. Thank you very much."

They finished their coffee. Bernhardt rose to hold Kläre's chair and help her into her coat.

6 March 1933, Hörde

The radio filled the sitting room with the sound of static and the dramatic voice of the newsreader. In Düsseldorf, another night of *Einzelaktionen*, acts of violence, had disrupted a meeting of Communists and resulted in the deaths of three men. Jakob Kohler sat oblivious to the shaking of his hands on the graceful arms of his walnut chair. With the next announcement, however, he gripped the chair and bent forward.

"True Germans! By Order of the National-Socialist Party! On 1 April all citizens are ordered to boycott Jewish shops, businesses, and legal and medical practices. The boycott will start at exactly 10:00 a.m. on Saturday, April 1. It will continue until the Party leadership orders its cancellation."

This, Jakob knew, was the Nazi response to the perceived disinformation campaign in the foreign press that the Nazis accused Jews of fomenting. The boycott was meant to bring German Jews to their knees economically, but was allegedly to exclude violence.

Jakob sat with his head in his hands, his thoughts piercing through a lacerating headache. *There are now as many attacks on Jews as Communists: artists, businessmen, and civil servants. The Brownshirts could show up here and pull me into the street! How is it possible that the Nazi filth took the election? The Social Democrats sued the Nazis in court, but they've stacked the court and disabled the constitution. What is left to do?*

Jakob rubbed his forehead as if to clear his thoughts of the confusion and disbelief competing with the shooting pain of his chronic headache. "Kläre," he called above the radio voice, "have you got a tablet there?"

The late March evening still held the cool light of lengthening days. Through the window over the large porcelain sink, Kläre noticed the carpet of snowdrops drifting across the garden as she cleaned the supper dishes. The winter aconites had closed their yellow cups to impending night and the cold wind that rose from the earth and drove through the streets in dank drafts. Brown leaves swirled into the corner of the garden wall and blew across the rhododendron bed. She could safely tidy the over-wintered garden now. Azalea buds were swelling and the first crocuses were nearly in bloom.

"Kläre! Have you the tablet?" Jakob's voice increased in urgency.

"Ya, one moment!" she called back. She swiftly put the last dishes into the cupboard before pouring water into a crystal glass and shaking a tablet of pain medication from an apothecary envelope into her hand. She crossed the hall into the sitting room, where Jakob sat hunched in front of the radio.

"Here, I have it," she said, holding the tablet in her open palm patiently as Jakob's hand lurched toward it. She gently folded her hand around his trembling fingers until he had grasped the pill. He nearly threw it into his mouth; she guided the water to his lips as he gripped the glass.

"Dr. Feuer said you can take another half if it doesn't help, you know." Kläre searched Jakob's face and saw the tension in his lined forehead. "Here, let me." She walked behind his chair and, closing her eyes, she drew him back until his head rested against her. She began to draw slow circles with her fingertips at his temples, and then strokes across his forehead to the sides and over the top of his head. The smallest of groans escaped as he breathed out and drew a long, slow breath. Kläre loved the softness of his thick thatch of dark hair, now shot through with silver. In their years together, Jakob hadn't often submitted to her stroking through it as she did now. She reached her fingers down into his heavily starched collar, drew her hands up the back of his neck, and then pulled her thumbs across the top of his head. He began to relax into her touch now; keeping one hand working across his neck, Kläre reached with her other hand and turned off the radio. The sudden silence filled the air like cotton, and they both breathed around it as if to cleanse the moment of fear and worry.

"You heard of the boycott, yes?" Jakob's voice was laden with dread.

"Ya, it's not to be believed. Thank God my father didn't live to see this day. Will you stay home?" This last question Kläre asked lightly, moving her fingers around the orbit of Jakob's eyes, which were no longer squeezed shut but gently closed. She kneaded the etched line between his dark eyebrows as if she could smooth away his pain and worry with her delicate fingers.

"I don't know. I suppose Krauss and I will discuss this tomorrow."

"My uncles are loaning seed to farms who barely made it through the winter. Does this mean those farmers must go elsewhere now? It's madness." Kläre kept the rigid anger she felt out of her fingers.

"The boys mustn't go to school on Saturday, and it would be best if you didn't go out unnecessarily yourself." Jakob spoke wearily but firmly.

"We don't want to live this way, Jakob, do we?" Kläre's hands continued to circle the orbits around Jakob's eyes.

"Kläre, please, not now, not again."

Kläre paused to channel the frustration that shot through her into the rhythmic movement of her arms, which were beginning to tire from their work. "Is the pain better?" she asked, gazing out the patio doors to the familiar landmarks of her garden, now vanishing into night.

"Ya, better."

"Come then, come to bed early."

Jakob rose slowly; it was a long moment before he could straighten and open his eyes. Kläre took his arm and turned out the lights as they moved toward the staircase.

An hour later, it was quiet but for the comforting noises of the settling house and the hiss of steam as radiators warmed the rooms. The sound of the wind outdoors mixed with the resting breathing of Jakob and his sons.

Kläre had remained next to Jakob until he slept, though they had not spoken or touched beyond the brush of a kiss that Kläre had placed on his cheek as he turned into the deep pillow. Now she rose and smoothed the starched duvet cover that Jakob had pulled up to his chin. He would sleep now, at least until the pill wore off, but it was too early for her to rest. She pulled on a dressing gown over her nightdress and tied the silk sash before sliding into house shoes and stepping noiselessly into the hall and down the staircase.

Again in the sitting room, Kläre sat in the Queen Anne chair that had been her grandmother's. The velveteen brocade on the firm seat was worn, but Kläre could not bring herself to reupholster it. The intricate carving of the short wooden back and the smoothness of the walnut in the graceful curve of the chair arms suited Kläre's slender body. Just as it was, the chair comforted her with the memory of the warmth and security of her grandparents' home.

She unlocked the side drawer of her desk and drew out a folio and a writing tablet with several pages already covered in her small, careful hand. Kläre had attended a meeting of the Jewish Agency for Palestine two weeks earlier, on an evening when Jakob had dined with a client in Cologne. She had tried to speak with Jakob about the possibility of leaving, but he had dismissed her suggestions that the danger for Jews in Germany was becoming intolerable.

"Klärchen," he had said, his voice softening as though he were speaking to a child, "these Nazis are only rabble rousers. They are only trying to bring down the republic because they are too stupid and simple to cope with people different from themselves. This will work itself out. Besides, what else should I do besides the law? I cannot practice elsewhere."

But Kläre's early misgivings had turned to greater concern and then to a low-grade but persistent fear that frayed her nerves. She jumped when the radiator clanged in the entry hall, and no longer allowed her children to walk in the streets unaccompanied, despite the humiliation this caused ten-year-old Erwin.

The evening meeting she'd attended had been held in the back of a small shop on Benninghoffer Strasse in Hörde. Typically, she would have told Jakob—perhaps even asked him—about participating in something of this nature, but she'd known she would go regardless of his opinion, and therefore had said nothing.

Kläre's links to the organized Jewish community had become tenuous in recent years. Since her father's death, no one in the family went to the synagogue, and the women's groups that educated the wives and mothers of the community in their charitable and domestic duties felt closed and irrelevant to Kläre. She did bundle clothing and food and donated it to the Jewish committee for the half-starved displaced Poles and Russians who poured across the borders, filled the streets, and incited the wrath of angry mobs. But as she sat now in a pool of lamplight at her desk, visions of Sabbath dinners at her grandparents' house, filled with delicious food, raucous discussions, and an under-the-table world of cousins, filled her mind. *That* had been her Jewishness. Not this dreadful identity, pressed upon them all by the Nazis with a broad sweep.

Still, when she had heard from her neighbor, Greta Friedman, that there would be a meeting with representatives from the Central Committee of German Jews and the Jewish Agency for Palestine to describe a new program for emigrating, Kläre had been intrigued. The thought of leaving Germany for a desert halfway across the globe was an outlandish idea, but there was no question that a Jew could go there. Jakob was clearly sick with the shaking palsy, and in the last months Kläre had begun to understand that she would have to take more responsibility for making decisions about their lives. So, though she'd been nervous about going to a meeting of Jews, as such gatherings were a target of violence, she went to the meeting to listen. She'd asked Etta to stay into the evening and come later in the morning. Etta, tired from her early pregnancy, had gladly traded the morning work hours for a relaxed evening.

The night had been cold with winter's last hold on the darkening street as Kläre entered the stationer's shop and moved into offices at the rear. There were perhaps a dozen people seated on hastily set-up chairs in the small space. They were mostly men, and Kläre was relieved that she recognized only one of them, and vaguely at that. She took a seat in the rear and spoke to no one. The room was strangely still, as if the audience were already listening to something complex—heads down, hands held tensely on their laps.

A distinguished-looking man stood and began to speak. "Good evening, ladies and gentlemen. Thank you for coming to hear Mr. Chaim David Weber talk about the opportunity to immigrate to Palestine and what is necessary to know should you choose to pursue this. The Central Committee will soon issue a statement and recommendations regarding our activities, which will necessarily focus on the need to provide assistance to the members of our Jewish community who are here and have lost their jobs. You should not interpret in this statement that we discourage people from leaving Germany." The man paused. "What is published under our name must be worded carefully." He lowered his voice but grew more intense. "Please realize that the Central Committee is well aware of the increasing restrictions being placed on Jewish commerce and the attacks that have occurred on individuals and businesses. Each family must decide for itself what is best, but do not forget your brothers. Those who still have must help those who do not. *Tzedakah,* ladies and gentlemen; justice and mercy must remain our guides even in these troubled times. Ladies and gentlemen, Mr. Weber." He stopped speaking then. When Kläre looked up from her writing tablet, he held her eyes briefly before relinquishing the floor to Weber.

What does he mean, this man? He spoke as though in code. Kläre knew that Jakob's practice now involved many Jews whose assets had been seized or who had lost their jobs and were seeking legal recourse through the very rule of law that appeared to be vanishing down the gutter drain of the new Nazi government. Jakob labored to think of new means to work on behalf of his clients even as the very avenues of justice were closed off, one by one.

But what of their own safety? Jakob wanted her to trust that the situation in the government would right itself, yet Kläre saw the hungry farmers in the streets—fed them at her own back door, in fact—read the vitriol directed at Jews and Communists in the newspapers, and shrank from the increasingly strident speeches of Adolf Hitler.

Chaim David Weber began speaking rapidly with no preamble, as though he might be cut off at any moment and therefore had to impart all the necessary information quickly and concisely. There were already some eighteen thousand Jews in Palestine under the British Mandate, with more arriving every day. The Central Committee and the Jewish Agency were negotiating with the German government to allow Jews to immigrate to Palestine freely. It appeared as though they would be allowed to leave with goods, though not with much currency, so individuals planning to leave should look toward placing financial resources in saleable goods in preparation. And there was more—the paperwork, the importance of building the country with hard work, agriculture, engineering, etc.

Kläre listened and wrote. The fervor of Herr Weber's talk cemented her understanding of the enormity of what might lie ahead. She gazed down at the pages now covered with words and shuddered as a stab of hopelessness coursed through her like a cold draft. Jakob would never agree to this. He had already dismissed the idea once. But Kläre sat up straighter and continued writing. It did not matter. Her job was to understand. She would prepare . . . It would be like a legal brief, with all the options and considerations laid out. She would write to Ernst in Berlin for advice. She smiled wryly. Wouldn't her brother think this legalistic tactic by his sister clever?

Now, two weeks later, she was preparing her notes to speak again with Jakob. She would wait until this business with the boycott was finished. In the meantime, she wrote to Ernst in Berlin, choosing carefully her questions for him. Was he thinking of leaving? Did he think his practice in danger? Had he heard about the Palestine possibility? She described the slow but tormenting progress of Jakob's palsy, and wrote news of the children. She sealed the letter and addressed it carefully. Ernst would give her questions serious consideration. He would understand her urgency.

Kläre turned then to her final task. She drew the application for the massage course at the hospital out of the folio and completed the forms, thinking carefully about each response. She needed a letter of recommendation. Tomorrow she would go to Dr. Feuer—but he was a Jew. Perhaps she should get a signature from a Christian. Perhaps the physician at the hospital she had worked in during the war was still there and would remember that she had worked well with even the most difficult patients. Then again, he might not be allowed to sign for a Jew. *I will try both. Massage is work that I can do anywhere.*

It was late, and the house had grown colder. Kläre replaced her writing things in the desk, put the application and letter in her handbag, and climbed the stairs toward a short night of troubled sleep.

7 May 1933, Hörde

Spring was in full flower in the city center of Hörde. Despite the town's growth and pending incorporation as a commercial and industrial district of Dortmund, the red brick of stately churches and granite entryways of dull, massive office buildings were set off by the leafy green of mature trees and spring garden grass. Walks and lawns were hemmed with beds of fresh-blooming tulips, daffodils, and hyacinths.

Kläre slowed for a moment as she made her way past a cramped wrought iron enclosure, its fastidious patch of grass marred by a tumbled pedestal and smashed bits of stone. A statue of Goethe, mistaken for a Jew by a drunken, raucous throng, lay destroyed. Quickly Kläre moved on, head held high, eyes cast down. These days she avoided the streetcar, preferring to walk, changing direction if need be. She inhaled the spring air, isolating the song of a lone bird in the city noise.

Bernhardt Steinmann had phoned this morning, only moments after Jakob left for work and the last breakfast dishes were wiped dry.

"Good morning. May I speak to Frau Kohler, please?"

"I am Frau Kohler."

Silence. Then, "Here is Bernhardt Steinmann, Frau Kohler. Kläre . . ."

"Oh yes, hello. How are you?" Immediately Kläre felt stupid with the formality.

"I am sorry to disturb you at home, but I wondered. May I see you today for coffee?"

"Yes of course." There was no point in pretending. She had to go to the stationer's and then to Jakob's office to deliver the supplies. She could do that and still finish preparations for dinner this morning, leaving the afternoon free until the children came home. "I could meet you at half past two."

"Café Hintz, half past two, then?"

"Yes, that would be fine."

"Thank you . . . Kläre. I look forward to speaking with you."

"Goodbye, Herr Steinmann . . . Bernhardt."

The rest of the morning had been impossible. She'd made *sauerbraten* and peeled potatoes for dinner, but in her distraction she had cut herself and over-salted the precious cut of meat. What did he want? What should she wear? It had now been over a month since she'd seen or heard from Bernhardt Steinmann, yet not a day had gone by in which she had not thought of him—thought of his graceful hand holding the coffee cup as he told her of the shocking discovery of his Jewish blood. She had worried for him only a few days ago, when the Nazis had burned books by Jews and other non-Nazis in great bonfires all over Germany. Why had he asked to call her? Why had she agreed? From where came her desperation to keep this man in the maelstrom of her life as it now unfolded?

The morning housework finished, Kläre had dressed and made her way into the town center. Now, as she approached the stationery shop—which she had not entered since the night of the emigration meeting—her thoughts returned to all she had heard and done in the weeks since. Ernst had written her back by return post. No, he did not think Palestine was the answer. Yes, he shared her concern at the worsening conditions, but did not feel the need to leave. He still believed that the rule of law would prevail and the country would right itself. Kläre was not comforted.

She had nearly reached the door to the small shop when it flew open and a man's body hurtled onto the street, followed swiftly by another. Kläre immediately recognized the smaller man as the stationer himself. He was bent over on his knees and his coat was half torn from his body. As he raised his head, Kläre saw blood oozing from his disheveled hair. No sooner had he started to stand when three brown-shirted storm troopers burst from the shop, shouting. They began to savagely beat the two men with clubs, and as one tried to regain his feet a trooper kicked his legs out from under him and continued the beating. The man fell heavily toward Kläre, who had backed into the doorway of the shop next door. Kläre looked wildly from the body, which now blocked the sidewalk in front of her, to the troopers still shouting in staccato bursts, "Communist! Filthy Jew! We show you what good Germans will do!"

Kläre felt the blood rush from her head. She stared at the man at her feet, his one eye bloodied and shut, his other eye wide with panic. A trooper shouted at her, "Don't touch him!" Kläre hardly knew that she had bent toward the beaten man. "He is a filthy Jew Communist," the trooper said—and, eyeing her honey-blond hair and smart dress, "You are a good German; leave him."

In that instant she felt the strong grip of a large hand on her arm, and a second later was fairly lifted through the air, over the body of the groaning, prostrate man on the sidewalk. Before she could understand what was happening she was being half-carried, half-dragged through the quickly gathering crowd, away from the dreadful scene.

"Don't look behind, just keep walking straight ahead," Bernhardt Steinmann's firm voice ordered from above her lowered head. "Where is your husband's office? Is it closer to go there or to your home?"

"Schildstrasse. Only there, next to the corner." Kläre heard her own voice as if at a distance; she was surprised that she could speak at all. Bernhardt held her fast, one arm around her shoulders, the other hand still grasping her arm so tightly that it hurt, even through the layers of her gabardine coat and knit dress. They walked for another 100 meters before he turned abruptly into a quieter side street. There he stopped, released her, and searched her face anxiously.

"Are you hurt? Did you get hit?"

Standing in the cool spring sunshine, Kläre's chest was tight with fear and an enormous shudder shook her body. "No, no, I'm fine. I'm not hurt." She answered in a shocked whisper as her eyes filled with tears. "Thank you. I . . . I didn't know. I . . ." She was crying now in short, jagged sobs. And then his arms went around her and she leaned into the fine light wool of his coat. They stayed that way for a long moment—until the rising noise of shouts and whistles and pounding feet from the nearby street caused Bernhardt to pull away.

"Kläre, you must go now to your husband's offices. It is not safe to be here on the street." Again he propelled her forward, down the block to the corner and around the next block, back toward the main street. Breathless from their swift pace, Kläre turned her face up to Bernhardt's.

"Later . . . will you go to the café?"

"I will go, but you must not come if you are feeling uneasy. You have had a shock just now. Here. Take my card. Phone me in the next days if you are not able to meet this afternoon."

They had arrived at the faceless, solid building in which Jakob's offices were located. Bernhardt paused, gave Kläre's arm a gentle squeeze, and was gone around the corner as quickly as he had appeared. Kläre wished desperately to call to him, to go with him—to stay in the protection of his strong arms. She breathed deeply for a few moments, composing herself, before opening the heavy brass door. The marble lobby was cool and dark after the sunlight outside, and Kläre paused while her eyes adjusted to the light. She walked to the rear, where she mounted worn stone steps to the second floor. There, the sedate office suite of Kohler and Krauss welcomed her with a calm order that contrasted utterly with the chaos and violence of the scene she had just left. She smiled gratefully at Fräulein Hildt at the front desk and waited as the secretary opened Jakob's door and announced her.

Jakob sat at his desk, looking tired, as he seemed always to look these days, but in command of the ordered work before him. His look as she entered was of one who dwelled in an alternate world of thought.

"Kläre, you're a bit early. Did you stop at Scheiner's?"

She paused before replying. "I started to go, but there was . . . an incident. The Brownshirts were there and I didn't dare go in. We will have to pick up your order tomorrow if we can. It was bad. Scheiner himself was beaten." Involuntarily she shuddered, and Jakob's attention turned to concern.

"Are you all right?" he asked, putting down his pen and moving his chair back from the desk.

"Yes, yes, I am fine, but it was quite ugly. It scared me, Jakob."

"Of course. Come, I'll just finish this one letter and we'll go home to dinner."

Kläre smiled weakly and sat in the deep leather of the client chair in front of the desk. She watched as Jakob concentrated on each word that he wrote, willing his hand to be steady with the concentration that was his great strength. It was not even eleven in the morning and Kläre was already exhausted. Closing her eyes, she immediately saw the brown-shirted arm, banded with a swastika, methodically raising and lowering the club over the bodies of the two men in the street. Her eyes flew open and she looked down to the handbag and gloves clutched in her lap. She focused on breathing steadily until Jakob rose—arduously—from his chair and made his way first to his secretary's desk and then to his coat and hat.

Before they exited the building, Kläre prayed briefly that it would be quiet in the streets—and it was. They skirted the main thoroughfare and did not see the hastily boarded storefront and swept glass around the bloodstains in front of the stationer's.

"Why were you there? How did you see me?" Kläre searched Bernhardt's face in the afternoon sunlight pouring through the window of Café Hintz.

She had only just arrived, later than he and with the beginning of an apology that she could not stay long. "You mustn't apologize, please," he had said. "Not ever."

"I had a meeting this morning at my bank," he began. His face hardened. "As I passed the stationer's, I heard shouting in the shop and saw the uniforms through the window. I must say I hurried on until I heard the men screaming. When I looked back I saw you. I circled back across the street. When I saw the filthy trooper looking at you, I had to do something."

Kläre sat back in her seat, living again the frightening scene from the morning. "I must thank you once more," she said. Bernhardt smiled and looked ready to speak when the words tumbled from Kläre: "In another moment I would have been in that shop. I would have opened the door."

"Yes," he said quietly.

"I cannot understand what is happening," Kläre rushed on. "How should we live?" She calmed her voice, looking around the café with its modulated murmurs coming from the many occupied tables. "How can we sit here this afternoon when what happened this morning is happening everywhere?"

Bernhardt stared silently at Kläre, his knowing eyes reflecting her frustration, her fear. "I don't know. Not at all." It was all he could say.

"Bernhardt," Kläre asked at last, "why did you ask me to come here?"

He thought for a moment and the faint lines across his forehead deepened. "You mentioned that you planned to take a massage course," he began. "My mother is quite uncomfortable. She has become terrified of going out, even for a walk, and has stopped seeing her doctor or her masseuse. She is fearful of being . . . found out." He was choosing his words carefully, watching her as he spoke. "I don't know if you have yet completed the course you spoke of, but if so, perhaps you would agree to work with my mother. She is a very good woman. Only now quite scared."

"Yes, of course. Of course she is scared." The day's terror, confusion, and helplessness suddenly converged in Kläre and created a powerful sympathy for Frau Steinmann's fear. It filled her with clarity of purpose, and the wish to be of service to Bernhardt—welcome feelings that displaced her helplessness. "I am finishing the first part of the course, and I must have practice. I would be honored to be of help."

A smile of relief played across Bernhardt's mouth even as pain filled his eyes. "Thank you," he said.

8 1935, Brussels

Light can be taken a thousand times from another light without diminishing it.
—Peter Paul Rubens, 1616

Kläre had chosen a dove-grey wool suit for the train ride. She smoothed the skirt across her lap, appreciating briefly the fine material and the skill of her dressmaker in the clean drape and perfect fit of the long jacket. Gazing at her reflection in the window, she noted the tilt of her hat; it was last year's, but still smart, a feather rising from the cloche at just the right angle. Across the compartment, Werner was already asleep, his body relaxed into the corner of the leather seat as it met the window, his head leaning into Erwin, who sat heavily in the center of the bench. Parcels and valises surrounded the three passengers.

Kläre took stock. First the gifts. Trude was in Belgium now, her husband Rudi forced to sell, at a fraction of its worth, his share of the furniture factory that his father had established. Brussels was a fine city, wrote Trude, but Rudi was badly depressed and though he had work in a factory there, he was bitter. The girls had learned French quickly, and were doing well in the Catholic school they attended. Flemish remained difficult even with their German, but that would come as well. What Trude longed for was the particular lingerie she was accustomed to: sensible German underclothes, and her favorite juices and tinned food that were local to Hörde. She missed items of home, and these Kläre had bought and bundled as gifts for her sister.

The door of the train compartment opened suddenly and an older woman hesitated in the entrance, looking first at the boys and then at the open seat next to Kläre. The train was crowded. Kläre redistributed her packages to the floor, under Werner's legs, and then moved the large valise so the woman could sit. This she did with a sigh of relief and a nodding smile. As she settled herself, Kläre stole a glance at her. The veined but shapely legs and the strong hands of the middle-aged woman were attractive; they bespoke a woman's life—the badge of childbearing or long standing hours and real work. The skin not taut on cheeks anymore, the silver curl in back of the ear, the body less firm than it once had been, all showed that some female qualities had been given over while some were yet preserved.

She is not young anymore, but is still strong and free and healthy. The thought was a comfort to Kläre, but took only a small bit of the anxious knot in her chest away.

It was becoming warmer in the coach and Kläre carefully drew off her gloves and tucked them into her handbag. The scent of oil rose faintly from her hands and she leaned back, eyes closed, and summoned the hour early this morning in which she had massaged Rosa Steinmann.

This had been her second visit. The first time, Kläre had gone at Frau Steinmann's request to meet the older woman—and perhaps, Kläre realized, to be approved for the actual massage work. It had been a short visit, but enough had passed in the silences between the niceties of conversation to trade knowledge of class distinctions known best to women.

"And where do you live, Frau Kohler? Is it nearby?"

"Yes, quite. We are in Virchow Strasse."

"Ah, I see. And Bernhardt tells me your husband is an attorney, yes?"

"Yes, he is in practice in the Konig building on Schildstrasse."

"Mmm."

A moment of comfortable silence ensued, during which time Rosa Steinmann looked appreciatively at Kläre, who knew the older woman had noted her fine suit and good posture.

"And how is it you have come to do the massage, Frau Kohler?" Rosa Steinmann asked.

Kläre spoke carefully now. "I worked at the hospital during the war, with returning soldiers. I began to learn it there, actually." She did not add how in recent months, Jakob's illness had worsened and it had become clearer to her that his deterioration matched the symptoms of soldiers who had been poisoned with nerve gas. At times the soldiers had uncontrolled palsies, and could not bear to be touched. At other times, their only solace outside of heavy sedation was deep, penetrating massage. This Kläre had learned to do with precious oil so as not to cause friction on the over-reactive skin of her patients. Sometimes she could massage Jakob in this way to calm him; other times he could not bear her touch. As he weakened and the Nazi threat grew more vicious and unpredictable, Kläre feared increasingly that she would soon have to support her family herself. This she did not impart to Rosa Steinmann.

"Frau Steinmann, can you tell me what manner of massage has made you most comfortable in your previous sessions?"

Kläre listened intently as Frau Steinmann catalogued her aches and pains and the techniques that provided relief. Kläre nodded, asked a few more questions, and then surveyed the sitting room, noting the daybed that would become the massage table.

The visit had drawn to a close when Frau Steinmann sat back in her chair and spoke pointedly, "Frau Kohler, I have been used to paying four marks for an hour massage." She paused and looked directly at the younger woman. "I am sure you must charge at least five marks, no?"

Kläre's eyes widened. Five marks! It was a handsome sum, more than she would have dreamed of charging on her own. Before she could answer, Frau Steinmann rose and extended her graceful hand.

"Wonderful, then. Shall we see each other next week? This same time?"

Kläre rose and shook the other woman's hand firmly, surprised at the strength of her grip. "Thank you. Yes, next week will be fine."

She had returned the following week to find her new client dressed in a loose-fitting silk housecoat that graced her tall frame well. Kläre wore a plain grey cotton dress, very much like her nursing sister uniform from twenty years ago. The daybed was low for Kläre, but she worked with it, moving Frau Steinmann and using pillows, towels, and sheets that she had brought to prop and bolster where needed. She murmured instructions and asked questions occasionally, exploring the aged but stately woman's body firmly and gently, easing tightened muscles and releasing tension in the fascia. Kläre straightened twice to roll her neck and stretch her back, tired from exerting so much effort in a bent position, but otherwise her hands worked until the hour had passed. As the last seconds ticked down, she reached under Frau Steinmann's shoulders between the woman's back and the daybed and slid her hands down to her waist. She then inched her fingers up the slender muscles along the older woman's spine and finished with a gentle cupping around the base of her white-haired skull, softly stretching her neck. She laid Frau Steinmann's head back on the pillow, her white hair spread on the starched linen. The look of ease and comfort across her powdery wrinkles and perfect half-moon eyelids made Kläre smile with satisfaction.

"*Aufwiedersehen,* Frau Steinmann. I will see you again in a fortnight."

Kläre smiled now as the train sped across the countryside, the station stops becoming less frequent, allowing long runs at full speed. She thought of Jakob, who had declined to accompany his family to Brussels, pleading work, though they both knew it wasn't work at all. Jakob had never been comfortable amidst the quick-witted banter of his in-laws. Even more, Kläre thought, he chose to remain home because it was becoming clearer that he was not well.

Originally, Frieda had planned to come on this journey, but at the last minute had to stay in Dülken as she was ill from trichinosis—no doubt from eating pork. Poor Frieda. Her luck was always the worst. Kläre thought with a pang of her grandparents' kosher home and the fact that none of the Ente households followed the kosher laws any longer. Frieda was weak from her illness and, though she desperately wanted to see Trude, had resigned herself to staying home. She'd sent along beautiful sweaters for each of her nieces in her stead, and Kläre had packed them carefully among the other gifts.

Kläre sighed. Frieda might have had an opinion about Trude's most recent plan, and Kläre needed someone to help her think it through. She had not even tried to tell Jakob of the idea to join Trude in Belgium and establish a guesthouse. It would have to be small, but she could work hard with Trude. Kläre could do the cooking, and Trude and she together could keep the rooms. Perhaps Rudi and Jakob would help with the business side. If not, she and Trude could learn. She knew they could. Jakob would manage what work he could and they could live in their own portion of the house. People still traveled to Brussels, so there was guesthouse business to be had.

The train sped through the countryside. They had left Germany and entered Holland. The border crossing was routine, nearly sleepy, and Kläre was relieved. She had heard stories of terrible harassment, but the Dutch border was still friendly. Venlo, Maastricht, another border crossing, and then Leuven all passed by like a moving picture in a theater. Flat farms and grazing land, low thatch-roofed houses, canals and irrigation waterways, and small towns with dull square housing all flew across the window. Everywhere, the verdant green of early summer and kilometer after kilometer of lushly tended flower fields colored the landscape with orderly beauty. The wide-open sky was a canvas for an advancing guard of billowy white clouds. Fields gave way to houses lined up on the edges of farms, which in turn became suburban tracts and then, finally, the solid outskirts of Brussels. The boys had awakened and Werner now sat, nose pressed to the window, as the train slowed and they entered Central Station. Suddenly shy, Werner turned to his mother as she caught sight of her sister on the platform, a bouquet in her arms.

"Mutti, I think I see Tante Trude, there. Don't you?"

Kläre and Trude abandoned the unpacking as sun broke through a roiling mass of clouds. Protests swept aside, the children were swathed in sweaters and slickers and turned loose on the beach below the house to run wildly after the long day of travel by train from Brussels. Arm in arm, Trude and Kläre fought the wind up the beach, practiced eyes on the children. They were intoxicated with the pleasure of each other's company absent the strain of their men or households to consider.

Erwin trudged silently apart from the rest, pausing occasionally to choose a shell for his knapsack. Werner ran with his cousins, exactly between them in age and giving over the requirements of boyish concerns to the curious delights of the girls. They were quick and smart and lighthearted, frequently too much for him to understand or follow—but they were kind to him, and so the three of them streaked down the wild, windy beach, throwing stones into the sea, gathering sea grasses and small, sturdy flowers into tiny bouquets that they brought to their mothers.

Off again running, always running, the children finally reached the Paravang. It was an elegantly wrought windscreen with benches alongside Leopold Park. Its roof, built in neo-gothic style, was decorated with glazed tiles in the form of shells. Certain that there were ice creams to be had, the children ran back to their mothers, heads bent together to be heard above the wind.

"Mutti, please!" Helga begged, her black curls flying about her earnest face.

"No, not now. You have a treat for after supper at home. Something special that Tante Kläre brought from Dortmund! But only for children who eat their supper, take their baths, and are ready for bed." Trude's eyes danced as they met her daughter's. Kläre marveled again that her wild sister had borne these two diminutive daughters, each with the same vivacious spirit as their mother's. She seemed less to raise them than to accompany them on each of life's adventures.

"You find for us the prettiest shells from the beach on the way back, alright?" Trude sent the children running again to the water's edge, studying the wave-smoothed sand.

They had arrived at the house by the sea in Blankenberge late in the day. With unpacking the trunks, the walk, and feeding the children, it was eight o'clock before the boys in their bunks and the girls in the double bed were settled under summer featherbeds. Before the last good-night was finished and Trude's clear, lovely voice had sung the final note of a lullaby, the measured, peaceful breathing of the young ones signaled the first chance at rest for the two mothers.

The sounds and sights in this house by the sea excited Kläre. Though it was still the summer holidays, autumn was heralded in the piercing wind that whistled through the crack between the glass doors leading out to the veranda. Steely light illuminated the wild evening on the Belgian North Sea coast. Trude prepared coffee as Kläre settled into the sturdy chair on the veranda. She pulled a second chair close and spread the fine Scottish wool travel blanket across her knees and onto the other chair for Trude. The narrowest of lines opened on the horizon as sky met sea and the light of the falling sun shone through between the cloudbank and the water. It was all she needed, that thinnest of beacons to turn the threat of storm into a powerful canvas of natural beauty. It filled her, strengthened her, but also brought on an exquisite loneliness. She often felt it. It was as though this power, this drawing from her connection to the natural world, was something she could not fully share.

Trude brought a tray with the coffee and settled into the chair next to her sister. "It would be nicer if the weather was fine, no?" Trude's pretty face frowned as she scanned the seascape.

"Oh, come now; it's fabulous. This is for me a wonderful gift. How did you manage it?" Kläre insisted.

Trude immediately broke into a satisfied smile. Kläre knew that it pleased Trude to have surprised her older sister with this small holiday. "It's all part of what I hope to do, Kläre. What I want to do with you." Trude leaned toward her now, the coffee forgotten. "This is the holiday home of the Oslers. As I told you, they wish to leave for America as soon as their visa is approved. They have already the affidavit from some family in New York. They want to sell their home in Brussels and this house, too. Leah Osler already runs the house in Brussels as a guesthouse. She takes guests in two of the rooms and they live in the rest. Ach, Kläre, I know we could do this! You mustn't stay any more in Germany. It's not safe. Not for you and not for the children. You must convince Jakob! And you must bring Mama as well. We can both look after her. Rudi says you could buy from the Oslers with a very good price. They are eager to sell." Even in the darkening twilight, the depth of Trude's enormous blue-grey eyes shined with excitement as her words tumbled out.

"A guesthouse. Yes . . ." Kläre worked the linen napkin absently around her fingers as she thought. *Perhaps Jakob will listen now.* She shivered as the words of the decree in the *Westfalian News* came back to her. *The Jew can no longer seek presence before the bar of the Court nor should he expect support of the Court behind him. As he who would deign to speak of German law, so must that person be a true German by law. On 15 September, all who are "not blood Germans" will be removed from the state Courts.* It had been some time since the heated debate over Palestine with Jakob, which she had lost miserably. They had barely spoken for days afterward, and Kläre had resigned herself to temporary silence on the topic.

But now it was different. While they were away, Jakob was to confer with his colleagues—Elias, Weiser, Ostwald, and of course Krauss, Jakob's long-time partner—over what the decree meant and what there was to do. Never, Kläre mused, would he agree to call on Louis, his own brother, a Rechtsanwalt and Notar, the same as Jakob, a year older, and savvy in the ways of politics as Jakob was not. The estrangement of the brothers was still, after all these years, incomprehensible to Kläre, though she'd learned early on that it was strong and abiding, and not a topic for discussion. Whatever the new edict meant, perhaps now Jakob would agree to listen to an idea for leaving Germany. Belgium was not far, was fiercely independent, and tolerated its Jews—and if Kläre and Trude started a business, it would give Jakob time to explore his own possibilities.

"Kläre! What are you thinking?" Trude put her hand on her sister's arm.

Kläre met her eyes. The enthusiasm she saw there made her smile.

Trude would embrace this experience first and foremost as an adventure—an opportunity. This Kläre loved about her younger sister. She did not crowd her thoughts with worry when she had a plan.

"I like it. We would work well, no?" Kläre sipped the cooling coffee. "I will have a job to convince Jakob. And Mama. I could also do the massage. I have begun, you know."

"Yes, of course. We should have to make rooms for you—in Brussels, but also here in the summer. We could bring people for a proper cure by the seaside." Trude was thoughtful now, and only the soundless wind, gentler now with descending night, drifted across the veranda.

Kläre closed her eyes and felt the breeze tease the wisps of hair that perpetually came loose from the knot at the nape of her neck. For just a moment she allowed herself to feel the exhaustion of the task that lay before her if they were to make this work. It did no good to dwell there, she knew. In contemplative silence, the two women finished their coffee and left the veranda for the warmth of featherbeds and heavy sleep.

The dream came to Kläre in the depth of night. A massive stone hearth stood at one end of a cavernous room, crowned with a ledge. A balcony ran above and behind it with a staircase to one side. An old and battered horn fell to the floor from the top of the hearth with a tinny crash. Kläre noted this within the dream with vague curiosity.

Other things—old, small musical instruments—began to fall, and then the dissonance of trying to make sense of the senseless began. It did not yet feel evil. As she stood beside the great hearth and watched, a strong, ancient hand grasped another small horn, tossed it over the ledge, and then withdrew. It occurred to Kläre that this disembodied hand was beckoning for her to discover more. Soon the hand appeared again, followed this time by a wizened old head and then the bodies of an old woman, several men, and a younger woman. They poured over the ledge and down the stairs into the hall below. One among them declared that they had been silent, in hiding, long enough.

Still the dread did not come—not until the younger woman approached Kläre and told her in threatening tones that soon enough she would do what was asked of her.

In the morning, during successive layers of waking memory, Kläre recalled the people as gnomish—like a band of travelers from a fairy tale. The unnerving sense of impending harm the dream inspired stayed with her into the overcast morning, but soon the demands of the children and the day by the ocean prevailed.

9 1935, Hörde

15 September—*The profession of Rechtsanwalt is closed to Jews. Existing professionals may continue to practice.*
27 September—*On order of the Riechsjusticeminister, all full-blooded Jews are forbidden to act as official Notaries.*

Jakob Kohler sat in the straight chair, hat in hand, briefcase placed on the floor next to him. The room was Spartan and dingy, not at all like the anterooms of the courts and judges' chambers where he was used to waiting. Blessedly, his hands betrayed only a slight tremor, and the headache that had plagued him the evening before had receded.

The door to the official's office was flung open, and an assistant shouted out, "Herr Doktor Kohler. Herein!"

As Jakob entered the office, the young man threw him a look of disdain. *Never before would this boy have spoken to me in such a way,* thought Jakob as he faced the man seated behind the desk.

"Herr Reichjusticesminister Heinrich Schloss," announced the assistant, "here is the Jew Herr Doktor Kohler."

The minister worked for another moment on the papers in front of him and then looked up at Jakob, who tipped his head slightly in a respectful nod. "Heil Hitler," the minister said forcefully as he rose, the accompanying salute pointed aggressively toward Jakob, who froze for an instant before bowing slightly once again, adding a heel click of his well polished shoes this time in deference to the authority of the minister.

He began speaking before his failure to return the salute of the Reich could become a topic of comment. "Herr Reichjusticesminister Schloss, I have here documents in which you will find substantive proof of my service as a soldier and my loyalty to the government. I have brought my Iron Cross, second class, from the war and also my qualifying examinations for Rechtsanwalt, citations from the Mayor of Hörde, and several letters from judges of the Court and the businesses which I have represented. I have also sworn affidavits declaring that I have no association with the Communists and never have, as well as . . ."

"Herr Dr. Kohler, my assistants and I are quite capable of reading what you have brought, are we not?" the minister interrupted in a soft voice filled with malice.

Jakob stood silent. Without taking his eyes off the minister's closed face, he placed his file carefully on the desk.

"You will be granted a provisional license to continue your practice only with the degraded title of Rechtsconsul," the minister continued, warming now to his officious task. "You will be allowed only to represent other Jews, and then only in the courts which may still be willing to tolerate Jewish cases. All other licenses are revoked. You will no longer wear the robes of a Rechtsanwalt, and you will announce as you approach a judge's bench, 'I am a Jew. I present to you my Jew card, and my Jew number is such and such.' You will be watched carefully to ensure that you abide by what I have said."

Before Jakob could even think, the minister spoke once more. "That is all. My assistant will show you out and draft the necessary papers." Without a further glance, the minister returned to his seat.

Jakob managed to murmur, "Thank you, Herr Reichsminister," before following the young man into the next room.

Thirty minutes later, Jakob Kohler was back in the streets of Hörde, the waning sunshine of late September welcome but no match for the chill that shook him from head to toe. He bent forward as he walked, as if fighting a strong wind, though the day was entirely calm. He felt the tension in his neck rise over the top of his head until it gripped the left side of his forehead and the eye below in blinding pain. He staggered once, but righted himself by force of will. He would complete the five-minute walk to his offices. He thought briefly of taking the streetcar home, but he couldn't wait that long to get to his pain tablets.

The thought of home shook him further with the reliving of the terrible argument he and Kläre had had the night before. She had returned from the holiday in Belgium with the fresh, windswept look of the sea in her eyes. The lines of worry that seemed constantly to rest on her face these days had been softened by the pleasure of the visit with her sister. Werner had chattered for days about the beach and his cousins and the ice creams. Even Erwin had been less sour than usual. It wasn't long, however, before the trouble began.

"Jakob, you must really listen, now," Kläre had begun urgently. They were drinking coffee in the sitting room after supper on the second evening after her return. "Trude and I have spoken for a long time. Even Rudi believes this can work. We can sell the house here and use the money from Papa to help buy the two houses in Belgium. The one in Brussels is in a fine neighborhood, and already Frau Osler takes guests in two of the rooms. The house by the sea is solid and large and in a very nice place. Rudi says we can have both houses from the Oslers for a very good price. They are eager to leave, Jakob."

"Rudi, Rudi. What does Rudi know? He is a stupid man, Kläre." Jakob spat out each word.

It was as if he'd hit her. He heard the poisonous tone of his own voice as Kläre sat back in her chair. Her cheeks reddened and her eyes flamed angrily. "He is at least smart enough to understand that his family had to leave Germany. His children are now at least safe. Do you understand that soon we cannot send the boys to a German school? Is it not enough that we live in fear every day of an incident in the street? Should the children learn to answer to 'dirty Jew'? Do you want one of OUR boys to be made to stand in front of the others and labeled as an enemy, a Jew, like the Newstadts' boy? Do we wait until you have nothing left of your work and no one to work for?" By now her voice was reduced to a choked whisper.

"Kläre, I go tomorrow to the Reichsjusticeminister. I believe I will have no trouble to get this new license. Sondheim, Simonas, and Meier have all received it. It is crazy to leave now. There is more business than ever. I'm needed here, Kläre." He had sunk into his chair in exhaustion, the headache already pressing with increasing urgency on his attention. "Please Kläre, not now."

She had straightened further, the animation draining from her face, replaced by a heart-sinking hardness. Noiselessly, she'd brought him his tablets and water. They had spoken no further.

10 1937, Dortmund

Rosa Steinmann fastened the last mother-of-pearl button under her chin with some difficulty. She smoothed the pin-tucked silk bodice over her ample bust and attempted to step into her soft leather shoes. Seating herself on the single metal chair in the small room, she spread wide the hooks and pulled the tongue of the boot as far out as possible before again placing her foot toe-first into the boot. It was no use. Even if she could get the boot on, she would never be able to hook it properly. A bitter sigh of frustration escaped her as she rose and opened the door. The nursing sister sat a few feet away at a small desk in the waiting room, but it was Frau Kohler, seated in the chair next to the door, who rose and looked inquiringly.

"Please, could you help me with the shoes?" Rosa whispered.

"Yes, of course." Kläre gathered her handbag and the letter she was writing and entered the room, silently closing the door behind her.

"I'm so sorry, Frau Kohler. I don't mean to ask you for so much help."

Kläre smiled. "But of course, it is difficult with the arthritis. My mother finds the same."

Rosa Steinmann's sadness welled up as she thought of her daughter, now far away in America with Alex and the two grandchildren. Their letters were regular but brief, as their lives were filled with the exhausting work of adjusting to a new country, finding employment, learning the new language, and becoming accustomed to what sounded like an entirely different world. If only Liselotte were here.

Bernhardt was a good son, but he could not care for his mother in the way that his sister had, and that Frau Kohler now did. In moments like this one, Rosa wished to reach out her hand and stroke the honey-colored head bent over her foot. For more than a year now Kläre had come to her to do the massage, and now also to help her when there was no one else. Only one of the maids remained in the Steinmann home, and she was becoming more unreliable by the day. Bernhardt came less often, and seemed to be working many more hours though he had less business.

"Come, I will take you now for a good cup of coffee and a pastry." Rosa smiled at her young friend.

Kläre seemed about to decline, but then changed her mind and responded, "I would like that, thank you." She helped the older woman into her coat and the two made their way across the street to the Dortmunder Hotel, where afternoon coffee was being served.

"Bernhardt will join us. He is today in Dortmund also," Rosa announced as she sat at the linen-covered table. She noted how Frau Kohler's eyes widened, and she smiled to herself. *I fancy that she likes Bernhardt. And why wouldn't she? She is young and attractive. She is gentle, but obviously a bright woman. She carries herself with an air of modesty but also self-confidence and perhaps also some passion. I hear little of the husband . . .*

She hadn't any more time to pursue these thoughts, as Bernhardt was already making his way toward their table. He caught his mother's eye, and she thought she saw him lift an eyebrow in question, but he bent dutifully to kiss her cheek and then turned his attention to her companion.

"Frau Kohler—a pleasure, I am sure." His smile was genuine.

"Yes, thank you, Herr Steinmann. Your mother has just had quite a good visit with the new doctor."

Rosa's previous doctor, Heinrich Stern, was a Jew, and no longer allowed to practice on "Aryan" patients. Rosa had been miserable for days after the notice arrived—she had actually cried as she'd spoken to her son over the telephone about it.

"I'm so glad, Mother. I trust he found everything in order."

"Yes, quite, for an old woman." Rosa smiled again at her son. He looked perpetually tired these days, but was relaxed for the moment.

"I saw Melisande Durr today, on the train from Düsseldorf." Bernhardt directed the information toward his mother, but Rosa noticed that he watched also to see Kläre's reaction.

"Melisande Durr? How interesting," Rosa replied. "I thought the Nazis condemned her. Does she have a show here, then?"

"No, it appears as though she has some other business in the city." Bernhardt seemed to be gauging something in the situation before continuing. "I believe there are dissenters organizing to help . . . those who are being persecuted." He had studiously avoided using the word "Jews," but his meaning was clear.

Rosa said nothing.

"She continues, then, to champion the political left?" Kläre asked after a quick glance around the room.

"Not exactly. She has moved more toward the network of people who assist with escapes and who care for children whose parents . . . cannot."

Rosa squeezed her eyes shut for a moment. One heard now about these children: Jewish children whose fathers had disappeared, whose mothers had been beaten or vanished. Murmurs, mostly, but the stories were alarming and increasing in frequency by the day. The Agency for Jews in Germany had been forced to step in to address the growing problem of Jewish orphans or children whose parents had been taken and then not heard from again.

"How brave," Rosa finally said, unable to mask the fear in her voice.

"Yes, she is very brave," Kläre said fiercely—then, rising from her chair, "I must really catch the tram for Hörde now. It is getting late."

"Allow me to see you to a taxi. Please." Bernhardt stood and was at Kläre's elbow. "You've been such a comfort to my mother. I am very grateful."

Kläre looked from son to mother and back again to son. "All right, yes, that would be very helpful. Good-bye, Frau Steinmann. I will see you again in a fortnight."

"Thank you very much, Frau Kohler."

After promising his mother that he would return quickly, Bernhardt guided Kläre through the maze of tables to the hotel lobby and helped her into her coat. His hands rested for the briefest of moments on her shoulders before he released her. "How are you, Kläre?" he asked.

"Everything is the same. I am only more frightened now." She could scarcely look at him, wishing neither to fight tears nor to tear herself away from his gaze.

"May I phone you soon? I'd like to . . . to meet. Could you do that?"

"Yes. Yes, I will. I will go to your mother in two weeks' time again. Perhaps when I am finished with her."

"All right. I think I can arrange to be free then. Thank you, Kläre."

Bernhardt then dipped and brushed Kläre's lips with his own. Before Kläre could open her eyes and recover from the jolt of electricity that coursed through her, he had already started toward the door to the street. At once the kiss became a strengthening pillar in the shaky structure that was Kläre's courage these days.

The doorman helped Kläre into the taxi while Bernhardt paid the driver, and soon she was headed to the east side of the city, and then into Hörde.

11 1938, Elberfeld

The sacristy in St. Stephen's smelled of stone damp and freshly ironed linen. Ansel Beckmann surveyed the vestments, monstrance, paten, chalice, ciborium, bowl, sprinkler, censer, flagon, and altar linens from his elevated perspective. Though he was tall for his twelve years, he still needed to step onto the wooden stool to place the sacred objects across the altar and ensure that each of them was clean, shined, and in its proper place. He was young to have been given this responsibility, but he loved the order of the ritual, the artisanship of the objects, and the disciplined care that made it possible for Father Sproll to close his eyes as he sang the Mass and reach to just the right spot for what was needed.

Satisfied that all was as it should be, Ansel stepped down from the stool and was headed toward the low doorway leading to the side aisle of St. Stephen's when he heard voices approaching the sacristy from Father Sproll's study. Someone unfamiliar was reading something in an angry hush:

"National Socialism is the fulfillment of the will of God which is demonstrated to us in our blood. . . . Christianity is not dependent upon the Apostle's Creed. . . . The true Christianity is represented in the Party, and the German people are now called by the Party and by the Führer to a real Christianity. . . . It is not the Church that has demonstrated that Faith which could move mountains; the Führer has. He is the herald of a new revelation." The man paused, then went on: "This is dangerous. This man Kerrl is trying to undermine the very connection of the Church to the people."

Ansel stole into the aisle, leaving the heavy door ajar. He heard the sounds of footsteps entering the sacristy from the other side. Father Sproll's deep, resonant voice answered the unknown speaker from only a few meters away.

"Heinrich, this is what I have been trying to tell you for months now. Why do you think I was sent away from Rottenberg? Now it is the Confessing Church that Kerrl is after, but it will only be a matter of time before the Nazis will come after the Catholic Church as well. Already we are forbidden to advertise our youth groups over the Hitler Youth movement. If we protest the activities of the Brownshirts, we risk becoming their victims. I tell you, Heinrich, to do our work—to keep this Kinderheim running and our boys safe—we must remain quiet. Do you understand?"

A long silence filled the room as Ansel stood motionless outside the door. Finally, the unknown voice spoke: "Yes . . . I don't like it, but I understand." The man's tone was weary.

One pair of footsteps retreated into the church, but Father Sproll remained in the sacristy, moving quietly around the room as he prepared for the five o'clock Mass. Ansel remained uncertainly rooted to his spot behind the door. He had understood only part of the conversation, but the danger that traveled like a crackle of lightning between the two men he had understood all too clearly.

"Beckmann," Father Sproll's voice commanded.

Ansel's heart jumped in his chest and fear sent prickles into his cheeks. "Yes, Father," he croaked, unable to move.

"Come in, Beckmann."

The priest's voice was firm, but not angry. Ansel drew a quick breath and stepped into the sacristy.

Father Sproll sought and held his gaze. "Did you hear my conversation with Herr Schmidt?"

"Yes, Father." Ansel gave no thought to any reply other than the absolute truth. Father Sproll was new to St. Stephen's, but Ansel had already formed a deep attachment to him, one born of respect and admiration. In the long and lonely years of his time here, Ansel had never felt noticed or recognized as anything more than a mouth to feed. It was different with Father Sproll.

The priest now regarded him as though a decision had to be made. Ansel's mind went blank with the fear that he had somehow violated the trust that was still so new and unfamiliar between them.

"I'm sorry that you heard us, but I appreciate that you removed yourself," the priest said. His response was totally unexpected, and Ansel struggled for a moment to think of what to say, but the priest continued. "Sometimes in the face of difficult things, we have to just continue to do our jobs—to do what we know is right. To discover what it is that God asks of us can be a comfort, Beckmann."

"Yes, Father." Ansel continued to watch the priest.

"Do your studies go well at the Gymnasium?" Father Sproll asked. Ansel was one of only two boys from the Kinderheim who were allowed to travel to Wuppertal to attend the high school there.

"Yes, Father, my examinations in history and literature and Latin are quite good. Maths are more difficult."

"Are your family in good health?" Father Sproll appeared distracted, though the question seemed genuine enough.

"As far as I know, Father," Ansel answered. "I haven't been home since Christmas." Ansel worked hard to keep his voice neutral, though he could see a troubled look pass fleetingly across the broad forehead and deep blue eyes of the priest—a look that mirrored the pain in Ansel's heart. After four years, he still missed his home and family. He had not yet mastered the control of that missing.

"You have been here for a long time already Beckmann, no?" Father Sproll asked.

"Yes, Father." Ansel did not trust himself to speak further.

"I expect it's still difficult, with your siblings remaining at home."

"Yes, Father. I mean, no. I am fine now." Ansel was confused; how did the priest know of his family situation? The sympathy with which Father Sproll spoke was unexpected. Ansel's face flushed with barely restrained emotion. But he had struggled too long to bury the loneliness and longing to air it now, especially in front of this man, by whom

Ansel wanted only to be regarded as strong and able. He straightened his shoulders and met the priest's gaze.

"Beckmann, you mustn't speak of what you heard today. Best not even to think about it. Do you understand?" Father Sproll looked at him gravely, his tone firm.

"Yes, Father," Ansel replied, though truly he understood only that he wanted to do precisely what the priest wished of him.

"The new boy, Krimm," Father Sproll continued, his voice once again soft and calm. "I'd like you to help him a little. He is young, as you were, and could use some kindness."

"Yes, Father." Ansel was relieved.

"You may go." Father Sproll turned back to his preparations.

Ansel exited the sacristy, walked quickly through the church, and emerged into the afternoon sunshine. He had nearly an hour before Mass; he had planned to use the time to study, but now he was obliged to think about Krimm. The boy had been at St. Stephen's for just over a week, and slept in the hall with the lower-form boys. Ansel left the grassy, sun-filled courtyard and climbed the narrow staircase to the lower-form sleeping room. Only the youngest boys would be in there now, as their day of classes, prayer, and chores finished earlier than the others'.

Ansel paused outside the door at the back of the sleeping room when he heard the sharp voice of a house sister—Sister Gertrude, he judged, from the sound of her raspy bark—emanate from inside. He waited until he heard the sister depart before stepping through the door. Only four of the twenty inhabitants were there, and they all froze in position, alarm flickering across their young faces, when they saw Ansel.

"Who is Krimm?" Ansel asked gently. Three heads swung toward a small boy who had been trying to place his book satchel onto the shelf above his bed. The boy neither answered nor moved. Ansel took in his fair skin and the light brown hair, poorly cut, that surrounded his large eyes, which were cloudy with unease. In a sudden rush, Ansel could picture his own days and nights in this room. He allowed the agony of the first weeks, four and a half years ago, to ooze, swamp-like, into his memory. The shock and strangeness of the new place, the strict rules that were far too numerous and detailed for an eight-year-old to apprehend, the sleepless nights of stifled tears, the endless hours of lessons and religion—all of it tumbled through Ansel's mind. The nuns were as close to the mothers left behind or lost as existed at St. Stephen's, but they were starched and removed in their vocations. There was no human warmth, no touching, and no comfort here. The impenetrable society of older boys seemed accessible only through cracking an as yet unknowable code. All this Ansel recalled now.

"There is extra polishing to be done in the sacristy," Ansel lied. "Father Sproll has allowed me to train an assistant. I will come for you after Mass tomorrow morning. My name is Beckmann." Ansel waited, half expecting to hear nothing. After a long moment, however, the boy whispered "Yes, sir," and began to breathe in small, shallow gasps.

Ansel turned and retraced his steps, a smile playing across his face. *I'll try to find a football to kick with Krimm.*

12 1938, Kühlungsborn

A steady southwest wind cleared the heat from the Baltic Sea beach where Kläre, Ernst, Ditha, and Margaret were nearly alone. After a bracing swim, the women joined Ernst, who had remained seated formally amid the cluster of rented chairs. Kläre lowered herself onto a seat beside her brother. The breeze was strong on her skin, skimming past her ear, playing it like an instrument, and drawing heat from within to dry her swimming dress. She sighed with a moment's contentment—a split second of near peace.

Kläre had joined in this vacation because she had a plan. Today was the day she would talk to Ernst—about the Kindertransport, about what she had learned, about what she and Jakob must decide. This would be her best opportunity to have that conversation with her brother, as she had come alone; Jakob, Erwin, and Werner had remained at home.

As the afternoon waned, the little group strode vigorously back toward their pension, Ernst quizzing Margaret on mathematics. They had all fallen into his familiar pace: measured, efficient, and of a speed that allowed for ramrod posture but purposeful progress.

"Look, he wants us to buy from him—the photographer there, in front," Ernst said, pointing up the beach as if routing out a conspiracy.

Margaret stopped mid-calculation, a frown of concentration still on her face, slightly breathless from walking swiftly enough to keep up with the adults. The photographer disappeared under his black cloth as they moved toward him.

"Straight ahead. Slowly as we pass by, shoulders back. Left, right, left, right," Ernst commanded.

Kläre fell into her familiar spot at his right, the favored younger sister, proud smile, firm lift of chin, matching his step perfectly. Ditha, who was used to humoring her husband, was the only one completely at ease in the wind and sand at the ocean's edge, and was dressed in trousers and a sweater for the windy weather. She was also the tallest of the group, and strode comfortably toward the photographer, between her daughter and her husband.

The small party made their way to their modest hotel, just beyond the photographer's lair.

Clothes changed, dressed to be seen at afternoon coffee, Kläre nervously pulled the few wild strands of her hair back from her face and resolutely pinned them into her bun. She would not risk caustic comments about looking like a gypsy from Ernst this afternoon.

She entered the hotel's sitting room and found him sitting across from Margaret with coffee and a newspaper. Ditha, it seemed, was still up in their room. Margaret was carefully sipping cocoa, visibly concentrating on holding the cup correctly and keeping herself tidy. Kläre was struck by the demeanor of this child, thirteen now, and grown taller since the last time she'd seen her. She was still serious and smart and radiated the brazen directness of an only child brought up to be clever and obedient but also to succeed. Her adolescence was pending, but did not yet weigh upon her. She had been sorely disappointed when Kläre had come alone; Werner was her favorite cousin.

Thinking of Werner snapped Kläre back to Ernst and what she needed to tell him. She sat gracefully in her chair and noted that as she did, Margaret looked expectantly at her father, trying to determine if this would be a time when she must stay at the table and listen to the interminable conversation of adults, or if this was not to be considered a meal and therefore subject to a relaxation of the rules.

"I'd like to speak with you about something," Kläre murmured to her brother.

Ernst raised an eyebrow, but looked at Margaret over his paper and dismissed her from the table.

Kläre knew the time to speak was upon her. The enormity of her plan filled her eyes and choked the words in her throat. But purpose drove back panic, and she began to talk, quietly and quickly.

"Ernst, Jakob has been again denied an affidavit."

Her brother closed the paper and repeated her scan of the room. "When? Who denied it?"

"The American consulate."

Ernst's thin lips pulled in and together, and fear flickered in his eyes—only for a moment, but long enough for Kläre to notice. Jakob had by now applied, belatedly but often, for chances to leave Germany, though mostly at Kläre's insistence. He had a growing tremor in his hands and feet, and because of it no doctor had dared declare him healthy—a prerequisite for a visa.

Ernst's hand gripped the arm of his chair. "What will you do now?"

Kläre saw her brother was trying to keep the urgency from his voice. It had only been a few weeks since his own desperation had caused him to engage in an unheard-of risk to obtain visas for immigration to America for his own family. He had told Kläre that after exhausting his high court contacts, he had waited in line at the American embassy—first outdoors and then in the immense lobby, standing and then sitting, until the office had finally closed and the other weary petitioners had left. But Ernst had resolutely stepped forward to the official still in the room, who was packing documents, ink, and pens back into boxes and files. It was May 31, Margaret's birthday, and an unseasonably cool day.

"Excuse me," Ernst had said, standing in his coat with his hat grasped in his hands.

The clerk had not even looked but said, "Closed—we're closed. *Geschlossen*. Come back tomorrow."

"Please, I have a special feeling. Today is my daughter's birthday. She is thirteen. I have an affidavit and all my forms and funds. Please."

His wide barrel chest had stayed straight and proud, but beneath the layers of suit and coat his heart had pounded. From behind the official, another man's tired voice had spoken, first in English—"I'll see him"—and then in perfect German: "*Kommen Sie herein.*"

The weight of the fine leather briefcase in his hand anchored Ernst's body, which had started to shake, and he stepped beyond the desk into the consul's office. Thirty minutes later, back on the street in the darkening evening, he'd had the visa.

Ernst had planned the trip to the Baltic Sea to maintain an impression of normalcy while clandestinely making preparations to leave. He had also needed to see his sister once more—to ask and say what could not be written or telephoned. He had spent nearly all his increasingly worthless money for black-market shipping of the fine antiques that would be his family's currency in America. Now, in this fine, peaceful guesthouse by the sea, Kläre sat before him, fearful but determined.

"What will you do now?" Ernst repeated. The question hung for a moment in the air between them. In the kitchen, noises and voices rose, signaling the switch to dinner preparations.

Kläre's eyes filled with tears, but she whispered fiercely, "We must send out the children." She paused to watch her brother's face as this declaration sank in. "And I need your help. In Hörde it is not so easy to find information. In Berlin, with your contacts . . . I must find out about the Kindertransport. There are more Jews in Berlin."

Kläre's hands, which had been frozen into fists in her lap, were now pulling and twisting the embroidered corner of her handkerchief. She locked her eyes onto her brother's face. "My Erwin is nearly old enough to be on his own, but Werner . . ." Her low, steady whisper caught in her throat and again her eyes welled up. Rigidly she brought the handkerchief to her eyes without breaking their hold on her brother.

"I will learn what you should do," was all he could say before they were joined by a maid who cleared their tea cups, signaling with her busy efficiency that it was time to remove themselves and allow dinner to be laid.

A week later, the letter from Ernst arrived in Hörde. Kläre opened it with dread.

Liebe Kläre,

I have asked a colleague to deliver this letter directly to you. You must read and act on the information quickly, but also then destroy the letter. It is dangerous for both of us.

The Kindertransport to England is done through the Judenrat in Dortmund and is a very good process. The children go to families, when they can be found, or to a group camp until homes can be secured. Also they help young adults to find work. Perhaps this is something for Erwin. But for younger children, they take at this time only those whose parents have been taken away or who can no longer care for them. There is some danger to represent yourself in this way if you do not meet the qualifications. Therefore, my dear sister, I worry that this will not work for Werner.

I did investigate another idea. It is perhaps dangerous. In Düsseldorf, a group of dissidents have begun an underground operation to help people escape. There is an artist who operates a bakery and café whom you must contact. Her initials are M.D.; more I cannot write for fear that I will endanger her if this letter falls into the wrong hands. Find her, Kläre. I believe she may be able to help you and Jakob.

Of our mother, I cannot write more. My heart is already too heavy. That we all leave you to care for her and for Jakob and your children is an onus I try every way to lift from you. We depart within the week, but I think of you day and night. I will continue to do whatever I can to help you from America.

G-d watch over you, my sister. If there is a G-d, truly you are one of his angels.

Your loving brother

There was no signature, and the letter was typed, but Kläre could hear her brother's voice speaking to her. She sat for several minutes clutching the arms of her desk chair, staring vacantly at the pages in front of her. This is what she had asked of Ernst, but suddenly she did not want to understand what he had written—did not want to move from reading to knowing and then to action. The desperation that she had lived with as one after another of her friends and neighbors had emigrated or disappeared, been beaten or terrorized, lost livelihoods and ability to send their children to school, suddenly gave way to a mounting panic. She could not send Werner away, could not begin to explain to him, could not herself live a day without him. A terrible nausea welled up in her and, nearly knocking the chair over, she ran to the toilet in the hall.

The retching did not last long, but was replaced with a cold sweat and fear unlike any she had known before. Weakly, Kläre climbed the stairs to her bedroom, where she closed the door and sank to her knees at the side of the bed. She cried then—long, jagged sobs. The minutes passed until, swollen and spent, she had no more tears. One by one, her thoughts returned like shards of glass, her eyes squeezing shut harder with each addition: *Go to the Judenrat first. Erwin will go to England now. I must find a way to get us all out. Werner can stay a little longer until . . . The artist and baker: It can only be Melisande Durr! I must see Melisande Durr! I will speak to Bernhardt.*

The thought of Bernhardt brought tears again, though now there was relief in them. She could ask him. She believed he would try to help her, as she had helped him. She need not be utterly alone in this. How she would handle Jakob, Kläre could not think about now. She rose slowly to her feet and smoothed her dress. She crossed the room to the fine old chest that had belonged to her great grandmother. On it sat a washbowl of Chinese porcelain, which Kläre kept full of clean water as much for its beauty as its utility. She splashed the cool water on her face, until she felt cleansed of her outburst. She breathed deeply into an embroidered face towel, sweet with the smell of lavender. She concentrated only on what she could do next.

Tuesday morning dawned slowly through a grey-felt drizzle. Jakob still slept, though he had tossed fitfully through the night. Kläre slipped noiselessly from the bed and quickly made her morning toilette. She would begin the long streetcar ride to Frau Steinmann earlier than usual today in hopes of avoiding the morning crowds, and particularly the Brownshirts, who were daily becoming bolder in their attacks. Only yesterday, they'd asked a woman in Dortmund for her identity papers and, seeing that she was a Jew, had dragged her off the streetcar and beaten her in front of her six-year-old child. True, she had been from the East and not a German, but the incident had added to Kläre's fear of moving about in ways she had always taken entirely for granted. She traded the more stylish hat she'd planned to wear for an ample silk scarf and her hooded gabardine raincoat, in deference to both the rain and her desire for anonymity. She took time for a good cup of coffee and a *brotchen* from the previous day before entering the wet morning and making her way to the streetcar.

The ride was long and uneventful, but Kläre very nearly missed her transfer, so preoccupied was she with thoughts of how she would contact Bernhardt. But no sooner had she arrived at his mother's house than she was shown to the sitting room—rather than the bedroom, where she was now accustomed to performing her massage—and there stood Bernhardt, a slow smile of amusement spreading across his face as he noted her surprise.

"Frau Kohler, good morning. I'm afraid I've astonished you . . . Yet I thought we had arranged to meet today. I'm so sorry if I was mistaken." His smile was replaced by a searching look as he stepped toward her.

"No, no. I mean, yes, of course, we did speak of today when I saw you last, didn't we? I quite forgot until now, but I am indeed very happy to see you." The maid who had shown Kläre in had withdrawn, and Kläre was suddenly very conscious of being alone with Bernhardt, out of the public eye and in the sitting room of his mother's house. Feeling confused, she sat down heavily in the chair nearest her. She struggled to find the words she had practiced, to find the tone that was a mixture of light inquiry and seriousness that would ensure Bernhardt's help yet preserve her dignity.

"What is it? Has something happened?" His concern now was open and genuine, and it gave her strength.

"I must ask a favor of you. And yet, as important as this is to me, I must also ask you not to put yourself or—or your family in any jeopardy . . ."

"Please, Kläre. What do you ask? I would like to be helpful to you if I can be."

Kläre's voice dropped nearly to a whisper. "I need to know more of the work that Melisande Durr is doing." Bernhardt's face became impassive, but Kläre pressed on. "I cannot leave—I will not leave—my husband and my mother. They have been refused visas yet again. And so now I must look to a way to send my children to safety. My older boy can go to England, but Werner . . . he is too young to go on the jobs program, and because we are still here and working, they won't take him." Kläre could barely eke out any voice through the constriction in her throat; she was barely conscious of the tears streaming down her cheeks. "He can not go on the regular Kindertransport. You said at the café that Frau Durr is working secretly to get people out of Germany, and my brother, too, has heard news of her work; since you know her, I wondered if you could find out what she does, and if it is safe for me to contact her."

Kläre's struggle for composure had left her sitting rigid in her chair, her tear-stained cheeks frozen in a mask of determination. For a horrible moment she panicked, thinking that Bernhardt's interest in her would not extend to helping her family, would not be worth whatever she seemed to give to him. She could not read the thoughtful look on his face.

"Ya, I believe I can find out for you what she is doing. How safe it is, I am not sure I can judge, but I will try."

Slowly, Kläre began to exhale.

"But this is . . . this is frightening. I can't imagine—" Bernhardt left off speaking mid-sentence as Kläre's face crumbled. "Oh my God." He crossed the room and pulled her into an embrace. "Ach, you dear, brave woman," he whispered.

Kläre was lost now in the safety of Bernhardt's embrace, lapsing out of time and task into his warmth and the resonance of his murmured words. They stood for some time together, until a nearly imperceptible tilt of Kläre's head brought them both back to the sitting room of Rosa Steinmann's home.

"Ya, your mother will be waiting for a massage, no?" Kläre replaced her handkerchief in her pocket and straightened the lapels of Bernhardt's jacket before lifting her eyes to his. The kiss came softly once again, but lingered for many seconds this time. Her lips responded with passionate hunger. With a sigh of simple longing, Bernhardt stroked an errant curl off her forehead before pulling himself away.

"Kläre, I think it best if you telephone me at my home at the weekend, maybe even Friday. I should have information by then. Is that all right?" he asked.

"I am most grateful. Thank you." Kläre managed a thin smile.

She made her way to the bedroom, where Frau Steinmann seemed particularly eager to see her and unusually contented to submit to her ministrations in silence, despite, or perhaps because of, the red-rimmed eyes that Kläre could not hide. Kläre was soon lost to the power of her own hands—working muscle under skin, gently moving across Frau Steinmann's body, bringing to them both much-needed relief and calm.

13 1939, Hörde

Jakob Kohler's newspaper lay unread in his lap, the weight of his hand insufficient to suppress the rustle from the tremor in his right leg. He had asked Kläre for a whisky tonight, but it remained untouched on the table beside him.

"I shall have to let Etta go soon. She is coming along with the second child, and her mother can not watch both." Kläre spoke matter-of-factly, her attention divided between her mending and her distracted husband. "It won't be so easy to find someone else," she continued.

Jakob did not answer right away, and Kläre's hands dropped to her lap as she watched him more closely. His trembling made the pool of light from the lamp beside him appear to flicker, as if he were in a film of poor quality. He sat this way often—sometimes staring into the dark, sometimes closing his eyes with his head leaned back in the chair. His knit brow and pale skin bespoke a pain for which his tablets brought no relief.

"It will be hard to replace Etta," Kläre repeated, louder this time.

"Yes, I suppose it will," he answered slowly. "I expect you will have to look for a Jewish woman, if you can find someone suitable." He turned to her, but seemed still preoccupied. "No 'Aryan' will be allowed to accept a job here any longer." The sardonic disgust in his voice was jarring.

"I could do without, if necessary; Werner is nearly old enough to stay here alone for a few hours if I am with a patient."

"No. You should try to find someone, if possible. We can still afford it, and you should have the help. It gives someone a job." She was surprised at the urgency of his response. He continued, more calmly, "I believe the Judenrat has begun to keep a listing of Jews looking for work. Maybe that is one thing our council can do effectively."

Kläre weighed her next words carefully. "Already, today, I went to the Judenrat to look for that list." She took a deep breath. "I found, also, information about the Youth Worker program in England. There is a journeyman program for boys Erwin's age. They go to England and have jobs arranged by Jews over there—perhaps in the trades, or in someone's shop or business. If we sent money with him, he could go to school also, although I shouldn't imagine he would be able to do it soon without English." She heard her own voice rising, and stopped. Allowing herself to speak with the full intensity, the importunity she was feeling would only upset Jakob and end any discussion before it began.

She waited, picked up the sock again, forced her hands to work and her chest to rise and fall with constricted breaths. She would try this once to persuade Jakob in the negotiating style of their twenty-five years of married life together. Kläre was gentle, clear, and articulate, and Jakob thoughtful but decisive. She rarely attempted to change his mind or counter a decision, but now she was aware that the onus of rescuing her children from the tightening snare of the Nazi threat lay with her.

Jakob said nothing; he only stared at her, as if wanting to keep from the quiet room the words that she now spoke:

"He must go. There is absolutely nothing for him here. He cannot work anywhere but for my uncles, and they could be driven out of Hörde at any moment. He cannot go to school. Jakob, you must speak to him. Help him to want to do this. He is already sixteen, and of the age to have an experience away from home. It will only be for a year or so, until this insanity is over with, no? Please, Jakob."

Their stares locked for a long moment. With unbearable sadness, Kläre saw not agreement, not dispute, but the draining away of any conviction at all in the deep brown eyes she knew so well. It bespoke the first intimation of defeat, the first ebbing of will.

She rose and gently took the trembling newspaper from Jakob's lap. Kneeling in front of his chair, she took his hands in her own and pressed her lips to his fingers. He pulled one hand free and stroked her hair. His voice shook.

"Ya, he is truly a young man now." Lifting her chin so that he looked again into her eyes, Jakob spoke more strongly. "It's perhaps only for the summer, or a school term. Of course we need to find out what is required. I know of this program. I have donated to it for several years now. I can make sure all his papers are in order. If you think this is the best for him at the moment, I will look into it. I will speak to him tomorrow."

Kläre kissed the hands in front of her again and squeezed her eyes shut for a moment before rising and turning away to her chair, where she busied herself putting away the mending and forcing down the sobs that threatened to burst from her. Having won the concession from Jakob, she would not burden him with her grief over the acts and decisions to come. Instead she thought of Bernhardt, and that brought her comfort. She could speak to him of her plan, and of her sorrow.

The next morning dawned sunny and warm—it was a day, Kläre thought, to venture into the garden to push aside and dispose of the detritus of winter. It was a day to find a snowdrop waving its small white flower, released from the dead leaves to glory in the fragile warmth of a March morning.

Instead, Kläre made her way to her mother's home. As she walked, she thought this was a day on which Grandmother Caroline would have had the maids beat a rug in the back garden while she surveyed every inch of her house with a practiced eye, formulating the tasks necessary to accomplish the prodigious cleaning leading to the Passover holiday. Her mother would begin a cleansing as well today, but without the strictures of Passover in mind. Instead, she would clean purely for the order it made.

Kläre worried over her mother. Since Jonah Ente's death, his brothers and nephews had provided a livelihood for Johanna from the business, but one by one the family had emigrated. Now only one uncle and one cousin were left, with fewer farmers willing to risk doing business with Jews every day. Johanna had grown increasingly withdrawn since first Trude and then Ernst had gone. She kept her house, and marked her days with the visits and telephone calls that Kläre made, the silent nods of shopkeepers and postal clerks, and tidings from her one remaining sister, whose letters from Steele still arrived each week. She would not discuss leaving her home or joining Ernst in America or even Trude in Brussels. If she was fearful of the rising influence of the Nazis in the everyday life of Hörde, she did not discuss it with Kläre, though she listened in strained silence to Kläre's worries and plans.

Kläre arrived at the house in Benninghofer Strasse and let herself in. There was no longer a maid living here, though a woman still came twice a week to clean. Johanna was in the kitchen, washing her coffee cup and plate from breakfast. Kläre kissed her cheeks and stood back to watch her finish her morning chores. Even now, her mother was still an imposing woman: A shock of white hair framed her large, strong face, and her black eyebrows commanded attention.

"Mutti," Kläre said, "Jakob and I have decided to send Erwin to England."

Silence.

"He cannot go to university here, and I don't think he would want to, anyway."

Silence.

"The Judenrat has organized a program to send young men to England, and Jews there help them to find a job."

Kläre stopped speaking and watched her mother wipe the perfectly clean counter with a starched tea towel. Anger suddenly welled up in her breast, such that she could scarcely breathe. She felt a shifting wall of opposition from her husband and her mother that took the form of tension, self-absorption, and critical judgments, leaving her alone with the urgent desire to flee the increasing nightmare around her. Her voice rose, and not in a musical way.

"He must get out, Mama. We all must."

Johanna turned toward her daughter and regarded her for a long moment. The harshness was gone from her face. In its stead were weariness and sadness, mixed with a flicker of fear. "You will send him by himself?"

"Ya. Werner is too young, and we have not got visas."

"Ya . . ." It was all Johanna said.

Kläre squeezed back tears with a discipline that she summoned ever more frequently these days, and helped her mother sweep the back porch leading to the garden.

Within the hour, she was once again on her way through the streets of Hörde, this time toward the tramway and the short ride to Dortmund.

A doorman ushered Kläre through the heavy glass doors of a fashionable apartment house. He nodded toward the marble staircase and she climbed steadily, glad for the exertion that gave her heart reason to beat fast and strong. The fourth-floor hall was flooded with morning sunlight from a large bay window. She paused to look down to the courtyard garden below, surprised to see crocuses and species tulips already dotting the orderly landscape with blues, reds, and yellow. It was a sanctuary of earliest spring sunshine and color, and she yearned to sit on the wrought iron bench placed among the tulips and lift her face to the warmth and light.

The heavy wooden door in the center of the hall opened, and through it walked Bernhardt, comfortably dressed in a tweed jacket and rich brown trousers. Though he looked more drawn than usual, his vitality and the pleasure writ large on his face at the sight of Kläre swept away the uncertainty and trepidation that had plagued her all the way from Hörde.

"Good morning, Kläre. Please come in. I am happy you could come."

Kläre took a deep breath and followed him into the apartment, knowing that in doing so—in coming here, alone, without Jakob's knowledge or permission—she was crossing yet another of the lines she had drawn in her head. She was acting now on her own, and it was both frightening and powerful.

By now she knew that Bernhardt lived in this apartment alone; that he never lacked for company and had many interesting friends, some of them lovers. He had come close to marrying once, but hadn't in the end. Kläre's massage patients tended to talk of their lives. The more she released the tension in their muscles, the more they unloosed the stories of their hearts. Rosa Steinmann had proved no exception, and so she had spoken of her son often. Kläre had listened without comment, but had hung on to the revelations Frau Steinmann had offered, storing them deep within her.

Bernhardt ushered her into a small reception area and gently closed the door behind her. Kläre noted the modern lighted cabinet displaying fine silver and a marble bust. Bernhardt hung her coat carefully in the coat closet, then turned to her and smiled, though he seemed somewhat anxious as well.

"Come, I will show you what I've learned." He opened the door to the sitting room, which was spacious and filled with light. The entire wall before Kläre was taken up with an enormous bay window, a seat fashioned across its expanse. Upholstered cushions invited the viewer to sit and gaze out over the square below, busy now with the traffic of morning commerce.

The room was furnished in fine walnut and caned pieces. Clean, curved lines carried the Bauhaus theme from the hall into the airy space. Bernhardt gently took Kläre's elbow and steered her toward a lovely table, its round glass top revealing the caned lattice underneath. There were coffee cups and small cakes waiting, along with a portfolio of papers.

"Coffee?" Bernhardt asked.

"Please," Kläre said, wondering at this man who was so gracious and comfortable in the role of host. Jakob would have been unable to produce a cup of coffee in the home he'd now lived in for twenty years. Bernhardt moved through an arch to what Kläre now saw was a paneled dining room and beyond it to a swinging door leading to what she presumed was the kitchen. This had all been much easier than she'd supposed—coming to Bernhard Steinmann's by herself, preparing to hear what she could not bear to think about but urgently needed to know. The tone of Bernhardt's greeting and his generous hospitality put her at ease. The warm flush that was always a part of being in his presence was today also a comfort. It replaced the cold emptiness that had filled her recent days.

The coffee service was simple but of fine silver. Bernhardt returned and expertly poured for them both, and then handed her a document from the portfolio.

"When you are ready, we will make an appointment with Melisande Durr at a café in Schwalmtal." The abrupt transition to the business of the morning startled Kläre, and all her anxiety returned to her. Schwalmtal, Kläre knew, was a small town an hour's distance by train from Dortmund. She was momentarily confused that Bernhardt had said "we," but he continued before she could ask what he meant.

"She has an underground network to move children out of Germany in the company of sympathetic companions. The children are using forged papers and the companions pose as parents, grandparents, aunts, uncles, etc." Kläre was listening, but she also found herself staring at the lock of soft brown hair that had fallen onto Bernhardt's broad forehead. She wished to reach forward and push it back, but the gentle command in his grey eyes brought her back to his words.

"Melisande creates a different plan for each child, using whatever people she can at the moment, and always uses different routes and trains to Switzerland," he continued. "When these so-called families reach Switzerland, the children are moved over the mountains into Italy and down to Trieste, where they then journey to Palestine. There, they are cared for in camps until their parents can join them or make further arrangements."

Palestine! God in heaven, it is so far! Jakob still thinks Palestine is ridiculous. If only we had all gone . . . But no. Stop it. It's at least a chance to get Werner out. Kläre's thoughts were now riveted on the details being presented to her, and she loosened her grip on the arms of her chair. The process of sending children to Palestine had become more widely known, as the German government's enmity toward England had decreased the number of available Kindertransports. Kläre nodded at Bernhardt to continue.

"It will be very expensive: 500 marks."

Kläre smiled ruefully. "Money is something we seem still to have." Jakob was being paid to help other Jews with their legal problems, even as he seemed paralyzed on his own, and on his family's, behalf.

"I told Melisande I would come with you." Bernhardt's warm voice was like a trapeze artist's harness, pulling Kläre through the air from above as she grasped for a swinging bar. "I have a motorcar available to take us if you wish. I thought perhaps it would be easier."

Bernhardt looked at her questioningly now, and Kläre saw that he genuinely worried for her. No doubt he already assumed that Jakob would not make this journey. Perhaps he knew that Jakob would not take the risk of being caught, of engaging in an illegal process. Kläre suddenly needed Bernhardt Steinmann to know that he had speculated correctly about Jakob, but that she could and would have gone to Durr on her own. She would find whatever strength she needed to move Werner to safety.

"I am so very grateful that you have discovered all this for me." The color in Kläre's cheeks rose further. "Bernhardt, I can see Frau Durr by myself, and I will if it presents any danger that you do not wish to take on." He looked as though he would speak, but Kläre stopped him, laying her hand lightly on his arm. She shook her head. "It's very strange that I've always been a Jew and paid no special attention to it, and now it determines everything about my life. And you . . . you were never one at all, and here you are, willing to take this risk for me and for my son. I remember my grandfather telling me that to save one life is to save the world. It's an important Jewish ideal. I am truly grateful to you, but you must not put yourself or your family at risk."

Again Bernhardt tried to speak, but Kläre pressed on. "You must also know that your help is not all I am grateful for." She spoke boldly, and reached now for the lock of hair that she found so irresistible. "When

I am with you, I feel alive, even when all else feels so deadened. We speak to each other without restrictions." Kläre's tears flowed. "Nothing makes sense to me anymore, but with you, I make some sense. I am a woman again." This last sentence she spoke softly; it was a seduction, but one with no artifice.

"I expect you are entirely a woman," Bernhardt said, bringing Kläre's hand to his lips. In a single fluid motion, he rose and pulled her to him. There was nothing hurried or furtive any longer in his touch. He kissed her slowly, with a longing that drew all the passion Kläre had felt for him from deep within her and spread it like a flowing river in streams and eddies throughout her body. He held the back of her head in one hand as his kisses traveled to her eyes, her ears, and the open neck of her silk blouse.

"I want to see your hair," he whispered.

One after another, the combs and hairpins containing her thick curls were laid on the table. She shook her hair free, pleasure flooding all her senses. They carefully undressed each other, stopping only to stroke a shoulder, a breast, the length of a back muscle.

Bernhardt sank to his knees and laid Kläre back onto the daybed behind her. He drew her stocking off with a hand running down either side of her leg. The couch's upholstery was fine but rough to the skin, and Bernhardt reached behind the cushion for a lap blanket of cashmere, which he spread over the seat. Kläre fell under the spell of his skillful pleasuring, her cares, her fear pushed away in the rush of sensation. She experienced the hunger to share passion again with a man. Jakob had been a tentative but surprisingly good lover, but it had been months since he had held her and nearly two years since he had made love to her. Kläre mourned the loss of their intimacy, particularly in the face of the grave concerns that occupied them both.

Now she rose to Bernhardt with passionate strength. When finally she arched her back in pulsing ecstasy, he joined her with a moan of pleasure. He settled her at his side, her head on his chest, his arm around her small back, while with his other hand he smoothed the tangle of hair off her face.

"Thank you," he whispered, and this did not seem odd to her.

"And you also," she murmured into his chest. Her fingers played across his muscled ribs. He shuddered and pulled her closer, kissing the top of her head and propping himself up on one elbow, when the telephone in the hall intruded with a jarring ring.

Bernhardt made no move to answer it, but the spell was broken, and Kläre looked about her for a clock.

"Kläre," Bernhardt said quickly. Turning her face toward him, he spoke with calm strength. "Whatever it is between us, it is good. It is real and good, no?"

Kläre smiled at him, though tears filled her eyes. "Ya, very good."

14 March 1940

The motorcar sped along the new road, slowing only occasionally to overtake a farm wagon. Kläre loved to watch the heavy draft horses patiently pulling their loads, reins bouncing with each step. A farmer perched on the wagon seat occasionally barked a command, but mostly the horse did what it knew.

After riding the elegant, high-spirited horses of the cavalry, Ernst had disparaged the work animals of the farm. He'd teased his sister, saying that farm life was beneath her, but Kläre had loved everything about the rearing and tending of crops and animals. She remembered the wagon rides with her father and grandfather at neighboring farms where the Entes had sold feed or bought grain; the balanced forces of human planning and hard work and the cycles of wind and weather, birth and death had always captivated her. The farmers around Hörde were a rough lot, but Kläre felt admiration, never scorn, for them.

The roadway, newly carved into the landscape, passed by fields, houses, and barns as timeless and orderly as the greening buds of spring swelling on the trees. The occasional stately manor house with brick patterns built into its tall sides and narrow window caps punctuated the traditional stucco farmhouses.

Kläre marveled at the speed and efficiency of the motorcar, and the ease with which Bernhardt drove. She studied his profile as he concentrated on the road ahead, relishing the captivity of their ride together. Already she knew his broad forehead, the skin softer than expected, knew his chestnut hair, thick but finely textured. He smiled, feeling her scrutiny.

"You have driven often?" she asked, breaking the comfortable silence.

"I enjoy automobiles, the speed and the design and the freedom to go where I like, when I like," he answered easily. He slid his hand to her thigh and rested it there; she closed her eyes and lapsed back into a contented silence. What lay ahead and what lay behind were mercifully absent in these hours of traveling through the countryside.

They reached Schwalmtal, and entered an establishment that served as both café and *stube,* the coffee service sharing a long bar with beer taps and steins. It was nearly deserted on this early spring morning.

A beautiful and earnest-looking young woman sat across the table from Melisande Durr. She didn't look Jewish—but then, Kläre thought, appearances meant nothing at all in Hitler's Germany. Perhaps this woman with her aquiline nose and fair skin was not a Jew at all; perhaps she was a Communist, or perhaps simply an art patron. Whoever she was, she had a sense of urgency about her that betrayed desperation of some sort.

Kläre renewed her own effort to appear calm as she waited outside the small room at the back of the café. Bernhardt excused himself and went out onto the street; left alone, Kläre watched through the window as the slow morning of the rural town unfolded. Tidy shop fronts and newly planted flower boxes hid the menace and unrest behind them. The occasional wagon or motorcar passed in the street as women with market baskets did their morning errands. There were no brown-shirted soldiers, but Kläre was not fooled. Small-town councils carried out with determination the same orders as those in the big city—expose Jews, harass them, expel their children from schools, restrict or eliminate their businesses. The small number of Jews who made their homes in country towns like this one did not even have the tenuous protection of urban anonymity.

Movement in the back room brought Kläre's attention back to the café. There was no sign of Bernhardt, and no time to ponder this. Her business concluded, the fair-skinned woman shook hands with Melisande Durr and turned to leave with a look of resolve.

Durr stood, and Kläre was surprised by her diminutive size. Otto Dix's well-known portrait of Durr represented her as corpulent and severe, nearly a caricature. Kläre had seen her in person only once before, months ago at Café Hintz, and there she had remained seated. Durr now turned to place her papers from the previous meeting in a briefcase, and as she did Kläre noted the maroon suit colorfully clothing the art dealer's shapely form, the fine stockings and stylish shoes on her solid legs. Durr, who still had yet to acknowledge Kläre's presence, turned back to the table and drank deeply from a stein of dark beer, then drew her hand with its fine gold and onyx ring across her face, kneading her forehead for a moment. Finally, she turned her attention to Kläre.

"Frau Kohler, please." The small but commanding woman pointed to a seat at the table and took her place again in the corner facing the doorway. "I understand you are interested in sending your son on a trip to Trieste with our youth mountaineering program."

Kläre was taken entirely by surprise by this bypass of introduction, as well as by the reference to a program of which she knew nothing. She remained silent until understanding dawned on her that her companion was speaking in some sort of code.

"Yes, I am interested."

"Then we must choose a host family to accompany him. Perhaps Herr Steinmann would oblige. I believe he plans to take his mother along for a mountain cure while he chaperones our young men."

Surprise broke through Kläre's look of concentration, and she sat back suddenly in her chair. "Oh, I see," she managed. Melisande Durr looked beyond Kläre to the door where a young man had just appeared.

"Mother Durr, we have secured your requested information."

"Thank you Laurent. Please meet Frau Kohler. She has a son who may be interested in our program."

The boy couldn't have been older than Erwin. He bowed politely as he shook Kläre's hand and murmured, "Frau Kohler." *Did he call Melisande Durr 'Mother Durr'?*

"Laurent is one of our leaders. He is in charge of the mountain activities. It is a very important job." Durr smiled, her clear fondness for the boy lifting some of the weariness from her face. No, the boy was not her son. Kläre felt with certainty that this woman had no children of her own. "Laurent works hard to keep all the children in our program safe," Durr continued. "He is very good at it."

Before Kläre had a chance to respond, Bernhardt joined them, carrying a tray of hard rolls stuffed with ham and cheese.

Melisande Durr's smile broadened across her large face once again. "Ah, I see Herr Steinmann has brought us some lunch! Come, Bernhardt, join us; Laurent will explain what your responsibilities will be, and Frau Kohler can decide if this will be the right program for her son."

Over lunch, as though this were a social occasion and not a coded conversation about a dangerous escape, Durr and Laurent detailed the plan. Bernhardt and Frau Steinmann would travel with two boys, "just as if they were family." Durr made this point with particular emphasis and pointed out that Kläre would have to secure papers with the "correct information," by which Kläre supposed she meant something other than Werner's real papers. The boys would be taken through Germany into Switzerland and then on a mountain trek to Trieste in Italy, where they would remain until joined by a contact. From there, the "option" existed for an extended trip to "the Mediterranean."

Kläre was working hard to absorb what was being presented. At the same time, dread was forming crushing bands around her chest.

". . . and a program of this sort is very costly due to the difficulty of all the . . . arrangements." Durr paused; clearly, Kläre was expected to say something here.

Kläre looked for the first time during the meeting into the impassive face of Bernhardt Steinmann, her eyes silently pleading with his. What was she to say?

"Frau Kohler assures me that such an opportunity will be well funded," Bernhardt said, his tone casual. "She and her husband have even offered tuition for another boy if you know of one who needs that help."

Kläre quickly added, "Yes, quite."

"Well then, it sounds as though we should proceed. Thank you, Laurent, and Frau Kohler—we will be in contact shortly. Bernhardt, if you don't mind, I have some other business I should like to speak with you about."

Kläre rose and went immediately to the washroom; she thought she might be sick. She leaned heavily over the washbowl, her head against the cool glass of the mirror, commanding the spinning to cease. She wet the corner of her handkerchief and wiped it across her forehead, pressing it hard into her eyes. There could be no tears now.

The early spring sun blinded Kläre as she stepped out of the dark café. She walked toward the town square and made her way to a small park, where she sank onto the nearest bench. She could still see the front of the café—even that made her nausea rise again. She turned her focus to breathing, forcing exhalations, trying to loosen the panic. *Bernhardt! Bernhardt will take Werner out. Did he know? For how long? Is he leaving with his mother for good?* Kläre bit her lip until the smarting brought tears that could not be held in any longer.

The second-floor windows of Bernhardt's bedroom were opened wide to the spring air, and the lacy curtain sheers made a delicate dance of light across the bedclothes. Bernhardt moaned into the goose-feather pillow as Kläre's hands moved up his back. She sat straddled across his hips with only a sheet between her thighs and his soft skin.

Their lovemaking had sent a flow of warmth around the stone weight of dread and vigilance that had settled in Kläre during the ride home from the meeting with Melisande Durr. Now, after his massage, Bernhardt would sign one last time, with yet another name, for the practice hours that would bring her closer to her full license. She traced down his spine with one finger, weaving back and forth across the vertebrae, which lay like ordered pebbles between his powerful back muscles. She closed her eyes and tried to memorize every inch of the warm, unfaltering body that lay beneath her. Could her fingers impart the gratitude she had for this man who would save her son? Or was she measuring into Bernhardt's skin the sorrow that stained her heart in inky pools? She could not bear to think of the missing that already tore at her. This would be the last time for a very long time, perhaps ever, that she would lie with him. In saving Werner, he was taking her last two comforts far away. She labored to keep her breaths slow and measured.

Kläre looked out the window into the warm sunlight of the afternoon. Across the square, a couple with a small boy stood huddled over a small collection of suitcases and bags—things that could be carried quickly. Jews. Fresh-faced German mothers on bicycles, with children perched between their arms, flew by the couple, whose faces, like a disappearing dream, were drained of expression. The boy, however, leaned out around his father's girth to watch the cyclists pass.

"Ach, no," Kläre cried, her hands flying to her mouth. "It's the Wachlenberg boy." Bernhardt lifted his dark head, roused by her alarm. "He is a deaf-mute. His brother has been a friend to Werner." Stricken, the respite of the afternoon gone in an instant, Kläre clutched the sheet to her breasts and stared down at the overdressed figures below.

Hans Wachlenberg had approached Jakob after the edict ordering the sterilization or euthanizing of "patients" who were "defective," including the deaf. Jakob had been able to do nothing other than give the names of sympathetic doctors, who were few now that all the Jewish doctors were gone. With no chance to send the deaf boy out, his parents had stayed, and now they had the dazed look of so many who had received deportation notices.

Familiar grief rose into Kläre's chest, cold and tight, and she sat next to Bernhardt on the bed, allowing him to move a feather pillow behind her back as she closed her eyes to the sunlight, withdrawing from the commingled smells of fear and lilac drifting up from the square below. There were no words.

They had three more weeks. With the tableau of the Wachlenbergs still occupying her thoughts, Kläre left Bernhardt's apartment in time to shop for one more set of heavy wool pants for Werner. It was a spring ski trip that was posited, and though none of the Kohlers skied, Werner had to have the necessary equipment and clothing and would likely have to trek on skis as part of his journey.

Streicher's was nearly deserted on this weekday afternoon. The "Aryanization" of the Jewish-owned department store had in truth been more a liquidation. Shelves were half-empty, the salesmen listless. Kläre had just paid for her purchases when she heard her name called and turned to see Amalie Beckmann waving. It had been months since the two women had spoken and nearly a year since they'd last seen each other.

Amalie looked thin and worn, but her smile was genuine. "Kläre, how wonderful to see you." Amalie held her at arm's length, and each woman tried to read the other's thoughts as they studied one another's face.

"How is Georg?" Kläre asked, giving Amalie's shoulder a squeeze. His oldest son, Joseph, had gone into the army at the start of the war and had been killed almost immediately. The news had brought to Kläre's mind Hans Hermann, Amalie's long-ago fiancé who had died in the last war.

"Ya, Georg is still grieving badly. The girls are now in St. Agnes's, working with the nuns. Ansel goes to the school in Steele, as he has quite good marks. He will take examinations for the university in Cologne after this year."

"Ach, good for him. Ansel must come to see us when he is at university. It's not so far with the train." No sooner had the words left her mouth than Kläre felt their absurdity. She had spoken as though there were no chasm between her world and the world of her Christian friend, who could speak of jobs, schools, and the lives of her children as if they had a future.

"Ya, I will tell him. He will like to hear of you." Amalie hesitated, then asked carefully, "And your children? Jakob? Are they all well?"

Kläre gave her a pained smile. "Erwin is working in England now, and Werner . . ." She couldn't continue; Amalie gripped her arms again.

"Ach, my God, what is happening in this country?" Amalie's voice dropped to a whisper. "Can't you possibly get out?"

Kläre simply shook her head and pulled Amalie close for a moment before turning away. "Werner leaves in three weeks," she whispered harshly. She moved then, toward the worn stairs, and descended to the exit. She stepped into the fresh air, grateful to be out of doors and on her way home.

15 April 1940

Bernhardt Steinmann entered the apartment house on Virschow Strasse and located Jakob Kohler's name on the directory inside the marble-floored hall. The simple fact of the man's name printed carefully next to "Apt. 3A" unnerved Bernhardt more than the many iterations of this meeting that had troubled his mind over the last weeks. The days and nights had become a blur of stealthy arrangements, of assurances to his mother that their escape would be successful. They were to leave in three days' time with Werner Kohler, whose papers now bore the name of Steinmann. Today, Bernhardt would meet the boy and his father, and they would take measure of each other as only the implausibly joined could do: openly, and without expectation.

Bernhardt knew from his terse conversations with Kläre that there had been no arguments with Jakob this time about sending Werner out of the country. Since Erwin's departure eight months ago, war had been declared, and each day had brought the older man further into retreat from a world he no longer recognized, one punctuated by agitated trembling, searing headaches, and lost bearings. Even so, he had doggedly provided the necessary papers and money drafts as Melisande Durr had requested them.

Bernhardt climbed the elegant staircase to apartment 3A, where a young woman nervously ushered him into a well-appointed hall. Bernhardt wore the uniform of an information officer of the Reich—an important component in his ability to travel over the border to Switzerland and then to Italy. He tried to smile at the maid, to reassure her, but she left him for the sitting room and returned at once with Kläre, who was dressed in a smart blue suit. Kläre also shuddered as she caught sight of his uniform. She quickly caught herself and gave him a welcoming smile, but the wan visage under the smile shocked Bernhardt.

"Herr Steinmann, I am so grateful for your visit today. Please, come in." Kläre led him into the sitting room.

Bernhardt noted the simple but elegant furnishings, everything in rich, soothing greens and golds. Kläre conducted him toward a sofa with its back to French doors and an outdoor balcony. A man who Bernhardt guessed to be fifteen years his senior sat next to the sofa in a graceful armchair.

"Bernhardt Steinmann, please meet my husband, Jakob Kohler."

"Herr Doktor Kohler, I'm so pleased to meet you." Bernhardt reached out to take the older man's hand. Despite his somewhat frail appearance, Jakob Kohler's long, dry hand had strength enough for a firm handshake.

"Thank you so much for this visit, Herr Steinmann. Kläre speaks very highly of you, and I understand we have much to thank you for in assisting us with the arrangements we've made for Werner. Please sit down." Jakob resumed his seat immediately, and gestured to the sofa.

Bernhardt turned to look for Kläre, but she had silently quitted the room, leaving the two men to make their way into conversation on their own.

"Have we now all the papers in order, and have all the costs been paid?" Jakob asked with quiet authority.

Bernhardt sensed that Jakob was asserting what little power he had over his son's destiny in his questions about these administrative details. "Yes, Herr Doktor Kohler," he replied swiftly. "All the papers are in order, and all the tickets have been purchased. We have Swiss francs and Italian lire awaiting us at appropriate points on our journey."

"Have you made such a journey before, Herr Steinmann?" Jakob asked.

Bernhardt searched Jakob Kohler's face for the meaning of this question; finding no clues, he answered, "If you are asking whether I have traveled to Switzerland and Italy, the answer is yes; I've been to both several times. My parents were fond of the rest spa at Glion, and we have visited the major cultural spots in Italy." Jakob Kohler seemed to be waiting for more, so Bernhardt continued: "If you ask whether I have"—he scrutinized Jakob Kohler once more before hurrying on—"whether I have escorted an aging woman and a child across two dangerous borders in an effort to escape a country gone mad, the answer is no."

Bernhardt felt sweat forming at the back of his collar. What this man before him did or did not suspect about him and Kläre made no difference to him at this point—but the danger of what he was about to do weighed immediately and heavily upon him, just as he supposed it did on Jakob. Bernhardt was responsible for saving his mother, Werner Kohler, and another boy, and he intended to fulfill that responsibility. Jakob had already played his part.

Kläre had exacted a promise from Bernhardt that in exchange for Jakob's cooperation in getting Werner's papers and paying Melisande for both boys' trip, Bernhardt would not speak to Jakob about finding a way to let Kläre come as well. It was a Faustian deal for Bernhardt, but the proud man with soft eyes who sat before him made a formidable impression, the recognition of which was actually a comfort to Bernhardt. He could understand why Kläre was so devoted to this man.

"The Babylonian Talmud says, 'Whoever destroys a soul, it is considered as if he destroyed an entire world. And whoever saves a life, it is considered as if he saved an entire world.'" A hint of a smile warmed Jakob Kohler's serious face, and his eyes left Bernhardt's to greet Kläre. She carried a tray full of coffee service and cookies, which she expertly set down on the table. Behind her stood a tall boy of perhaps twelve years.

Kläre introduced them. "Werner, this is Herr Steinmann. He is the man who will be taking you to Switzerland and then Italy."

The boy stepped forward and offered his hand with a short bow. "Good afternoon, Herr Steinmann." His face betrayed nothing of his feelings.

Bernhardt saw no reason to delay discussion any further. He began to lay out the plan for the Kohlers, keeping his explanation as simple and direct as possible. "We will leave from the Bahnhof on the early morning train to Frankfurt, and travel the length of the country from north to south. It's the slow train, and may take most of the day and night. We cross the Swiss border at Basel, then continue to Bern and over the mountains to Lugano in Italy and eventually Trieste. There we will meet the group that will continue to Palestine."

Kläre listened carefully, matter-of-factly. Bernhardt could see the mask of grief spread across her features, and he sensed the wall she had built around her thoughts, the event itself. As they spoke over coffee, she made notes of items she had yet to pack, occasionally asking a clarifying question of Bernhardt. Werner's eyes were lit with the excitement of the adventure ahead of him; this, Bernhardt saw, pained Kläre greatly, though she hid it well.

"Werner, it's important that you behave in your most grown-up fashion, and that you do exactly as Herr and Frau Steinmann instruct. There may be danger to you at any point," Jakob said to his son in a quiet but firm voice. "What is your new name?"

"Werner Herbert Steinmann."

"Parents?"

"Otto and Lissie Steinmann."

Jakob continued to quiz Werner, who spoke eagerly even as his father sank back into his chair and Kläre's fingers worried a handkerchief in her lap. Bernhardt watched her barely contained grief with a feeling of helplessness, trying silently to transmit the love he felt for her, the bravery she would need for what lay before her.

The meeting finished in an hour's time, and Bernhardt rose to leave. Jakob also stood, looking more frail and haunted than he had at the outset.

"Thank you Herr Steinmann . . . Thank you," was all he could utter.

Kläre followed Bernhardt into the entryway and then out to the hall. She took his hand in both of hers.

"I also thank you . . . from the bottom of my heart," Kläre said.

"Kläre. . ." Bernhardt's voice caught, but Kläre placed a hand on his chest.

"No, please . . . You mustn't say another thing. Please."

Bernhardt nodded once and took his leave. As he headed toward the tramway, he could see nothing but her tortured face, surrounded by honey-colored curls.

16 1941, Hörde

Early darkness fell unnoticed in the rear of the drab truck. An unseen hand grabbed Johanna Ente as she clung to the bench she had fallen to, stabilizing her there. Her left thigh had hit the wood painfully; she clutched her cane and tried to brace herself. Still breathing heavily, she squinted to adjust to the canvas-covered dark. She gradually made out a figure to her left: a man whose strong hand still held her arm. She saw only the outline of a coat and hat, an upright and vigorous form—she could not make out his features.

"Many thanks," she ventured.

"No worry." The man's tone was ironic, polite.

"Do you know where we go now?" Johanna worked to keep her voice steady as the truck lurched along an unknown route.

"No." The answer was abrupt and leaden.

Other voices resumed urgent conversations and stifled weeping. Johanna pulled her shawl closer under her chin, leaning back into the side of the truck bracing as best as she could without being able to touch the bed of the truck with her feet. She felt the man's hand loosen from her left arm, though she remained wedged against him in the dark. She waited as she often did in these days for her momentary confusion to clear, but it had all happened too fast and she did not understand.

"Frau Johanna Ente!" the soldier had shouted at the door. "Open up!" It was a cold evening in February, damp with rain and smells of a city absent its greenery. She had only just finished washing her plate and fork from the evening supper. She didn't remember having spoken, only moving as the orders were barked out.

"You have been ordered to the office of the SA. You will be relocated. You may bring one valise. In ten minutes' time, we must leave."

She had stared blankly at first, trying to sort out what was happening. She stood staring at the mud from the soldier's shoes on her kitchen floor, absently moving toward the cleaning cloth hanging from the hook near the sink.

"Quickly!" the man had shouted. She had hurried then to the hall and up the stairs, the soldier following closely. The stairway had become a chore with her advancing years, and Johanna was conscious of the young legs impatiently following her old ones.

"Bring something warm," he said, some of the harshness leaving his voice as he looked around her bedroom, a hint of embarrassment showing on his youthful face. This lapse was followed quickly with more angry orders to hurry, to not keep the others waiting. *What others?* Fear crippled Johanna's typically adroit hands, and she fumbled with the latch of the valise, unable to think properly about what to place in the heavy leather case.

In the end she grabbed only what she saw that seemed comforting and warm: her grey wool suit, her black day dress with the lace collar she'd made herself, the fine old woolen shawl with cashmere in it that Jonah had brought her once from a trip to Amsterdam. In went the silver brush and comb set, her warm woolen stockings, and her new high-topped black shoes. She was wearing her heavy old brown shoes and a brown tweed housedress. Over these she put on a wool jacket and shawl and her winter coat, pinning a sturdy hat on before her vanity mirror. As she turned, she swept the fine triple-silver picture frame with photos of Jonah, Ernst in uniform, and her three daughters into a large handbag. From her glove drawer, she drew the two warmest pairs and a small pocketbook containing fifty marks.

The impatient soldier motioned to the door as she turned. Johanna dragged the heavy valise to the floor, her handbag clutched with it.

"I'll take that," the soldier snapped; he pulled it from her roughly and steered her out the door. A moment later they were downstairs in the hall where the second soldier was waiting, leaning against the doorframe of the sitting room and studying its contents.

Johanna stopped before the telephone. "My daughter must know that I am leaving."

"We leave here in two minutes. You had better pack something to eat rather than speak on your Jew telephone," the second soldier sneered.

Johanna squeezed back her tears and entered the kitchen, where she filled an oilcloth bag with a cold potato, a small chunk of bread, some cheese, and a small packet of sliced meat. She maintained a steely calm, wearing her years of practiced reserve like a web of tangled vines around the thicket of her fear.

She had barely locked the door when the soldiers pulled her down the stairs and toward the large truck in the street.

The truck veered around a corner and someone fell from the other side. A woman wailed—an outburst that was followed immediately by a thumping from the cab.

"Quiet!" shouted a soldier.

The woman's cry instantly turned to muffled sobs. Johanna no longer tried to keep her own tears from falling. She gripped the sleeve of the man's coat next to her.

"God help us."

Kläre held the postcard from Werner, reading it for what seemed like the thousandth time. It had been ten months and only this message had come from him.

Liebe Mutti und Papa,

The train brought us to our holiday after many delays. We are in Italy now preparing for our further journey. Onkel Bernhardt and Oma Rosa send their greetings. I am well.

Hugs and kisses,

Your son, Werner

Kläre wept holding the card, which had taken two months to reach her and had obviously been restricted to a simple, non-identifying message. They had been together when the card was written—Bernhardt, Rosa Steinmann, and Werner—but it was impossible to know what had happened since. She had heard nothing else from Italy, and could only hope that Werner had made it to Palestine. With Italy's entry into the war, it was no longer clear what safety might exist for a family hiding Jews. Perhaps Bernhardt had found a way to take Rosa to America. *But no, no thoughts now of Bernhardt, or even Werner.*

Kläre placed the card next to the photo of Erwin, whose latest letter had been brought to Germany by a stranger. After two years, Erwin was now a recruit in the British Army. It made Kläre's head ache to think of it, and so she did not.

It was time to go to the shops to try for food. Herr Tischmann still allowed Kläre to visit the door in the alley behind the Hauptstrasse to buy small, tough pieces of meat. She had first to draw her shawl across the yellow star sewn neatly to her overcoat before she approached the store, in case someone should see her. Better to look like a beggar than a Jew, though in truth she had become both. It didn't matter now. She had to buy food for her mother and for Jakob and herself. Only twice a week did she venture out to the streets: on Tuesday to the butcher and bakery, and on Friday to the market square for cheese and the meager produce still available from the farmers' stands.

Today she would go to the butcher and then to her mother's with a meat soup that was thin but tasty. She hung her apron behind the door, retrieved her shopping bag from its hook, and had just stepped into the hall when a quiet knock on the door froze her mid-step.

"Frau Kohler. It is Herr Licht. Are you there?"

Kläre composed herself and moved quickly to open the door. Her neighbor from the flat above stood nervously in the hall. He wore only the brown shirt and pants of his army uniform, the brown tie neatly knotted at his throat.

Herr Licht had been an administrator at the hospital where Kläre had provided massage during the war. He knew that she had worked many more than the required hours on the wards and that she had been of great comfort to the patients. Kläre and Jakob had moved to this apartment after the Nazis had begun to seize Jews' homes at an alarming rate. Jakob had managed to sell their house to a young attorney, and though they hadn't gotten nearly the proper value from the sale, they had gotten enough to buy the antiques and jewels that were helping them to live now, just as Ernst had suggested.

Licht had greeted Kläre in the entrance hall of the building shortly after they'd moved in. His polite reserve had surprised Kläre, as her star had been as clearly evident as his officer's uniform.

Now he stood uncertainly outside her door. "Frau Kohler, may I . . . may I speak to you?"

"Yes of course, come in, Herr Licht. Is everything all right?" Kläre asked, her fear returning as the slight man moved past her into the hall.

Herr Licht waited until she closed the door before speaking: "I am sorry to tell you this, but I have just learned that there are orders to move a number of elderly people from Hörde to a relocation camp in Linkheim. I'm afraid your mother's name was on the list. I believe she may have already been taken."

Kläre grabbed for the side table. "Ach, no. No, they can't!" Kläre pressed her shopping bag, which she still held in her gloved hand, to her mouth, as if to keep more words from spilling out.

Herr Licht stared at the floor. "I don't have access to more information, and it would not be good for me to inquire too much. It's best to ask at the Judenrat . . . I'm sorry." With that, he moved to the door.

"Herr Licht." Kläre stood behind him, her voice shaking with tears.

"I thank you. You have been very kind to tell me this. Please, if you hear more . . . I would so appreciate . . ."

He looked briefly over his shoulder at her and then immediately back to the door. "Yes. Yes, of course." And he was gone.

Jakob. I must phone him. Kläre dropped her shopping bag and struggled with her shaking hands to dial the telephone. Jakob went less frequently these days to the offices of the Judenrat—the only place he was allowed to work. The regulations and prohibitions had become increasingly draconian and the proceedings he submitted ever more useless, to the point that even there he could do very little. But he had gone there today, and he must do something—anything—to find her mother.

6 March, 1941
Dearest Klärchen,

I saw today Herr Rauch, an old customer of Father's, and bless him; he will bring this letter out to you. The last days have been fearful, but I am all right still. We were taken to Linkheim, where we are staying in a dreadful house, many of us to one room. It is cold and we have not enough blankets, but so far I stayed warm using what I brought. We are not told why we are here or where we will go and they are beating the ones who ask too much. Only once in a while a soldier comes and shouts orders. I cannot write more as I must give this to Herr Rauch, and the men here say it is dangerous to write at all. I beg Jakob to try and get me back home!

Kisses,
Mutti

Jakob's shoulders slumped forward as he reread the scrawled note. Next to him, Kläre's muffled sob struck a further blow. The letter from Johanna Ente had been written a week ago, and it had now been nearly a month since she'd vanished.

Jakob's inquiries had been methodical, insistent, and utterly ineffective. The Judenrat had told him nothing of value: A transport of older adults had been relocated to Linkheim. No, there was no process to secure the release of Frau Ente. There was no one to pay, no one with whom he might negotiate. Didn't he understand? The assistant to the director of the Judenrat had himself been beaten on the street, and a truck full of women and teenage boys had been gassed to death near Frankfurt in the last two days. Linkheim, a small, drab town with few if any Jews, had no underground contact.

"Jakob." Kläre's voice was low and ragged. "Perhaps we can contact Louis. He knows people still in the underground, doesn't he?"

"Louis is in London. We are bombing London. How can he help us now? Why would he try?" Jakob spoke this last question with bitterness.

"He is your brother, Jakob. He has helped once with Erwin. Perhaps . . ."

"No! I will not waste time with him." Jakob spoke angrily.

Kläre's head dropped nearly to her chest, her hands clasped tightly in her lap.

A finch's twitter broke into the fierce quiet of the room. *Grünfink,* Klare thought, the identification coming to her unsought. Kläre let the lovely sound of the finch's song expand in her head, pushing back her fear and anger. Almost immediately, the idea followed: *Rauch! I will find Rauch and he will return to Linkheim; he can bring to Mutti some food and perhaps money and more warm clothing.* Rauch—a former employee of the Entes' feed business—came from Linkheim. He had seen Johanna once; he could find her again.

She smoothed her skirt and raised her eyes to study her husband, lost now in his own thoughts. She would not press him further—but neither could she find it within herself to place a comforting hand on his shoulder as she rose to leave. The finch's song finished as the morning sun filled the room.

Two hours later, Kläre made her way down the Konigs Strasse, folded into a gabardine coat that Ditha had sent from America six months ago. The yellow star sewn carefully to the lapel was nearly covered by a plain brown scarf that draped Kläre's head and hid much of her face. She smiled in spite of her anxiety as she thought of her sister-in-law. Almost as soon as Ditha and Ernst had gotten to New York they had begun to send her packages, mostly with clothing: last year's coats, dresses, hats, and gloves. Their reduced circumstances hadn't changed Ditha's routine of seasonal replacement of perfectly good clothing. By some happy accident, the woman from whom they had received the affidavit to immigrate had been wife to a vice president of one of the largest department stores in New York. One of the woman's first acts of largesse had been a shopping trip with Ditha and Margaret. Ditha had written, *I cannot correctly boil an egg for breakfast yet, but we look very smart on the street.*

Kläre continued walking, banishing thoughts of everything but the task she had just accomplished. The ban on Jews using public transportation meant that Kläre had walked for more than an hour with her package. She had had to look purposeful and invisible at the same time. She had found the feed store of Axel Rauch and had waited until he was alone in his back office. Boldly, she had handed him an envelope and a small parcel that she had carried under her arm. She had worked hard to persuade Rauch to risk taking the clothes and the envelope stuffed with bank notes to her mother, but in the end he had agreed.

Now she was returning home, searching for the sound of a bird to accompany the rhythm of her moderate stride. Taking the back streets, she would be safe at home in an hour. *There! Not a Grünfink this time. A simple sparrow, singing in the morning.*

Kläre had only just hung her coat when Etta's voice startled her from her thoughts: "Frau Kohler!" The girl's face was frozen with fear. "There is an officer."

As the words left her lips, the soldier burst in from the room behind her. Kläre lowered her handbag to the table before her without taking her eyes from him.

"Frau Kohler," he began forcefully, though his darting eyes betrayed an uncertainty. "You were seen delivering a package in the Norden Strasse to a grain broker's business. Why were you there? Are you spying on a good Christian's business?"

Kläre continued to stare directly at the officer—a boy, really, not much older than her Erwin. She remained outwardly impassive as she sought frantically for an explanation that would save, disguise, and parry, all in the same moment. How had this happened so quickly?

Etta backed against the wall, making herself as invisible as possible. Kläre knew all too well that Etta's mere presence in the room, in defiance of the order banning Christians from working in the homes of Jews, put the girl at great risk. Etta—her young husband at war, and her children at home—had defied the law, partly to keep milk in her larder, partly out of her loyalty to Kläre.

"My father used to be a colleague of that feed establishment," Kläre said calmly, intentionally avoiding using Rauch's name. "On his death, I found some accounts that I believed belonged to that business. I was merely delivering them."

The young officer looked straight at her now with shrewd eyes, gauging the level of her understanding, if not her truthfulness. "Perhaps this matter may be settled with a fine . . . say of fifty marks," he concluded.

Now Kläre dropped her head and, after a moment, turned to Etta. "Please, Frau Schmidt," using the first false name that came to her mind. "If you would be so kind as to take the message to Herr Licht regarding the rental check, I will telephone Herr Kohler about that matter, as well as this one, immediately."

Etta paused for only a fraction of a second before leaving the room and then the apartment with purposeful dispatch. Kläre rose and entered the front hall, crossing directly to the telephone. She rang the Judenrat and, forcing her voice to remain calm, asked to speak to Jakob.

"Jakob," she said clearly and loudly. "An officer is here regarding a fine for . . . for delivering the accounts information to the feed business in Norden Strasse. Will you bring home fifty marks, along with a draft for the rent for Herr Licht? Ya, he is here now."

Kläre replaced the receiver in the cradle and had barely turned toward the sitting room when the door to the outer hallway opened and Herr Licht entered. Etta remained outside. Licht barely looked at Kläre and said nothing as she gestured toward the door to the sitting room. He entered the room, and the young officer, who had been scrutinizing the artwork, the books, and the antique silver in the cabinets, scrambled to attention and saluted his superior officer. Open fear alternated with wily calculation before his expression settled into blank formality.

"Name!" barked Licht.

"Lieutenant Armand Holz!" responded the younger man.

"Excellent work, Lieutenant!" responded Licht. "You will wait here for delivery of the fine, and then report to me at 1600 hours at the district offices. If there is a problem I will communicate with your superior. Otherwise, I assume this matter will be finished!"

"Yes, sir!" Holz saluted smartly, though his eyes smoldered with resentment.

Herr Licht turned on his heel and left the apartment without even glancing at Kläre. She sat at her desk. The officer sat awkwardly on the sofa. Kläre looked steadily at him and asked, "May I offer you some tea? I haven't any coffee."

Half an hour later, when Jakob arrived, the officer had finished the cup of poor tea that Kläre had prepared for him and was fidgeting in his place on the sofa.

"Officer—" Jakob began.

"Holz," Kläre broke in.

"Officer Holz, I believe you will find what you require in this envelope." Jakob handed him a bulging packet, standing straighter than Kläre had seen him do in some time, his face drawn but resolute.

Holz took the envelope, rose uncertainly, and then, straightening his shoulders, brushed roughly past Jakob to the front door. "Dirty Jews!" he spat as he left.

Kläre sank to her chair. "Thank God, Jakob," she whispered. "Thank God."

17 June 1941, Palestine

"Kohler, I have never had such a meal. An orange, Kohler. So juicy! And the cucumber: fantastic!" Avery Frey sat with his eyes closed, head tilted back, face to the sun.

Werner smiled at his friend and shook his head. "Ya, this is really something. I would have eaten more, but I actually got full." The wonder of such a statement struck both boys and they were silent again.

Like their companions, they had shed their heavy clothes, shoes, and socks upon their arrival at the beach. Some, like them, were sitting in the sand; others were walking or dipping their toes in the water. They had been given twenty minutes' time to stretch their legs and enjoy the beach. Soon, they would load the truck and set off for the Ben Shemen Youth Village and its agricultural boarding school in the central part of Palestine.

Werner stood and waded into the ocean in the blinding light of the Mediterranean spring day. The wind was hot and strong over the water's salt-heavy, brilliant surface. Avery, a few meters away, looked every bit as stunned by the heat and the intensity of the colors surrounding them as he was. They still wore the long trousers they'd needed for the journey to Haifa from Trieste—four hundred children on an old tourist boat. They had arrived the day before.

"This is Caesaria, Kohler." Avery's sense of wonder moved from food to history. "Herod the Great probably stood right here."

Werner was not thinking of ancient Romans. He was thinking of their voyage from Trieste. For nearly a month they had traveled south through the Adriatic Sea, had anchored endlessly in waters off Greece, Cyprus, and Turkey, and had finally arrived outside the harbor at Haifa. Always there had been delays for more payments, more paperwork, more unloading and searching of luggage.

"Frey . . . Did you get to Trieste before I did, or did I get there first?" Werner asked.

Avery looked back at his friend, eyes huge behind his spectacles. "I was there before, Kohler. We had come already in the winter. Why are you asking?"

Werner sat heavily in the sand, the water lapping at his feet. "I'm trying to remember each step. I already can't remember things. Do you remember Trieste? When they brought us to the ship and we saw all the kids stacked on the wooden platforms and they wouldn't allow any more? Can you believe we are actually here now?"

Avery stood above his friend, silent, expectant, so Werner continued.

"I didn't think we would make it through Cyprus. How long were we there, rotting in the sun?"

Avery nodded his head. "Two weeks. Ya, but that wasn't the worst that I can remember. I saw the ship *Aparta* on the Danube. It was frozen in with all the people from Poland. They couldn't get permission to move on. I heard they starved. I saw them jumping into the freezing water to try to get to us. I still think about it."

"Don't, Avery. Don't think about it."

"Right, Kohler. We didn't all get a ski holiday on our escape to Trieste, did we? Tell me again about pulling the old lady on the sled and staying in the barns with the cows."

So Werner launched into the tale of his travels with Bernhardt and Rosa Steinmann, omitting the first long train ride through Germany, when apprehension and heartache had replaced the anticipation of adventure. Even now, in the sparkling sunshine, the long hours in the train compartment with his arms wrapped around the sack of food carefully packed by his mother were vivid and disturbing. Düsseldorf, Cologne, Bonn, Koblenz, Frankfurt, Mannheim, Baden Baden, and Freiburg. Long past the point of hunger, he hadn't wanted to eat a single roll for fear of losing something she had touched. Posing as Herr Steinmann's nephew, he'd sat stoned-faced as soldiers had come and gone on the train, asking for their papers over and over again as they moved toward the border. After an interminable stop in the middle of the night—accompanied by much stamping and shouting and collecting of passports—the train had moved across the border and they had disembarked in the cavernous central Bahnhof in Basel, Switzerland.

Werner picked up his story with that night in Basel, regaling Avery with their movements from home to home, first to Lucerne and then to nameless towns and villages, traveling in carts and on foot over the mountains—the faces changing, the food meager but shared, the care of the aged Frau Steinmann becoming the connection between Werner and Herr Steinmann. The elderly woman was brave and kind and treated Werner with the respect befitting a young man assisting her on a perilous journey. Werner, accordingly, rose to the occasion.

One evening, a long walk between two mountain villages ended with an unexpected spring snowstorm and Frau Steinmann slipped and fell. Herr Steinmann insisted that she sit on the sled they were using to drag their belongings.

"I pulled her myself for at least a kilometer," Werner boasted. "The snow was so thick you couldn't see a meter ahead."

Instead of finishing the journey to the safehouse in the village ahead, they stopped at a humble farmhouse close by the road and asked for shelter. The farm wife took in the unusual travel party and, without a word, showed them to a small loft in the cow barn that comprised the ground level of the house. Even with the snow outside, it was warm with the smell and heat of animals, and they all slept immediately, a precious ladleful of fresh milk brought by the farmer's wife filling their empty bellies.

"Frau Steinmann leaned over the edge of the loft and said, 'Thank you for beautifying our evening' to the cow." Werner mimicked Frau Steinmann's elegant, clipped speaking voice for this part. While his friend chuckled, he turned his face to the sea to hide the tears that sprang to his eyes.

In the short weeks it had taken to get to Trieste, Werner had come to love Bernhardt and especially Rosa Steinmann, and leaving them had been nearly as difficult as leaving his parents. More than once, Werner had caught Herr Steinmann watching him with a look on his face that Werner didn't exactly understand, but was nonetheless comforting. He closed his eyes to the sea breeze and the memory.

The two boys continued talking, speaking in short ellipses, comparing stories of the odysseys that had brought them here, a lifetime away from their homes and families. Their stories wove them together, but had forever separated them from all that they knew before. They could not bear to think of their mothers, their schools, their friends, or their towns. They concentrated only on newer memories. There was the guilty pleasure of the excitement they felt in having journeyed to a young country that they already felt chosen to found. The danger and discomfort fed their sense of adventure. Even at thirteen and fourteen, they understood that in exchange for the saving of their lives, they would devote all that they had to moving forward and building. They could not think of what they had left; the past was sealed off as surely as a cave covered over by a rockslide.

Nevertheless, thoughts of the photograph in his pocket broke across the vivid seascape lying before Werner. It was a picture of his mother, windblown and beautiful, striding abreast of her brother, sister-in-law, and niece, smiling in the bracing wind on another beach, on another sea. *Mutti, Onkel Ernst, Ditha, and Margaret—where was Father? Where was Erwin, and where was I? Already gone? Margaret was there. Why was I not there with her, searching for shells and the next forbidden adventure?* It was the last photo he'd had from his mother, sent in a letter that he'd gotten when the representative from the Palestine Office had boarded the boat in Trieste. He sat on the hot sand, his feet burning, and willfully sealed away the questions with the memories.

At the sound of a whistle, the boys gathered their things and moved toward the truck. They lined up, their new rucksacks on their backs.

"Kohler!" a voice shouted from the front. "Werner Kohler!" Werner looked at Avery, who shrugged, and stretched around the other boys to see the man who had called. Werner stepped forward toward the doctor whom he had seen in the morning.

"I am Kohler, sir."

The man's face was tired, but kind. His shirt had no doubt been properly ironed at some point, but was now creased from a long day of checking all the children. Stains had appeared under the short sleeves of his open-collared shirt. Werner had never seen a doctor without a jacket and cravat. This man was deeply tanned and his shock of sand-colored hair curled wildly around his hatless head. He pointed toward a young girl at his side, holding a large bag.

"Here are some eyeglasses I found for you, Kohler," he said in German. "They aren't exactly the same as your old ones, but they'll have to do until we find better ones." The girl handed Werner large, horn-rimmed eyeglasses, and reached for his old ones, which had glass on only one side, and which were lopsided on his face, the left arm of the frame attached with a piece of wire. They had been crushed by the boy who slept next to Werner on the ship from Cyprus. All night the seas had rolled heavily, and at last a heavy pitch had tossed several boys from their crude bunks. Werner woke to his neighbor thrashing atop him; his eyeglasses, carefully tucked next to him under his towel, had been ruined.

"Thank you very much," he said as he adjusted the glasses on his nose and over his ears. They were too large and one eye was not strong enough, but he could see more clearly now. He fixed his gaze on the smiling girl in front of him. "How did you find them so fast?" he asked her.

"My father is very good at finding things."

Watching her, Werner could not move, and he said nothing.

The girl smiled. "How do you do? I am Hannah Kiewe. I help with the new pioneers at Ben Shemen."

"But you are German, no? You speak perfectly." Werner felt rooted to the sand.

"Yes, we came from Düsseldorf nearly two years ago now, but I hardly remember it anymore. I like it here now. If it weren't for the war, we could be doing even more, but it has become difficult with the English." Hannah's open face became fierce, and she shook her blond hair back over her shoulders.

"Hannah, Hannah! Leave the poor boy alone with your chatter. Let him find his place on the truck so we can get going now."

Hannah lowered her head as Dr. Kiewe turned Werner back toward the line of boys. Werner walked two steps and then looked once more at the doctor's daughter. She, too, was stealing a glance at him.

"Thank you for the glasses," Werner called. "It's much better." He stumbled for a moment on the uneven ground as he returned to his spot next to Avery.

"Look at you, Kohler!" Avery exclaimed. "Now we have to call you the Professor!"

Werner pushed Avery ahead in the line that was now moving toward the rear of the truck. At the front, someone began to sing *Ha Tikva:*

As long as deep in the heart,
The soul of a Jew yearns,
And forward to the East
To Zion, an eye looks
Our hope will not be lost,
The hope of two thousand years,
To be a free nation in our land,
The land of Zion and Jerusalem.

One by one, the pioneers took up the song as they boarded the truck, repeating the words they had practiced for a month now with no idea, as yet, what it would cost them to embrace the hope of this new country. They were fervent as only the young can be, and also delirious with the heat, the light, and fatigue.

When the anthem drew to a close, one of the leaders began to speak. "We go now to Ben Shemen, a youth village for those of you whose good fortune allowed your parents to send you here. Aliyot ha-Noar welcomes you, and asks you to remember it is our goal to save children from the evil in Europe and to build the future of Palestine! You are the pioneers who will go on to build *kibbutzim* and *moshavim* all over the country; who will fight, farm . . ."

"Avery, I met a girl," Werner whispered to his friend. "She's beautiful, Avery. I think you'll like her. Her name is Hannah."

Avery nudged his friend. "My God, that didn't take long, did it? You are something else, Werner Kohler!"

". . . bear children, and fight more to be masters of your own land, your own lives."

Werner leaned forward as the leader went on, craning his neck toward the back of the truck to try to catch a glimpse of Hannah.

". . . Neither the British nor the Arabs can challenge you with hardship and hazard the way that the deadly rumors from Europe can . . ."

Werner met the rolling eyes of a number of boys and then leaned back toward Avery and spoke softly. "Not Werner anymore, Avery. No more German names. From now on I am Avraham. Avraham Kohler."

Avery shook his head but smiled at his friend. "Okay, Avraham. Avraham! God in heaven, why Avraham?"

18 1941

"In other words, what did not lie in my plan lay in God's plan. And the more often things happen to me, the more lively becomes in me the conviction of my faith—that from God's point of view, nothing is accidental, that my entire life, even in the most minute detail, was pre-designed in the plans of divine providence and is thus for the all-seeing eye of God a perfect coherence of meaning."
—Edith Stein

Amalie Beckmann absently rubbed the dull finish on the old bureau as she watched her stepson pack neatly pressed shirts into the old valise. The tiny room barely contained his tall, ungainly frame, and despite the care with which he dressed, his long arms and large hands seemed to belong to another, bigger man. The dawning day lit the room with a dim glow as Ansel prepared to depart for Cologne and his university studies there.

He had already been up for hours. This Amalie knew because she had woken in the darkness of pre-dawn and heard his quiet movements as he began packing and then carefully made the narrow single bed, its springs sighing softly. He had washed before dressing and then there had been the long silence, during which time she knew he had been on his knees on the bare, scrubbed floor. His was not the prayer of the casual believer, performed dutifully en route to a day of worldly tasks. His supplication was long, dreamy, and deep, with recitation of the rosary on either side.

Amalie had never understood him, though surely the praying had been instilled by the nuns who had raised him. After the death of his mother, Ansel had been sent, alone among the five children, to be raised by his aunt, a nun in a Kinderheim. One by one, Amalie had found her way to each of Georg Beckmann's children, but Ansel had been the hardest. He was never rude, nor was he unappreciative, but on his rare visits home he had kept his distance. Amalie had had no part in Georg's decision to send Ansel to the Kinderheim, but the move had coincided with her entry into the family, and she hadn't had the opportunity to provide the mothering to him that she'd developed with the other children. She liked Ansel—liked his seriousness, his discipline, the respect he effortlessly afforded and commanded even at a young age.

She wished they could become closer. Each of them had suffered loss and had developed the skill to accommodate, most recently in Georg's death, and there was an unspoken understanding between them, an agreement to settle for what was. Amalie turned to her stepson.

"Ansel, it is hard in these days for a student at university. I know how much your father wanted for you to study. I wish I had more money to send with you, and I wish . . . you could be closer."

Ansel halted his packing and stood, waiting.

Amalie continued, "Do you remember Kläre Kohler, my friend from Hörde?"

Ansel answered with polite interest. "Yes, of course. We visited her several times in Hörde. She has two sons."

"Yes, that's right. Well you know, she lives much closer than we do to Cologne. You enjoyed her quite a bit when you were younger. Perhaps you might visit on a weekend."

Ansel searched Amalie's face for a moment. "Is she safe, then? From the Nazis?"

Amalie hesitated, but answered him directly. "I don't imagine any Jew is safe. But if she has a piece of bread, she will share it with you. Her own children are gone—sent out of the country—and I hear her mother has been deported. I have some things I'd like to send to her if you would be willing." Even as she spoke, Amalie wondered that she asked this of a seventeen-year-old boy. Always, Ansel seemed older than his actual age, and she was speaking to him as if he were a grown man.

"I remember her kindness, and it is very good of you to think of her now. Give me what you have for her and I will see to it."

Amalie looked and listened for any irony or hesitation in his expression, and finding none, she descended the stairs to the kitchen to bundle together a small packet of sugar, one of tea, and a pair of sturdy woolen stockings she had knitted using wool from an old vest of Georg's.

She heard Ansel's heavy steps on the stairway, and met him in the cold hallway. She tucked the bundle into his rucksack as he wrestled himself into the coat that had been his father's. It was a good, thick herringbone tweed from before the war, and Amalie was pleased that her tailoring had transformed the garment suitably for Ansel's tall, thin frame. The autumn had not turned cold quite yet, but the coat was too bulky to pack, and Ansel buttoned it carefully. He arranged his bags next to the front door and turned once more to Amalie.

"I must go now. Thank you for helping me. Will you be all right? I know my sisters are nearby . . ."

Amalie looked into his limpid brown eyes. They were Georg's eyes, but with a softness that had gone out of—or had never been in—her husband's look.

"Ach, you mustn't worry about me. I am fine here. But you must be careful going to Cologne. One hears so much about the unrest there."

"I go to study. Politics do not interest me. Religion and philosophy are quite gone from most people's attention. I'm certain to be fine as long as I stick to my program."

For a moment it looked as if Ansel would bend down to kiss her cheek, but the moment passed and instead Amalie reached out and patted his arm awkwardly. He gathered his belongings and walked down the front stairs into the cool morning. Amalie waved.

Ansel's journey to the train was short but arduous as his bags were heavy and his coat very warm for the sunny morning. Fine beads of perspiration covered his forehead and he was breathing heavily by the time he approached the old station. He stopped to readjust his load, and a flood of memories filled his heart with pain. The many times he had walked with his father just this way to the train to return to the orphanage, or afterward to boarding school, had always been sad, though the sadness was always left unspoken. They would shake hands at the end of the platform, with Ansel often fighting tears, and then his father would hand his bag to the conductor. Ansel would climb the steps and enter the second-class compartment, then find a window seat on the platform side and watch his father pace up and down the length of the car. He waited for the conductor to check his watch and the large clock at the head of the platform, then raise his whistle to signal the on-time departure. Georg Beckmann would lift his hand in a reserved wave and then walk quickly away as the train pulled out of the station, leaving his son to watch from the window until he was out of sight.

Sometimes, on a visit, this would be the only time Ansel had alone with his father, and he remembered longing for the walk to double in length. He would tell a story or ask his father questions, just to share the time, and then he would replay the conversation over and over during the weeks and months that went by between visits.

Now his father was gone, and Ansel felt the ache of loneliness. He was truly an orphan. The visit with Amalie had been affecting for each of them. He'd felt her reach across the breach of time and history in search of a connection to him in the loss of his father, but he'd had nothing more than the conventional platitudes to give her in return. It was not in his nature to dissemble, and the truth was, their opportunity for connection had always been limited in time and scope. Amalie was a good Catholic, had been a good wife to Georg, and had done her best with his children, eventually becoming close to the girls—but Ansel had been kept from the center of things and so had only peripheral attachments. And while Amalie had been both kind and deferential to him, she had stayed in the background when he was home, allowing him to focus on his sisters, brother, and father. As such, the two of them had maintained a polite distance from one another.

The train station was busy on this Monday morning with soldiers, businessmen off to the big city, and common travelers, all with a wariness cultivated by war, shortages, fear, and suffering. This time, Ansel thought, he would build a new life entirely on his own and of his choosing, and into his sadness crept an excitement that he quickly moderated with careful expectation. He would study hard and do well, and his mind would dwell in the company of the world's greatest thinkers and believers.

Ansel's first week at university was exhilarating, but also unnerving. The many young men who had joined the army left the lecture halls half-empty, and those that remained wore worried looks of preoccupation—or perhaps guilt. Girls now attended classes as well, and this Ansel had not expected. His had been a focused, serious education, first at the orphanage, and then in the Gymnasium in the nearby town. There the monks and priests had taught most of the classes, and only to boys. Ansel's experience with women had been limited to the nuns and to his sisters, all of whom were years older than he and of a subdued and distant nature.

On the second day of classes, Ansel found his way to a hall for a philosophy lecture. A disturbance at the entrance had drawn a small crowd, and Ansel instinctively stepped away from the mass of people to stand in the shadow of a doorway. The crowd shifted, and a diminutive nun, whose ardent voice echoed in the hall, became visible through the shoulders of the young men and women who surrounded her.

"My sisters do vigil to atone for the insults that the divine heart of our Lord must endure!" The gap closed as the students shifted, but the voice still rang strong and clear. "By their steadfast invocation, they draw down God's grace on we who sin, and mercy on we who need. In our time, when the powerlessness of all natural means for battling the overwhelming misery everywhere has been demonstrated so obviously, an entirely new understanding of the power of prayer, of expiation, and of vicarious atonement has again awakened." The small figure again shifted into view, her wimple vibrating with the strength of her commanding presence. Ansel stood, transfixed, until a passing student blocked his view. He fell into step with the other boy, moving toward the crowd and the captivating voice.

"Who is she?" Ansel asked.

"Ah, that is Sister Benedicta of the Cross. She is a Carmelite. Crazy, actually. They say she was born a Jew and the nuns want to send her to a monastery in Holland; she is hardly safe here." The boy glanced back at the entryway and continued, his voice rising as his subject's did. "She did a doctorate in philosophy in Freiburg. I guess she can't just leave well enough alone . . ." He moved past the crowd and into the lecture hall of the School of Philosophy.

A moment later, Ansel watched as a clutch of nervous students shepherded the slender figure of the nun down a back stairway, leaving the crowd to murmur and press into the hall. Ansel remained for a moment, dazed. *In our time, when the powerlessness of all . . . means for battling the overwhelming misery everywhere has been demonstrated so obviously . . . new understanding of the power of prayer.* The words spun through his mind and lodged in his heart with the warmth of recognition.

Ansel was still thinking of Sister Benedicta as he rode the train from Cologne to Dortmund. He had sent a short note to the Kohlers, announcing his arrival in Cologne and suggesting a visit to deliver his stepmother's greetings. Immediately, he had gotten a reply.

> *Dear Ansel,*
>
> *I would be most pleased to have you visit with us next weekend. You must forgive me in advance that I cannot prepare for you such a sumptuous meal, as we suffer as everyone does the shortages in the shops.*
>
> *You must come and stay if you like overnight.*
>
> *Best greetings,*
>
> *Kläre Kohler*

Now he stepped from the streetcar and walked the short distance to 17 Furchler Strasse. It lay in the middle of a quiet section of Hörde, and spring rain made the streets glisten. Ansel noted the pavement with approval; he hadn't extra shoes to change into, and was happy not to have to brave a muddy road. The apartment house was imposing but narrow, and not as ornate as those that surrounded it. He climbed to the third floor and rang the bell, noting that the carpet in the hall was scrupulously clean if somewhat worn.

"Yes?" a muffled voice spoke just as he was shifting the package to his other hand to knock again.

"Frau Kohler, here is Ansel Beckmann."

The bolt was swiftly withdrawn and the door opened to reveal a smaller, more drawn version of the woman he remembered from years earlier. Her eyes filled as she reached for him and, drawing him in from the hall, she exclaimed, "Ach, look at you. What a grown man."

As she re-bolted the door, and they stood in the warmth of each other's smiles, Ansel extended his package. "Here. My stepmother wishes to send you all her best greetings, and these few things from her kitchen and her hand."

"Oh, she shouldn't," Kläre murmured, holding the packet to her chest. "And I am most grateful that you should come to see us. Come, I have a special tea for you."

War, deprivation, and fear hadn't kept Kläre Kohler from filling a slender vase in the center of the glass table in the sitting room with daffodils and cornflowers, cheering the damp darkness of the cloudy spring day. She and Ansel quickly launched a spirited and wide-ranging conversation. Ansel was astonished by the depth of what passed between the two of them: talk of his studies and the privations of war, but also of music, books, theater, and film. She drew from him not just what had happened and what he'd done, but how it felt and what he thought, all with an ease and interest that filled him with confidence and expectation.

"Have you had any letters from your son in Palestine?" he asked after exhausting reports of his own activities.

"Ach, no, I have not received news since two months ago. He got there safely and is in a boarding school now at Ben Shemen. It's a community for children who came from all over Europe."

Kläre volunteered no further information, so Ansel asked, "Is he happy there? Is he doing well in the school?"

He watched Kläre work to compose herself before answering, "I don't really know. I have had two short letters through the Red Cross. They said only that he is at this new place and that he is well. Also, that he has a friend—a boy from Hungary."

Ansel struggled to find something of comfort to say. "A boy of thirteen will certainly have many adventures to speak of when you see him again, won't he!"

Kläre closed her eyes and smiled, even as she drew her handkerchief from her sleeve and wiped tears from her cheek. "Ya, and he will see it that way, I suppose. Not like Erwin. Do you remember him? He complains in his letters of the hard work he must do as a landscaper for the family he is staying with." Kläre shook her head. "But with the bombing now, I hear nothing from Erwin. The last letter said he was thinking to join the army, the British Army. Can you imagine?"

Ansel could not imagine. He invented a response almost as he spoke: "He must do something to fight back against what has happened, mustn't he."

Kläre looked thoughtfully at the boy in front of her. "Yes, yes I suppose he must."

Ansel cast about for something more to say, and told Kläre of his visit with Amalie before leaving for university. She asked about the house and garden in Beilefeld, and about his sisters.

"They both still have their work," he said. "I hope they will take care of Amalie now that my father is gone. She has been good to them."

Kläre leaned forward in her seat. "You know, she knew nothing of children when she married your father. They were both so sad—your father with losing your mother, and Amalie with losing her fiancé. Did you know that she was to be married to a soldier who died in the first war?"

"No, I didn't." Ansel glanced down. "They didn't speak to me of such things."

"Ach, ya, you were such a little boy. Do you remember when you first came to me for a visit with Amalie?"

"Yes, of course, I remember the *lebkuchen.* It's still the best I ever had, I think." This made Kläre laugh outright, and Ansel colored with pleasure.

Kläre's face became serious again. "She had to learn everything about being a mother and a wife overnight. It wasn't so easy, you know. I suppose she did the best she could. Still, I believe it was very hard for you, wasn't it, to leave the family."

Ansel didn't answer for a long time. When at last he spoke, it was to say simply, "Ya."

"I'm so sorry." Kläre reached to place a hand on Ansel's arm.

He didn't move a muscle, but stared long at the woman sitting across from him. His heart beat strongly in his chest, pumping warmth through every inch of him. Perhaps he'd waited a lifetime to hear the words "I'm so sorry."

"And I am so sorry that you lost your brother, and now your father," Kläre added.

Ansel sank into the moment as he looked at Kläre. She was lovely in her grace and warmth and animation, though the strain of her difficult circumstances showed in a sadness that hung about her like a light mist. He imagined her as a mother, a wife, a friend. She sat quietly as he gazed, her face framed by a halo of hair that was lit by the fading afternoon light. He realized how entirely comfortable and alive he felt in her presence. He had spoken to no one about his brother's death in the first weeks of the war, or his conviction that this horror had hastened Georg's death only months later.

"They were so close, those two." He felt as though he needn't say more. He had new thoughts to consider now—about Amalie, and how these deaths must have hurt her more than he knew.

He stayed for nearly two hours sitting in the same fine walnut chair.

"Frau Kohler," he said finally, with more force than he intended, "it has been a long time since I have been in such a lovely room with such interesting conversation." He was shocked to find himself on the verge of adding "and with such a lovely woman." It was an unseemly thought.

"You must return soon," Kläre answered, and this Ansel vowed to himself to do, a decision that rested like a warm ember at his center.

19 1941

"The more powerful the perpetrator, the greater is their prerogative to name and define reality, and the more completely their arguments prevail."
—Judith Lewis Herman

The weeks flew by as Ansel devoted his time to studying and attending lectures, and to exploring the city of Cologne in his free time. A term break came, and with it a short holiday, which Ansel spent in Beilefeld with Amalie and his sisters. In the evenings they listened to the news of the expanding war. Ansel was discomfited by the hyperbole of the reports and the strangeness of the names of battle sites in Africa. What had Germany to do with Iraq or Syria? His sisters nodded and knitted their socks, but Amalie watched him with a careful eye. He sheltered her from the horror and dismay that he felt for the war that the Nazis waged against Germans themselves even as they created carnage around the rest of the world.

One evening, the radio was particularly full of the attacks in the Ukraine and the achievements of a new group, the Einsatzgruppen. The droning voice of the announcer read that they were "dedicated to the annihilation of Jews in Latvia, Ukraine, Estonia, and Lithuania," as blithely as if he were speaking of the latest football game. Ansel scowled and rose to leave the room. Amalie followed him outdoors to the garden, where the early evening light illuminated even the tired shrubbery with gold.

"Ansel, you mustn't let the news upset you. Leave the war to the soldiers."

"It becomes harder each day," he said.

"But you mustn't think to join the army. You mustn't allow them to take you."

The fierceness of Amalie's tone touched Ansel and he turned to her in the fading light.

"We lost first your brother, and now your father," she said. "You must remain with your studies and build a life for after the war. It's all we have left." Her face contorted with the effort to withhold the tears that welled in her eyes. Strong Amalie was frightened, in ways different from Ansel's own fear. He suddenly understood that she needed him, just as his sisters did.

Without thinking he reached out and touched her shoulder. "May God save us," he said. It was all he could think to say.

On his return to school, he found Cologne in a heightened state of disquiet. Soldiers were increasingly visible, and disruptions at the university more frequent. Ansel applied himself with renewed intensity to his studies, and narrowed his wanderings in the city to a nearby café and to the Kölner Dom. He found himself repeatedly drawn to the imposing cathedral. Its sheer magnitude sent a jolt through him, a thrilling disorientation of which he never tired. He welcomed the cool vastness of the ornate interior; he felt small and safe in the ordered beauty of its lofty lines.

On an early September day, his mind full of Humboldt, Weber, and Schopenhauer, Ansel walked the busy streets toward the Dom for afternoon Mass. He liked the smaller Mass, held in the side chapel near the brilliant gold sarcophagus housing the relics of the Three Kings.

Ansel had crossed the nave and was nearly to the chapel when he heard a groan coming from a pew in the rear of the cavernous center aisle section. Seeing no one nearby, he entered the row nearest the source of the sound. Lying on a bench was a boy of perhaps fourteen or fifteen years. He lay curled on his side, his clothing streaked and torn. Ansel crouched next to the boy, who clutched his hands to his groin and tried to rise. His trousers flapped around one bare leg as he sank back to the bench and groaned pitifully.

"Dear God, you're injured," Ansel whispered, his words echoing weirdly in the giant space. "I must get help!"

"No," the boy gasped, a bloody hand grabbing at Ansel. "They'll kill me if they catch me again."

"What happened? Who?" Ansel was looking furtively at the worshipers as they passed across the aisle further down.

"I'm from the other shore," the boy spat out.

Ansel stared at him uncomprehendingly.

"*Schwul* Homosexual. They tried to cut my sacs off. Now get out of here. My brother is coming with help. I can't be discovered. Go!"

Ansel was on his feet running, his stomach lurching. He burst through the side entrance and vomited over the steps as three men rushed past him with a small bundle and entered the church.

Ansel sat heavily on the steps to recover. As soon as he could stand, he headed back to his room, rinsed his mouth, and slumped into his desk chair, looking wildly for something to save him from the horror that dizzied him. At the corner of his desk was a letter from Kläre Kohler. He would go to see her again—get out of this place, if only for the day. He hadn't enough for the ticket if he wanted to eat for the whole month, but his desperation overruled his usual careful consideration. With a shaking pen, he wrote a quick note begging her leave to visit on the weekend. If he rose early and posted the letter first thing, she would have it by Friday.

He prepared hastily for bed, then sank gratefully to his knees in prayer. For the better part of an hour, he tried and failed to cleanse his spirit. At last, he crawled into bed and fell into a troubled sleep.

The next morning, he felt ill even before he stumbled out of bed to the water closet down the hall. He forced himself to eat the meager breakfast of hard rolls and pork fat that the landlady provided—eggs, cheese, and butter were long delicacies of the past—then posted the letter to Kläre and moved on to his morning lecture.

The weekend came, but Ansel did not board the train. An extra lecture was required of all students on Saturday to announce the imposition of new restrictions on student activities and the creation of a special registry and student papers. Ansel quickly wrote again to Kläre and apologized for not coming, promising to try again soon.

But it was not soon. Rather, it was two months before examinations were past and the scrutiny at the university relaxed in the days before the Christmas holiday. Finally, on a Saturday in early December, he boarded the train in Cologne, sinking gratefully onto the leather seat. He felt battered, eager for the respite of a visit to the Kohlers followed by Christmas with Amalie and his sisters.

The radiant winter day cleaned and cleared the air. Carrying only a small valise, Ansel chose to walk from the station to the apartment on Furchler Strasse. If he closed his eyes, he could almost believe that there was no war. The sounds of autos, of the shops closing for the afternoon, the housewives chatting in doorways, were the comforting sounds of daily life. With eyes open, however, Ansel saw the frightening signs of war everywhere. A huge swastika banner decked the Bundesbureau building. Soldiers moved in jeeps, and posters everywhere in the streets proclaimed progress toward the conquering of Russia and celebrated the Japanese bombing only days before of the American fleet in Hawaii.

Turning off Kaiser Wilhelm Strasse onto Furchler Strasse, Ansel noted immediately that the street was deserted, and he hesitated, watching. He faced the cold wind with watering eyes, watching for any sign of danger. Seeing none, he continued to the Kohlers' building. The entrance door was ajar, and as Ansel entered, he heard the door of the first-floor apartment slam. He mounted the stairs to the third floor.

As he arrived onto the landing, Ansel froze. The hall table lay shattered on the ground, and the hall carpet was pulled to the side opposite the Kohlers' door, which hung, splintered, from a single hinge. Ansel clung dizzily to the banister, his heart pounding into the turned oak. The silence frightened him, and he stood, unable to move either forward, through the door, or back down the staircase. After a moment he heard the chime of a clock and, as though it were a shot from a race gun, he lurched forward into the apartment, looking wildly into the hall and beyond to the sitting room.

The apartment was empty, silent, save for the savage sight of a slight man—dressed in a German officer's uniform, his hands bound behind him—hanging from the chandelier in the center of the sitting room. The name label, sewn neatly to the dead man's jacket, said "Licht." A woman's—Kläre's—suit coat, with a yellow star beside the left lapel, was draped over his shoulders. Kläre was gone, Jakob was gone, and in no time Ansel was racing down the staircase and out into the street, running blindly back toward the station, slowing only to dodge the streetcars and autos in the main thoroughfare.

20 1942

Kläre lost count of the trains, the days, the schedule of her hunger. She knew from the path of the sun that she occasionally glimpsed through a crack in a door that they were headed east. Where they were going they'd not been told, nor did they dare to ask. What they'd left had become immediately unspeakable between her and Jakob; they were both devoted to a frozen watchfulness for what lay ahead.

On the night they were taken, they had been dropped by truck at a station on the outskirts of Dortmund, then moved in a freight train to this country station where they had now been standing for more than an hour, waiting to board the next train, their valises between them. Without speaking, each knew that the other was cold and afraid, still in shock. The conviction that the less reaction shown the better lay between them like a vapor. They breathed the danger—felt it pass before their eyes in sickening waves, chilling them more than the cold—but they neither moved nor spoke.

By now there were hundreds of people standing in the mud and snow. Soldiers shouted, beat with their fists, and stabbed with their rifles to move the silent crowd ahead. As the point of convergence came into view, it became apparent that a selection was taking place. Jakob looked at Kläre, and his eyes spoke urgently of his fear and then of his plan. She had none—she could not think any longer of plans or options. But Jakob held her gaze and slowly moved it first to one officer, and then, with a minor sweep of his eyes, to another. *Study!* his eyes said.

Many families with children and older people were directed toward a distant car on the train, while a few men and even fewer women were sent to a closer one. These fewer chosen ones looked younger, stronger, more confident. Jakob had already placed one hand behind his back, the other weighted by the valise. He had decided that they would be younger and stronger, and he stood with his strongest posture as they arrived at the front. He handed the paperwork to Kläre and took her valise to place in front of himself.

Kläre understood. She was to hand the papers to the officer; she was not to talk first.

"Next! Move it forward, assholes." The foulness of the man's language belied his mechanical delivery, and Kläre carefully emptied her expression without dropping her eyes.

"Papers," the officer demanded.

She handed their passports and a special paper Jakob had gotten to the soldier, careful not to meet his eyes. His vacant face did not fool her. As he read the letter and looked Jakob over from top to bottom, a sly smile snaked onto his face that alarmed Kläre more than his cursing.

"Well, we'll see about your usefulness, then, won't we Herr DOKTOR Kohler. I certainly hope you're of some use to your Jew wife."

The comment stung Kläre deeply, but she said nothing and moved slowly toward the closer car with Jakob. Though it was old and cold, the car was not yet packed with other people, so there were still seats available. Immediately, Kläre worried about the toilet. As they passed the WC, she looked in and saw a bucket next to the overflowing commode. She would use it; she would do anything if only she could sit for an hour and sleep. Jakob shoved the valises overhead with her pushing behind him, and they sank as one into the bench seat in a half-filled compartment. They were asleep in seconds, and Kläre awoke again only when the train groaned and screeched to a halt in the middle of a deserted field.

The wind blew across the stopped train with a steady hum. Occasionally it surged, causing wraiths of snow to move like quicksilver over the empty landscape. Pressed into the corner of the compartment, Kläre leaned against the glass, her cheek chilled. The closed, airless space now held five people besides Jakob and herself, cramming the seats and the floor.

For now, she did not want to look at the people, or care that they might look at her. She wanted simply to look out at the swirling white and listen as the wind whistled through unseen cracks and shook the window frame in small bursts. She felt Jakob's slow breathing and his heavy weight leaning into her. A brief commotion in the hall outside the compartment preceded a slight, uniformed man who pushed his way through the tangle of people and baggage. For a moment Kläre thought it looked like Herr Licht, but then memory crashed in and sucked the air out of her so that she nearly fainted.

Jorgen Licht, her neighbor and former colleague, who had helped her twice with the Nazi bureaucracy, had been brought to the door of her apartment by three Brownshirts, drunk with violent malice. Accused, tried, and convicted of aiding her, a Jew, on more than one occasion, Licht had been beaten, first by one officer and then another, as Jakob and Kläre cowered in the chairs they'd been thrown into.

"See what you sold yourself away for," the officer shouted as he tore Kläre's jacket from her. Pulling her to stand in front of Licht, he wrenched her arms to her back so that she thought they would break. Licht's tormenter pulled him up to face Kläre, his jaw hanging lopsided on its broken hinge, and for an awful moment their eyes met as he groaned in pain. She could not bear the agony of those eyes.

"Stop! You must stop!" Kläre heard a voice like an animal's rising in pitch from an unearthly screech. Before she understood that it was her own voice, a Brownshirt's stick struck a blow to her chest and she bent in breathless pain.

Jakob whispered harshly, "Shush, Kläre. Say nothing more."

The beating of Licht continued until one of the soldiers snarled, "Let's give Mr. Licht here a last chance to live up to his name." A moment later, Licht was strung up to the light fixture, and then Kläre and Jakob were ordered to pack a valise for deportation. One of the men grabbed Kläre's suit jacket and hung it amidst raucous laughter and taunts onto the twitching body before she and Jakob were dragged to the bedroom.

Kläre squeezed her eyes shut and returned her head to the cold window in the train, then opened her eyes again and stared into the white field, fixing her attention on a lone tree, an apple tree perhaps, far in the distance. She had begun to tremble, causing the paper in her hand to rustle. She hadn't known that she still held Jakob's letter and their billfold of passports and papers clutched at her side. Slowly, she drew the letter out and silently unfolded it. It was written on the official stationery of the city of Dortmund.

> *Re: The Jew Herr Doktor Jakob Kohler, Rechtsanwalt und Notar*
>
> *Let it be known that the above named individual provided useful services to the resettlement office of the Reichstag, Dortmund. He may be trusted to provide similar services elsewhere.*
>
> *Heil Hitler,*
>
> *Leut. Ambrose Halter*

Kläre frowned. Jakob's 'useful services' had been his attempts to interpret the avalanche of regulations and restrictions for Jews who came to the Judenrat. He had been shunned from the courts and city offices. He had tried to help find vanished people. Perhaps his calm plodding efforts had been considered useful. She hadn't time to think further as the train lurched and began to creep forward. Jakob shifted to the far side of the bench and Kläre sat straight, surveying the tumble of people and bags stretching around the door to the hall and beyond. There was no food or water now, and she could wait another sleep's worth to use the bucket toilet. Moving only slightly, she placed the billfold into her handbag, which she had wedged between her leg and the arm of her seat. She slowly rolled her head in a small circle around her neck, rolled her shoulders inside her heavy suit and coat, and leaned once more into the cool glass, concentrating only on breathing slowly and deeply. Sleep came again immediately.

Theresienstadt was an ugly town with ugly houses and ugly streets. The train slowed as it passed one colorless block of row houses after another. Perhaps the town had turned malevolent with its masks of evil—Nazi soldiers visible everywhere, the Czech citizens replaced with a ghetto and work camp that had tripled the population. Or perhaps the simple harshness of winter cold and deprivation had bled the town of interest and color. In reality it wasn't terribly different from Hörde—a town full of solid, boring stone buildings.

The train stopped outside a barricaded square with a large guard post fronting the main building. Other than a small detail of raggedly dressed women sweeping the building's steps, the square was deserted. In a moment, soldiers in Czech uniforms boarded the train and shouted orders, which a gaunt Jew in a colorless jacket with a tattered star sewn to its lapel repeated in German: "Gather your parcels and prepare to present your papers."

The next hours were filled with tedium and horror in equal parts. Like animals, they were herded into an endless series of selections, with no apparent reason for the different dispositions. Children and parents were separated, men and women sent to different places—but some couples, including the Kohlers, were permitted to remain together. In another endless line, they were forced to give up many items from their baggage, and to pay for the ones they were allowed to keep. They were asked endless questions, and Jakob, always watchful, often answered for them both, but sometimes turned to Kläre, silently indicating that she should speak. They were registered, given numbers, told to report for a work detail the next morning, and sent finally to the second-floor apartment of a squat house with a narrow door and a steep flight of stairs.

Jakob barely managed to climb the last stairs; at the top, he collapsed on the floor and leaned against the wall. Kläre knocked at the door, and after a few moments of muffled movements the door opened and Kläre found herself looking into the gaunt faces of four people.

"Here is house number 6, second floor?" she asked nervously. "We were told to come to this apartment. I'm sorry, they didn't say it was already occupied."

"Certainly not. That's only the beginning of what they don't say. I don't know where we're supposed to put you, but come in, Frau . . ."

"Kohler. I'm Kläre Kohler. And here is my husband, Jakob. He's feeling a bit weak."

Jakob struggled to his feet, and pulled their suitcases into the tiny room, which felt as cold as the hall.

"I am Karolina Rosenfelder. This is my brother, Max Lowenthal, and these are the Hertzes, Walter and Erna. Come, we haven't any tea or coffee, but there's some warm water and a bit of bread. Are you more exhausted or full of questions?" Karolina stopped on her way to the stove at the end of the room and looked directly at Kläre.

"I want to find my mother. Do you know a Johanna Ente?"

Karolina's eyebrows shot up toward the white curls drawn into a loose bun on top of her head, which barely reached Kläre's chin.

"Come," she ordered, and marched Kläre back into the hall and up to the third floor, where she ushered her into a garret room lined with a row of beds, a table, and a few old chairs. Five women lived in this room, one of whom sat in a chair by the single window. She was tinier even than Karolina Rosenfelder, though her snow-white hair was drawn back in a neat bun. Kläre looked at the woman in the nearest bed, and at a third woman in a chair by the table. She did not see her mother until the tiny woman by the window turned toward them, her heavy black eyebrows knitted in a squint.

"Oh my dear God in heaven! Klärchen, is that you?"

Kläre's hands flew to her mouth as she gasped. "Ach, Mutti." In a moment she was across the room and on her knees next to her mother, drawing the starving woman into her arms, their tears mixing in the fading light.

"I'm here now," Kläre repeated, over and over again.

The morning was brilliant and icy. The guard who had abruptly pulled Kläre from her table in the laundry just minutes ago now disappeared just as suddenly, leaving her standing before the commandant's office door in the camp headquarters. The commandant had summoned her, for reasons she could not fathom.

He opened the door and beckoned Kläre inside.

"I see here that you have the certificate of massage training," he said, glancing down at a paper on his desk. His eyes rose momentarily to her body, registering neither appreciation nor dismay. Perhaps he was calculating whether her sinewy arms could perform at all.

Kläre stood before him, breakfast scraps still heavy in her queasy stomach. "Yes, Herr Commandant, I have done the massage."

Another moment of his impassive gaze, during which time she met and returned an unspoken, half-comprehended message, and the interview was complete.

"You will begin work as my house maid. I will request your services for massage as necessary. The head of staff for the house waits for you now in the butler's pantry." He looked at her one last time. "That is all."

The trembling did not begin until she had left the elegant study and followed a uniformed young man down the polished floor of the main hall toward the commandant's private quarters. She was grateful that she had used a swipe of precious lipstick that day, reddening her pale lips enough to make her look healthy. Her curls were tightly pinned into a loose bun at the back of her neck, and she wore a clean dress, an important benefit of working in the laundry.

A new fear crept into her already crowded chamber of worries. She would be given only one chance to attend the commandant successfully. One moment of hesitation, a touch too penetrating or too soft, the wrong muscle worked, and this possibility of a lifeline could vanish as quickly as it had just now been created. As Jews were never allowed to care for the children, the bedroom, or the wardrobes of the commandant and his troubled wife, she would know nothing of his physical effects. No extra pillow or bolster among the bedclothes, no reading chair beside the tall windows would provide her with clues of where he might ache or cramp. His perfect military demeanor and studied movement masked even the possibility of analyzing a certain walk or posture.

She suppressed this new fear with the others, and by the time the soldier turned the polished knob of the commandant's sitting room door and she stepped soundlessly across the thick carpet, only quiet readiness could be seen in Kläre's hazel eyes. She must earn more food with her efficient deference, her perfect folding, straightening, and cleaning and her wordless foresight in preparing the family rooms for the next activity, meal, or visit. For a Jew to be allowed to work as a parlor maid was a near impossibility, Kläre knew. She guessed her careful conduct in the last months, her appearance, and her status as a Prominente, based on Jakob's Iron Cross from the war and his work for the Reichsbureau, were how she had gained this privilege. Jakob, too, had a coveted job—supervising loading and unloading of supplies in a warehouse, teams of younger workers serving under him. Kläre observed a stray flick of ash in a silver-rimmed crystal ashtray; she made a mental note to polish it.

She was led to the kitchen, and in short order given a clean, starched apron, instructions for her dress, and orders to return in the morning before 6 a.m. She carefully avoided looking toward the stove, where pots of steaming food were being prepared for the family dinner. The smell of roasting meat nearly caused Kläre to cry out. She remained resolutely silent, determined to do whatever it took to work here. As she prepared to step out into the cold afternoon, the head cook handed her a heel of bread, its open side smeared with chicken fat.

"You must keep your weight. Don't give this away, or you won't stay here."

"Yes, thank you," Kläre said without emotion.

She waited until she was far enough from the commandant's house and out of the courtyard of the small prison, on the road to the ghetto, before even looking at the bread again. The returning work crews had not yet filled the Hauptstrasse, though they would shortly. Slipping the loaf end out from the expanse of her coat sleeve, she sank her teeth into its fresh crust.

The fat was cold but delicious, and Kläre was careful not to waste a morsel of it. Though she understood what the cook had said to be true, she also knew she would save a third of what was left for Jakob, another third for her mother, and the last bit for Frau Neustadter, her mother's roommate, whose kindness and care had helped keep Johanna alive. Only last evening, the lively older woman had engaged Johanna in a spirited discussion of the making of the *knaidlach* for the Sabbath soup. Should the matzo balls be small and dense, or large and fluffy? What they could not make in reality at the camp, they made instead in their conversations with each other, keeping alive in the harsh emptiness of the ghetto the worlds that had defined them. While Kläre understood the policy of larger rations for children and working adults, she could not bear to see her mother wasting away, and had already found ways to increase her nourishment.

Kläre returned the bread to her coat sleeve, careful not to look furtive as a truck passed her in the road, the open back a wretched tableau of gaunt faces headed for the prison. Trucks never brought people back from the small prison, and stealing food was a one-way ticket into it, though the occasional supervisor looked the other way.

Evening approached, and Kläre quickened her steps, wishing to be back in time to receive her meal ration. Jakob and Johanna would be worried, too—particularly if they heard a soldier had taken her. Only yesterday, four people from the apartment below theirs had been roused early in the morning from their beds and hustled into a waiting truck. No one in the house had returned to sleep. No one knew where the truck had gone. People came and went. More people came. Each person had less food.

A winter goose honked high above—then another, and another. Kläre's thoughts escaped to a memory of the winter nights she had ridden in her father's wagon at the end of a Saturday delivery to a nearby village, warm under the wagon rug, high on the seat next to her father. Then the geese had been exciting, their black lengths outlined by the darkening sky, and she recalled the prickle of a soft shower of snow on her upturned face. Now the geese sounded forlorn and distant, but they were in the evening sky, and she was alive to hear them.

21 1943

True history is the history of the spirit, the human spirit, which may at times seem powerless, but ultimately is yet superior and survives because even if it has not got the might, it still possesses the power, the power that can never cease.
—Leo Baeck

The cracks in the floor seemed to widen daily, as though even the floorboards wanted to send a message of increasing peril—the crevices of fear and filth encroaching on the shrinking solid ground of existence in Theresienstadt. Kläre stepped carefully to the corner of the room, where she had made what little comfort that could be made in the crammed apartment for Jakob and herself. Thin mattresses, a set of small shelves nailed to the wall, a drawing of Kläre done by an artist one evening at the meeting house nailed to the right of the shelves, neatly stacked piles of clothing, a mismatched set of bowls, spoons, and forks, and a single pot formed almost the totality of their possessions. Kläre's eyes rose to the top shelf, on which rested a precious photo of Erwin and Werner taken long ago on the beach at Norderie. Seized with longing for her children, Kläre stared at their happy, wind-burned faces.

The Kohlers were still considered "Prominente," and they had this lodging with three other families as a result, though it remained unclear whether it was Jakob's former work or Kläre's position in the commandant's house that maintained their prominent status. Rumors flew that with the swelling of new arrivals, even these accommodations would be seized and changed, to billet an increased number of guards and troops or to create barracks for inmates. Kläre could not think about that now, as she wrapped the heel of bread from the commandant's cook in a scrap of laundry paper and placed it in the cooking pot.

Jakob had not yet returned from his job filling in for a sick neighbor. He was to sort clothing, then package it for dispersal back to Germany. It was rumored that the clothes were confiscated from Jews and distributed to Germans suffering losses from the Allied bombing. Jakob could barely speak for humiliation at what he did each day, it being no comfort to him that he was still able to work at all. Kläre sought to engage him with a distracting story as soon as they were together each night, though in truth, they were always so exhausted that they could barely eat their ration of dinner before they fell to the mattresses and slept.

The sound of Jakob's heavy tread on the stairs brought a sigh to Kläre as she gave over her brief solitude to thoughts of caring for her husband. He entered the room, ashen with the effort of climbing the stairs, hunger written in the hollows of his cheeks and the frailty of the folds of skin at his neck, which no longer filled the prim circle of his collar and tie.

"Good evening, my dear," Kläre said as she helped him remove his coat. "I have a treat of some bread from the commandant's kitchen for you. You're late today."

"Ya, the Council of Elders was just finishing as I passed and I talked a while with Edelstein." Kläre's eyebrows rose. Edelstein was a leader of the Ältestenrat, and some said he took orders for managing Theresienstadt from Adolf Eichmann himself. Renowned as a Zionist, Edelstein had traveled often to Palestine and centers throughout the sphere of German influence to persuade Jews and governments to expedite Jewish immigration to Palestine.

Jakob continued, "He wants me to consult on the proposal to develop the youth Aliyah immigration forms for Palestine." He stood a little taller, and Kläre's heart tugged in her chest. From what shreds came the hope of salvation!

As though bidden, the sermon of Leo Baeck from two nights ago floated into her mind. It was the second time she had gone to hear Baeck at a secret lecture in the Community House. Chief rabbi of Berlin, noted philosopher and essayist, he had refused to leave Germany and had eventually followed his flock to this desolate place. Kläre had never learned much about the Bible or the works of philosophers. Jeremiah, Ezekiel, Plato, Kant—these were all names of which she had heard, but Leo Baeck brought their works to life. More than five hundred people had crowded into the hall, Jewish guards standing sentinel all around the square, though Baeck's oratory was couched in such elevated polemics it was doubtful that any soldiers would understand their seditious intent. Indeed, Theresienstadt, the "gift" of Hitler to the Jews, was full of fakery designed to disguise its true purpose as a labor camp and transit facility. Many of the finest creative minds from Germany, Czechoslovakia, Austria and Holland were imprisoned there, forced to give concerts, art exhibitions, plays and lectures – all pretending against the inexorable march toward death that awaited most of the inhabitants.

When Baeck spoke, the people listened, some straining just to hear, some to recognize anything familiar, some to understand his exposition of ancient thought, and many to wonder what good could come of his words. Some were too exhausted even to follow the train of thought. It comforted Kläre, as it seemed to do others, just to be sitting in the presence of the great and compassionate man, who would not join with other elders in administering the ghetto because he would not join injustice, not even to save himself. His international fame kept him alive, and with his words he wove a web of metaphor and subtle subversion mixed with comfort and hope. Listening to him, Kläre found herself thinking of her Judaism for the first time in her life.

"Jakob, Leo Baeck spoke to us about how important it is to survive . . ." Suddenly Kläre needed to impart to her husband what had happened to her two evenings ago. They were lying on their narrow pallets, resting before making their meager dinner.

"Something about Dr. Baeck's talk the other night went beyond thoughtful or interesting, Jakob. It felt hopeful and somehow elevating . . . I think it's perhaps the first time I felt proud and inspired by something Jewish." Kläre's voice was energized.

She turned to look at Jakob, whose hand rested on her arm. His eyes were closed in his gaunt face, but she knew he was listening.

"He's a German, Jakob, like we are, and he talked about how Jews interweave themselves into the lands that fate takes them to: We breathe the air, learn to think in new languages. But when we confront evil, and the collective society around us fails to live in justice, then we have to return to the deepest mystery of our identity for our moral compass. And he says the idea of death and rebirth into an elevated existence subordinates the pain we experience now. Living means living for justice, goodness, and truth. Our true history is the history of the human spirit." Kläre's voice rose musically as she was filled again with the comfort of the rabbi's words. "He made it feel like the camp doesn't exist where he is, as though the filth doesn't touch him. Everyone listened quietly. We listened for a bit of peace."

Jakob grunted. "Everyone listened for one more bite of food, or one more day to live. Will we prepare before the Hertzes?"

Kläre rose slowly and brought their dishes and her pot to the stove, its brick-and-tiled bulk occupying the corner of the room. A basket of shriveled potatoes, a half cabbage, and two carrots waited for the ministrations of the three women to make into their families' dinners. Kläre scrupulously cut and divided their portion, and lit the coals of the old fire in the stove to begin her preparations. She would climb the stairs with a dish for Johanna, whom she had not yet seen today.

As she worked, Leo Baeck's words floated back to her: *The way shown by the revelation . . . A voice cried out for the mystery. . . . When the people heard it, they knew in days of confusion where clarity was, and in days of darkness where light will shine.* Like a prayer mediated by her hands and her breathing, Kläre repeated to herself, *clarity, light, clarity, light . . .*

She hadn't expected the commandant to call for her already on the second day. Kläre was in the sitting room—straightening, polishing, and noting every detail of placement and use—when another maid noiselessly entered and spoke briskly: "Go to the commandant. He wishes to see you in his office."

Kläre's heart sank. Was she ready? Could she find any healing power in her hands? There had always been an automatic transition into that mode where time and the careworn world faded and the gentle curative force found its way through her heart, into her body, and then into those whom she touched. How could she navigate to those deep, gentle places when there was no calm, no ease here?

She stood by the door until an assistant motioned for her to enter. The commandant was still concentrating on the words of a soldier, and Kläre avoided looking at either man, staring instead at the picture above and behind the commandant. It depicted with some skill a vase of bountiful roses arising in lush strokes of pink, cream, and deep vermillion. She stood blankly, part of her attention yearning for the world of beautiful roses, while another part heard portions of the urgent young soldier's words.

"Herr Commandant, paratroopers from the government in exile are landing every day. We caught . . ." his voice lowered, and she heard only murmurs. Then, ". . . in Lidice, Deputy Mende has ordered spies put to death . . ."

Kläre continued to stand motionless, invisible, until the commandant waved the young soldier away and closed his portfolio over the sheaf of papers on his desk.

"Leave me," he said flatly to the soldier, and a moment later, only Kläre was left in the room with him.

"Herr Commandant," she said steadily, bowing her head slightly.

"Come here . . . please. I have a headache that is blinding and pain in the back of my neck." His voice was surprisingly quiet, but matter-of-fact and full of calm authority.

Kläre crossed the carpet noiselessly, moving to the back of the desk behind his chair. *Come now, Kläre. Find your hands. His is just the body of a man . . . in pain . . . Breathe . . .* She breathed deeply into her belly—a breathing entirely opposite the high-chested, straight-backed, shoulder-squaring breaths she had trained herself to use since she'd started making war against this life of oppression and danger—and laid her hands across Commandant Sternkopf's forehead, summoning the knowledge to impart comfort and relief. Her fingers spoke in a low, prayerful voice, dictating relaxation of one muscle after another, beginning at the top of his head and moving down to his jaw and back to the nape of his neck. Now her hands reached down into his collar, which he loosened in one swift motion.

"Let your tongue relax," she murmured as she released the muscles of his face, his forehead, his scalp with her other hand. At each breath's apex she emptied her mind of thoughts and opened herself to feeling. It was grief that stole through the breaths, surrounding her diaphragm with a vise grip of pressure. *Not now! No!* But she was helpless as her thoughts flew to Werner. For just one second, an infinitesimal relaxing of her guard made space for the paralyzing grief and longing that she felt for him, immediate and lacerating. The expansion of her spirit as she worked her magic was crushed as surely as a hand closing around her heart, a stone on her chest, gravity pulling her lungs back into her core.

The commandant exhaled slowly and deeply. With Kläre's hands on either side of his head, gently rotating, he spoke: "Your touch is skillful. You will return this afternoon at two thirty." He slowly pulled one of her hands away and drew her to the side of the chair. He rose then, standing for a moment before walking to a door at the far end of the room. He motioned Kläre to his side as he opened the door to a small inner room, equipped only with a table, lamp, chair, and tall single bed. "Ask Frau Hertzmann for whatever you need for . . . a full massage."

"Eat," is all he said when later he entered the small room. She had gotten from the housemaids sheets and a soft blanket, as well as pillows to place under and around him as she worked. She knew to be frightened of what the other maids would know—what they might tell—but she had no choice.

She sat at the table, waiting, and the commandant put a plate in front of her on which lay a small slab of cheese, coarse bread, and, impossibly, some dried apricots. She stared first at the plate, and then at the commandant.

"Eat," he repeated, and she took the cheese with the bread and raised it to her mouth, concentrating on exhibiting no particular energy. While she slowly chewed and then took an apricot, the commandant removed his jacket and then his shirt. Kläre left the food and drew back the sheet on the bed.

"Lie here," she said. "On your stomach." She had created a rounded cradle out of fine linen towels for his face, which she held as he positioned himself face down. This man was no stranger to massage. She began to work on his back, and studied him. He was tall and thin but well-built, with strong, sinewy muscles. His narrow waist and hips gave way to long legs. It was a body built for movement with grace, and even lying prostrate, it showed imposing strength. She worked up his vertebrae and across the muscles of his shoulders, then up the sides of his torso. Again, she concentrated on her breathing, and sought a place to dwell beyond thinking—of where she was, and what might happen to her at the hands of this man. She could not help but think of the only other man whom she had ever fully massaged, whose broad, passionate body had cared for hers so fully, and whose every muscle and bone she had memorized. She willed Bernhardt Steinmann from her mind and from her hands, lest danger penetrate her defenses. Her guard must be complete even as her hands worked deeply and automatically across the commandant's body.

22 1943

Dulce lignum, dulce ferrum, dulce pondus sustinet. (Precious the wood, precious the nails, precious the weight they bear.)
—San Diego de Alcalá de Henares (St. Didacus)

The July evening was warm, even deep in a trench outside Vilna. Ansel Beckmann lay waiting, the sweat from the day's march and battle preparations drying under his field uniform. The MG 34 stood mounted at the ready on its tripod, and silence replaced the rumble of tanks of the 18th Army. All that remained was to wait.

Ansel shifted his weight onto his left elbow and reached into the cargo pocket of his jacket for the last of the hard dinner roll with dried beef that had been his only food all day. His jacket, snug when issued a year ago, now sagged loosely on his frame. The rock-hard roll was the first bread he'd had in days, and the dried beef the only meat he had tasted in weeks.

"A lucky find, that one," offered Reiner, the gunner in Ansel's company. "That old cow of a woman hardly put up a fuss."

Ansel did not answer. Images of the morning's operation in Vilna rose like the dank night air to sicken his heart. No luck, no sense, no accomplishment attached itself to the preying on local populace that had become routine in this abominable war. The army had simply scoured Vilna in the morning and brutally commandeered what food they could find, just as they did in every other place they had gone. Starvation had nearly emptied the town, and the bakery's proprietress had turned over a forlorn tray of leftover rolls with no hope of payment or recourse. Ansel had lurched out of the bakery and stumbled up the street, queasy from hunger and disgust, when his eye caught a scrap of cloth along the narrow cobbled lane. He'd bent to pick up a faded yellow star, recognizing immediately the mark of a Jew, no doubt already slaughtered or expelled from the once-prosperous town. He squeezed his eyes shut as images of Kläre Kohler and the horrible, hanging body of the officer in her apartment appeared in rapid succession. Clutching the tattered star, Ansel had retched, though in truth there was nothing in him to vomit. Gasping for breath, tears watering the dust blackening his cheeks, he'd thrust the star deep into his chest pocket, near to his heart.

Ansel could not get used to this rape of the downtrodden. He had no loyalty to the Führer, no sense of mission as a soldier. He lay in a trench waiting to defend the occupation of Vilna from the attack of the Red Army. No matter the shouted commands of the officers, the men knew in their hearts that it was futile. The East was already lost, and with it the war. He saw that to remain alive and keep his soul were all that were left to him, though he barely knew how to accomplish either.

Ansel ate as the clear sky began to flicker with tiny points of light. Vilna and other ghetto towns, once the seats of Jewish scholarship, mysticism, and culture in Lithuania, were empty of their thousands of Jews, all massacred or deported in the previous two years. He stopped chewing as he thought of the sages of Vilna he'd studied at university, in tracts that had escaped the purging of all things Jewish in the library. Under this very sky had lived the Vilna Gaon, a saintly genius who, as a child, had memorized vast biblical passages while studying science and mathematics. He'd become the most influential rabbi of his century. Ansel had heard of the Gaon's works, and much of it was inscrutable, but its power and depth had intrigued him. Now he lay in a muddy gash in the very landscape through which the Gaon had walked and thought.

Reiner lazily reached for the machine gun and patted its side. "How many red asses will we get you tonight, my little steel angel?"

Ansel squeezed his eyes shut and prayed: *Dear God, if I live, if I but have the courage . . . it will be to serve You and to bring the heavenly lights back to our poor earth!*

The attack came swiftly, snapping Ansel out of his reverie. He grabbed the magazine and shoved it at Reiner, who immediately began to spray the advancing enemy. In mere seconds, the twinkling night sky became an inferno, and Ansel felt the cold sweat of fear. Blinded and deafened by successive blasts of mortar, he nonetheless saw the look of simple surprise in Reiner's eyes as he disappeared from his place across the trench. Amidst exploding earth and human parts, Ansel himself was lifted and thrown.

Perhaps it took moments. Perhaps hours. From a great and muffled distance, Ansel heard more than felt a steady beat and rushing. He woke to searing pain that he could not localize. As he moved his legs, the pounding increased, pain tearing into his belly so fiercely that he succumbed to the rushing noise and descended again into blackness.

When next Ansel swam to consciousness, he opened his eyes to a night sky still filled with stars, the points of light pulsing and swirling in waves. He gingerly moved his hand to the pain in his belly and felt the viscous warmth of blood. He tried to reach across his body for anything to staunch the blood, and a second, stabbing pain radiated from his shoulder, threatening to send him again into blackness. Methodically, he assessed his injuries, eyes staring into the sky, willing the stars to cease their wild gyrations. He lay still until he could move, this time in tiny, slow increments.

The field was silent, the forms surrounding him motionless. If any of the unit medics had survived the attack, they would not venture from behind the lines in the darkness to find the wounded. In the eerie silence, Ansel heard not the slightest sigh—no groan or rustle that bespoke another living soul. The moon rose and cast a low blue light across the top edge of the trench. Ansel directed his gaze to a single stream of light that seemed to radiate upward in a soft column from where he lay before shimmering into a thousand points of light in the night sky. Despite the cool breeze and his constant shiver, unreasonable warmth coursed through him all the way to his fingers, toes, and the roots of his filthy hair.

I am dying, Ansel thought, even as he held his arm to his belly and, using his right leg, pulled himself to a crouch, his eyes never leaving the electric night sky. Counting to ten before each move, using breath to counter the waves of pain and nausea, he dragged himself over the lip of the trench and toward the only lamps he saw, nearly five hundred meters distant. He stopped, prostrate, once, twice, and each time rested until his breath quieted, praying to the God whose pulsing Presence filled him with strength. He strained to keep his face to the fullness of the jeweled sky and crawled through the ruined fields until at last he heard shouts amidst flickering lamps in the distance. He prayed one last time for the strength to move the last meters, even as the lights danced above him. *Let me live to bring the beauty of Your Light to others.*

23 1944

Karolina Rosenfelder pulled a shredded shawl tighter around her shoulders. The women of Dresdener barracks crossed the hard, damp ground of the yard toward a small fire outside the kitchen house where a soup pot hung.

"What will Max get for his dinner?" she whispered to Kläre Kohler, who walked beside her. Karolina had not seen her brother in more than a month. No longer afforded the privilege of being crammed with three other families in a small apartment, the women and men had been separated into rough barracks, dozens of people stacked up the walls like discarded warehouse items.

"Perhaps he is starving as I am, not more than three hundred meters from here. I suppose he is finishing work now," Karolina continued with a heavy sigh.

The old woman stepped deliberately, breathing weakly, eyes cast down, moving with the other inmates in their listless mass, tin cups in hand. Obsessive thoughts of hunger and food had given way to the mindless exhaustion of starvation. Six or seven meters away from the soup pot, Kläre's hand took Karolina's arm. The two women's eyes met in a sideways glance. Karolina felt but did not see a small bundle slipped into the folds of her shawl by the younger woman who had become her friend and protector. Involuntarily she gasped and clutched what was surely forbidden. This produced a trembling fear that she willed away lest the hard-eyed kitchen worker detect something worthy of cruel play and single her out. Wordlessly, Kläre merged back into the silent sea of women. In another moment, Karolina had her soup of potato peels and had started the trudge back to the barracks.

The sickly broth was warm this evening—nearly hot—and Karolina felt a desperate urge to wrap both her hands around the cup and hold it close to her chest as she walked. Instead, she focused on the package in her other hand, which burned with danger and importance. She tilted her face toward the cup to feel the weak steam and began to breathe more slowly as her fingers worked around the rough burlap under her shawl. A small lump and the crinkle of paper gave the only clues to its contents. Entering the low-ceilinged dim, she made her way directly to a center row of rough wooden bunks. She sat heavily on a bottom one.

As an older woman, the unwritten but strictly adhered-to social order of the camp meant that she did not have to climb to reach her cramped platform and threadbare blanket. Neither did the rats and the lice. Karolina bent her head and reached for her spoon at the foot of the bunk. As others moved about her, she ate quickly, not even savoring the moment of warmth traveling through her body. She carefully cleaned the spoon and cup with her tongue and set them aside.

Looking out and up into the aisle, Karolina glimpsed Kläre in her bunk against the wall, high on the third tier. It had been three months since they'd moved from the relative comfort of the crowded apartment house in the town to this desolate barrack. The population of Theresienstadt had doubled and then doubled again as deportees poured in from Germany, Holland, Denmark, and Belgium. More and more Jews, gypsies, and mixed-race people arrived; people whose protections had run out. Even with the increasing number of transports east to Poland, the camp and the town were crowded to bursting. Meager supplies and conditions had engendered increasing illness and privation.

Karolina remembered when Frau Kohler came with her sick husband. She knew that Kläre worked now for the commandant, and therefore got enough to eat. Even as Kläre cared for her own mother lovingly and cleverly, she had made time to care for Karolina as well, whose own two daughters were lost to her—one so young, her breasts eaten away by cancer, the other gone in time to America. *God keep her safe,* Karolina prayed, grateful for Kläre's willingness to risk her own safety and take advantage of her access to the town outside the bunkers to carry messages, food, and medicine.

The two women's eyes met, and wordlessly the younger nodded, conveying from her perch that Karolina could safely open the packet. She quickly bent over and unfolded the burlap. With a soft cry she held a small square of old cheese wrapped in a piece of bread crust. Beneath it her brother's writing, though nearly illegible with poor ink and shaky script, covered a stained brown wrapper.

Dearest Karolina,

Yesterday the refuse fell from the garbage wagon, which I pulled, and this treasure I found for you. The guard did not see me bend to grab it, but I fell and now my foot is crushed. I fear your foolish bird of a brother, who has loved you always, and was in my time a fine acrobat, has fallen to my own final peril. I have here a friend of my kind who will hold me in my pain until the end, so do not worry my sweet, clever sister. We have made a cigarette from the last chestnut leaves and we will share it this evening.

He will take to the headquarters this treasure for you, and if Frau Kohler works today, I know you will receive it. Angel that she is, she has found the smallest vial with two pain pills, which she gave to Axel for me, and I will have the second tonight.

Always, I have loved you best.

Your devoted brother, Max.

Karolina slumped forward over the letter and cradled the dirty pieces of food. Moments later, she felt Kläre slide onto the bunk. Silently, Karolina cried, Kläre's thin arm wrapped around her shaking shoulders until even tears were exhausted. Kläre's strong hands worked across her back until she sighed with a deep shudder and allowed her legs to be swung up onto the bed, under the dirty blanket. Karolina heard Kläre carefully wrap the gift of food and place it under her pillow.

"Thank you, Frau Kohler. Thank you so much."

"Sleep, now, Frau Rosenfelder. Sleep," Kläre replied.

The commandant asked for Kläre regularly. At times he wished only for her to release the tension in his shoulders, neck, and forehead as he sat at his desk. Other times they removed to the small room, which she kept stocked with towels, sheets, oil, and pillows that suited him and the full-body massages that occupied hours of their late afternoons. Kläre intuited that silence allowed them both to avoid the realities of their association. She could transport herself to the place where her hands could do their job by themselves. The commandant did not use cruelty as the basis of his conduct, and silence obviated the need for explanations, permission, resistance, or acceptance. Only their bodies spoke, and each spoke a truth understood by the other, beyond the sickening reality of life outside the room.

On this day, Kläre was called to the commandant earlier than usual. She stood near the door, waiting as she often did while he finished his work. Today she waited nearly an hour as he discussed a new order with an assistant. The painting of roses behind his desk had become Kläre's secret ally. It was full of beauty and impressionistic sensuality, the painted porcelain vase a stable base for a riot of deep pink and creamy white blossoms. She could fairly smell the pungent perfume of summer roses.

Kläre had not yet finished the careful work of cleaning and straightening the sitting room when the commandant had called. There was a real bouquet of roses on the glass table there, which gave off a faint, fresh scent. Kläre had squeezed her eyes shut to contain tears of longing for her own garden, her own roses and the impossibly remote life of safety and comfort that the aroma summoned. When she returned, she would reward herself with a visit to the table where the roses spilled opulently from a crystal bowl. Would she touch them? Straighten them? Perhaps she would only stand above them, and breathe deeply.

"Herr Commandant, this messenger insisted stubbornly. He brought roses and an important message regarding Dr. Baeck and several other inmates. He says it is urgent to speak to you before the visit of the Red Cross," the commandant's assistant was saying.

"Roses? Whatever did he bring roses for?" the commandant asked irritably. Kläre could see the lines tightening across his forehead, signaling a headache.

"He said, 'Ladies of the house should have beauty even in a war,' Herr Commandant."

The commandant paused and looked at his assistant for a long moment. "What did you say his name was, then?"

"Lieutenant Stein. Bernhardt Stein."

"Tell him I will see him tomorrow at ten. That will be all."

Kläre stood frozen to her spot. The man had said Stein, not Steinmann. Could Bernhardt possibly be here? What business would he have with Leo Baeck? Could he know she was here?

"Frau Kohler!" The commandant spoke sharply.

Kläre's attention snapped back to the room and the commandant. Had he asked her something? "Yes, Herr Commandant," she answered quickly.

"I am ready."

"Yes, Herr Commandant."

An hour later, Kläre slipped through the door and down the hall into the sitting room, straightening her dress and apron and tucking a stray curl back into her cap as she went. She resumed her cleaning and after ten minutes stood at the table, polishing the ashtrays, the glass tabletop now shining and spotless. The roses were beautiful. Kläre's thoughts had settled. She could make no further sense of what she had heard in the commandant's office. The very idea that Bernhardt Steinmann might be close sent such a jolt through her chest that she banished all thought of him. Instead, she gazed at the roses.

If only Frema, who taught drawing to the children in the camp, could see these flowers! There was so little beauty to work from. In one swift motion Kläre snatched a fading bloom from the bowl and plunged it deep into her pail, beneath the polishing rags. Trimming brown petals from several of the other roses, she worked at the arrangement until its ordered pleasure reached perfection. When finished, she went to the scullery and thrust the faded rose into her coat pocket before returning to the kitchen to help with the midday meal.

That evening, Kläre whispered to Frema as she passed her in the darkening bunkroom, "Here is a rose to draw with the children."

"Ach, thank you, Frau Kohler. Such a thing! How did you get it? They forget already things of beauty. This is wonderful! I must have something for the children to draw that I can show to the inspector. He wants only the pleasant pictures."

"I found it. I thought of you, but be careful, yes?" Kläre smiled and continued through the barrack.

She reached her bunk and saw that her mother was already sleeping, clutching the tattered sacking that acted as her only blanket. Too tired to do more, Kläre climbed to her own platform and slept instantly. Not more than an hour had passed when a shrill whistle and the shouting of guards woke all the women in the block to dread and confusion.

"Get out! Now! In the yard, all!"

Kläre slid down into the aisle before she could think, pulling her clothing and shawl around herself before nearly lifting her mother first to sit and then to stand beside her. Johanna weighed no more than a child, but her head sank to her chest and she leaned forward, unbalanced.

"Mutti, you must wake quickly. We have to stand."

"No, no, I cannot." Johanna shook her head and seemed to have no strength to return her head to center.

"You must, Mama, please." Kläre walked mechanically forward, her arm under her mother's shawl, supporting her frail body. Frema appeared on the other side, whispering "Come, Frau Ente," and Kläre felt her mother straighten and move between the two younger women like an aged marionette.

The night was mild for March, but it was damp, and Kläre shivered. The moon hung low and huge between the buildings as the 130 women shambled into the yard. A prickle of fear fanned up Kläre's scalp as she noted the unusual number of guards. *It can't be another transport already. We lost twenty women only this morning*. Keeping her eyes down, Kläre moved silently, running the possibilities through her foggy mind. *Someone tried to escape. Something has gone missing. There are new orders.*

"You. Out!" an officer shouted, pointing his club at a woman in the front row.

"No, please . . ." Kläre could hear the woman pleading, her voice rising.

"Silence!"

The woman could not stop. She no doubt knew better but could not control her fear. The tension rose in the air until the inevitable crack of a rifle silenced her and she dropped to the ground.

"You, move." The officer continued, choosing women in what appeared to be random fashion as he pushed through the silent crowd. He neared Kläre, who stepped quietly in front of her mother. He was an officer who met with the commandant from time to time, and Kläre watched him until she knew he recognized her. Only when he was directly in front of her did she drop her eyes. Pausing for only a moment he turned to Frema and shouted, "Jew, whore, MOVE!"

Frema's arm slipped from around Johanna Ente, who by now stood weakly on her own, head down. Passing in front of Kläre, her face expressionless, Frema whispered, "God bless" and joined the other women. An hour later, the selected women had been marched away, and the remaining inmates returned to the bunk after being made to stand and listen to screamed insults and escalating threats for the duration.

Kläre returned Johanna to her platform and listened. She heard only the distant rattle of a truck somewhere in the town. There were now at most two hours until she had to rise again. She climbed stiffly to her own bunk and, within moments, slept.

"*Aus!*" shouted the guard. Kläre's legs began to straighten and search for ground before her eyes opened, before she'd cloaked her consciousness in narrowed vigilance. This time, nothing more than the normal waking routine followed. Up the aisle, carefully avoiding the sight of Frema's empty bunk, Kläre made her way to the shower, shedding her rough dress to stand for an instant in the icy sting of water. As she braced for the physical pain of the frigid needles of water, she played one of her mental games: She summoned an image of plunging into the Swiss mountain lake at Lauterbrunnen where she and Jakob had once vacationed. Too soon, her attention returned to donning her sack dress, and she stepped out of the barracks toward the Command House, where she would dress in her uniform, left spotless and pressed last evening.

Hurrying through the low doorway in the half-light, she did not see the bodies until she'd tripped on a splayed leg, caught herself, then fallen flat onto the next. Five bodies lay naked in the blue light of dawn, blood drying like blooms from bullet holes in heads, chests, and groins. As if burned by the cold flesh, Kläre leaped to her feet and stifled the scream that roared from her chest as she spun away from Frema, the slightest of the bodies, her legs broken open, a bloodied rose stuck between them.

"Move along, Jew bitch!" shouted one of the soldiers. "We can give you a rose too," he taunted, and the other men laughed.

24 April 1944

We create dramas and the dramas that we have no control over create us.

Andros Savcik bent low over the young lettuce, scanning expertly in the outer leaves for telltale signs of slugs or disease. The late April air filled his head with the scent of open earth and floral perfume that bypassed his wily prisoner's vigilance and filled his chest with the promise of spring. In another five meters he would arrive at an older row of fat, buttery lettuce heads that he had come to harvest for the officers' kitchen. He had nurtured the greens since seed planting in early March under cover of wooden hoops and oiled cloth, and now they stood, fulsome, in the afternoon sun. Ordinarily, Andros would focus only on the plants and the elaborate mental game of ignoring the penetrating hunger cramping his belly while thinking how best to enhance the garden produce. Today, however, was no ordinary day.

A snatch of breeze rolled through the kitchen garden, lifting daffodil heads lazily on their long stalks. Andros straightened and casually stretched his shoulders back, turning his head slightly to the left where the burlap sack of straw lay. Pulling the sack toward him, he began to scatter its contents along the row he had just tended, working with studied deliberation, expertly meting out the straw until he had emptied it all exactly at the row's end. He studied his work with a critical eye; then, lifting the sack, he carried it up the garden path to a wooden garden cart standing ready for the lettuce harvest. He smoothed the sack along the bottom of the cart, immobilizing his face as he felt around the outlines of the packet hidden in a pocket at its bottom. Reviewing his plan to himself, Andros began to pick the grown lettuce heads and place them gently onto the burlap bed in the cart. *Deliver the lettuces; return the cart; go to the barracks of the elders; request to see the rabbi; deliver the mail, the contraband newspaper; then pass the packet to the agent. But only if the timing is exactly correct . . .*

Concentrating on making sure that no sign of the fear that crossed his heart would cross his face, Andros left the garden with his cart of lettuces, past an officer's wife who was indelicately cleaning her fingernails with a knife, her job as a warder ignored for the moment.

The rooms of Leo Baeck were sparsely furnished, but they were clean, and the celebrated rabbi had been allowed to keep a small library. He sat at the simple table, his eyes traveling repeatedly over the text of his recent address at the Community House. *The prophets . . . turned against every misdeed of history that sought its vindication in success of expediency. They turned against the sort of politics that creates its own moral code, they objected to any justification of right by victory . . .*

It wasn't working. The erudite, elaborate polemic was designed to bolster spiritual resistance—to demand the continuation of Jewish identity and of life itself based on the principals of justice, goodness and truth. Nothing he had ever done surpassed this work in importance, this willing of survival against impossible odds. Yet doubt, fear, and horror of what he saw happening filled his own heart. The very survival he insisted upon to his followers grew more dubious in his own mind daily.

A sharp knock at the door jolted Leo out of his exhausted reverie. "Come in."

The door opened and his assistant ushered in a German officer Leo had never before seen. He rose to greet the man, who started toward him but appeared to think better of it and stopped several meters away from the simple desk.

"Dr. Baeck?"

"Yes . . ."

"Lieutenant Stein." There was a pause as Leo waited for further identification from the lieutenant, but as none came, he moved slowly around the table and gestured to the two wooden chairs that served as the only other seating in the room.

"Please sit. I am sorry that I have nothing to offer you, Lieutenant . . . Stein." Leo thought he saw a grimace of pain cross the expression of the younger man, but perhaps not. Tall and ruggedly handsome, his brown hair shot through with silver, his guest was in his mid to late forties. His grey eyes, deep and luminous, caught Leo off guard, yet somehow relaxed him as well. The rabbi waited for the other man to speak.

"Commandant Sternkopf directed me to you as I am seeking some reading material, and he thought I might borrow a book or two."

Leo paused for only a fraction of a second, quick to cover his surprise. "But of course. I haven't much here, but I am happy to loan whatever you wish. Did you have something particular in mind?" It seemed this question put the younger man at a loss. Another knock at the door interrupted them.

"Please . . . come in," Leo Baeck called.

The assistant entered again, great consternation written across his face as he darted a fearful look at the lieutenant. He spoke quickly: "I am so sorry, Dr. Baeck, but the gardener has arrived with your post and insists upon seeing you immediately. I told him you had an important meeting just now, but he is adamant."

Now both the assistant and Leo looked to the strange officer, who spoke immediately: "Please, I have time to wait."

Leo regarded the man quizzically, but instructed that the gardener be shown in.

Andros Savcik strode across the threshold, clutching a bundle in his hands. "Dr. Baeck. I beg your pardon for interrupting, but I have acquired the items you requested, and have your mail, and I must return quickly to the garden . . ."

Leo felt astonishment pass across his face like a film. The gardener had obtained a strictly forbidden newspaper, and now here he stood, insisting upon delivering it in front of a German officer. If anything went wrong now—if their elaborate ruse unraveled—it would mean disaster for both of them.

Andros carefully withdrew a bundle from his burlap garden sack and handed it to the rabbi, shielding it from the officer's sight with his body. "A message also, Dr. Baeck, from Frau Kohler," he said, looking directly into Leo's eyes. "She wishes you to know that your lecture at the community house inspired her, and that she takes strength from all those who work to preserve body and mind in these troubled times."

Leo returned the gardener's gaze and then, with a brief glance at the officer, took the bundle from Andros and calmly put it out of sight on a shelf behind him, leaving Andros with only his sack, which he folded neatly and placed on the table.

"Perhaps I can return later to finish the business we were discussing, Dr. Baeck," the officer said.

"No, no," Andros cut in. "I must return to the garden and have no wish to interrupt you further." Bowing slightly, Andros turned to leave, raising his eyes for a single moment to meet those of the lieutenant before leaving the room.

Leo watched him go, then moved to the bookshelves and pulled out several volumes to offer the lieutenant. He returned to the table and found Andros's burlap bag still sitting there. "Ach, the gardener has left his sack," he said, reaching for it.

"Please, Dr. Baeck, I am happy to return it to the gardener," Lieutenant Stein said, stepping forward and picking it up. "I wish to visit the garden next in any case. It is a relief to see something growing amidst a war."

Again silence fell like an evening snow.

"Quite," Leo responded at last. "Perhaps, then, it would interest you to read essays I wrote about the Book of Creation. The tension between Commandment and mystery and the Greek and Roman connections . . ."

"Thank you, yes, that would be most interesting," Lieutenant Stein replied as he reached for the book and picked up the folded sack. He met Leo's eyes and said, "I hope it is of some comfort that even here—no, especially here—your work provides strength to your flock. The Frau . . . what was her name, Kohler? It seems as if you've lightened her load."

Leo did not reply at once. What was it about this German soldier that put him at such ease? He met the younger man's gaze and said, "She is a woman who supplies more strength than she ever takes in even the most unbearable of situations."

"A woman of valor," said Lieutenant Stein, and Leo marveled at this use of the language of the Sabbath prayer for wives and mothers. "How fortunate in the midst of such misfortune."

With that, the lieutenant rose to leave. The two men regarded each other openly, and Leo felt with certainty that something important, something he did not entirely understand, had happened in this unusual meeting. His faith in the mysteries of life and God allowed him to smile warmly at the lieutenant. Reaching for his hand, he held it in both of his own. "May the Lord bless you and keep you. May his countenance shine upon you."

The lieutenant returned the rabbi's smile and departed, book and bundle in hand.

Bernhardt did not return the sack to the garden, but instead walked directly to the small anteroom he had been given to prepare the reports that his sham orders requested. Stepping into the washroom next to the offices of Sternkopf himself, Bernhardt withdrew the packet Andros had secreted in the burlap sack and stuffed it into his jacket. Names of prisoners, names of officers, descriptions of the camp, copies of transport lists—all were to be smuggled to the underground resistance.

That Bernhardt had succeeded in maintaining his cover as a German officer and had finessed the transfer of documents from the gardener in his meeting with an unknowing but canny Leo Baeck did not occupy his thoughts. Kläre Kohler did. The mention of her name had unnerved him in a way that the danger of his mission did not. Somewhere, very close by, she was surviving in this wretched place, and he could not risk his mission or her precarious safety by seeking her out. Yet with all his heart, Bernhardt wished to see her, to hold her in his arms, to tell her each detail of how he had delivered her son to safety in Trieste. He wanted to tell her that he, too, worried each day as to Werner's whereabouts and safety, that those weeks posing as the boy's uncle had connected him more deeply to Kläre. Most of all, Bernhardt wished to take her away with him and out of harm's way.

He had another life now, with other commitments and his own danger to navigate. He closed his eyes, composed himself, and gathered his papers. He returned the sack to the garden shed, and departed through the ghetto for Dresden.

25 July 1945

My Dear Ones,

Yesterday I received, to my huge surprise and still greater joy, your first letter for nearly six years. You are alive!

It wasn't only the sudden appearance of your letters that joyfully shocked me, but much more, their content. In Ben Shemen I have gotten to know many survivors of Buchenwald and other camps. I can only say that I could never have imagined how much one can destroy in a human being and have them still survive. But now I believe it. Therefore, I cannot adequately express my joy that I found so much confidence and will for living in your letter. I don't believe there is anyone to thank because after all the things that have happened to the Jewish people, and that they have withstood, in Palestine and in Europe, each one who has made it through or helped another has himself to thank. I can only say that I am proud of this.

Many times people ask how our life is in Palestine. The answer is, it depends on whose life. There is one group, fortunately very small, who try to live again like in "the good old days," but slowly they must give in. The rest know, thank goodness, what to expect when living among foreigners in a strange land, and they build here in Palestine a homeland in which they have self-determination. I can only say that it takes nearly superhuman strength to again make fun and cheerful people out of them. But it must be done and so it is—without any foreign help!

The life in the kibbutzim is not easy. It requires doing without a lot, but almost because of this it is more beautiful. Along a smooth road one can slip easily! I have left Ben Shemen. For the last year I have not gone to the agricultural school where I started, but instead have become responsible for a fairly large experimental station. I have learned a great deal about agriculture. I am with a group of nearly 70 youths at Kibbutz Eilon near the Syrian border. At the moment, we are doing preparatory work on the land. If we are lucky, in the next year we will start a new kibbutz. Our average age is 18 ½! In normal times, one would have had to wait at least until age 25 to be in charge of a job like this. This is one of the most beautiful regions in Palestine, with an unusually large water supply (which is a major issue here). As soon as you acknowledge receipt of this letter, I will send you pictures.

Our daily schedule is very comfortable for us compared to Ben Shemen. There, we received in the last year apart from Saturday, one day off in the week. On that day, they taught us agriculture and humanistics. Besides that we worked 10–12 hours a day, sometimes even more. So we were pretty tired when we came home in the evenings. The work was at the very least not the easiest. Under such circumstances it is also not so easy to absorb additional subjects.

Now, we work only 8 ½ hours per day. We begin from 6:30–12:00. During this time we also eat breakfast (8:00) and then we work again from 1:00–4:30 in the afternoon. After 4:30 we are free and can do what we want with our time. At 7:30, we learn together or one of us holds a talk about different important questions. These talks are alternated so each person has to prepare a theme once in a while. I can tell you that one learns a lot this way. Anyway, we stand on our own two feet. We provide for ourselves well from age 15 on and feel wonderful.

There is so much more to write, but first I must see if you receive this.

Many greetings and kisses,
Your Avraham
Address: Avraham Kohler
Garin Mir
Kibbutz Eilon near Naharia, Palestine

Kläre no longer cried each time she read the letter, and had brought it to the hospital each day since she received it. She read it daily to Johanna, who sometimes remembered what it contained, and other days wanted to hear again why Werner was in Palestine, and why he signed the name Avraham. For Jakob, Kläre held the letter and if he felt strong enough, he read it himself. Now the wonder and the worry set in: wonder that this mere boy had created a new life on his own with other mere children, and worry that they'd done so in a wild and unsettled land.

Kläre replaced the letter in her pocketbook next to her ration tickets, and wished first her mother and then Jakob a good evening. It was time to leave the hospital and stand in the long lines with other exhausted housewives at the shops that reopened at 3:00 p.m. She hoped for a loaf of bread or an egg, but resigned herself to whatever tin or produce might have appeared since morning.

Descending the stairway, Kläre marveled again at the order that had been created in this convalescent center in the few short weeks since the buses had brought them here. Those days were still a blur, with no order to the memories and impressions that alternated with hours of exhausted sleep.

In the end, as the German soldiers fled Theresienstadt, dysentery had taken over as the omnipresent killer. Kläre had found an abandoned room in an apartment for herself and Johanna and Jakob, both of whom had fallen desperately ill. Rumors of the American Army coming brought fear as much as any other reaction to the thousand people who could still move or think. Their safety now rested with the unknown. More than all she had endured, this uncertainty unnerved Kläre so that she didn't know any longer how to regard the rising of the sun, the spring rain, or the gentle chill of the nights. In place of the bitter cruelty and precision of the camp, only the random misery of the sick and dying contorted the impossible beauty of another spring. Kläre scavenged food from the commandant's kitchen. His May garden, which had barely begun to produce, was soon savaged.

Then there was the day the Americans came, their shocked faces and incomprehensible speech present and soon gone, with the news that the war was finished, and that the Russians were to follow. The first deliveries of water, food, doctors, and other relief workers arrived. Kläre tried to remember when there were suddenly hands other than her own feeding her mother and her husband, when they had been led out of the apartment to a hastily put together field hospital. Always she insisted on being near Jakob and Johanna, and miraculously they listened. But days dissolved into each other and into sensations of warm water, cleaning, and sleep; of real soup and fresh bread. There were forms and more forms, and then, one day, the International Red Cross asked questions about family members.

Kläre remembered clearly the afternoon when a young man came to her section of the shelter and asked about children. She had spoken wildly, her fingers clawing at his arm—but his German was not good enough, and she had been forced to slow her speech and speak more clearly.

"WERNER KOHLER," she'd said, exaggerating every sound. "K-O-H-L-E-R. Birth date October 14, 1927. He went to Palestine." She could tell that she looked mad; could hear herself that she sounded like a shrieking skeleton. "Also I have a son in England: Erwin Kohler. He is twenty-two years old. He is in the British Army." The man wrote, asked more questions about their last address in Hörde, but Kläre could remember nothing after that.

Weeks had gone by—a month, even—in which the sick were cared for or died, and the transports out of the camp began. Each day, it seemed, transports left in different directions. Finally the day came when six battered busses arrived from the city of Dortmund to claim its citizens. Kläre had watched in a daze as the nursing sisters and relief workers prepared Jakob and Johanna for the journey and provided

Kläre with a sheaf of papers and permissions. She hadn't even had the energy to read them all. She'd gathered the items of clothing that remained to her and that she'd been given for her husband and mother, put the few papers she had saved during the two years of their internment, and then they were driving slowly toward Germany on an early June morning.

The buses had crawled through the countryside, following the Elbe River amidst the stunning green beauty of renewed life. Trees were in full leaf, occasional fields filled with early hay, and dazzling red geraniums spilled from the window boxes of farmhouses. Jakob and Johanna had slept constantly, and Kläre had also dozed. She'd tried to think of Hörde, of where they would go, but had given up exhaustedly. She had learned too well to operate only in the reality of the moment.

Well into the afternoon of that long day's drive, they had eaten lunch in the basement of a small town church in the center of Saxony. A strong sun had shone as, resuming their travels, they passed a group of men repairing a fence at the roadside. It looked to be a father and his sons, big, strong boys. The one closest to the road was tall, with a mop of brown hair which he threw back in laughter as the bus passed. He looked to be Werner's age, and for a moment Kläre had believed it was him and craned her neck around to watch him through the window. Realizing her mistake, she pressed her eyes shut, and a small prayer formed at the corners of her heart as tears did in her eyes. *Let him be alive, dear God.*

And he was alive. The letter in her pocketbook had come less than a week after they were returned to Hörde. The displaced persons' shelters, set up in what had been army barracks at the edge of the city, were spare but well organized, and the Red Cross workers were efficient, even kind. Those first days were filled with registrations, supplying of cots and blankets, and food—simple but nutritious food. Dortmund lay in the British sector of the newly carved devastation that constituted Germany.

"Frau Kläre Kohler." The voice from the front of the dining tent struck fear first, but then she had seen the sheaf of letters and heard other names called. There had been more news as well: Erwin was also alive and actually somewhere in Germany, still with the British Army. The note from him was simple:

> *Mutti,*
>
> *I am not far and I will come to you as soon as possible. Use these ration cards. Thank G-d you are alive.*
>
> *Erwin*

Kläre descended the final steps into the lobby of the hospital and made her way into the warmth of the summer afternoon. The barracks were far enough out of the city center that the devastation of the bombing was not everywhere visible. The subdued movement of citizens and British soldiers was eerie. Shortages of petrol and damage to roadways limited motor traffic. Shops opened only during circumscribed times, and even then had little to sell. But it was enough for Kläre to raise her face to the warm sun and breathe deeply before making her way to the shops. It was more than enough.

The July day dawned bright, and Kläre gazed into the opulent blue of the sky. Her eyes were weakened, and she had only a second-hand pair of eyeglasses. The relief of staring into blue space without needing to focus and refocus was a small gift of the morning. She noticed these small gifts as she took back the days of her life. But only the days had returned to her conscious possession. The nights were still rigid affairs at the end of exhaustion, fraught with frightening dreams or sleepless vacancy.

Feelings stole across the fences of her routine endeavors, waltzed through the garden gate of her self-control like a bold suitor with designs on her time and heart. Only this morning, surrounded by blue sky, the idea occurred to her that she might possibly have already experienced her best days. The notion settled on her as she pulled her attention back from the sky, adjusted her eyeglasses, and returned to mending Jakob's shirt, so worn that the mending was nearly useless. She stopped as a revolt from somewhere deep inside her shouted, *No! That will not do! I haven't come this far to live in the past!* Her own passion discomfited her, and she waited until calm returned.

It was nearly time to make her way to the hospital. The weeks there had sustained Johanna in the way of an autumn garden kept tidy. She was weak and slipping away, but comfortable. Kläre searched each day for a way to help her mother want to eat. She found a flower to put on her tray, or a special sweet when she could pay for it with the meager scrip given to her. Today she was bringing a letter from Ernst and Ditha in Detroit to rouse her mother. She would read it to her between mouthfuls of soup or bread.

Kläre placed her mending and the letter into her basket, and found her cardigan. It hung on her shrunken frame like she was a child wearing her mother's clothing, but Kläre hadn't time for thoughts of her body or her clothing. She stepped inside the barrack she shared with fifteen other women and saw that her bed and chest, chair and table were orderly. She left then, and walked to the entrance of the camp, across the commons area.

The hospital was a kilometer and a half down the road, on the other side of the town. A convoy—a combination of trucks and soldiers on foot—seemed to be crawling at a snail's pace ahead. Mostly the soldiers near the camp kept to themselves and left the displaced persons in the camp alone. Occasionally a regulation had to be introduced or a new form filled out. The British had been quick to find Germans, some of them the liberated Jews themselves, to run the day-to-day operations of the care and feeding of these broken and lost souls, ever mindful of what "camps" had meant to so many of them. The word "displaced" was so British, Kläre thought—as if *place* had a thing to do with what failed the people around her. These people were sick, shocked, deranged—any of a dozen maladies of body and soul combined to betray them over and over again. Place hardly mattered anymore. At least they were fed, and dogged efforts were being made to reconnect them with their lives. Kläre was dumbly grateful for every bit of assistance.

She picked up her pace in the dazzling sun, filling her lungs with fresh air, willing strength to return to her legs. She began to pass the soldiers as they moved slowly toward the town center: they in the dusty road, and she on the newly built cobblestone walkway. She had nearly reached the greengrocer's shop when a group of soldiers halted beside her and a solid young man broke from the group and walked tentatively toward her. Involuntarily, she stiffened and turned her head toward the shops, maintaining her quickened pace.

"*Verzeihen sie* . . . Excuse me, ma'am . . . May I ask you, please?" the soldier called in perfect German.

Kläre slowed and, seeing no other pedestrian nearby, turned to look at the boy, who was now only five meters from her.

"Yes, can I help you?" she asked tentatively, adjusting her glasses. She studied him for moment before her hand flew to her mouth and the boy reached out toward her.

"Oh my God, Mutti, is that you? Mutti! Is it really you?" Erwin Kohler pulled his emaciated mother into the folds of his summer uniform on the dusty street of Hohenstadt.

The nursing sisters whispered excitedly as Kläre entered the ward on the arm of the young British soldier—her son. She fought to keep tears from spilling down her cheek. Erwin's serious face was filled with an emotion he did not seem quite able to contain.

They reached the bedside of Johanna Ente, and Kläre took the older woman's sliver of a hand. "Mutti," she whispered in a choked voice, "Mutti, look here. Look who I have brought to you today."

Johanna opened her eyes to her daughter's face and held her gaze for a long moment. "What . . . what, Klärchen? It is you, yes?" She looked around and saw the young man at the foot of her bed. She returned her gaze to Kläre, a look of confusion and mounting alarm filling her eyes. "What is it, then?"

Kläre stroked a thick thatch of steel grey back from her mother's forehead. "Mutti, it's my Erwin. My son, Mutti. He is here from

England with the army. He found me just now in the street. It's my Erwin."

She saw her mother's eyes dart back to Erwin, who stood smiling uncertainly, hesitant, as always, to intrude. Kläre could see that her mother was working to sort out that it was her grandson who stood before her. Suddenly recognition broke through and Johanna cried out weakly. "*Ya sicher* . . . of course! My God, here is Erwin." She lifted her arms then, and Erwin stepped forward and bent down to gather his tiny grandmother gingerly into his arms. Her hoarse wail of joy was muffled by his jacket.

Kläre stood back, suddenly weak with the fullness of this moment. She held to the end of the bed to steady herself. "Erwin, stay here with Oma, and I will bring down your father." She knew Jakob would want to be sitting rather than in bed when his son saw him.

She raced to Jakob's room, where she found him reading a newspaper, a small pillow helping to control his trembling hand. His worn, palsied face acquired a look of wonder as he saw her radiant happiness.

"Jakob . . . Jakob, it's Erwin. He is here. Right here in Hohenstadt. He is downstairs with Mutti. Come, I will help you now to dress and we will go to them."

Jakob looked from his wife to the wall in front of his bed and then back to Kläre before whispering, "Thank God . . . Thank God." In the next moment he was working to move his trembling body out from under the blanket and into the clothing that Kläre had gathered for him.

Jakob sat tall in the wheelchair. Kläre wheeled him into the curtained area of the women's ward where her mother's bed stood. Midday sunshine streamed through the window, lighting the scene of Erwin sitting at the bedside and holding his grandmother's frail hand, speaking to her quietly. Johanna, now fully alert and propped up on her pillows, eagerly watched her grandson.

Kläre heard Jakob sigh as he beheld his son, flushed in the warmth of the sunny room, his uniform tightly buttoned and his tie neatly tied. Erwin looked up then, and was neither clever nor fast enough to mask the look of shock that registered as he recognized his father and took the measure of his decline. Jakob winced as if stinging nettles accompanied the traverse of his son's eyes over his wasted, trembling body. Erwin's soldier's impassivity returned to him as he rose and moved forward to first grasp his father's hand and then bend to kiss his cheek. His customary awkwardness had been eased by the deliberation with which he now engaged in every task. Kläre's eyes filled again as the recognition washed over her that her son had grown into a man—one whom she did not know.

The family Kohler moved onto the veranda overlooking the hospital grounds, green with the life of early summer, though the gardens had only recently been tended and the neglect of all the war years was still evident. An hour later, an exhausted Jakob had to be returned to his room. The halting stories, the exchange of news, the detailing of circumstances which is the manna of loved ones starved of each other was also an exercise in frustration as they advanced toward and retreated from topics of great immediacy to great anguish and back.

Kläre and Erwin left the hospital as they had come, walking slowly arm in arm and speaking softly. He would rejoin his unit to assist in the town. He would expedite the resettlement of his parents and grandmother as fully as possible. Kläre would bring the two letters from Werner and would try to answer the questions Erwin could not ask but which haunted his eyes when he looked at the three members of his family. Where had they been? What had happened to them to create these ravaged versions of his loved ones?

For now, Kläre too was exhausted, and it was all she could do to cling to her son for another five minutes as they reached the edge of town. He turned back there, and she continued until she entered the displaced persons' camp and found her way to her cot. She played over and over again Erwin's words: "I will see you tomorrow, Mutti. I am here now to help you."

One more time, tears spilled down Kläre's still-sunken cheeks, but they followed the curve of her smile before they dropped to her pillow.

26 September 1945

After the doings of the land of Egypt, wherein ye dwelt, shall ye not do; and after the doings of the land of Canaan, whither I bring you, shall ye not do; neither shall ye walk in their ordinances. Ye shall do my judgments, and keep mine ordinances, to walk therein; I am the Lord your God.
—Leviticus, 18:3

Ansel Beckmann pulled the wide lapels of his father's old coat closer around his shoulders. Where his father had been wide and stocky, Ansel stood tall and round-shouldered, and he had lost solidity and strength. Sharing rations with his sisters and his stepmother and the meager fare at the seminary had left him chronically underfed. He gazed out the window of the train as it slowly made its way through the countryside. Rain fell steadily, coursing down the windows of the coach, cold and dismal. Ansel shut his eyes in a prayer of thanks that he sat in a train at all, that the train ran, that the British soldiers mostly slept or looked out their own windows. The war's end was nearly as hard to believe as its having been waged for so many wretched years.

The end had brought a new kind of chaos to Westphalia. In the fading days of September, many small farms lay fallow or in ruins. Ansel had grown used to the sight of bomb damage in Cologne. The shocked faces of its nomadic residents were a part of the broken landscape. He had not yet steeled himself to the misery of the starving animals on farms, the abandoned tractors, fields gone to weeds, and worst of all, the knots of travelers on foot along the roads. They carried what they could, and if they moved at all it was slowly, the grief, hunger, and exhaustion of their disaster hanging like a fog around them.

Ansel's long fingers pulled the worn Bible in his lap open to *Leviticus* and he re-read the passage that had compelled him to make today's journey:

> *But the goat, on which the lot fell to be the scapegoat, shall be presented alive before the Lord, to make atonement with him and to let him go for a scapegoat into the wilderness.*

Allowed to live, the goat was an atonement for the people's sins. Ansel pondered this improbable way of thinking about Kläre Kohler, and how to approach seeing her. Where she had been and what she had suffered had been the topic of intense speculation during his recent visit to Amalie in Beilefeld. Ansel had learned quickly what little Amalie knew: That Kläre, Jakob, and Johanna had been in a camp for more than two years, and had been brought back to Dortmund after liberation. That Kläre still resided in a displaced persons' facility near the hospital where Johanna and Jakob lay. That Amalie's cousin in Dortmund had heard that Kläre's son Erwin was a British soldier stationed in the area. Beyond that, nothing more was known.

"Go, Ansel," Amalie had instructed her stepson. "As a priest you have the possibility to find her. Perhaps you can help."

Whatever evil she had encountered, Kläre had survived. Was her survival atonement for the sins of others, countless others? What wilderness would he find her in now, if he could find her at all? Ansel could not redress the suffering that Kläre had borne, but he wanted to try or at least bear witness with her.

A mixture of confusion and dread lay upon Ansel like a leaden vest, yet urgency drove him to spend a week's worth of food money on the train ticket and delay for two days his return to the seminary and the final months' preparation for his ordination. He would spend the last days before taking his final vows in seclusion. Whether for the sake of his vocation or in response to the rare pull of Kläre's spirit, reaching to him across the years, Ansel felt compelled to find her. He had no plan, but trusted in the will of his God.

He returned his gaze to the empty landscape outside the window. In another half-hour, the train would be at the outskirts of the city, and scattered hamlets and larger roads would replace the fallow fields and open sky. The rain had stopped, but the skies remained cloud-covered, with only an occasional break in the grey.

> *For the life of the flesh is in the blood: and I have given it to you upon the altar to make an atonement for your souls: for it is the blood that maketh an atonement for the soul. Therefore I said unto the children of Israel. No soul of you shall eat blood; neither shall any stranger that sojourneth among you eat blood.*

Ansel gently closed the Bible in his lap and once again closed his eyes. The spilling of blood in all manner of the ways of war had left the taste of it everywhere.

Gutersicht, Rheda, Oelde, Neubecke, Hamm—the towns became larger and stops more frequent until finally the train reached the station at Hohenstadt and, carrying only his Bible and a small valise, Ansel descended the train steps and strode off toward the town center.

"Sergeant Kohler will see you now," the officer's assistant said.

Ansel looked up to see Erwin Kohler striding through the lobby of the office building that served as the unit's temporary headquarters. Erwin studied him closely. What must he think? Ansel saw himself as Kohler might: his height, his thin paleness, his ill-fitting clothes, which were currently soaked from the rain that had resumed just after the train pulled into the station. He looked expectantly toward Erwin.

"Yes?" Erwin said in English.

"I come here to ask after your mother, Officer Kohler," Ansel said. "I have heard that she is alive, and has returned to Dortmund. I would very much like to see her, and perhaps help her if I am able."

Erwin looked surprised, not only at the personal nature of this request, but by the strength of feeling Ansel had not been able to keep out of his tone. "Who are you, and how do you know my mother?" he asked, his tone harsh.

"My name is Ansel Beckmann; my stepmother is Amalie, a childhood friend of your mother. I have met Frau Kohler several times, and she has been very kind to me. Our family wishes to do what we can to help," Ansel replied steadily. He smiled faintly. "I came once as a child to your house. You let me play with your very fine train set." Ansel watched as Erwin searched his memory, his hand worrying the button on his uniform jacket.

Erwin glanced at the officer's assistant over his shoulder. He seemed reluctant to proceed any further with an audience. "I have work to finish," he finally said. "Meet me here at six this evening. We will speak further then."

Ansel bowed his head slightly in assent and turned immediately to the door. The hour and a half passed quickly, and at six precisely, when Erwin had completed his day's work and returned to the building lobby, Ansel was there waiting for him.

"Perhaps we should find a beer," Erwin suggested, and relief flooded Ansel.

They were seated in a crowded *stube* within minutes. Even the starving citizens of Dortmund found time and resources for the occasional beer now that the presence of the British Army had put the bars back in business.

"I have this one," Erwin offered, and Ansel again felt relief. He sipped his beer and waited. Erwin did the same.

After a long silence, Ansel ventured, "I would like to be helpful to you, and to your mother, if there is any way to do that . . . and I would like to see her, if that would be all right. I don't know what has happened to her in the last two years since she was . . . since she was taken."

Erwin Kohler hunched down in his chair, his neck disappearing into the collar of his shirt, his hand absently rotating the glass of beer.

Ansel decided to continue. "Where is she living?"

"My mother lives in a displaced persons' camp at the edge of town, not far from here. My father and my grandmother are in hospital, also nearby."

"Are they well? I mean . . . are they stable?" Perspiration broke out on the young priest's forehead. Erwin had not yet decided to be helpful, and Ansel understood that he had to make himself of some use to the dour young man before him. "Your mother took care of me a bit before the war. I'd like to return the favor." He watched Erwin's face carefully, hoping he had struck the right balance between sincerity and insouciance.

At last, Erwin spoke: "If you are certain that my mother will welcome your visit, I will give you directions to get to the camp. The gates are locked after dark, so you'd best wait until morning. She generally goes to the hospital in the afternoon. Will you have somewhere to stay?"

"Yes, thank you," Ansel replied, surprised. "I spoke with the priest at St. Stephen's, and he will keep me for the night."

"When is the last time you saw her?" Erwin asked suddenly, the hunger in his eyes signaling the final departure of his reserve.

Ansel lowered his head and turned the beer stein in his hand for a moment before responding. "I visited when I was a student in Cologne, just before they were taken, and before I went to the army. It seemed like they were doing okay—worried, yes, but your father still had a job at the ministry, and your mother made me feel so comfortable, so welcome. And then the next time I went, they were gone . . ." Ansel leaned over the table and locked eyes with Erwin. "It was awful; the Gestapo had hanged a man in their apartment. I didn't know where your parents were taken or if they were even alive." Ansel realized he was breathing heavily now; he strove to maintain control as he continued. "After that I was sent to the Eastern Front until I was wounded. When I got out of the hospital, I went straight to the seminary, and I'm only just now finishing."

“Right, well, I guess that’s it then.” Erwin rose to leave.

Ansel rose as well, a little startled by Erwin’s abruptness. He bowed slightly, with the formality of a stranger, but his hand gripped Erwin’s warmly.

Ansel watched as Erwin walked away. Sadness hung around the young soldier like a heavy blanket.

The next morning, sun slanted from the east as Ansel entered the barracks kitchen. Across the room, Kläre Kohler was scrubbing potatoes, concentrating on each one as if she were investing it with nourishment. Her drawn face and bent frailty struck his heart. She looked up at him as though he’d spoken, though he’d not made a sound. For a moment he feared that she did not know him, but suddenly her face broke into a kaleidoscope of astonishment and delight. He had crossed the room and taken her hands into his own before he could think of anything to say.

“Frau Kohler.” Ansel realized he was crying, and that Kläre was as well. “I am so very glad to see you.”

Kläre looked up at him and reached her arm through his. “Has God kept you safe and sent you here, then?”

Ansel helped Kläre into her coat and, drawing her arm through his once again, walked with her into the morning.

27 September 1945

"It's better that it's gone . . . Isn't it?" Ansel asked as Kläre clung to his arm and Erwin strode around the ruins of 17 Furchler Strasse. The patchwork of broken walls and shattered windows stood in relief against the clear sky. A crater beside the building marked the spot where an errant bomb had fallen, no doubt intended for the steelworks half a kilometer away. Ansel shuddered as images of the horror he had witnessed on his last visit to the Kohler apartment seeped out of the locked vessel of memory. He wondered suddenly if Kläre knew—if the hanging had happened in her presence. He had not yet dared ask her anything about the time since last he'd seen her. She needed to find her way forward now, and it had become his mission to help her. It seemed likely to Ansel that the humiliation and punishment of Officer Licht was only one of an unnumbered catalog of atrocities that Kläre kept locked inside.

"Yes," Ansel answered himself resolutely. "It is better to look forward now." Erwin Kohler stopped a worker one hundred meters down the road, near the far side of the crater, and spoke to him intently. The man gestured toward a neighboring apartment house and then back to the Kaiser Wilhelm Strasse. Catching sight of Kläre, he tipped his hat before continuing to speak with Erwin.

"Do you know that man?" Ansel asked.

"I cannot see him properly," Kläre responded. "I haven't the right eyeglasses." Ansel added to his mental notes to find an optician.

Erwin walked purposefully back toward the two of them, his

expression grim. "I have inquired from the fellow working at the crater. He is local and says many of the apartments were looted before the bombing. I have the names of people to . . . consult regarding the possible disposition of furniture and housewares. The army has set up an office in the Kaiser Wilhelm Strasse. We will go and investigate," he said, his voice stern.

"Will they pay attention to someone . . . like me?" Kläre asked, disbelieving.

"There are compensations for leap-frogging to the rank of Company Sergeant Major, Mother. I am needed because of my German, and therefore suddenly of value. And I suspect the presence of a priest will help gain the attention of the locals who have been brought in to deal with all of this."

Erwin drove directly to the Kaiser Wilhelm Strasse. Kläre and Ansel remained in the car as he strode into an appropriated storefront, one of the few operating on this once-thriving commercial avenue. Where only a few months ago, a Nazi banner had hung, the flag of the British Army of the Rhine now flew. Erwin remained inside for nearly twenty minutes.

Kläre spoke first. "I didn't understand—or even dream—about how confusing it would be to return here . . . how changed everything is." She turned to Ansel then. "I'm so grateful for what you and Erwin are doing. He seems already so burdened by adulthood. He always carried a heavy spirit, but I scarcely recognize the boy we sent to England six years ago. And you, Ansel, what has happened to you, dear boy?"

Ansel reached for Kläre's gloved hand. This was not the time to speak of all that had happened to him in the years during which he had completed his studies, fought in the army, and entered the seminary. Not yet. Here they were, together, forming a bridge toward a new life, whatever its form. "You are not alone, Tante Kläre. That is what is important now."

Ansel talked to her, mainly about Amalie and his sisters, Kläre asking after each of them in succession. At last Erwin reappeared, and when they were once again underway, he reported what he'd learned.

"I have the names of several people to contact for an apartment. It won't be much; there's so little available, and so many people displaced. But we should be able to find something fairly soon. Tomorrow, Ansel, perhaps you and I will spend some time following leads I've gotten about my mother's furniture and other possessions. The neighbors appear to have been quite willing to care for your household in your absence." The sarcasm in Erwin's voice was tired but vicious.

"My silver . . . It's buried in the garden of the Kleinschmidts. Unless, of course . . ." Kläre spoke just loud enough to be heard above the roar of the engine. "Unless nothing is there anymore."

"We'll check," Ansel said immediately, and saw Erwin's corresponding nod in the rearview mirror.

"Mutti, tonight you must make a list of important items for me to look for," Erwin instructed. "An inventory, if you can, of what was lost. It will help me to remember." Erwin then glanced at Ansel. "Can you stay for another day or two?"

"Yes, of course," Ansel replied. "I've told the abbot not to expect me until Saturday."

"Good," Erwin said. "I'll need you tomorrow."

The day dawned as clear and cerulean as the previous one. The September air was warm with the full sun. Kläre had her lists ready when Erwin and Ansel arrived punctually at 8:00 a.m. She examined the two of them—the compact British soldier, his uniform tight around his hefty middle, and the tall, thin priest—and thought what strange partners they made.

Kläre had worked late into the night, visiting each of her home's rooms in her memory with painful clarity, seeing the warm afternoon light in the sitting room falling on the Liebermann painting of a peasant woman. The seventeenth-century carved oak chest in the dining room creaked in her mind's ear as she opened the door to reveal photos, serving dishes, and table linens. Jakob's study with its Bauhaus furnishings, the marble-topped reception table in the front hall, and the steady tick-tock of the long wall clock's pendulum—each appeared in her recollection. She had been beyond missing the beautiful artifacts of her life for a long while. Now, she detailed them as though for a school lesson, with as much energy as she could muster.

Erwin skimmed through the pages briefly, and said only, "We'll do our best."

When they had gone, Kläre turned back to finishing her letter to Werner and preparations to visit Jakob. She worried about Johanna, whose health declined by the day, though she never uttered a single complaint. Kläre put aside thoughts of the morning's work upon which Erwin and Ansel had embarked.

In the evening, Ansel returned alone to tell Kläre of the day he had spent with her son—how they had walked the disrupted neighborhood around Furchler Strasse, speaking by turns with former neighbors, petty officials, and opportunistic strangers, until a story of loss, abandonment, theft, protection, moral provocation, and dissolution had coalesced around a plan for restitution; how, as the items appeared, one by one, he and Erwin had loaded them into the truck that Erwin had commandeered for this purpose.

They would move Kläre, and possibly even Jakob, he told her, to a small but light-filled apartment with the items they were recovering from former neighbors.

"I cannot thank you enough for what you and Erwin have done in these last days." Kläre held the priest's large hand fervently in both of hers. "If I knew a prayer, I would say it for you."

Ansel smiled and, bending his head to join Kläre, he prayed aloud, "O Lord Almighty, we have been bold enough to pray this prayer because you built a house for the people of Israel. Your words are truth, and you have promised these good things to us, your servants. And now may it please you to bless this family; for when you grant a blessing to your servants, O Sovereign Lord, it is an eternal blessing."

In less than a week the move was accomplished. On an evening that came early, Kläre sat alone at her desk. Her tears fell uninhibited. There was much to do. Jakob was settled for the night in the next room. He had taken a sleeping tablet, which would guarantee a few hours of uninterrupted sleep. Kläre tried to lay aside the letter from Werner. She could not yet get used to this new name, Avraham. She still did not understand who this boy, her son, had become. In this moment alone, the ache of missing him, at a distance of half the globe, compounded by his description of the foreign life in Palestine, bore into her chest. She could not imagine how to tell him of all that had happened—did not know the words to convey pain as well as comfort across so vast a distance of time and change, nor did she know how to keep the heaviness of her longing and missing out of what she must write. She read his letter again.

August, 1945
My Dear Ones,

I received your letter of 28 July. I am very happy that the wonderful family in America is taking such good care to send you packages and funds, and that Erwin could be of so much help recovering some of your belongings and securing an apartment. I don't really remember Ansel Beckmann personally, but of course I know who Amalie Beckmann is, and remember her visits to us. A Catholic priest? Doesn't our world throw the odd associations our way! If he is helpful to you, I mustn't hold him responsible for his church or his nationality. I have learned here to first look at the person.

I hope that soon, postal connection here will improve and I will be able to send you more regular mail. I wish I could send fresh oranges to you . . . They would give you strength and pleasure for the winter. Our orange business isn't working at the moment because none grow in this new place, and I think that export is too hard now. Oranges have to be shipped refrigerated.

I hope I can send pictures in the next few days, when I can travel to Haifa. To answer your questions: At the moment, my area is peaceful. However, even though I heard they want to authorize 100,000 visas, I am not much in favor of your entering Palestine. All immigrants are being held right now in camps, and it is not at all sure what will be done with them later on. There have been escape attempts and fugitives have been seized with warships and planes; sometimes they are freed with violence. I don't really think the circumstances are suitable, but if you want, I will try everything for you.

As I said before, things elsewhere in the country are unstable. Not only are the politics of the government a big mess, but some of the leaders who are great patriots are dreaming of a Jewish State without Arabs. Not to worry, dear Mother, because, thank G-d, I have a reasonable mind, though I will say that many of the young people from the camps are idealistic and daredevils.

Speaking of the Arab question and the terrorism, my movement, the Shomer Hazair, is fighting for a dual state for Arabs and Jews and against all who resort to terrorism. The terrorists, by the way, are a consequence of the British. There wouldn't be assassinations if the British weren't working so hard to subjugate.

I think you have misunderstood the situation with Ben Shemen and my education. Most children stay with their parents until they are 18. Ben Shemen was a school for young immigrants without parents. As far as high school and university go, I could attend if I paid for it myself. I was never attracted to university. I respect anyone who studies to prepare for a profession, but many cabbages get their brains stuffed full of academics to avoid real life.

You are mistaken if you think agriculture was forced on me. I am too stubborn for that and I love farming! I wanted to learn it and I had to literally force my way out of the university track and into agriculture classes! It has been a hard battle and hard work for me to achieve my current position as an agricultural specialist. Even as a student, I was responsible for the research station in my area, and I had no one to help me, even though I am only 19. (Not everyone was pleasant about that.) Don't worry that I am too conceited; I know I still have a lot to learn. A small group of us will leave Ben Shemen and will be going to the south somewhere to learn more techniques so that we can come back to the north and start our own kibbutz!

As for music lessons, the answer to getting those was "money." Three years ago, I started to sing in the choir. The orchestra lost some members and they needed new people. That's when they offered me music lessons. But since I didn't want to have anything to do with them any more, I declined. That doesn't mean I love the arts any less than before.

Regarding my comment about the hardships of my youth, I didn't mean any offense at the time. What I can see is how easily people get derailed when an obstacle lies in their path. The boys and girls whom I have lived with all this time at Ben Shemen stand tall and strong as oak trees. Even though it was hard, we stayed together and achieved much. We surmounted the difficulty and are stronger for it.

In any case, I am healthy. Please write how Father and Oma are. I so treasure Father's sweet words. I haven't heard from the Sterns and I miss the writing of my cousins. I hope, dear Father, that you got my birthday wishes, and I wish the same for you, Mutti and Oma, and excellent health, now that all of you are together and establishing a new life. May it be the best.

Many regards,
Your Avraham

Kläre put the letter aside and wished with all her heart that she could respond in kind with news of their day-to-day activities, the hardships and the progress. Instead, her letter could only contain the one piece of news. She took up the notice on her desk to read one last time in preparation for the printer and the newspaper tomorrow.

Johanna Ente, (geb. Loewenstein)
b. 21 November, 1868, d. 18 September, 1945

The quotation that should follow, an expression of hope or comfort or of summation of the mourned one's essential quality would not come, did not arise from the sorrow that lay listless on Kläre's heart.

Johanna's death had been peaceful. The evening prior she had been no more or less responsive than at any other time in the last month. Kläre had kissed the soft skin of her cheek and smoothed a steely wisp of hair back from her forehead, and then had gone home to tend to Jakob and supper. The nursing sister had found Johanna dead at the midnight rounds. She had simply slipped the final bonds of bodily life, having given over in spirit long before. This Kläre knew and understood, but she could not keep the grief at bay. For six years the survival of her mother had been at the center of her life, and now she did not know how to relinquish that organizing feature of her days—the vigilance, the intimacy. The victory of having kept Johanna alive became sadly irrelevant in the natural simplicity of her passing.

Erwin had returned with his unit to England, Werner/Avraham was committed to his life in Palestine, and Jakob was still weak and fretful in his first days at home after the months in hospital. *But there is Ansel.* She had phoned the seminary and within a few hours had gotten a message that Ansel would be allowed to attend the funeral tomorrow. Perhaps he could help her navigate these days of the funeral. The smallest seed of comfort settled into Kläre's disturbed spirit. Her bitter tears ceased, and she rose from her desk, at last able to move toward the brief respite of sleep.

28 February 1946

Everything can and will be transformed in life and in art, if we speak the word LOVE without shame . . . In it lies true art."
—Marc Chagall

"Okay. We have it now, ya?" Kläre took her hand from the top of Jakob Kohler's for the tenth time and stood up to knead the strained muscles of her lower back. She surveyed the product of their labors over her husband's shoulder. Together they had signed and notarized ten documents without betraying the severe palsy that undermined Jakob's solitary attempts to write his own signature.

Satisfied, Kläre said brightly, "It's fine, isn't it?"

Jakob attempted to sit a bit straighter. "Ya, it will do." He could muster no more toward their joint goal of resuming his work and restoring some normality to his life— their life.

Kläre bustled the papers into a stack. "So you rest. I will type now the envelopes and take the ones to the post office which we must send." They kept a small schedule, an hour-by-hour plan for the smallest inroads into a life no longer dictated by deprivation and fear.

Soon, Kläre would meet with Ansel. His solitary months at the seminary had drawn to a close, and Kläre had attended his ordination—a solemn but joyful affair, the limits of the British occupation and chronic food shortages notwithstanding. It was held at the beautiful church in Aachen, which had escaped damage in the bombings. Amalie and Ansel's sisters had attended, and Kläre had joined their proud pew, watching as the initiates chanted their vows, the sun streaming through the stained glass windows and dappling their white robes with a jeweled light. Kläre's late train back to Hörde had allowed her to share the meager cakes and ersatz coffee at the reception. For those few hours, she and Amalie had clung to one another, exchanging stories and sympathy and establishing, in the way of women who have known pain, the sharing of a common joy.

While Ansel awaited assignment to his first pulpit, he had time to spend with family. He visited his stepmother and sisters often and Kläre and Jakob even more often. Whenever he had the train fare, he came and helped. It was he who had finished securing what furniture and household goods they had recovered. It was he who had encouraged Kläre to respond positively to the offer from Jakob's former employee, a young attorney who had spent the war in England and who wanted to return to his old post.

What was there to return to? Slowly the calls had come. The first halting attempts to discover what was left of their former lives were being made by returning Jews and other refugees from the labor and concentration camps in the East. Some, like Kläre and Jakob, had been brought back officially by the city of Dortmund. Others were finding their way on their own, individually or in small family groups, drifting into the city like brown autumn leaves drained of color and held together only by the most fragile skeleton of veins and gossamer tissue.

Displaced Germans, locals who had lost their homes and livelihoods to the bombing and the brutality of defeat, also filled the city. Their misery played out alongside that of the gaunt, lifeless trickle of Jews who had survived—Jews who were increasingly seeking out Jakob Kohler to ask for help.

The British attempts to organize relief for the crushing need all around were dogged and well-meaning, if inadequate. German municipalities were quickly granted agency to dispense goods and services that were now arriving, though the occupying forces first had to root out Nazis and their sympathizers.

Kläre and Jakob had heard the speech of the British zone commander on the radio: "We should constantly try to free this government of every Nazi trait and any other aspect that militates against the democratic ideals we fought for . . ."

As issues of property seizure, business loss, and restitution began to be raised, the British discovered in Jakob Kohler one of the few remaining Rechtsanwalts and Notars from the Jewish community in Dortmund. He knew all too well what had happened in the years leading up to the war, and what the community had suffered during the Nazi reign. Erwin's position in the British Army cemented the connections that brought in his father's first clients.

While the clients were few, with proper food and sleep, Jakob's health had seemed to improve, and he had easily hidden his infirmity. Before long, however, it had become noticeable that he couldn't sit in a chair for more than an hour at a time and that he could no longer write on his own.

So Kläre began to assist him. At first she only performed basic secretarial functions in a small corner of the sitting room she'd organized into an office. Then the number of clients grew, the trickle becoming a small but steady stream, and Jakob could no longer keep their stories committed to memory. Kläre began to take notes during meetings. She would not have chosen to do this, but it allowed Jakob to work. Though the stories of their clients brought back painful memories, Kläre did not speak about it.

Jakob, by nature a patient man, and fueled by gratitude for the semblance of usefulness and a return to an ordered life, withstood the humiliation of having to rely on his wife not only for his personal care but now also for the conduct of his legal practice. But when the letter from Hans Heymann had arrived, inquiring about rejoining the practice, Jakob had resisted accepting his offer.

"We manage well enough now, Kläre," he said.

"We do, Jakob. But each day we have more to do, and I am no lawyer. You are only now regaining some health, and Heymann is someone we know and can trust." Kläre had held her breath, and noted how quickly Jakob relented.

On this day in February, Kläre finished tidying Jakob's office space and saw him to his room for an afternoon sleep. She looked forward to meeting Ansel, who was due to arrive on the one o'clock train. He had a surprise for her, he had written. He'd asked her to go to the station and free herself for an afternoon away from home.

Kläre stepped into the cold, crisp air. It excited her to pursue the smallest of adventures on a winter day. She had taken extra care preparing for the outing, using some of a precious stub of lipstick to color her wan cheeks and lips. A package from Ditha and Ernst in America had included a winter coat of rich camel-hair wool, and this Kläre wore, though it had obviously been meant for a much larger woman. She felt safe and warm, all but hidden in the great coat. It still felt like a gift to walk the streets boldly in daylight, her chin high, a smile ready for even the most bedraggled passerby.

Barriers and piles of debris obstructed the way down Virschow Strasse, though the worst of the demolition had been cleared in the nine months since the war's end. Gone also were the roving bands of refugees and displaced persons. The Russians in particular had been frightening—violent in their looting and desperate to avoid being sent back to Russia to what they knew would be worse than what they suffered in Germany. The first signs of reconstruction now appeared in the form of neat stacks of reclaimed stone. Kläre stepped carefully around them as she made her way to the train station.

She immediately spotted Ansel on the platform, and waved her arm until she caught his attention. Her cheeks colored a shade deeper than even the winter air and brisk walk had produced. In a moment Ansel stood before her, waiting, as always, for her to reach up and embrace his tall, lanky body, bent low and passive. She gave him gentle but firm hugs that she always held a moment longer than necessary in recognition of the deficit of warmth and touching that still needed replenishing in the boy.

She held his large face in her hands. "You look good!" she exclaimed happily. "Have you more to eat now?"

"Ya, it gets a little easier. We have more food coming into the town and the seminary both," Ansel replied. "And you? How are you two doing?"

"We are so lucky. Jakob has more work, and the municipality allows him a greater allotment of food. Next week will come Hans Heymann from England to discuss his return to work with Jakob. I'm really not an attorney! And not much of a secretary either." Kläre knew she was chattering. She happily matched two steps to Ansel's one as he linked his arm into hers and they exited the train station. He steered her toward the Haupt Strasse.

"Where are we going now?" Kläre asked, her eyes shining.

"It isn't far now, come along. Do you remember I told you of my friend Theodor Jager? He is a fellow priest with the Church of St. Martin here in Dortmund. He has interest as I do in the Hebrew Bible and the history of Judaism. We studied sometimes together when he came to the seminary to teach."

"Yes, I remember your speaking of him." Kläre was listening intently, aware that the otherwise cheerless February afternoon had closed in a bubble of contentment around her and the young priest.

"He is something of an art aficionado," Ansel said. "When the local offices and residences of Nazi officers were raided, the British found great stashes of artwork . . . much of it no doubt stolen from people sent off to the camps." At this, Ansel's voice dropped and his shoulders stooped, a look of misery stealing, shroud-like, across his face. "Jager means to see as much of it returned to rightful owners as possible."

Ansel turned to her, and Kläre saw in his eyes that she need say nothing; there was pain and anguish there to match that in her own heart. Ansel had anticipated the blackness of her thoughts. Where had this knowing, loving understanding come from? No matter, it brought tears to her eyes, and she squeezed the arm on which she hung with fierce gratitude.

"Anyway, he is given the job to sort and identify the work. He has something special to show us! Here we are." They had arrived at a side entrance to the Church of St. Martin. Kläre hesitated, but Ansel gently pulled her into the side chapel, empty except for the waiting priest. He was short, only a quarter of a meter taller than Kläre, and his thick, sandy hair framed his face in an elegant style. With a small shock, Kläre realized he was wearing a toupee, but she did not betray her amusement. He wore spectacles that were large and dark, making his enormous blue eyes look even larger. His jacket and collar were of fine material and well tailored. He looked altogether more like a curator than a priest, an impression made stronger by the contents of the small room into which, after warm greetings, they were led.

Soft light flowed into the office of Pastor Jager through leaded windows, and Kläre stood for a moment inside the door, waiting for her eyes to adjust. Carefully hung paintings covered the simple, whitewashed walls of the room. There were nearly a dozen of them, all by the same artist. Astonishment grew to thrill as Kläre recognized the work of Marc Chagall, whose exhibit in Berlin she had heard about, and whose single works she had seen before the war. Here were ten paintings, rich colors bursting from the canvasses—bold figures, some portrait-like, others suspended above scenes of villages. The visual feast of vibrancy and inventive composition, fused with nostalgia, exuded a spirit of fantasy and a palpable spirituality. The world of feeling and wonder swept Kläre up as if she rode in one of the zeppelins that had floated above the cafés years ago to the delight of the people below.

Ansel and Pastor Jager spoke in low, excited tones about one of the paintings, which depicted Jesus on the cross wearing a loincloth made from a Jewish prayer shawl. The suffering Christ was surrounded by scenes of the persecution of Jews throughout the century: Russian pogroms, the burning of a German synagogue, the stealing away of townspeople with their sacred scrolls. The sounds of the priests' talking faded, and the mists and smoke of the painting's night fire surrounded Kläre. At the bottom of the canvas, a woman clutching her baby appeared to stare straight out at her, and Kläre thought she could hear her ask, "How must I save them?" An answer flew to Kläre from a place of deep knowing.

"With a strong heart," she said quietly. Firelight, moonlight, and the sighing of misery and wind tumbled the other figures in the painting through a whorl of confusion, but Kläre locked eyes with the young mother until she resumed her place in the corner of the canvas.

"Kläre . . . Kläre! Are you all right?" Ansel's concerned expression came into focus beside her as she returned to the reality of Jager's study. She felt unsteady until she'd sat down and Jager had brought her some water. After repeated questions, Kläre smiled at the anxious young men.

"I'm fine. Really, quite fine. You were both saying about Chagall something interesting, no? I quite like these works. I'm afraid I was a bit overwhelmed with . . . their beauty and their power."

Ansel stayed next to Kläre as she listened to Jager's enthusiastic narrative about the paintings. An hour later, their private showing ended, and Ansel insisted on accompanying Kläre all the way to her apartment, murmuring polite responses to her comments when necessary, his words punctuated by thoughtful, watchful pauses through which Kläre felt him reaching into her very soul for an explanation of what had happened.

She served Jakob and Ansel small cakes and weak coffee, and then it was time for the younger man to catch his train. He allowed Kläre to fuss over his coat and scarf, and accepted an oilpaper packet of bread and sausage for the train ride.

"I will come back soon, yes?" Ansel said, watching Kläre closely.

"Yes, of course, and thank you so much for the surprise today," Kläre responded.

"God blesses us in mysterious ways, I think. You were given a shock today, no? But perhaps also a calling."

Kläre nodded thoughtfully. "Yes, perhaps."

"Stay well, Tante Kläre," Ansel said as he hugged her.

"You also." She reached up and kissed his large cheek. "Until we see each other again."

The images of the Chagall paintings returned to Kläre for days and nights after the showing in Pastor Jager's study. She experienced repeatedly the soaring into the air of the fanciful figures as she dreamed at night or in quiet moments during her day. She would be striding purposefully toward the market when the images—of the perfect symbiosis of lovers, the burdened face of a rabbi that burned with internal light, the joyous colors, the whimsical animals—would arise. Most often she remembered the painting of the crucifixion. Images of the frightened townspeople soaring above and the inferno of fires, the smoke and mist, would rise in her mind at night as she tried to sleep or when she entered a shop filled with strangers. She could always see most clearly the figure of the young woman and her child. Kläre realized that she had answered the woman's question, *How must I save them?* but now had to answer her own heart. She began a letter to Werner.

My dearest Avraham,

It is still so difficult for me to call you by your new name, but I shall become accustomed to it I am sure. We received your letter of 12 January. It took only five weeks! You are very wise to realize that Oma hadn't the strength any longer to adjust to our freedom and return to Hörde. I was able to make her comfortable until the last. I enclose a separate letter from Father. He has difficulty now with writing so he mostly dictates to me. He begins to return to some work as a lawyer and notary. He isn't well enough to do it alone, so I help, but also a former associate from his office will return from England and perhaps help us.

You said in your letter that you are mostly "a threesome." Is it still the boy Avery and the girl Hannah? Imagine our surprise when her parents wrote to us last week! They have returned to Düsseldorf, where her father will resume his medical practice. They plan to make a visit to us and tell us all about life in Palestine, which is so nice of them.

I saw this week an extraordinary collection of paintings by the Frenchman Marc Chagall. Ansel Beckmann took me to his friend, another priest here at the Church of St. Martin. This man has been given charge of all manner of recovered paintings taken by Nazi officers or found in abandoned buildings. He first asked if we were missing any work and when I told him the names of our paintings, he assured me he would keep an eye out for them. I especially miss the Liebermann of the woman seated in a courtyard. I miss her quiet and her elegance.

In any case, he then brought us to his office and there was a collection of paintings like I've never seen. I must say the power of Chagall's work quite overcame me. One painting in particular seemed to pull at me. You will think it particularly odd, but it was a picture of Jesus on the cross, but represented as a Jew, with Jews all around him in different scenes of persecution. I think I must have had a near fainting spell, but I actually felt as if I were flying into the painting and speaking to a woman who was clutching her baby.

I told her that following her heart would save her, and then I missed you so painfully, my boy. Through all that we suffered, holding you in my heart kept me going, and now I long to see you again, and put to the test of my eyes my imagining of looking up to your face instead of down. I wish to see all that you have built and accomplished.

So please, try again to work on a visa for us to visit. Perhaps you are right that Father cannot adjust to the harder life there, but since you cannot leave, I must try to come to you instead. We don't have reliable news of the events in Palestine, so your letters are of great interest. Sometimes it seems safer and sometimes more dangerous for you. I see that it is just one more excitement for the young people building new communities there. How ironic that just as the British are putting this part of Germany back together, they are causing difficulty for you in Palestine. The Arabs, I confess, I don't understand much about at all.

There! Enough of your pleading mother. The news from England is that your brother has found a sweetheart. Her name is Betty and he sounds quite serious about her. Perhaps he is writing you directly by now. He couldn't write easily in the army but he is now established back in the landscape business of the people who took him in during the war.

Food is still very scarce here, though each day is a little better. We look forward to spring, when the farmers will again be able to plant.

Perhaps I will do a little salad garden for us here at the back of the apartment. No one cares for it now, and maybe it will be all right if I put in some plants.

I worry that you had such a bad flu, but I suppose you have taken good care of yourself for a long time now without your worrying mother. Write again soon, my dear son, and send my regards to all of your friends. I look forward to meeting them myself someday soon.

Many kisses,

Mutti

Kläre sat back and straightened her shoulders. It had been a long day. She read through the letter in front of her one more time. It satisfied her, so she folded it into the airmail envelope. There was more to say—much more—but she sensed that this would be enough for one letter to Werner, whose own letters had the jaunty, racing quality of the driven young. She missed the quieter, more contemplative observations that had sprung from the uncannily wise younger Werner—but then, he was no longer a sheltered twelve-year-old but a young man of nineteen, and experienced beyond his years. She would have liked to tell him more of Ansel, a boy not many years older than himself and a priest, no less, who somehow seemed to know a great deal about things which he himself had not experienced.

Kläre's thoughts returned to a dream she had had several nights before in which she found herself floating, anchored with something that felt enduring amidst the upheaval, in a Chagall-like world of topsy-turvy symbols and figures, menace sharing the timeless space with whimsy. In her dream, the figure of Christ, which had so centered and lit up the canvas in Jager's office, had awoken and descended to her in the corner of the painting previously occupied by the young woman. Startled, she realized that he had taken the form of Ansel, and he drew her into his embrace. Even now, in the gathering darkness of her apartment, she felt the flood of warmth that had come in her dream. It was passion of a sort she had not felt in so long she had nearly forgotten its source. What she felt was love.

29 September 1946

When Kläre answered the knock on her door, she could see immediately that Hans Heymann did not recognize her. She'd become used to former neighbors' and shopkeepers' initial looks of noncommittal politeness, followed by the shock of recognition and the attendant embarrassment, ending swiftly with an overabundance of enthusiasm. Though much stronger and healthier now, Kläre was still thin, and her honey-colored curls were shot with grey and pulled sedately in a bun at the back of her neck rather than dressed in waves around her face. Attention to her clothing and toilet might come again; for now, though, it was enough to wear clean clothes and continue to establish a normal life. It took but a moment for Heymann to recover, and by then Kläre had invited him into the sitting room, where the delicacies of real coffee and homemade cakes were waiting.

"Are you much shocked to see Germany in this state?" Kläre asked after Heymann had adjusted his trim, well-dressed body into a formal pose on the chair across from Jakob. She may just as well have asked the same question regarding Jakob's condition. Kläre noted Heymann's efforts not to stare at her husband, whose tremor was only somewhat concealed by the artful placement of his hand under a heavy book in his lap.

"In a way, yes, of course, although London is also more or less in ruins," he replied.

"What made you think of coming back? And will your wife and children want to return?" Kläre asked, though she'd surmised already that the young lawyer was unable to practice law in his broken English in a foreign judicial system.

"I had heard that the British were making initial efforts to repatriate Rechtsanwalts in order to help with the resettlement of Jews and other refugees, and thought I'd investigate, as peddling furs doesn't appeal to me." As an afterthought he added hurriedly, "Though I'm most grateful to the Meler family for giving me the opportunity, and I've made a decent living." Kläre looked at him expectantly, and he continued cautiously, "I won't be moving my family back to Germany. Helga won't hear of it, and the children have learned English and are doing well in school." He spoke directly to Jakob now: "If it should work out for us to work together, I propose to live here for several days at a time, and then return to London at the weekend or every other weekend as necessary."

"By aeroplane?" Kläre asked, "Can such a thing be done?"

"Yes, actually, there are a good number of flights from London these days! I became quite the aviation bug during the war; I volunteered at the local airbase. I believe the government is eager enough to retain our services, and that it will be possible to make the commute. There will continue to be a great number of flights available as long as the British remain here."

Kläre did not miss Heymann's use of "our services," and she was grateful for it.

She was trying not to conduct this interview for Jakob, but she had to feel comfortable with Heymann's intentions if the arrangement was to work. In fact she liked him. He was pleasant, well-spoken, and confident, and did not speak too aggressively or dismissively. He could take over much of the public face of the law practice—something Kläre could not do—yet he was clearly considerate of Jakob's dignity.

"I am interested to assume as much or as little of your work as you feel you need me to," Heymann said. "Under the circumstances, I expect I could do more of the court and government work, while you perhaps could do more of the local client work. But I'm most eager to hear what your thoughts are."

Kläre turned to Jakob, who had all this time been studying the young man. He of course knew Heymann; he had hired him as an associate, but had lost him a year later when the Nazi rise to power had convinced the younger man of the need to leave Germany. Jakob appeared to be preparing to speak when Heymann surprised them both with a question of his own: "Why have you stayed?"

There it was, asked gently but clearly. This question, in one form or another, had been asked of Kläre repeatedly in the last eighteen months. It first came in the early days of liberation, after their starved bodies had been fed and cleaned and the Joint Distribution officials in Theresienstadt had addressed their immediate medical needs. The question had come again when they'd accepted the city of Dortmund's offer to resettle them, and had returned to the destruction and deprivation suffered by the local populace. Werner had asked them this in his first letters, fervently offering to pursue visas for them to go to Palestine. Erwin's offers to bring them to England had been less enthusiastic, as if he knew that he had never been, would never be, equipped to help his parents surmount the difficulties of establishing a new life. Her brother Ernst had actually succeeded in getting her mother a visa to America, though only weeks before she died. He'd then offered to try the same for Kläre and Jakob.

Each time, Kläre had tried to present Jakob's dogged insistence that he could not adjust to another life as more than the failure of spirit of a sick and disheartened man, but that was in large measure exactly the reason they were here. She would have gone to Palestine—would go still, if Jakob were willing. Increasingly, however, he was not only unwilling but also unable. His smooth forehead and proud bearing still called upon her love and loyalty, and she hadn't the energy herself to force a showdown.

Heymann looked from Kläre to Jakob.

"If we can but establish even a small normal life, and do our bit of useful good here, that will be enough," Jakob said, his words quiet but strong. With a lawyer's care, he had intimated with his simple, hopeful statement a contrast with the long, chaotic years of evil through which they had come.

Kläre smiled at her husband and turned the remainder of the interview over to him. "Shall I get some more warm coffee while you two discuss arrangements?"

The afternoon post brought three letters, and after preparing and cleaning up supper, Kläre settled into her chair to read them. First was a letter from Erwin in England. He asked after their health and reported that he'd had a letter from Werner, which he'd enclosed. He then complained at some length, first about his job, which he hated and planned to leave as soon as he had another, and then about the moods of his girlfriend, Betty.

Kläre put the letter down and felt a pang of guilt at her lack of sympathy for this son for whom life seemed always to hold more problems than pleasure. He had worked dutifully on their behalf in the first months of their return to Hörde, but had seemed to slip back into a civilian life of little inspiration upon arriving back in England. He had sent a photo of Betty, who was classically pretty, but all his descriptions of her had been empty of interest or true vitality. The one note that Betty had herself written to Kläre had been self-deprecating and needlessly defensive. Yet it seemed as if Erwin would choose to marry this girl. When Kläre spoke in her own letters about visiting England, Erwin demurred, citing shortages, his intense work schedule, the lowly rooming house in which he lived. He wrote that it would be better to wait.

Hungrily, Kläre took up the enclosed letter from Werner and smiled as he gallantly sparred about his brother's sweetheart and then bubbled forth with more news of his latest agricultural feats and adventures.

Finally, Kläre read the letter from America, containing Ditha's colorful narrative of Margaret's wedding. Kläre could scarcely believe that Margaret, only twenty-one, had married. A young German refugee from Munich had first approached Ditha at a German self-help club dance, thinking the beautiful woman his own age. When gently apprised of her status as a matron with an eighteen-year-old daughter, he asked, undaunted, to meet the daughter, and had courted her ever since, despite her father's thinly veiled disapproval. Walter Rosenfelder came from a Bavarian Jewish family, and Kläre's brother was not above the old regional snobberies of German society. The Entes and Ditha's family were "high" Germans from Berlin and Hamburg. The Rosenfelders were from Munich and the surrounding farm villages, and considered less cultured and sophisticated. But Walter was persistent and obviously a bright young man. Energetic and entertaining, he had spirited Margaret out of the captivity of her father's household, and with what little money they'd managed to put by, Ditha and Ernst had held a beautiful wedding, flying a German rabbi in from New York to perform the ceremony.

Frieda, Ditha wrote, had baked for days, and the ballroom of a fine hotel in Detroit had been the scene of the June festivities. Kläre sorely wished to have been there. Tears for the chasm between the life of her brother and her own filled her eyes, but she hadn't time now to cry. She rose, changed into her house shoes, and drew down the sitting room shades before making her way to Jakob's room to prepare him for the night. When she finished, she would pack for her trip to Brussels. At long last she had arranged a visit to Trude.

A priest had hidden Trude and Rudi in the countryside near Brussels during the war years. Their daughters, Edith and Helga, had gone to a Catholic boarding school and been protected by its network of sisters, who had arranged a foster home for them. Rudi had been taken away twice to work camps in Germany and France. Each time, through cunning and bribery, he had managed to free himself. Trude had suffered poverty, occasional hunger, and the fear and uncertainty of her husband's detainment, but they had survived.

Trude had come to Germany once since Kläre's return from Theresienstadt. Erwin had secured a special pass from the British Army so that Trude could see her mother in the hospital. Kläre had still been living at the displaced persons' camp. Seeing Trude had produced a mixture of longing, relief, and strangeness that highlighted the gulf that now separated their once fully connected lives. How could Kläre tell Trude, her closest sister, what she had seen, what had happened to her, what she had done to save and be saved?

During the visit, Trude had clung to Kläre, had wept at her mother's bedside, and had then tried to bring cheer through lighthearted reminisces. Kläre saw that Trude feared the darkness that lay over her sister like an inky veil, and she had not probed or asked to be brought under that veil. Instead, Trude sang to her mother in her sweet, high voice and brought comfort to them all. After two days, she had returned to her family and their struggles.

As the months went by, the sisters had written to each other and even occasionally phoned when that became possible. Trude chattered about the girls but mentioned Rudi less and less, and became quiet when Kläre asked after him. To be sure, the family had all expressed their collective dismay at the aggressive personality of Rudi Stern at one time or another. Kläre had never discovered exactly what went wrong between Rudi and her brother Ernst, but they had never gotten along.

Then Johanna died. Kläre would never forget the conversation with Trude. She had gotten permission to use a telephone in the bureau that contracted with Jakob. Trude's priest had a telephone, and allowed her liberal use of it. Kläre had called on the evening of Johanna's death, and eventually reached Trude. She imparted her news and the sisters wept over the distance with each other.

"We arranged to bury Mutti next to Father," Kläre reported tearfully. "The cemetery was nearly destroyed, making the burial difficult, but one of Erwin's soldier friends helped us get the necessary permissions. We made the funeral Thursday, to give you time to come . . ."

Silence opened a vacuum at the other end of the phone line.

"Klärchen, I don't know . . . I'm not sure." Trude spoke haltingly.

"Trude, I can give you the train fare. You can stay here with us."

"No it's not that. It's just that Rudi . . . He doesn't . . . He has said there are no more visits to Germany."

"But it's safe now. You needn't have special permissions any longer. I will meet you directly at the station and—"

"Kläre, he has gotten so difficult about the family," Trude interrupted, speaking in a painful rush. "I cannot understand why, now, but he blames Ernst, and all the family, for losing the business and having nothing here to start with. I know it's crazy, but he feels so violently about it. I can't . . . I can't." She was sobbing now and had difficulty speaking.

Kläre could not process what she was hearing. She could not bear to understand what her sister was saying. After everything, must she now lose Trude? Anger burst like a dynamite blast from her chest, and she pulled the telephone receiver to her breast with both her hands as she tried to suck breath back into her body. She looked wildly around the room for anything to stabilize her. Her hand flew out to the arm of the chair behind her and she fell into it.

"Hallo? Kläre? Hallo?" Trude sounded panicked now. Slowly, Kläre pulled the receiver back to her ear.

"Ya, I am here." Kläre's voice was small and tight. The room cleared, but her throat burned with the effort to speak. "It's okay. We can manage it. Give Rudi some time."

"I love you Klärchen," Trude whimpered. "I'm so sorry. I don't know what to do. I want to come, but I can't if he says no."

"It's okay. I will phone you again afterward, all right?"

"Okay . . . Kisses."

"Kisses," Kläre replied, and the conversation was finished.

In the following months, Kläre had written and spoken to her sister whenever she could, but there had been no further mention of Rudi or of visits between the sisters. Then suddenly, two weeks ago, Trude had written that Kläre should come to Brussels.

It was a long train ride for a two-day visit, and there had been a lot of arranging to have Jakob cared for, but the September day was lovely, and Kläre was happy to be going to see her sister. Venlo, Maastricht, the border crossing to Belgium, and then Leuven passed, film-like, through the window of the train. The specter of a village church, once imposing in the landscape, crossed the screen of Kläre's window, only a curved staircase rising to nowhere left among broken graves in the churchyard. Memories of her last journey to see Trude in Brussels floated through Kläre like a fog. The war and the horror it brought were still to come at that time, and the beautiful countryside had showed no signs of distress. Now, the harvest hayricks dotted the fields with the promise of returning prosperity, but they were surrounded by grim reminders of the bombings and fighting that still scarred the landscape.

Kläre was surprised again, upon arriving in the city, at the beauty of Brussels. The industrious Belgians had restored many of the buildings already, and everywhere were signs of vitality. Trude brought Edith and Helga to the station, and Kläre was struck by how much they'd grown. They were young women now, these two girls who so closely mimicked Kläre and Trude's own relationship: Edith was the energetic, intelligent, and practical sister while Helga was the beauty and the free spirit. They bundled Kläre off into the waiting taxi and showed her the sights along the way, the girls bubbling over with news of their lives and questions about their cousins.

When they reached the small apartment that the Sterns had moved into several months ago, there was a festive dinner waiting for them. Trude's eyes shone as Kläre complimented her creative menu and table setting. Shortages and financial limitation still governed the lifestyle of most people in Brussels, and Rudi Stern had not regained his place in the furniture business. He worked only as a simple salesman.

Afternoon passed into evening. Conversations flew like swallows in the darkening sky among the four women. Gently, Trude and her daughters asked more about the years of the war. Kläre knew to tell only what the most sensitive among them could tolerate, and therefore left much unsaid. Even so, tears flowed, and in turn the small and large losses of their experiences in Belgium were shared.

When at last the girls rose to clear away the coffee, Kläre asked her sister, "When will Rudi come home for his supper?"

Trude cast her eyes down and sighed heavily. When she looked up there were tears where before there had been sparkle. "He's gone away for several days. He won't be here during your visit."

"Trudchen, does he know that I am here?"

"No, and he mustn't. I know it seems crazy but he still is so angry about the family . . ."

Kläre fixed her expression; as pain seared through her, she fought back the tears that rose from the inexhaustible well deep inside her.

30 February 1947

By the reach of the Great Hand, he will be relieved from solemn grief through a gentle death.
—Psalm 144:7

The stroke had violated the symmetry of Jakob Kohler's pleasing aquiline features. His right jaw had wilted, the closed eye above it drooped into lines of what had been, even at seventy, a firm cheek. Kläre stood rooted to the spot where the morning sun lay in a pool on the bedside floor, the jewel reds and blues of the Persian rug lit around her. Jakob was gone. That she could see immediately. No death mask of residual struggle or torment, no transfigured mantle of peace graced the face of her husband. He was simply, irrevocably gone, as though the stroke had siphoned his very soul through the drawn folds of his sagging face.

For the moment before shock set in, before the soft rubbing of the lamp at the center of her heart set free the genie of her grief, Kläre stood as though paralyzed herself. Then tears came, and they fell unheeded as she lifted Jakob's cool hand in both of hers. The stroke had accomplished with merciful speed and totality what nerve gas, years of battle, disease, indignity, and suffering at the hands of Nazis had been unable to bring about. The struggle to keep and care for was over. For long moments more, Kläre could only weep in small, choking sobs as she stood and held her husband's hand.

As from a far away place, the voices of "must do" and "manage" took root in her consciousness, forcing the genie back into the bottle at her core. Kläre turned to the hall and the telephone. Whom to call? Momentary panic gripped Kläre. *There is no one here!* Erwin had made many of the calls when Johanna died, but he was back in England. It was still early there; perhaps he had not yet gone to work.

Kläre sat heavily on the seat of the phone bench as the operator rang the number. Betty was newly pregnant. Kläre scarcely knew her and already they had married and were expecting a child. Kläre prayed that Erwin would answer. The funeral home—yes, she remembered the name, as well as the awkwardness of their not knowing the customs for burying Jews.

"Hallo?" answered a sleepy and querulous voice.

"*Ya, Betty? Is Erwin da? Here ist Mutter.*" Kläre spoke loudly and distinctly, as though to a child. Betty understood no German, and Kläre's new English failed her. To her great relief, Kläre heard the rustle of the phone being put down and Betty's voice calling to Erwin.

"Ya, Mutti?" Erwin's weary voice already held the knowledge of unwelcome news.

"Ach, Erwin . . . Papa has had a stroke. He's—he's gone." Kläre was losing the struggle to keep the stranglehold of tears from her voice. "Just now . . . He's gone."

Kläre heard the depth of the sigh that escaped from her son. He must have held the phone away as he told his wife, "My father has died."

Kläre could not understand the whole of Betty's response, but heard the fretfulness of her voice, along with the words "have to leave" and "feeling so poorly," and then, more clearly, Erwin's response: "Yes, of course I must go. You needn't come if . . . Never mind, we will discuss this later."

Then he was speaking to Kläre again. "Mutti, I'll come as soon as I can get an airplane. Will you telegraph Werner?"

"Ya, of course. You come when you can." Kläre replaced the phone receiver and tried to breathe again.

Ansel returned from his interview in Dülken to two versions of the same message, one from Amalie and the other from Kläre. Jakob Kohler was dead of a stroke. Could he come to the small funeral in two days' time? Could he perhaps say something?

The delay in his return meant he had only a day until the funeral. Ansel sought and received permission to go and spoke briefly on the telephone to Kläre, whose tearful gratitude pulled at his heart. What must he say tomorrow? He found the prayers for the dead from the Jewish tradition. Now he must find words to bring comfort to Kläre. But how? This would be his job often, to bring comfort to the bereaved, but in this instance he found it hard to stand apart from Kläre's suffering. He did not understand the power in his connection to her, a commonality of spirit that he did not question and had no desire to resist. He sat down in his room at the seminary that he would soon leave for his first pulpit in Dülken. He would write a letter to Kläre from his heart, and see what words arose.

My dear Tante Kläre,

The great sorrow that you and your dear sons have suffered weighs upon us today. I know very well how impossible it is to be comforted over such a loss, in view of the fact that the death of such a loved one creates an irreparable wound in our inner life. All words of consolation ring like that much noise next to the inner feelings. We have ultimately only ourselves for comfort. The strength of our own hearts is all there is to combat the enormous pain that always and again storms within us.

The manifold darknesses of this life are for us indescribable; you can certainly confirm that with all that you have had to suffer. But perhaps you are also, in your life, even with the pain you must experience at this moment, illuminated with a higher sense of your thread of fate. This light shines out from you perhaps only for seconds at a time, but it does so with enough certainty that we who are in the room of your heart feel its glow. And when we remember in difficult hours that blessed certainty, so may it bring from our hidden, beloved Source a healing peace to settle in us.

As humans, we feel our pain deeply, feel it with the utmost sensitivity, drilling to our very core and draining us of our strength. But if we undertake the quest earnestly to feel also our own light, we find that we don't lie down and die but instead draw on a hidden wealth which no pain and no fate tears down. And when we embrace this inner treasure it will be to our everlasting comfort.

Perhaps in my words, which hold my honest conviction, you can find your way in your connection to your dear Jakob. Nothing would give me more joy than to restore the whole of your peace of mind and deepen your certainty of spirit.

To you, dear Tante Kläre, and your sons, I give my wish for peace of heart going forward.

Your Ansel

Ansel shivered as though recovering from a trance. He had written a truth that stunned him even as it filled him with joy. He had put into words his recognition of Kläre's God-given gift of spirit. He prepared for bed then, knowing that he had the words he needed for the morning.

The weeks after Jakob's death were filled with lonely decisions that Kläre made in dull succession throughout the days. The flat, which only recently had begun to feel like a home, now felt vacant with the sensation of one recently dead. Jakob's presence remained in the arrangement of chairs, in the pipe rack on the sitting room table, in the bolsters, pillows, and the cashmere throw that had warmed him over the cold winter. Kläre felt no urgency to the sorting, no deadline to the packing and disposal of his possessions.

The March weather was by turns stormy and brilliant, with the transitions full of white and grey clouds roiling across the sky. A Sunday came when all that needed to be done had been done, and only a visit from Ansel, whose new position in Dülken was keeping him busy, broke the emptiness of Kläre's day.

The warm and sunny afternoon called forth the scent of wet earth coming to life. Kläre prepared her special apple *kuchen* and set the sitting room coffee service with care. Her weariness gave way to the anticipation of Ansel's visit.

The young priest arrived and wordlessly drew Kläre into a soft embrace. She remained there for several long moments before pulling away to smile at him through her tears.

Ansel hungrily ate and drank, and then sat back and asked earnestly, "Tante Kläre, what will you now do? Have you thought to go to live with Erwin in England or perhaps with Ernst in the United States? Do you wish to go even to Werner in Palestine? Will you not want to go to your family now?" When Kläre did not answer immediately, he rushed to add, "I can help you . . ."

Kläre studied him. His sincere questions touched her, but why did he ask these things now, today? Was he so eager to relinquish the job of assisting her? Had she been too much of a burden for him?

Her thoughts must have shown in her demeanor, because Ansel did not wait for an answer before saying, "I should miss you terribly if you went, but perhaps you will want . . ." His strong, well-trained voice faltered then, and he reached forward to cover Kläre's folded hands with his large ones.

She answered in a firm but low voice, "You are very good to ask, Ansel, but I cannot do such a thing now." Her voice became softer still, so that Ansel had to lean forward to hear her. "I do not wish to make another change just now. I am fifty-two years old. I've . . . I'm so weary."

A smile filtered through the look of concern on Ansel's face and he began to speak, a note of eagerness in his voice. "Then come to me. Come to live with me. I need a hausfrau in the rectory at Dülken to look after me—someone with whom I have a real connection, someone with whom I can have a real conversation. And perhaps you need someone to watch out for you also," he rushed on, "perhaps you need someone to care for." He stopped then, an achingly pure look of pleading and conviction written on his young face.

Though fatigued, and somewhat dazed at this new idea, Kläre could not help smiling at Ansel's youthful ardor. "Ansel, I can not imagine . . ." She chose her words carefully. "A Jewish woman keeping house for a young priest? Would that not be unseemly? Would the Church allow it?"

Ansel thought seriously for a moment. "I will go to the bishop," he said finally. "If I obtain permission, will you then accept?" His brown eyes were full of excitement.

Kläre answered slowly, taking in a deep breath. "Yes—yes, I think I would." She was stunned by her own words, but a broad smile lit her face. The first ember of a joyful future began to glow at her center.

On a cold day a week later, Kläre and Ansel went together to the bishop's offices. Kläre wore a grey suit, a small hat, and no ornament. Ansel shepherded her into the outer rooms of the bishop's office. She sat on an ancient settee, he on an oak-framed chair to one side of her. Kläre twisted her handkerchief in her lap to calm her nerves. Ansel seemed absolutely at ease and confident. *He already is at home in this world!* Kläre thought as the young priest offered her yet another reassuring smile. *What am I doing?* Before she had a chance to answer her own questions, the door to the inner offices opened and a short, dignified cleric emerged with a sheaf of papers.

"Frau Kohler, Father Beckmann, good morning. I am Father Lerner. Please follow me." The priest shot a quizzical look at Kläre as Ansel rose and moved to her side.

They entered a study, well appointed with a massive desk of mahogany, walls full of beautifully bound books, and a kneeling bench in front of a small altar. A simple but evocative crucifix hung on the wall. A vase of the spring's first crocuses stood in the center of a table by tall windows through which light poured.

When Kläre had finished surveying the room, she found the bishop's secretary studying her more openly. "Frau Kohler," he said, "you must know that it is quite an unusual request that Father Beckmann and you have made." His voice was calm and steady, and Kläre could read nothing to fear in his face. "I see you are from Hörde . . . I grew up in Hörde, and had a classmate there by the name of Kläre Ente. She was very kind to me and especially to my sister, who was a bit slow. She would, no doubt, be the sort of good soul who would care well for a fine young priest, would she not?"

Thus, by pure chance—springing up in the sorrow of Kläre's life like a woodland flower through dead leaves—it was Kläre's childhood classmate Gustav Lerner who had become the bishop's secretary and would process their appeal. The father promised to confer with the Bishop of Paderborn and see quickly to the approval of the arrangement. Kläre did not trust her hand to hold the cup of coffee that he offered to her.

In the quiet of the light-filled study, the priests went on to speak of the initial details: a change in household allowance, the monthly stipend to be paid to Kläre for her services. As they finished with a plan to discuss further details at a later time, Father Lerner turned again to Kläre.

"I have asked Father Beckmann to make an appointment for you with Frau Schild here in the rectory at Paderborn," he said kindly. "She has cared for the bishop, and me, for many years, and will answer any questions you may have regarding the details of a priest's household. I trust you will find her advice informative."

"I thank you for your help, Father Lerner," Kläre said. She at once understood that he meant for her to learn how to run a Christian household—a Catholic priest's household. She turned to Ansel, whose beaming face shone with contained pleasure, the great brown pools of his eyes full of contentment. Kläre relaxed into the embrace of the serenity that filled the air around them.

31 April 1947

Two weeks later, as if in a dream, Kläre Kohler moved to the small, solid rectory in Dülken and established a household with Ansel Beckmann. They had chosen to move nearly all of Kläre's furniture there, as Ansel had little and the rectory had a hall, a sitting room, a dining alcove, and a study on the main floor, with three bedrooms on the second floor. The day of the move was a dreary one, and though the rectory looked out over the main park at the front, and St. Cornelius Church over the back garden, the thoroughfare was a busy one, and the movers' truck had to be squeezed into a spot two houses down.

Kläre arrived just as Ansel was returning from morning Mass. His first Easter at St. Cornelius, just a week ago, had been a great success. Kläre had gone to the morning Mass and was astonished at the beauty of the gothic sanctuary, the geometric colors of the newly replaced stained glass windows with jeweled facets blessing the morning light in patterns on the stone floors.

Today was the Saturday before the second Sunday of Easter and Ansel arrived full of energy and excitement for the task ahead.

"Tante Kläre," he exclaimed, animation bringing color to his pale cheeks, "isn't this a wonderful day? You come today to live with me and we begin together a wonderful life."

After speaking to the movers, Ansel pulled Kläre into the house. He ceremoniously took her coat and hung it not in the guest hall closet but in the family closet next to the kitchen door, and then began consulting her on the placement of furniture and of the boxes of fragile objects being carried in by the movers. It took several hours, but eventually the last of the heavy footfalls of the movers departed, and Ansel ushered Kläre to the newly arrived dining table, where he seated her and brought in a delicious cold supper prepared by the local woman he engaged to clean and cook. Kläre's own dishes were still packed in the boxes that lined the dining room wall, but Ansel took special care to set the table decorously with his own small set of plates and glasses.

"Tonight we have a fine wine," Ansel proclaimed as he poured the late-harvest riesling into Kläre's glass.

Kläre proposed a toast. The marking of momentous occasions with a formal toast had been the habit of the Ente family for as long as Kläre could remember. The thought of her family, gone and dispersed, sent a shiver of panic through her. What would they think of her? Her brother and sisters were each carefully reproducing in new countries the fine, sophisticated family lives they had all enjoyed in Germany. She, meanwhile, had come alone to live with and care for a Catholic priest. One day she would explain to them. The panic passed and in a strong voice Kläre declared, "To you, Ansel, who have so welcomed me into your life. I wish for us a life of health and comfort . . . and of peace."

"And to you, dear Kläre, I offer the prayer of thanks to the God of us all who brought us both to this day to celebrate a new life together. *Baruch Atah Adonai Eloheinu Melech Ha-Olam Shehehchiyahnu vekiyamanu vehegianu lazman ha-zeh,*" Ansel said, his face shining.

Kläre closed her eyes as the faces of her grandfather and grandmother, and then of Leo Baeck, floated up in her memory, their lips chanting this iconic Hebrew prayer of recognition and thanks. Kläre would forever remember the first time she had heard Leo Baeck recite the prayer with his explanation that even in the camp there were occasions to mark with thanks. It was the first time that Kläre had understood in the depths of her spirit the power to mitigate life's setbacks with gratitude and blessing that was inherent in the faith of her forefathers. There, the embracing of contradiction, the parceling of pain and hope, had been a key to her survival. Here, Ansel had brought that thread to their first meal in their new life together. All the losses filled her heart alongside all that remained to be lived and loved.

In the following days Kläre spent her time organizing, arranging, finding shops, observing the rhythm of Ansel's daily life, and listening to his reports of his new role as pastor of the lovely church towering across the garden. She served breakfast precisely at 8 a.m., dinner at 1:00 p.m., and supper at 7:00 p.m. She learned which of the bakery's *brotchen* pleased Ansel the most, and found thinly sliced cheeses and fine cured ham, more available now as conditions in the country improved. She scoured the butcher and greengrocer shelves for the best cuts of meat and finest produce to prepare their dinners. She was an excellent cook, and Ansel an appreciative diner. Before even a month had gone by, the new household was settled.

In the last week of April, Amalie Beckmann came to visit. Kläre looked with satisfaction upon the sitting room table she had laid for coffee, her fine antique furniture placed artfully in the rectory's small but gracious spaces, and a new lithograph, a Chagall Ansel had purchased, hanging in the entry hall.

Kläre had been grateful for Amalie's eager telephone call a week earlier, and had quickly invited her old friend to see them. Amalie had seemed to fall in with the implausible logic of Kläre and Ansel's decisions with ease. Her enthusiasm was a comfort and support—and Kläre's spirits were further buoyed when her friend arrived with a lovely African violet in full bloom, her face shining at the sight of her friend and the prospect of an afternoon together. The two women embraced, and Amalie's spirited compliments warmed Kläre further.

"Ach, what a sweet and lovely home you've made here, Kläre."

"Oh, it's not just me," Kläre replied. "Ansel takes a great interest in every decision. I'm so glad you like it. We haven't yet had many guests. Come, let us take our coffee. I made an orange *kuchen*. Is it still your favorite?"

"Yes, how sweet of you to remember." Amalie sat on the Queen Anne armchair. "I remember this chair from your home in Hörde. It's unbelievable that I sit in it now in a rectory in Dülken and you are here with Ansel. Life certainly brings us to strange places, doesn't it?"

Kläre nodded slowly. Amalie's face was open and warm, and showed no trace of reserve or skepticism. "It was very important to Ansel and to me that you favored this idea of our joining our lives," she said. "The idea might not have been so easy for you. And I'm not sure you understand how important you are to Ansel."

"No, perhaps I don't understand it. I always felt so badly for him, though I tried my best. He is so deep and keeps so much to himself. I've always worried that he blamed me for the hard things in his life, though he never said so and has always been good to me. If I've learned anything, it is that we must take advantage of the things that connect us to each other when they come, and I see only good in the connection you and Ansel have found with one another. It makes me very happy for you both. And Ansel certainly can benefit from your good taste and your skills as a hausfrau."

The two women fell to talk that always came easily to them: of family, friends, housekeeping, memories, hopes, and dreams. When two hours had flown by and Amalie needed to leave to catch her train, Kläre embraced her for a long time.

"Thank you so much again," she said. "I look forward to seeing you soon, perhaps with the girls also."

Amalie returned the hug. "Give Ansel my love, and tell him how very proud and happy I am for him."

Kläre could see that she was, and she savored the anticipation of being able to relay her friend's message at supper that evening.

Ansel came home from an important meeting at the church, one attended by many of the diocese officials in the area. He strode into the dining room and, after kissing Kläre's broad, high forehead in what had become his habit of private greeting, he said a brief grace and eagerly took a spoonful of lentil soup. He closed his eyes in obvious pleasure.

"Tasty, very tasty," he enthused.

Kläre smiled and nodded her thanks. "And how did your meeting go?" she asked.

"Very well, Frau Kohler! It must have had something to do with my fine new coat and collar." Kläre saw to the cleaning and starching of Ansel's shirts and priestly collars, and had recently persuaded him to replace the ones that were too worn. The intimacy of this task, and of arranging the breadbasket for breakfast, and of Ansel's choosing a wine for supper that he knew would please her, filled Kläre with a joy she had thought utterly gone from her life.

Kläre related all that had transpired in her visit with Amalie. Ansel beamed, and Kläre thought again of her good fortune.

"Kläre," Ansel asked tentatively, interrupting her thoughts.

"Yes, my sweet," she replied, surprised though comfortable that the endearment fell so naturally from her lips.

"At Mass this morning, during my homily, I was troubled. The topic was giving thanks. It's wonderful that Amalie came today and spoke of finding happiness in our lives where we can. I worry that if I only say to you how wonderful it is that we have made this little family, you and I—if I don't allow for the possibility that for some reason you might not be happy, because I am *so* happy—I worry that perhaps you won't say something . . ." Ansel's voice trailed off, his large, open face troubled.

Kläre did not rush to answer. Instead, gazing steadily at the young man before her, she rose and rounded the table so that she stood next to his chair. She gathered his face into her hands and turned his chin up before she spoke. "God has given us to each other; I am sure of it. You must never worry about what might happen, but only cherish this blessing. It's just as Amalie said." She bent slightly and graced his forehead with a gentle brush of her lips, then held his head to her bosom, the contented chirping of nesting chickadees outside providing harmony to her own heart sounds.

The last day of April was brisk and clear, blessedly absent the dull, listless clouds of the previous week. Kläre and Ansel traveled to Dortmund and she marveled at the way the war-scarred city bristled with purpose and bustle. They needn't any longer search for an open shop with goods to sell, needn't avert their eyes from ruined buildings. Her step quickened with optimism as the healing city poked up new buildings along with the springtime bulbs.

Ansel had business for the church and would be busy for two hours. He had hesitated to leave her outside the train station, and only her smiling promise that she would find a special treat in one of the newly reopened shops assured him. It was their first outing since Kläre had moved into the rectory in Dülken.

Buoyed by the sun and the colors of early spring, Kläre stepped along the street toward the Konditerei, where she hoped to buy a torte. Jakob had met her there often for coffee, but memories of those old familiarities led to darkness, and today was a day of light. The distractions of the sun playing over the city scene, the sounds of building and traffic filled her consciousness.

Her errand at the Konditerei finished, Kläre walked down Berliner Strasse, where she found that a small gallery had bravely opened, alone on a short block of darkened and boarded windows in the once fashionable commercial district. Kläre stopped to appreciate the wholeness of the small storefront, itself a framed picture of sorts. The spotless glass of the small display window gleamed. The wooden door still needed varnish, but its brass handle shone furiously, and the street before it had been swept clean. "*Kunst*" was lettered freshly and simply in an arch on the glass. A stab of relief and pleasure went through Kläre at seeing art once more set forth in the everyday world.

Yielding to impulse, Kläre stepped into the richly lit gallery. As her eyes became accustomed to the warm darkness, she saw that the small collection was hung tastefully in two rooms.

The proprietor stepped forward to greet Kläre, appraising her well-tailored suit and carefully polished shoes in one swift glance.

"Good afternoon, Madam. Is there something I might show you?"

"Good afternoon. I just passed by in the street. I haven't been to a gallery in . . . in a long while."

"Please, have a look around. I am most happy to answer any questions for you." The man left her then, busying himself nearby as she began to study the walls.

Some of the paintings were the typical German and Dutch landscapes of tranquil farms and mountain forests. Some were quite good. She recognized a Jedocha De Mumpa almost immediately. Ernst and Ditha owned two of them—large, vaguely sinister, ethereal things that had hung in their dining room. There were some modern portraits by artists Kläre did not know, and then some German versions of the Cubist work that had so enraged the Nazi Nationalists. Kläre did not like them, but it pleased her that they hung here.

She had just entered the second room when the bell above the door to the street jangled and another customer entered. Kläre turned back toward the archway and a painting in the corner of the room caught her eye. It was a medium-sized canvas, framed simply in grey. The subject was a bouquet of flowers, perhaps asters, white and spiked with dark yellow centers. They were surrounded by six yellow roses. A blue pall infused the canvas; what could have been vibrant in color and mood was dulled, the yellows faded. The flowers appeared to float above a dull black vase that seemed small for the arrangement, which hung on a mere suggestion of stems. In the space where greenery might have been, dark, radiating lines diminished into a miasma of paint. Did it contain a figure?

Kläre moved closer. She couldn't tell. The paint suggested a lone person, perhaps a man. The canvas's unearthly night sky seemed lit from above by an argon lamp, suggesting a sourceless menace. Where there should be simple beauty, something difficult lurked. In an instant, Kläre knew she had to have the painting.

"Would you care to see it in a brighter light?" The gallery proprietor appeared at Kläre's side, startling her.

"Oh! Why thank you. But no, actually, I don't think so. A brighter light seems quite beside the point to me," Kläre said.

The proprietor now watched Kläre closely as he spoke. "It's not a work for everyone, is it? It's hard to tell exactly what we're looking at."

"Quite," Kläre said. "One has to choose the flowers, or it would be quite easy to get lost in the darkness, wouldn't it?" A moment of doubt crept into Kläre's thoughts. What if Ansel disliked the painting? Never far from her mind, the question of how to reconcile her past with the life that they were building together weighed upon her. She had to trust that Ansel would understand what spoke powerfully to her in this painting. If he did not care for it, she would hang it in her own room.

Kläre arranged the purchase for a reasonable sum. Her finances were still quite confused in the aftermath of the war and Jakob's death—but Hans Heymann had been extraordinarily generous in promising Kläre an income from the practice going forward, and Ansel's household allowance provided all that they needed from day to day. As a result, Kläre had money—more than enough money. She arranged for delivery of the painting, and as she collected her bag and gloves, the proprietor offered her a copy of the newly resumed publication of the arts journal *Kunst Zeitung*, which she took with her.

Ansel had arrived early at the train station. His eager face greeted Kläre as she stepped onto the platform. Shortly, they were settled onto the train.

"I've done something quite unexpected," Kläre began. "Perhaps unwise."

Ansel waited, curiosity registering in the rise of one eyebrow and the tilt of his head.

"I've bought a painting," she said. "It's very modern and a bit disturbing. If it isn't to your taste, perhaps I could put it in my room. It is your house, and—"

"Not at all," Ansel interrupted. "It is *our* house, Kläre." They were sitting opposite each other in the compartment, and Ansel leaned forward, his hands on his knees. Kläre smiled tentatively, and then more deeply.

They each sat back in their seats then, Ansel to read through papers from the bishop's office, Kläre the arts journal. The photo plates of new artists' work were mixed with articles on museum restoration work and announcements of exhibitions. As Kläre leafed to the back, a black-bordered announcement leapt out from the page. She gasped as she read:

> *With sadness we announce the death of*
> *Melisande Durr*
> *Artist, Dealer, Heroine*
> *Mourned by all whose lives she touched and saved*
> *Lost at sea 27 April*
> *Also lost,*
> *Bernhardt Steinmann*
> *Publisher, Investor, Hero*

"Oh my God in heaven," Kläre cried, her voice strangled behind her gloved hand. She looked at Ansel, drawing jagged breaths. She handed him the journal, the announcement somber in its black outline.

"But I don't understand," Ansel began. "Who are these people?"

Kläre fought tears as she struggled to speak. "They saved Werner and saw to it that he reached Palestine. Bernhardt was a friend to me . . . I met him when we lived in Hörde. He owned a publishing company, and he learned his mother was Jewish just as the Nazis became more threatening. We were very close . . . before . . . and he introduced me to Melisande Durr."

Kläre read the concern on Ansel's face, but this was a grief she could not entirely share, not yet. Though she loved and trusted Ansel, he was still young. She did not know how to communicate all that Bernhardt Steinmann had meant to her. "Melisande Durr was a patroness of artists and thinkers before the war, and was also a dealer. She then became part of the resistance. She ran a bakery café in Düsseldorf, but eventually she helped Jewish children to escape. Ach . . . they were good people." Her voice was barely a whisper. "It doesn't end, this losing."

I mustn't burden him so much, Kläre thought. *He is so young. And the church* . . . Her disquietude sent a tremor through the clutched fists in her lap.

Ansel leaned forward again and met her eyes. "One to whom God gives much love has also much to lose."

32 July 1948

Will God or someone give me the power to breathe my sigh into my canvases, the sigh of prayer and sadness, the prayer of salvation, of rebirth?
—Marc Chagall

Ansel Beckmann sat at the massive oak desk in his study. The song of cicadas surged into his consciousness with the harmonics of summer, and he closed his eyes to let the sensation resonate around his head in a moment of escape. He breathed in slowly, then exhaled as he let the insects' hum retreat and the murmur of the voices in the sitting room next door reenter.

Dr. and Mrs. Kiewe had left after seeing to it that Kläre was safely asleep, with instructions to Ansel to continue administering the sedative for the next twenty-four hours. The Kiewes had come as soon as their daughter Hannah had sent the telegram. The local woman who worked as the maid in the rectory was preparing a light supper under Amalie Beckmann's supervision, and Ansel's sisters were sorting telegrams and answering the telephone. It had rung incessantly for the last day. Erwin Kohler was due to arrive in the morning, but just now Ansel had an hour alone in his office.

Dully, he examined the walls and furnishings of this room that ordinarily pleased him so much. His diplomas, the beautiful crucifix Kläre had bought him on their first vacation in the Black Forest, the etchings of the cathedral in Cologne he had saved for as a student, all hung in their appointed places, yet the sense of constancy and accomplishment they normally represented were gone.

In front of him were the letter and telegrams and the file folder with Kläre's arrangements to travel to Palestine. Their contents threatened to overwhelm him entirely, as they had Kläre. He mustn't succumb. He must pray for strength and wisdom for himself now, just as he had often prayed for others. He was thirty-three years old, the head priest in a small but fine church, and the master of his own household—but in this moment he was master of nothing save the need to bring Kläre out of the abyss into which she had just been thrown.

The letter from Werner had come in yesterday's post. Wearily, Ansel picked it up and read it again as if it might this time reveal the secret of God's purpose in what was to follow.

18 June 1948
Dear Mutti and Ansel,

Ansel's face crumpled as he felt again the surge of pleasure this greeting had given him only yesterday. That Werner should include him in the family letter as an equal meant more than he could say even to Kläre. But now . . . He read on:

I received your letter of 31 May only two days ago. I hope that you have gotten all my previous letters. Unfortunately, I couldn't write you for the last two months as our entire province was closed. There wouldn't have been much to write anyway because I was sick for nearly all that time; now I can stand somewhat weakly on my legs. I think it was mostly from overwork. Since we got to the Crusader's fortress on the land we bought for the new kibbutz, others have gotten malaria and other high fevers that lasted from 6–8 weeks. What angers me most is no one seems to have any medicine for this illness. In any case, they moved us out of the fortress into a tent camp, and since then, there have been no new cases. Then came the cutoff of the new road. Not even mules were getting through. But now the Haganah has secured the road in our district.

It took a terrible misfortune to bring them here. The Arabs and Jews had closed each other's road access down. Finally both sides saw that they couldn't continue. They formed a treaty in which both sides would let traffic go in peace. Instead of peace, one of our convoys was attacked. The Arabs were plowing next to the road looking totally innocent, and their women were walking in the road. Our trucks came and thought nothing of it because we had a treaty! Suddenly more than 100 of their men attacked. 15 Arabs were shot, but 50 Jews fell. In one tank, wounded soldiers fought from 3 p.m. until midnight. They broke through but were surrounded. They fought until the last bullets; the last ones were for themselves. I thought things like this happened only in books.

You know, when the attack on the prison occurred that made so much news across the world, I thought it was a huge mess, an action without purpose, and it made many more Arabs into terrorists. I thought then that the weapons the Arabs used against the English could also be turned against us. Anyone's car can be exploded and in this way, many peaceful citizens have lost their lives. It's no big act of heroism to let a truck drive over a land mine. And remember that this isn't a fight between two sides. The terrorists are getting help from the outside, from America and from France! The Americans' "love" for the Zionists is only shallow politics.

Good will not prevail as you suggested. We may be convinced that the Jews have a "right" to Palestine, since we have no other place; but we in our own right do harm to some of the Arabs. We say we are right. The Arab, who had a stupid law forced on him, doesn't understand that. When our area was bought in 1939 there were Bedouins here, who were given the right to let their herds graze on undeveloped land. They've done it for 50 years. Then we came and told them that they were in the way of our building projects. From the other side they were incited by the gangs, so what meaning did our "law" have? When they were then given grazing lands in the Arab territory, their "brothers" received them by burning all their belongings. We are only in the right because we can't survive any other way. It's simply a fight for survival, but it's not "good," mother.

Enough of the politics! Thank you so much for the books on mushrooms. Along with the help from the experimental agricultural station, I have started a growing cave. I plan to try seven varieties! Please ask Erwin to send whatever books he can find in England. I can read English even if I can't write it. Speaking of Erwin, I'm sorry to hear that he is not happy. Getting married quickly is an after-the-war manifestation. In a kibbutz, the matter of getting everyday needs met is much easier, but I can see among my friends that a wife can be a big help. But usually it is the opposite. Having children early is even worse, because usually you regret having them. In any case I hope that everything will be OK for him.

Mutti, I think you misunderstood me in the matter of money. Since everything is communal here, everything we receive is also communal. Since there are many people among us who have no way to get outside help, it wouldn't be right if I would accept money and clothes from America without sharing them. The KKL gives us a large sum of money to help us get started, but we live very frugally. We are making progress. Yesterday we got a big tractor. It has 40-horse power more than the one whose picture I sent you. It performs much better and it seems as though we will be able to make more area arable than we thought. Soon we will be getting a diesel engine with a generator that will give us electric light. Now that the road is open, we will be getting our next shipment of chickens. We haven't been able to expand the chicken and geese flocks and cattle herds because we haven't been able to rely on feed getting through. The beehives are doing very well, and soon we will be feeding ourselves all year with our vegetables. We can't plant orange trees here because of the climate, but apples, plums, and grapes will thrive. We are still drilling to find more water, but with the new tractor and explosives we're hoping to expand the water basin and keep the ancient cisterns full all year around. The Crusaders did some good after all!

So even though there is confusion from time to time, I am not near the big cities. In fact I'm not near anywhere, so for the most part, our life goes on uninterrupted. But I don't think it is a good time for a visit. The disputes are becoming serious.

I am nearly healthy again, and send you a 1000 hugs and kisses,

Avraham

Ansel had seen how Kläre had struggled not to cry as she read her son's words, and had sought to comfort her, even though he understood that she must grieve this setback in her endeavor to reconnect with her son.

"He looks to protect his mother, of course," he'd said, choosing his words carefully. He wanted to soothe her, not to increase her worry. "It isn't so safe for a woman to travel now."

"Ya, and why then won't he come home? It isn't safe for him either," she responded.

Ansel had remained silent then, not knowing what to say. Werner had insisted that he would not be allowed to leave—that he was needed and was loyal to the youth movement and his fledgling kibbutz. So Ansel had risen and come around the table to place his hands on Kläre's shoulders as she fought tears, his large hands kneading the neck muscles at either side of her spine where knots of tension formed. He had been devotedly offering this service to her since Jakob's death. He had watched her do the same for her husband many times, and was pleased that in nearly any situation he could give comfort with his strong hands. If only this had been the worst of the day's news.

The telegram had come late, after the evening coffee, from Kibbutz

Yechiam. Some of it was in English, some in German, but the message was savagely simple:

> *Avraham Werner Kohler, age 21, died 22 July, 1948 - Rambam hospital - Haifa - day after - "accident" - explosives - Kibbutz Yechiam. Further information forthcoming.*

The swollen skin around Kläre's eyes did not mask the dark rings from her sleepless nights. The hair with which she had all her life fought a losing, daily battle of control hung undressed and unbound, the managed curls replaced through inattention with a wiry tumble around her shoulders. Ansel was frightened by the listlessness she'd shown in the last weeks, but doggedly kept to the pattern of days, coaxing her to eat a butter bread here, a slice of her favorite cured ham there, to discuss the shopping list, or to hear a story of a parishioner family.

Erwin had come for the memorial service and gone. Amalie and Ansel's sisters had stayed longer but were also now gone. Ernst and Ditha had simply not had the money or time to take away from their jobs to travel from America. Trude had come with her girls but had required as much comfort as she had given. Through it all, Kläre had risen each morning, dressed, sat, and allowed herself to be kissed and touched, spoken to softly and briefly.

Then the visitors and mourners had gone and Kläre had taken to her room and let go. Long silences behind the closed door were punctuated with the strangled, unearthly noises of depthless grief. The sounds of a drawer shutting, the scrape of a chair, or the flush of the toilet in the hall were sometimes the only signal to Ansel that she was still there. When, after two days, she began to come to meals, he spoke quietly of the day's events and of household matters, watching her. He expected nothing in return, and got nothing but an occasional, dispirited nod. Ansel knew she had retreated to a place from which she must return before her spirit could heal. No matter that his faith taught him that if only she could turn to God, He would show her a path. Ansel the priest read the book of Job and prayed; Ansel the man lay awake at night, lost in inadequacy and the power of his love.

A morning came when Ansel went to Kläre's room to ask about sending the maid to the market, and he found her staring out the window into the back garden with unseeing eyes.

"Good morning, dear Kläre. It is warm today, no?"

She turned to him, and he worked to control the wince that froze in his expression as he looked at her haunted face. He was drawn to touch her, to hold her arms. Her chest heaved with the effort of breathing, and she looked wildly around as if to anchor her pain somewhere other than in the anger that fought with sorrow in her eyes.

Ansel steadied her trembling body and now she clutched his arms as well, turning her face up to him.

"I didn't have time to tell him not to hurry so much with that girl. No time to get to know her. He could have gone to university." Kläre spat the words out between jagged breaths.

Ansel was frightened now. "Kläre, Kläre, you couldn't. You tried. You . . ." Ansel stopped, stunned into silence by the raw agony that contorted her face. She was not thinking, not hearing. "Klärchen, you must take a tablet."

"No, no more tablets," she hissed.

Not knowing what else to do, Ansel pulled Kläre to him with a strength that brooked no opposition. With an enormous shudder she drew in breath and coughed out a sob whose source was far deeper than one human's pain. Ansel did not know that place, but he could hold Kläre, smooth her hair down the back of her head. He knew enough not to speak; he waited for the softening of her rigid muscles, waited until she went limp against him, folded into his tall, stooped embrace.

"Ya, ya now," he whispered.

Her crying gave way to a low animal moan that rolled from her center to every part of her body and then resonated into his.

"Ya, ya, this is good," Ansel whispered again.

Kläre's knees gave way and Ansel caught her around the shoulder with one arm and, bending, swept her legs up with the other. He cradled her against himself, swinging slightly back and forth from his waist, his cheek against the top of her head, thinking only to draw the pain from her. He laid her gently on the bed and took a clean, pressed handkerchief from his pocket to wipe her tears. Kläre turned and curled onto her side and Ansel lay next to her, enclosing her form with his own. He breathed in the sweet smell of Kläre's favorite soap and it dizzied him for a moment. He had love and comfort to give, and the power of it filled him with strength and purpose. He was no longer scared.

"*Liebchen,*" he said. "Do you remember the story of King David?"

Kläre did not answer, but the shaking of her shoulders lessened and her sobs abated.

Ansel settled into the low, sonorous tones of a master storyteller. "David, most beloved of kings, was worshiped by his people for his strength, his wisdom, and his love of beauty. The son of his heart was Absalom, borne to him by Maacah. As a very righteous person, David led his nation towards a spiritual existence even as he led them in war. He wrote beautiful psalms reflecting his life, which consisted of many personal entanglements . . . of great highs but also of tragic lows. In the way of God's will that no man understands, David's beloved son Absalom met his death in the strife of warring loyalties."

Kläre now lay utterly still under Ansel's protective arm. He continued, "David was tormented with grief at the death of his errant son. He cried from the depths of his heart, 'O Absalom, Absalom, my son Absalom! Would God I had died for thee.' But God had other plans for David. The strength of his grief led the king to seclude himself from everyone—but as a great leader, David did not have that luxury. Joab, a commander in the army came to David and told him the people needed to see him, to know he was still in charge. So the king mustered the courage to go out to the gate so all could see him. With great bravery, he endured the heartache that went with the mantle of the life he had chosen.

Ansel paused and sat up at the edge of the bed as Kläre turned toward him. Her eyes were no longer vacant, but he found her look of anger, pain, and sorrow unbearable. Still, he held her gaze until she said, "Finish the story . . . please."

He drew her hand into his own and, holding it gently, continued, willing the life that had returned to her eyes to remain. "David had won his place as king mostly through his own courage and his trust in the Divine. He declined to wear the heavy, ornate armor that others would have worn to meet the giant Goliath in battle. Instead, he relied on his skill and strength to win. And though David suffered greatly in the loss of Absalom, he became stronger still, and a better man. He found eternal grace in the descendants of Solomon, his son with Bathsheba, and his role as ancestor to our Lord Jesus. As the Lord said to David, '*If your sons take heed to their way, to walk before Me in truth with all their heart and with all their soul, you shall not lack a man on the throne of Israel.*' And so you see . . ."

"Yes, I do see," Kläre said. She squeezed Ansel's hand and closed her eyes. "Thank you."

Ansel recognized that he had been dismissed. He rose, and left Kläre to her thoughts.

Ansel was taking his seat at the dining room table at one o'clock when the door opened and Kläre entered. She was dressed in a soft blue skirt and sweater, and her hair was drawn back into a loose knot. She surveyed the table, laid carefully with the midday meal.

Ansel rose and walked around the table to the chair opposite his, pulling it out. "Won't you please be seated?"

Kläre smiled as she walked to her seat. Once settled, she pulled the linen napkin from the silver ring that bore the initials of her grandparents and placed the napkin on her lap. "Wherever have you found such a beautiful *sauerbraten?* Did you shop for it yourself?" she asked.

Ansel smiled broadly and, bowing his head, recited a heartfelt blessing for the gifts at his table.

33 1952

"She does not take Communion. Ever."

"But she comes each week to Mass."

"I tell you there is something false here."

"I saw once that she lit a candle with Pastor Beckmann. I heard her son died but she did not go to a funeral."

The two women spoke in low voices as they cleaned and polished in the sacristy. The vaulted ceiling amplified their voices. Kläre had just emerged from Ansel's office, the door only a short distance from the room in St. Michael's where the two local women came each week to clean and prepare the vestments and sacred objects for the weekend Masses.

Kläre hesitated in the hall, uncertain whether she should proceed or retrace her steps to the security of Ansel's private room. She had come to bring him a book, glad of the chance to walk across the snow-covered path between the rectory and church. The icy air and deep blue sky enhanced the beauty of the hemlocks forming their own green cathedral overhead, boughs laden with snow-lace patterns that sparkled in the sun. On her way in, she had nodded to the women with a quiet "Good morning" as her eyes adjusted to the dark church.

Perhaps they thought she would be longer with Ansel. She had only come to deliver the forgotten book, and had quickly left him deep in study, closing the door softly behind her. Now she stood frozen to her spot as the women continued.

"I heard she came from Dortmund, but no one knows where. I'm told she has coffee with Frau Kruger from time to time, but otherwise, no one really knows her. She is very proper, I know, but I just think there is something the canary isn't singing."

"You know, I asked her once where her children were baptized. She didn't really answer."

"No answer is also an answer, don't you think?"

Kläre had heard enough. She cleared her throat, stamping her galoshes lightly to make noise. Immediately, the women in the sacristy went silent. Kläre returned to the snowy afternoon and the short walk home, the beauty of her path dimmed by the overheard conversation.

Over dinner that evening, Ansel suggested they discuss the events they would host and attend in the upcoming Lenten season. "Ash Wednesday is on the twenty-second, so our program at the school will be that day, but will we attend both the carnival in town and the one at school the weekend before? Kläre?" Ansel stopped, surprised at her inattention. "Do I bore you already? We've barely started all there is to plan."

Kläre blushed and straightened, returning her attention to the social management that she did so well. "Yes, fine, either one or both, as you wish." She prepared to continue the discussion, but changed her mind. "I didn't care for Purim as a child—the false celebration of it, the attempts to turn it into Fasching like the other children celebrated. The story of Queen Esther saddened me, no matter that it ended well for her."

It was an odd turn to the conversation, Kläre realized, perhaps not the time to unburden herself to Ansel, who had so much on his mind, but he warmed to the topic immediately.

"How interesting," he responded. "I actually didn't much like Carnival myself as a child. I rarely traveled home for it and though we received extra sweets from the nuns, it actually made me feel quite lonely in the orphanage." His look turned thoughtful. "Our religions wish to brighten the darkness of the winter, but we rather like that time, don't we? It seems enough, doesn't it—to fast and cleanse in preparation for spring, without all the noisy public display."

How does he know so well how to put me at ease? Kläre thought. *How can it be that we are so much the same way?*

"Do you wish to have more of the Jewish celebrations in our home? You have never asked, but neither have I asked you. Should we prepare a seder for Passover?" Ansel's question held no artifice or restraint, and this deepened Kläre's love for him.

"Yes, I should like that very much, just you and me." Kläre's next words tumbled out: "Ansel, I heard the women who clean the sacristy talking about me today. They see that I do not take Communion, but that I am in church each Sunday. One of them finds something false in my behavior." She looked at Ansel and saw the smallest irritation knit his brow, but she raced on. "Do you? I mean, do you feel what I do is false somehow?"

Ansel sat back in his chair. "Kläre, you know I care nothing for what the women gossip in the sacristy. There are no rules for our situation save those we make for ourselves. I feel . . ." He struggled to find the correct words, and his face lit up as they came. "I feel that we are very true here—as far from anything false as I can imagine. I can understand if you do not feel comfortable with public expression of your Judaism. With all that has happened, to be in a small town in Germany might bring discomfort and uncertainty to you. But not to me, Kläre. It makes no separation for me, your Judaism and my Catholicism, and therefore no falseness exists. You are a woman of God in every way that is important to me." As Kläre relaxed into her chair, Ansel smiled. "Perhaps over time, it can be my gift to bring your Jewish faith back to you. But for now, be gentle with yourself, Klärchen."

Kläre sat next to Father Theodor Jager in the church nave. The early spring morning was cool, and the church still held the musty smell of stale winter days. Sun streamed through the simple stained glass windows, creating warm patterns on the stone floor. Ansel's sonorous voice filled the sanctuary. Theodor had been the concelebrant with Ansel at early Mass, but sat now in the second row, between Kläre and

Agnes Hintz. It had been five years since Ansel and Kläre had moved to Baumstadt, and Ansel not only had the pastorate of this lovely old church, he had also become principal of a new comprehensive high school.

Agnes sat primly beside Theodor, her blond hair pulled back, her lovely face raised toward Ansel as he gave the homily. Theodor's pleasure in the picture of Agnes's reverence lit his face. Kläre watched until he turned toward her; eyebrow arched, she smiled and gave him a small nod. The priest colored and bent his head. Kläre's smile remained as she thought of the events of the previous evening.

Theodor and Agnes had arrived from Cologne an hour before the evening meal. The young priest was Ansel's closest friend, the only one whom he considered worthy of drawing into the warm circle of his home with Kläre. Theodor had captured Kläre's heart early on, years before, when she'd found him in the sitting room, holding a photo of Werner, sadness clouding his wide, solid face.

"There is no answer to the pain of this loss, is there?" he whispered.

Kläre could only shake her head and take the hand he extended to her into both of her own.

He had arrived on this visit in the company of Agnes Hintz, introduced as a distant cousin who would be assisting in the research for a book on which he was collaborating with Ansel. Theodor was an accomplished painter, and an artful orator with an active life as a pulpit priest and scholar. Perhaps it should not have come as any surprise that he was creative in his relationships as well, particularly when it came to lovely women. Yet Kläre was momentarily astonished and then amused by his boldness at bringing the girl for the weekend. Kläre noted an electricity between her two guests that was not cousin-like.

It had been Theodor's rollicking, wicked sense of humor that had set the tone at dinner. His booming laughter rose above his hosts' during the leisurely meal and evening walk. He and Ansel had retired to Ansel's study after their walk, and when Kläre brought them cognac, she had stayed to listen. Theodor was a brilliant theologian and lover of the arts, but it had been Ansel's idea to write a book about kings and prophets in the art of Marc Chagall. Ansel and Kläre had remained interested in Chagall since Theodor first brought them to see the collection of paintings in his church immediately after the war in Dortmund. Their first joint purchase of an artwork had been a lithograph of King David and his harp, followed a year later by one of the prophet Jeremiah. The human themes expressed in bold colors and fanciful religious images embodied emotional and spiritual contrasts that spoke to each of them.

"Come now, Ansel," Theodor said. "Is your publisher really interested in this? It's certainly not the stuff of traditional church scholarship. But this is truly exciting. Our crisis in the German church must also be the chance to make room for thinking differently. Kings and prophets, power and visions: What a fantastic metaphor for seeing and doing things a different way. I look forward to this!"

Theodor's contagious passion had ignited Ansel's excitement.

Theodor is right, Kläre had thought as she watched the two men talk. *Even with the school, Ansel would do well to have a project outside of his official responsibilities.* She smiled at the two young men.

Ansel had already published *The Unspoken Word*, a scholarly analysis of a Baltic physician who had attended one of Hitler's most powerful aides. The book had been well received, though its sympathetic portrait of the doctor, the aide's confidante and masseur, and its subtle condemnation of the Catholic Church brought criticism from far-flung quarters. It was still very early in the establishment of German scholarship concerning the nightmare of the Nazis. Kläre had been Ansel's first and closest reader as his manuscript took form. Reading it had made her acutely aware of the pain he'd relived during his research, but also of the pride he took in exposing truths that the reading public might not want to face. Now, Kläre realized, he needed more. And Theodor, the genius terror of the bishopric, had agreed to join his friend on the journey.

Kläre's attention returned to Ansel as he finished the morning Mass and strode to the sanctuary doors. After saying good-bye to the last of his parishioners, he hung away his vestments and joined Kläre, Theodor, and Agnes. They walked down the wide, tree-lined gravel path from the church toward the rectory, where a fine dinner awaited them.

Ansel and Theodor immediately launched into a discussion of the homily, oblivious to the rather comic pair they made: Ansel, tall and thin, stooped slightly forward with his hands clasped behind him; Theodor, short, broad, and erect, his toupee slightly askew, also clasping his hands behind his broad back. Kläre and Agnes walked behind them.

"So, Fräulein Hintz, are you an art scholar?" Kläre asked her young guest, her tone friendly and gentle.

"Call me Agnes, please, Frau Kohler. I shouldn't say an art scholar, really, but I've become a sort of sleuth for Theodor in the past few years, as he has worked on the Church's art collections. I've done a good bit of writing for him as well." Seeing Kläre's smile, she continued with more animation, "He is truly a great thinker . . . I have never met anyone else in the Church with such a passion for interesting ideas. His appreciation of art is so connected to what he believes and his commitment to God. He isn't so tied to Catholic dogma, you know? And he can conduct such a wonderful Mass. I love to listen him. But you must know all this as Pastor Beckmann is his close friend, isn't he?" Agnes gave Kläre a worried look. "I hope I haven't spoken out of turn."

"Not at all." Kläre took the arm of the young woman and continued walking. She spoke slowly, "When we find a person whose passion for what is good and important speaks deeply to us, and this is offered to us, it seems to me that we should be grateful to accept it, shouldn't we? Theodor"—Kläre paused to look at Agnes—"Theodor is a very special man. He has been a wonderful friend to Ansel and to me. He was so very helpful when I lost my husband and my son."

By now the walkers had reached the rectory. The two women went straight to the dining room to begin preparations to serve Sunday dinner.

"Theodor told me about all that has happened to you, Frau Kohler," Agnes said, continuing their conversation. "Forgive me for asking so personal a question, but how is it that one can move on from such loss and suffering? I mean, you and Pastor Beckmann have made such a wonderful life here!"

Kläre looked at the painting above the dining table, and Agnes followed her gaze. It was the still life with the suffering asters and roses suspended before a dark and uncertain background, a hint of a figure to the right of the painting. "Sometimes the mouth laughs and the heart cries," Kläre said. "It isn't always the one or the other." She had never spoken in this way to anyone about her thoughts, her choices—but something told her to risk what she said next: "We're lucky any time or any way we are loved and have the chance to love another. I've learned this because in many ways, even with all that has happened, I have had this kind of luck in my life."

Agnes was thoughtful. At last she turned to Kläre and said simply, "Thank you."

They continued their preparations, and shortly the foursome was seated at the comfortable dining table where Kläre's special veal cutlets were the centerpiece of dinner. Kläre was particularly pleased to have been able to find good veal. She basked in the exclamations of appreciation from her guests. She watched Theodor's animated discussion with Ansel, and Agnes's quiet contributions. She quite liked the girl; she hoped that both spoken and unspoken messages between them had put her at ease.

After dinner, Ansel retired to his room for his afternoon rest, and Kläre excused herself to put the kitchen in order. She, too, was ready for a rest and was just passing through the front hall to the staircase when she heard voices in Ansel's study.

Agnes spoke first: "The portrait is fabulous. You have caught her absolutely. It's . . . it's her eyes. They are truly full of light. It's as if she knows everything . . . You don't want to look away from them. "

Kläre smiled as she listened. Theodor was working on a portrait of her for Ansel's study. Ill at ease with the idea for a long time, Kläre had eventually been persuaded by the enthusiasm of both young priests for the project. Theodor had spent the last several visits working on the painting, sometimes asking Kläre to sit, other times using a photograph clipped to the corner of the easel. In the work, she sat slender and tall, a white suit softly draping her shapely torso. Her reddish waves, streaked with white, were caught into a loose bun. Red chair, blue wall, thin mouth, long nose were highlighted by her brown eyes.

Now she heard the smile in Theodor's voice and the intimacy of his response to Agnes: "He who knows, sees. It pleases me if the picture pleases you."

"Pastor Beckmann must be thrilled as well," Agnes continued.

"That you must ask him. He's far too good a friend and careful a priest to reveal otherwise." Theodor laid down his ready banter, and emotion rose in his voice. "He loves her very much, and she him. I am fortunate to have become close to them both."

"I quite think they feel the same about you, my dear," Agnes replied.

"I've often thought their love and devotion is redemption for the pain they've each suffered," Theodor said. "Sometimes this kind of love comes in unexpected ways . . ." His tone changed. "I have only the last touches of white here, and now I'm done for today. Come, my dear. Ansel will have an especially good bottle of wine for us tonight at supper. We should have a rest now, no?"

Kläre smiled and silently mounted the stairs, the dull pain in her joints no match for the warmth that filled her heart.

34 July 1954

A clear and sunny mountain morning and the distant clang of cowbells accompanied Kläre's fairy tale view of the Jungfrau, its icy splendor visible behind the lacy sheers of the hotel window. Kläre luxuriated in the sweet softness of the feather duvet and the oversized pillows. She had rested deeply all night. The hotel was small but fine: excellent food, immaculate service. Ernst and Ditha expected no less, and it pleased Kläre that her recommendation, which had come from Theodor Jager, had turned out exactly as billed.

The sounds of Ansel stirring in the room next door were what had woken Kläre. As she stretched one last time, his knock on the door between their rooms sounded softly before he entered. He padded across the carpet in the new pajamas she had bought him and sat at the side of her bed.

"Good morning, Frau Kohler; it's a beautiful day in Wengen, isn't it? Did you sleep well?" He bent and kissed her forehead.

"Yes, very well, and you?"

"Quite well. Come, I will fetch your shoes." In two long strides he reached the door to the hallway and retrieved Kläre's shoes, polished to a furious shine. Kläre closed her eyes and sighed with contentment. Placing shoes in the hall outside her room at the end of the evening and having shined shoes reappear in the morning was a small thing, but small things struck her regularly with darts of gratitude. Ansel returned to her side.

"You are very good to me, Father Beckmann. Doesn't it bore you to travel with an old woman?" Kläre's eyes danced as she sat up against the propped pillows.

"Ah, but such a beautiful old woman, *liebchen.*" Ansel grinned.

An hour later, Ansel and Kläre entered the breakfast room and joined Ditha and Ernst, who were settling into their seats.

Ernst rose quickly to greet them, placing Kläre next to himself. She watched her brother exchange pleasantries with Ansel. Silent, she let Ditha and Ernst engage the young priest and learn of his character, his intellect, and—most interestingly, she was sure—his relationship to her.

Kläre and Ansel had arrived at the Swiss mountain resort the evening before, two days after Ernst and Ditha. The train trip from Düsseldorf to Bern, and then to Interlaken, and finally the slow, spectacular climb in the tiny cog train to Wengen, perched on the mountainside, had been exhilarating but exhausting. Kläre knew it would take at least two days to become used to the altitude. The ascent to her second-floor room had left her breathing with difficulty.

The two couples had gathered the evening before in the lobby for schnapps. Ernst and Ditha had been warm and polite during the introduction of Ansel, but it had been clear that their real joy lay in their reunion with Kläre in this place of heart-stopping beauty. Kläre had seen Ernst briefly in Dortmund, months before, on his first appearance in the German court after his re-admittance to the Bar, but this was the first time they had all been together since the desperate days before the war.

He has changed, Kläre thought of her brother. *He is not so intense, so impatient. He looks good, but older—though not so old as I. Ditha looks not one bit different. How is it possible? What must they think of me? Of Ansel?*

Once seated in the large wooden easy chairs, schnapps in hand, the conversation had begun with news of Margaret and her two young children, with pictures shown and favorite stories shared. Then Ernst had steered the discussion to Ansel. Much of what had transpired since the war Kläre had written in letters, but Ernst now wanted his own assessment of Ansel, and of the status of his sister's life with the young priest.

"Kläre tells us that you are now both a priest and a principal, and an author to boot. That's quite something for a young man. I am interested to read your work," Ernst began.

Ansel sat formally, his cheeks coloring modestly. "It would be my honor to give you a copy of my book. It has mostly been well received, though some on either end of the political spectrum have found fault with it. Recently, the editor of the *Frankfurter Allgemein* did quite an interesting review. I'd like to show it to you." They continued to discuss the research Ansel had done in order to write his book.

Ditha had tried to engage Kläre, but Kläre's attention had remained on the interaction between the two men who were so important in her life and were just now meeting. Their polite sparring had been brief, as the hour was late and the travelers weary. As they rose to go to their rooms, Kläre had watched Ernst take the full measure of Ansel's height—always a sensitive subject for Ernst, whose short stature so thoroughly contrasted with his sense of himself.

"Shall we breakfast at half past eight?" Ernst offered.

All had agreed, and as they climbed the steps, Kläre was already imagining the conversation between her brother and sister-in-law.

"He's a nice-looking young man, and so tall."

"Can you imagine? He's just Margaret's age, and already has his own church, he's the principal of the local Gymnasium, and he's done scholarly research."

"Do you suppose the townspeople know that Kläre is Jewish? Could we ask?"

"They actually look very happy together, don't they?"

"You don't . . . It wouldn't be possible that they're . . . No, no!"

"Ernst!"

Now, at breakfast, Ernst and Ansel engaged in lively discussion about the future of Germany, the economies of Europe and America, and the group's plans for the day. Ansel spoke deferentially but comfortably with Ernst, who was flushed with pleasure at having found a worthy conversational partner. Kläre, beaming, turned to the news of all the family from Ditha, who occupied the center of communication from every source.

"Frieda still lives in the city, near where we used to live. It's a very nice flat on the second floor in a good neighborhood. All her boys have found work now. You know Hans married that Dutch girl and they have a boy, and Charles and Jenny have Elaine and Steven, and a new baby, Alan. Frieda is busy with them all, and still doing some sewing and baking for extra cash. There's always something happening there, though. Frieda caught her finger in the sewing machine. We try to help, but Ernst still isn't very patient with her." Kläre made a mental note to talk to her brother, her old role as the voice of his conscience falling onto her shoulders like a well-worn cape. But first she had a more important task to attend to.

"Ernst, I have something I must show you. I found it stuck among papers from Mutti that I only just looked through." Kläre unfolded a large, worn piece of bread wrapping paper, covered on both sides with fading, water-stained script in her mother's tiny, spidery hand. "It is a letter Mutti wrote to all of you—you and Frieda and Trude and the children—while we were in the camp. Much of it makes no sense . . . she had already become so weak and sick; but I've copied out what could be understood." Kläre handed several sheets of writing paper to her brother, and watched as he read.

To you my dear children and grandchildren,

Now I will tell you about my life in Theresienstadt. Jakob and Kläre are in my area, and we are safe, thanks to Kläre's wonderful care.

You will surely be interested to hear more details about my journey. As I am certain you heard, I was taken in the middle of the night to Linkheim. After a fortnight there, I got the news from the Jewish Agency of my deportation to Theresienstadt, which is in Bohemia. We traveled for 24 hours in a packed train (third class so that you often had to stand) before we finally arrived. The train stopped in Bauschowitz-Schleuse.

"Get out! You are now prisoners of war! Suitcases stay here!" one of the soldiers shouted. I didn't believe my eyes and ears. By paying the money I had brought, I thought I would be able to stay in a pension. But in spite of immense exhaustion, I had to walk, leaving the luggage behind as well as my well-made sandwiches, which became the property of the guards.

There was no pension. Theresienstadt had 8,000 inhabitants. Now in the same area there are 170,000 Jews. There are 68–70 people in one room. There is a garrison church, and a post office arranged by Jews. It serves the purpose of forwarding letters and packages, which come off and on. The city is built like a square. It has long and cross streets. I live at Lange Strasse 25 in a blockhouse. This house that used to hold 68–70 per house now houses 600 people, women and men.

Today on my birthday, November 21, I feel very close to all of you. You have to stay well, dear children. I feel closely attached to you. You must feel it, dear children. You were my luck, my good fortune, and my joy. My thoughts circle between Theresienstadt, Brussels, and Detroit. Pray for we three as I always pray for you.

Ernst stopped reading, tears filling his eyes as Kläre met his gaze.

"Finish it later. It's so very sad, but also truly Mutti. I'm glad to have even this piece of her back with us, no?"

Breakfast gave way to an hour-long morning stroll across the gentle face of the mountain plateau, which rose in an easy slope to a café, where the talk continued over coffee. Ditha spoke of Margaret and her two children. Her husband Walter had left his chemist job at Ford Motor Company to go into his own business. Ditha spoke glowingly of Margaret's cleverness in decorating her little flat, and the plans to move her young family to a house near Ernst and Ditha in the near future. Ever warm and sensitive, Ditha asked carefully after Erwin and his family.

"Has Erwin been to see you recently?"

"He came for several days in February, but now that the third baby is here, it's so much harder. Betty hasn't really recovered from the birth and her mother is with them often. I don't think Erwin feels he can leave, and says they aren't ready for a visit. The girl has never been terribly . . . stable." This last Kläre uttered with a sigh, and Ditha took her arm as they walked. A head taller than Kläre, and a vigorous walker, Ditha paced their progress to account for Kläre's arthritic hip and strained heart.

"The picture of the baby is beautiful. The older girl looks quite like her mother."

"Yes, Betty is lovely and Josephine promises to be the same." Kläre smiled wistfully. "I don't dare to hope of a strong connection, but I would so love to watch a little granddaughter grow." They walked a ways in silence. The staggering beauty of the snow-adorned mountain peaks filled Kläre with awe, providing a needed escape from thoughts of her life without her children compared to what Ditha and Ernst had. Warm sunshine set off the green of the nearby fields and the brilliant red geraniums tumbling out of the town's myriad window boxes.

"Trude's Edith had her first child," Kläre finally said, her face brightening. "A girl. Trude is busy with them, and Edith's husband, Herbert, is also a chemist with an excellent job. Helga gave up singing to marry someone that nobody seems to approve of. Trude says he drinks too much. I'm invited there in September to see them all."

Ditha smiled and squeezed Kläre's arm, though she didn't question further. The two women had an unspoken pact regarding Trude and her family. There was no communication between Brussels and Detroit: Rudi Stern, though aging and infirm, refused to allow Trude to communicate with her brother, continuing to nurse his bitterness over their pre-war disagreement. Trude submitted, though she grieved the loss, and Kläre had given over her attempts to foster reconciliation. Instead, she transferred information to and from Ditha and Trude, both of whom were hungry to know of each other's lives.

The morning walkers returned to the hotel with just enough time to rest and dress for midday dinner. Ernst dropped back to join his wife and sister.

"I like that young man," he pronounced, taking Kläre's arm.

"I also," Kläre replied.

35 September 1955

Kläre had had a very successful day in Dortmund. She had eagerly agreed to accompany Ansel on business, as it had been months since she'd been able to travel to the city. They had the train ride together to speak without interruption, and then Kläre had arranged a visit to the dressmaker and a meeting with Hans Heymann. His ten years in Jakob's former practice had made him a wealthy man, and even after all this time he continued to provide a nice stipend for Kläre.

Now she was eager to rejoin Ansel and to lunch at their favorite restaurant. The tender beef roulade always pleased, and Kläre enjoyed the wonderful service—and how Ansel teased her about the lavish attention paid to her by the young waiters. In truth, the artful dance of gentle flirtation, small extra flourishes of serving and clearing and high compliments traded back and forth, made Kläre feel appreciated and special. She loved that the escalating gallantries entertained Ansel, and he inevitably joined in. They made room wherever possible in their small world for appreciation and good humor.

Today they were meeting later than usual, as they'd each had much to do. Kläre was walking through the park that bordered Hörde toward the restaurant when she stopped, suddenly riveted in front of a bench under the linden trees. So much had changed around the bench over the years that she'd nearly missed it. The double row of trees had been reduced to just a few on each side of the central promenade. The bench itself had endured, but its wrought iron was scratched, its wooden slats grey with age. Nevertheless, Kläre recognized the spot, and events of thirty years past came flooding back as she stood before it. Here she had come with her young children. Before her eyes she could see gangly little Werner chasing after a pigeon and Erwin worrying a stick through the iron fencing. Here she had met Bernhardt Steinmann. The casual elegance of his long body comfortably arrayed across the bench stole into her memory with a sigh. A stab of longing for her younger self, for her family, and for what might have been shot past her careful filters to the past.

Kläre had kept her grief over Bernhardt's death shelved away with others in her library of sorrows. Now it shook her like the autumn leaves in the afternoon wind. She sat on the hard bench and shed tears of simple sadness. The flowerbeds on either side of the bench held the last stalwart blooms of autumn, and Kläre's gaze rested on their beauty until the ache and trembling subsided. Then she rose and walked with resolve toward Benninghofer Strasse and the restaurant where Ansel awaited her.

He was already seated at their favorite table. The simple severity of his black suit and white collar enhanced the healthy glow on his cheek and the eager light that sparked in his eyes as he rose to greet her. Kläre quickened her pace as she approached the table.

Her fall was simplicity itself: graceful, really, as her leg seemed simply to fail her. She dropped to her side, cushioning the fall with her arm. Immediate, excruciating pain robbed her of breath. An involuntary gasp became a moan that she tried to stifle as Ansel, other diners, and waiters rushed to aid her. Someone's jacket quickly made a pillow, and another draped her legs after an initial attempt to move her induced a cry of pain. Ansel, on his knees beside her, held her hand as they waited for help. One of the diners—*a doctor,* she thought—barked orders to the manager. Kläre squeezed back tears.

"Ach. What have I done?" she whispered.

"Shhhhh. It will be all right, *liebchen,*" Ansel assured her, his face close to hers. "Don't move. I am here."

The ambulance took Kläre to St. Josef's on Wilhelm-Schmidt Strasse, where she remained for three weeks. She remembered little of the first few days. Familiar faces, along with cartoons of past events, arose through a daze of morphine. The boundaries of sleep and wakefulness were indistinct. Ansel's voice ascended through her dreams, and often she felt his hand holding hers.

"Klärchen, I am here now. You must eat soup now for the nursing sister," or "Here is Dr. Kiewe. He has come to visit . . ."

Slowly, she grasped at moments of lucidity and clung to them. On the day in which one such moment coincided with an injection of yet more morphine, Kläre uttered thickly, "Please, not so much." The sister nodded, and Kläre traded eerie stupor for more painful sentience.

Ansel visited often, though the train ride from Baumstadt was an hour long, and his responsibilities at both church and school were pressing. Kläre saw past his unfailing cheerfulness to the fact that he was tired and worn. She willed herself to heal quickly, and worked diligently at rehabilitation. At her request, Ansel began to bring small tasks for her to accomplish from her hospital bed. One day, she wrote a guest list for a Sunday tea a month hence. When Ansel brought her small sewing basket, she began to darn socks.

She still could not bear weight on her hip. In the midst of a bedside physical therapy session, a nursing sister came to the hospital room and announced a visitor.

"Dr. Kiewe, Frau Kohler."

"Oh please, show him in. Would you help with my bed jacket?"

The nurse assisted Kläre as she donned the pale green quilted jacket that Ditha had sent for her last birthday. Kläre had only time for a quick sweep of her hand over her unruly curls before Günter Kiewe entered, his doctor's coat spotless and starched, his tie perfectly knotted, a reserved smile softening his heavily lined face.

"Frau Kohler, how good to see you mending and looking so well."

"Dr. Kiewe, how kind of you to visit again. I'm sorry—I'm afraid I was more or less unconscious the last time you were here. Do tell me, how is Frau Kiewe, and what have you heard from Hannah?"

The doctor's smile widened and some hesitation on his part seemed to dissolve.

"Ach, thank you. My wife is well, and sends her wishes for a speedy recovery. Hannah . . . Hannah has married. She and Avery decided to marry, and they are staying on the kibbutz together."

Kläre became very still, her eyes absently resting on her folded hands. The girl Hannah, who had loved her Werner and who had written every few months since his death, had at last found consolation in his best friend. And this dignified father—who had seen Werner in Palestine, had known him there, had cared for him long since Kläre had seen her son—bore this bittersweet news. After a moment she raised her head and extended her hand to the doctor, who had moved closer to the bed.

"Dr. Kiewe, that is wonderful. I am so very happy for her . . . for them. Congratulations to you and to your wife."

"Thank you," he nearly whispered.

"It's very hard to have her so far away, no? Will you return to Palestine? I mean, to Israel?" Kläre spoke gently but with warmth and squeezed the doctor's hand reassuringly.

"We will go for a visit in spring. I have work I will continue there, and my wife will surely want to see her married daughter."

"Yes, quite. I'm certain of that."

"Avery is a good young man, Frau Kohler. They have poured all that they are into the building of Yechiam. It was Avraham's dream too. To hear it from them, you would think it is the rebuilding of the holy temple itself. They are already one of the most productive kibbutzim in the north."

"So I have heard, and one day I will go to see it for myself. Ansel has all his life wished to go to the Holy Land, and I believe we shall do it. Of course I must finish mending from this silly fall."

"That you will, Frau Kohler. That you will. I have spoken to your doctors and they say you are healing very well. You should be able to return home within the week, though it may still be a while before you can walk properly."

"I will be most grateful for that, Dr. Kiewe."

In fact it was less than a week later that Kläre rode again in a medical taxi, this time home to Baumstadt. Ansel had taken the train from Hörde so that he could ride with her. The housemaid, with Ansel's instructions, had prepared a veritable feast for her, and a temporary bedroom had been created in the sitting room. Ansel had set up a dressing table with her brushes and combs and toiletries, and the hall closet now contained a basic wardrobe of dressing gowns and robes.

As they entered the house, Kläre exclaimed over all that had been done, but also protested, "You mustn't let me interfere with your work!"

"Ah, but I will be working," Ansel said. "I wish to finish the Chagall book with Theodor. We're nearly finished with the writing, but now we must propose the plates to be included. Won't it be fun to look at all the pictures together and choose our favorites?"

"Ach, ya, it will be fun, dear one. Most fun for me, though, is to be home here with you." Kläre's eyes gleamed as she settled back into her chair.

"And don't think it will be so easy for you, Frau Kohler. You have a mountain of mail to read, and I'm afraid my bachelor ways have not kept the house up to your standards. I'm guessing you'll have much to put right, now that you're home. And remember, you have only five months until it will be time to go to America. The Entes won't rest until they have you there for a visit. Are you exhausted just to think about it all? I'm truly worried for you." But it was hard to see worry in Ansel's dancing eyes.

Weeks passed, and with each one Kläre grew stronger, though a residual limp marred her complete recovery. She was just beginning to prepare the house for Christmas when she received a phone call from an unknown English-speaking woman.

"Mrs. Kläre Kohler, please."

"Here is Kläre Kohler."

"One moment, please . . ."

A new voice came onto the phone line, this time speaking in German. "Frau Kohler. Here is Leo Baeck. Do you remember me?"

Kläre sat down heavily and swallowed hard before answering. "Yes, of course, Dr. Baeck. How absolutely wonderful to hear from you."

"I am here in Düsseldorf at the moment, and I was wondering if I might make a visit to see you."

Kläre looked around at the rectory, the church spire towering out the living room window, before responding, "Yes, we would be so very honored to have you come."

Arrangements were made for Dr. Baeck to visit two days hence, and to the extent that her limited mobility allowed, Kläre engaged in a frenzy of preparations. *What will he think, coming here to find me in the home of a priest? Will he be disappointed? How did he find me? Why does he want to see me?* The questions unnerved Kläre, but she imposed outward calm.

Ansel, at least, was eager to meet the great rabbi. He had become a student of Dr. Baeck's work after hearing Kläre's stories of him from Thereseinstadt, and looked forward to his visit with great anticipation.

When Dr. Baeck and his assistant arrived for midday dinner two days later, Ansel greeted them personally at the door. Baeck immediately noticed the Chagalls in the marble entry hall, and after the rituals of welcoming were concluded, he engaged Ansel in a lively discussion about the artist. Ansel's book interested the older cleric immediately.

Kläre had prepared a pea soup and her finest veal schnitzel. The entire meal was cooked to perfection, and both men lavished compliments as they ate. When they had finished and were installed in the sitting room with cognac, Dr. Baeck finally volunteered the reason for his visit.

"I had to find you, Frau Kohler, because I am writing of my time at Theresienstadt, and I cannot forget your impact." Baeck trained his gaze on Ansel. "She really was the angel of Theresienstadt. She helped so many people—was so kind even in her suffering. She gave so many hope where there appeared to be none." He turned back to Kläre. "I want you to know that you were an inspiration to all who tried to bring comfort in that horror."

Kläre was humbled into silence.

“We are each of us angels with only one wing, and we can only fly by embracing one another,” Ansel remarked gently.

Baeck’s face broke out into a smile. “Lucretius.”

“Yes, that’s right,” Ansel laughed, and, drawing Kläre’s hand into his own, he gave it a gentle squeeze.

36 June 1956

In forty years of being photographed, Kläre Kohler never looked directly at a camera. She chose instead a profile pose, which she struck with great purpose. On a late spring day, in her voluminous gabardine coat, she stood in that pose, waiting for her photo to be taken in the weak but welcome sun. She had come to visit Ditha and Ernst in Michigan on her first trip to the United States, and they were recording the occasion.

The photographed outing took place at the Detroit Zoological Park, one of the Entes' favorite spots, located between their home and Margaret's. Margaret's two children seemed to be accustomed to grownup chatter, much of which was in German. Kläre watched where the little girl's interest lighted, and in her careful, singsong English discussed with the child the finer points of polar bear antics, repeating often her standard cache of German exclamatory words and phrases.

"Is it not *grossartig* how such a big bear makes a jump to the water with hardly any splash. *Entzukend!* Do you think he makes fun with us for a laugh?"

The girl concentrated, clearly adept at translating fractured English into intended meanings, pleased to apprehend that "*grossartig*," "*entzukend*," and "*fabelhaft*" meant "clever," "sweet," and "fabulous." The six-year-old took Kläre's hand and led her to the next exhibit. Kläre sighed with pleasure, the small hand in her gloved one as they walked along the cinder paths.

The well-kept zoo represented an outpost of wilderness to the city-bred, sophisticated, and German-cultured elders. *Die Tiere*—"the animals"—referred to any creature larger than an ant, but the towering giraffes, the bored lions, the antelopes, were as personal friends to these two children. Though Kläre could not follow all their chatter, she watched and listened in fascination.

Determined to reduce barriers to contact with her own grandchildren in England, Kläre had begun to improve her English. She had already once visited the town south of London where Erwin and Betty lived with Josephine, Clare, and Andrew. The visit had been acceptably pleasant, but had left Kläre exhausted. Betty had not fared well with the third childbirth. She was once again under medication and bed rest with depression. The children were fine-looking, and well behaved, but she had not experienced the inquisitiveness of these American children. Kläre had been frustrated at the distance that Betty insisted upon, preferring that only her own mother help with the children's baths or serve them their evening tea. Still, they were Kläre's only grandchildren, and she saw in a movement here, an expression there, traces of Jakob in the little boy, and of her own broad forehead and large eyes in the oldest girl—and though he maintained a stiff formality with them, Erwin clearly loved his children.

Kläre's thoughts of her own family terminated with the end of the excursion to the zoo. She returned with Ditha and Ernst to the Entes' auto for the short trip to Margaret and Walter's house. The number of gleaming new automobiles seen everywhere on the streets in Michigan astonished Kläre. Ansel was keen to have an auto and thought that by next year they would be able to afford it, but here everyone drove an auto and many families had two. Earlier, at the luncheon Margaret had prepared for them, she had announced that she could never live without her car. She used it many times each day to do the shopping, drive the children, visit friends, etc. The nearest public autobus stop was nearly a mile's walk away—not only inconvenient, but also infrequently serviced.

After dinner, Kläre helped Margaret remove the dishes from their meal to the kitchen. The gangly, intense teenager with black hair and huge green eyes who had left Germany had become a tall, beautiful, and self-confident young woman. She had strained the family budget to complete her university degree in French language and literature, and now presided as mistress of a solid brick home in the suburbs of Detroit. As they washed dishes, Margaret chattered about their friends, many of whom were either fellow immigrants or members of the fledgling Jewish temple they had helped found in the last year. Margaret asked after Erwin and his children, and either did not notice or chose not to respond to Kläre's hesitation in answering her.

"My parents very much liked Ansel Beckmann when they met him," Margaret volunteered. She paused, dishtowel in hand, and faced Kläre. "I actually used to love going to Mass when we had to go in school before the Nazis came. I found it much more comforting than the Jewish services, though don't tell Walter I said so. He's very much into the religious part of Judaism. We go to services every Friday night, if you can imagine. Do you . . . Does it help you forget about your old life? I mean with Erwin in England and Werner . . . gone?"

Kläre watched the young woman return to her dishes. She seemed confused and discomfited by her own question. Emotional intimacy didn't come to her naturally. "There isn't a day I don't think of Werner, or Onkel Jakob, or Erwin." She placed a hand on Margaret's shoulder. "But Ansel and I were lucky to find each other for a life together now. It makes us both very comfortable."

Margaret smiled in relief, and the conversation moved on to the discussion of Frieda's son George and his wife Thea, who had just had their second baby.

"You are fortunate to have your cousin and your *tante* so close that you may see them frequently," Kläre commented.

"Yes, I suppose we are," Margaret responded, though her tone made Kläre question whether she truly felt so.

"I will have a visit with Arne Ente in Philadelphia before I return to Germany," Kläre said. Margaret smiled, and Kläre knew that her careful pronunciation of the strange city name amused her niece. "You know, Arne has been very successful there. Do you remember that his brother

Paul lived with my parents before the war, and that they helped Arne emigrate? Arne sent for Paul after he got established. They both live now near each other, and they write it is a beautiful city. I wish only that Ansel could be here to see it with me. I will bring him back here."

At the end of two weeks' time, Kläre's suitcases were bulging with the proceeds of several shopping trips, and with the last season's coats and clothing that the Entes were sending to Germany. There had been two huge dinners with Frieda's family—who now numbered eight young adults and as many grandchildren—and many afternoons of coffee and *kuchen* at Frieda's or the homes of the many German friends they had found in Detroit. Everyone warmly welcomed Kläre, and she loved the brash, young excitement of America.

On Kläre's last evening, over a particularly good white wine, Ernst began speaking almost as if he were facing a jury he needed to convince of a difficult point.

"Klärchen, it has been absolutely wonderful to have you here! It's hard to believe that from the little family we started with, we now have so many. I know you have made a wonderful life with Ansel in Baumstadt, but I have to ask you, now that you've been here and seen what the life here is like—would you like to come here to live? We would so much love to have you here."

Kläre knew that Ernst was serious, and that if he was making this offer, he must have discussed it at length with Ditha. "That is so very kind and thoughtful of you both," she said, her gratitude shining in her smile, "and I hope to come here often and that you will come to visit me as well—but my home is really now with Ansel. It fills my heart to be there, and I think it is the same for him. I know perhaps it is hard for you to understand—"

Kläre would have continued, but Ernst interrupted: "Asked and answered, my dear sister. Let's have a toast, then: To many long and happy years to come with frequent visits and much love! *Prosit!*" The glasses clinked with the ring of fine crystal.

Airline travel still frightened Kläre, but she was now comfortably seated on the Lufthansa flight to Philadelphia, where she would have a brief visit with Arne and Paul before the long overnight flight to Frankfurt. She had taken tablets for her arthritis, as the sitting would cause her hips to stiffen and hurt, but as she turned toward home excitement filled her. The airplane soared above spectacular piles of white clouds, stacked like huge cotton curls below the intense blue of sky above.

Ansel would take the train from Düsseldorf, and would be there waiting for her at the airport in Frankfurt. She would tell him about the clouds, about each detail of her visit, and she would hear about his days—whom he had seen, what had happened in the town and the school and the church. They would return to Schulstrasse 25 in Baumstadt, to the marble floors, the Chagalls, the green of the living and dining rooms, the begonias lined up under the bottle-glass mullioned windows. Ansel would make *schinken* on butter bread sandwiches for their supper. He would place a bottle of mineral water, and perhaps a chocolate box as well, in her room to greet her.

The plane cruised high above a great lake, and Kläre's heart soared as well. The adventure of her visit to America had gone very well, and she felt the pull of her loved ones there, but now she was headed home to Ansel and the life they had built together. A lovely line of the hymn that Margaret had sung at temple the Friday before settled into her center as she floated off to sleep: *May peace fill the earth, as water fills the sea . . .*

37 1962

And to them will I give in my house and within my walls a memorial and a name (Yad Vashem) that shall not be cut off.
—Isaiah

The Avenue of the Righteous Among Nations at Yad Vashem stretched before Kläre and Ansel like a magnet. It pulled them toward the dark building that hung on the edge of an arid hill, overlooking the hills of Jerusalem, and Hadassah Hospital rising in the light. They had heard that the architect had designed the Holocaust Memorial to face the maternity ward of the hospital below.

Although it was still early in the morning, the fierce Mediterranean sun delineated each carob tree leaf, each detail of the beautiful sculptures, and each word of the monument inscriptions along the walkway. Kläre was winded from the steep walk up the hill from the car park and because she could hardly bear the weight of feeling in her chest. The sun burned through her silk blouse as though to ignite her heart.

The Avenue of the Righteous—how grateful she was that the designers of this museum of the Holocaust honored first those non-Jews who had saved others. Before descending into the building that would display and explain the darkness and horror, visitors walked down this promenade with trees, benches, and sculptures named for those who worked against the deadly progress of the Nazis. Carob trees, chosen for the hard, bent fruit they grew containing seeds that endured forever, were planted for each honored person.

Kläre hung on Ansel's arm. "I have names to add to this avenue," she whispered.

Ansel stood close, with his head bowed as if in prayer.

"Jorgen Licht," Kläre intoned, the name ringing in the morning sunlight from the clear bell of her voice to float among the trees and flowers. The two of them stood in silence then, opening their memories of the reluctant soldier who had paid with his life for his aid to the Kohlers—for his humanity.

"Melisande Durr," Kläre's voice rang again, loud and clear, though her chest heaved with the heaviness of her heart.

"Bernhardt Steinmann," she cried once more, and now tears flowed, though she stood straight and strong at the top of the promenade. She turned her face toward Ansel, whose eyes were closed, though he held her arm firmly and had grasped her hand in his own. "He saved my heart, Ansel. He saved my son's life, and others' too, but he saved my heart." She looked down the walkway. "I should like to remember him here."

They sat on a bench and Ansel turned to Kläre as if to speak, but he remained silent, watching her deep in thought, her mouth working slowly as if to rehearse how she might tell Ansel what she had kept to herself for so long. The memories of another park bench miles and years away, and memories of other breezes that had traveled over her bare skin in the midst of passion, played across the cinema of her face as Ansel looked on.

"Ditha and Ernst have often said that I've had luck in my life," Kläre said at last. "For example, I found you." She patted Ansel's hand and searched his face. "I loved my husband, Ansel. I devoted my life to him and to my family, and we had a good life. He was a good man. But where I have been lucky is to have found others who learned to know me . . . and I them . . . in just the ways that are most important to me: what I believe, what my dreams are, that landscape on the inside that we are only very lucky to ever be able to share. I know this is hard to understand, but I feel that way about you, Ansel." Kläre's voice faltered as she worked to think of another way to communicate this fundamental truth. She gripped Ansel's hands in both of hers and sat at the edge of the bench, twisted to face him. She grimaced slightly and shifted the pressure off her hip.

Ansel placed a finger at Kläre's lips to silence her. Seeing her rising consternation, he spoke quickly: "I understand entirely. After all, you have made me a lucky man in just the same way. And I'm sorry that you ever had to lose such a one, and so much more."

They sat for several more minutes in silence, Kläre leaning against Ansel in the shade of the young trees planted to remember good in the face of unspeakable loss and horror.

At last Kläre said softly, "Ya, I'm ready now." They would tour the museum, and then lunch with an archivist with whom Ansel had arranged an interview. Kläre had a story to tell, and Yad Vashem's mission was to memorialize such stories.

The next day dawned as bright as the previous one. Kläre and Ansel rose at first light and, after a large breakfast of delicious fruits, vegetables, and fresh eggs, found their way to the Lion's Gate in the old city of Jerusalem to begin their pilgrimage along the Via Dolorosa, the Avenue of Suffering. The Stations of the Cross along the Via marked Jesus's path to crucifixion. The forbidding heat of the day was still hours away, and Kläre felt a surge of energy as they approached the gate. In the airplane from Frankfurt, Ansel had spoken of this walk as a spiritual journey that he approached with both eagerness and trepidation.

"The archeology of this path doesn't fit. This we know, but the concept that we can walk with Him, feel His pain and His grace, this is powerful to me," Ansel had said. "It's like the passage in the Passover seder: 'Tell the story to your children; experience the Exodus *as though it was you, yourself.*' But it's still now just a street and some churches that all of Christendom have laid claim to. It's busy. I don't know how it will feel. And I believe it is narrow and perhaps not so steady for you. We will see how you feel when we are there, ya?"

When Ansel had again questioned whether Kläre was up to the

walk that morning, she had silenced him. "I wish to go with you on this walk, Ansel," she'd said firmly. She felt responsible to support him, as he had done for her at Yad Vashem. Not only that, but from the moment the bus began the climb toward Jerusalem from the plain below, its spiritual power had washed over Kläre like a fragrant spring rain. Beyond knowing the Holy City's importance to three major world religions, Kläre felt in her bones the vibration of a common essence of humanity, built and lived in the city of golden stone.

They stood now at the Lion's Gate, and Ansel folded Kläre's arm into his own as they began their walk. The first station was easily missed, and Ansel explained that it was where Christ was condemned to death. Farther down was an archway where Pontius Pilate gave his Ecce Homo speech and crowned Jesus with thorns, bound him, and gave him the cross. Ansel's tall frame seemed to bend with the weight of Jesus's burden even as the morning sun shone and the merchants set up their wares on the side of the narrow street.

They continued, noting Polish churches, Franciscan monasteries, and then the Armenian church where Jesus was said to have met his Holy Mother. Kläre stood silently, her face turned up to the sunlit relief of the Virgin Mary and Christ, suspended for all time in marble above the arch of the door. The unbearable suffering of sons and mothers sucked the sounds of the city away and darkened the dazzling morning with an oppressiveness that pulled at Kläre through the cobblestones beneath her feet. Ansel, too, seemed rooted to the spot.

Why? Kläre thought. *Why must our sons suffer and we with them? What does God mean by such agony?*

"It's just so that I have come to understand Christ," Ansel said, his face still turned upward.

Kläre was momentarily confused, not knowing whether she had spoken or whether Ansel, in the transfixing moment, had heard her anguished thoughts.

"In holding the suffering of all his people," he went on, "in bearing it until the end, he gave hope and comfort in the midst of evil and uncertainty, and in this was elevated to the Kingdom of God." Ansel's face was infused with the light of his epiphany. "Perhaps here it is Mary who truly understands the meaning of what Jesus has done and can give to him, and to all of us, a mother's love and comfort and recognition of our pain. He accepts this from her, and it helps ease him . . . Do you think?" he asked, turning to Kläre, and it was as if his words had returned the light to the morning—they lifted the oppression from her heart.

"It would be any mother's wish to bring relief to a suffering child. I suppose that is what we must each try to do for the other, no?" Kläre reached to Ansel's smooth, shaven cheek and stroked it, and they both smiled.

They continued to follow the twists and turns in the Via Dolorosa until they reached the last four stations in the Church of the Holy Sepulcher. Ansel prayed for a long while, kneeling under the dome, its four points and gilded blue creating a heavenly surrounding for the central image of Jesus, floating above. Kläre sat in the pew beside Ansel, trying to understand all that had happened that morning and feeling grateful for the warmth that suffused her. The power of facing pain, of accepting love and forgiveness, had never found its way into her heart with such strength before. She knew, however, that to find true peace, she had one more visit to make in this remarkable country.

For the journey to Yechiam, Ansel secured a private car and driver, still a rarity in Israel. Moshe, their tough-looking guide, picked Kläre and Ansel up from their hotel early the next morning and they began their descent on the highway to the west of Jerusalem. On either side of the road they saw burnt-out tanks and jeeps, evidence of the two wars that had been waged to gain and then defend the young country's independence. These symbols of sacrifice, Kläre knew, were purposely left for tourists and Israelis alike to see and be reminded of the costs of freedom.

"I think we are going to the north for getting to Yechiam, no?" Kläre asked in halting English.

"We cannot drive safely through the Arab lands so we go west first to stay within Israel's borders," Moshe responded in flawless German.

"Ah, you speak German," Kläre said gratefully.

"When I must," the driver responded.

Kläre cringed. It pained her that her language alone caused discomfort to this man, whose story no doubt included a flight and then a fight and a rebuilt life.

"I come to see the grave of my son," she murmured. "He came here as a child, but grew to start the Kibbutz Yechiam. He wanted to farm. He was killed by an explosive in 1948."

"I'm sorry." Moshe's voice softened. "The land in the north is good land and Yechiam has become a fine kibbutz. They were very brave, those boys and girls in Hashomer Hazair Nahal. I was part of the liberation force that secured Yechiam after the siege . . . and the massacre. Perhaps I met your son."

The car fell silent but for the roar of the engine and the sounds of the undercarriage complaining at stray rocks thrown up by the wheels. Kläre called back the images of Mary and Jesus from the Via Delarosa, and the peaceful interlude with Ansel at Yad Vashem along the Avenue of the Righteous. "He died doing what he loved and building something he believed in," she finally said, her voice strong and clear.

Ansel covered Kläre's hand with his on the seat between them.

Within an hour, Moshe was pulling the car into a *moshav* not far off the main road north. The village of Ben Shemen lay before them in the sunlight. The agricultural training program and boarding school had been Werner's first home in Israel. He and Avery had become fast friends here, and Werner's love of the land and his Zionism had been instilled within these walls and in these fields. As they left the car to tour, everywhere around her, Kläre saw flowers, trees, crops, and animals being coaxed to grow in the dry heat. Healthy-looking children of all ages were at work in classrooms, in the dormitories, and in the fields.

Kläre presented a donation to the director of the school and politely declined his invitation to stay longer: They had many more hours to travel north. For a long moment, though, Kläre closed her eyes, breathed the rich air around her, and stored the memory of the sun shining down on her and this land that had felt her son's footsteps, nurtured him, and set him on the path to a future he embraced. *If he'd been sent elsewhere, perhaps to learn a different trade or go to university . . .* But no, the time for ifs and whys was long past. She was here to see and connect to the life Werner had lived and been happy in. She opened her eyes, and with a nod to Ansel, they returned to the car and the next stage of their odyssey.

The journey took all day, north through reclaimed land planted to orange groves, avocado trees, miles and miles of vegetables, and then more miles of parched, arid countryside. Everywhere there were signs of building, bustle, and transport. Soldiers appeared everywhere as well—strong, healthy boys and girls in uniform with rifles slung over their shoulders, at ease among their fellow citizens. The sight of them reminded Kläre with a pang that here, like everywhere, children were sent to fight wars.

At noon, they left the main road and travelled a short distance to the Mediterranean coast, where Ansel wished to see the ancient site of Caesarea, the Roman ruins and living history arrayed along a beautiful harbor and the brilliant blue sea. A hot breeze blew off the water, and behind her dark glasses even Kläre's weakening eyes were stunned by the white light, the bursts of color in the sea, and the powerful evidence of Roman culture and industry from 1,500 years earlier. It didn't end, the clash of successive powers, religions, and cultures, here in this tiny country. It all seemed to melt and erupt together in the heat and light, the vortex of all the energies vibrating in the very air.

It was late afternoon when the car wended its way down a last dusty road in the far north of the country and Kibbutz Yechiam came into sight. The old fortress rose behind it, its restoration underway. Twenty years ago, this place had marked the site of the pioneers' first housing. Sickened by the water or the fetid air, the young people had been ill continuously until they had managed to build the first buildings and blast into the earth for fresh water.

As she had been doing all along this journey, Kläre fit the snatches of geographical information from Werner's letters, which she had nearly memorized, into the landscape that unfolded before her. Everywhere were the rocks that stymied each building project, starting with the road they'd just travelled. The arches framing the entrance to the main building of the kibbutz and the stone walls containing gardens and animal pens were a testimony to the victory of human sweat and ingenuity over the harsh realities of the landscape.

Moshe disappeared into a building and soon emerged with a young woman, deeply tanned, wearing shorts and a work shirt, her hair tied back in the ubiquitous bandana scarf.

"Mrs. Kohler, welcome to Yechiam. We are so happy that you came." Though the girl's English was accented, Kläre understood her perfectly well, even without Moshe's quick translation.

Moshe continued in Hebrew. As he spoke, the girl's face became openly curious, and she looked from Kläre to Ansel and back. Kläre guessed that Moshe had just explained that Ansel was a Catholic priest.

"Welcome to you both," she said in English, once the introductions were done. "Come this way. I show you to your room."

Moshe helped Ansel with the valises, and they walked a short distance to a small cottage at the end of a path. Flowers grew on either side of the doorway, and though the rooms were small and Spartan, they were meticulously clean.

"This is wonderful. Thank you very much," Kläre said in her careful English. "If you please, when it is possible, can you let Avery and Hannah Frey know that we have arrived?"

"Yes of course," the girl responded. "And please, join us for supper in thirty minutes' time."

Kläre nodded, and the girl departed. She and Ansel confirmed with Moshe that he would return for them in two days and bid him goodbye with thanks, and Ansel brought their luggage into the rooms.

"*Liebchen,* dear one," he said, "lie down for a few minutes and rest. We will go to see Werner directly after the supper, I promise."

The large dining hall shone in the full daylight when Kläre and Ansel entered. Immediately, the young woman who had greeted them earlier rose from a table and approached them. Behind her followed a young couple—the man of medium height with close-shorn blond curls, and the woman, also fair, with her long hair pulled behind in a scarf. They were dressed in clean working clothes and held hands.

"May I introduce you to Avery and Hannah Frey?"

The couple stepped forward hesitantly, and for a moment no one spoke. Then Kläre reached out to Hannah, who took Kläre's hand into both of her own.

"Frau Kohler, I am so pleased to meet you. This is my husband, Avery." The young woman spoke in halting German and paused for a moment.

Kläre's response was immediate and heartfelt: "Oh Hannah. I have waited for this day for a long time. I have visited many times with your parents, and your letters have been wonderful for me to receive. And Avery"—Kläre turned to the young man—"you have been such a wonderful friend to my son when he came here all alone. I have for so long wanted to thank you." She reached up to his strong shoulders and looked into his sharp blue eyes. "It means more to me than I can ever tell you."

Hannah quietly interpreted into Hebrew, and Avery's eyes filled with tears.

"Come," Avery said. "You should forgive my poor German. Let us eat something, and then we walk to see Avraham's grave and we talk."

The food was simple but delicious—all grown and produced on the kibbutz, which was now known for its kosher meats and fine vegetables. After finishing their supper, Hannah and Avery ushered their guests out into the early evening cool and began a walk down the main road of the kibbutz, past all the buildings, pointing out the children's house, the barns, the members' houses. As they walked along the hillside and up the ridge toward the ancient fortress, Hannah explained that the fortress had been built in the twelfth century by German warrior monks. It had then been captured, destroyed, and rebuilt by a succession of Arab and Persian rulers. It was finally purchased in 1937 by the American Jewish National Fund for the purpose of establishing agriculture in the north of Palestine.

"We will tour it tomorrow. It is where Avery and Avraham and I first lived when we came to settle Yechiam. But now come to see Avraham," Hannah said, leading the small group to an enclosure fenced in by wrought iron and shaded by young trees overlooking the valley below. "This is the cemetery remembering 1948," she said, bowing her head.

Kläre had seen photos of the monument made from the golden indigenous stone and the Hebrew letters on the bronze plaque: *Avraham Kohler, born April 17, 1927, died July 22, 1948.* A riot of different-colored cyclamen raised their blooms above heart-shaped leaves in the planter formed by a rectangle of stones. Kläre had not understood from the photos or descriptions the profound sense of peace and tranquility that pervaded the small cemetery, and the beauty of the vista out and below the ridge. The early evening light turned golden and played in lengthening shadows along the valley floor, lush and verdant like nowhere else they had seen so far in this country. Ansel busied himself taking photos of the gravesite. Kläre turned to Hannah and Avery, searching for words, but Avery began to speak quickly in Hebrew, Hannah translating quietly into German when he paused.

"I met Avraham for the first time at the children's camp of Aliyot Noar in Trieste. As children, we didn't exactly know the meaning of the separation from our parents and our warm homes. The tourist boat we took to Palestine was among the last ships to make this trip. At first we were sent to Ben Shemen, and our situation—being in this strange country with its strange customs, language, and clothing—drew us closer together. I know it's hard to understand, but because of all that we had to learn and adjust to, our connection with Europe was severed. We considered Europe under the Germans as the enemy. We could only send letters through the Red Cross, where we were restricted to writing only that we were alive. Then even that connection was cut off. We heard nothing about our parents and relatives. This reality caused us to block out our past so we didn't speak about it. We studied agriculture.

Avraham excelled at it. He was always investigating new plants and techniques. As boys of seventeen, we organized a common way, and as our education was Zionist and prepared us to settle the land, that is what we chose to do."

Avery paused to breathe but immediately continued, as if his words and the memories that formed them were air in an overfull balloon that he could finally release. "We came here to build our own kibbutz. Avraham was very active and popular. He learned on his own how to raise mushrooms and he established a farm in the caves nearby which became a source of money for all of us. At the end of the war, we started to get information about what had happened in Europe and who was left of our families. To tell the truth, it was so painful, we didn't talk between ourselves much. I lost all of my family."

Kläre laid a sympathetic hand on his arm, and Avery kept talking, as though he needed to finish getting out every part of what he had to say. "Our life taught us to deal with the reality of the present and to accept the verdict of life, each person to himself, quietly. Avraham devoted himself to working the fields. On Shabbat, we would find him asleep between the rows. He was always there for us, motivating us by his example. He was an honest and loyal friend, open-hearted and bright-eyed. He always wrote little stories and songs to entertain us at parties that everyone loved."

Avery's eyes bored into Kläre's. "Avraham and Hannah and I were together all those years, friends in every way. We struck out on our own common destiny and we built a new settlement here in the heart of Arab country. Avraham never stopped thinking and dreaming of building the kibbutz, but he accepted with love, like everything else he did, the dangerous responsibilities. On the morning of the accident, we still talked about the tractors, and the future." Avery was openly weeping now, wiping his face with a large handkerchief. "He died just before the chance to see Yechiam liberated and his dreams come true. We had to realize his dream for him . . ."

Kläre stepped forward and pulled the young man toward her, heedless of her own tears. His heart beat solidly as Kläre's cheek lay on his chest, and for a single moment it was as though Werner were standing in her arms, young, healthy, and strong. Peace flooded through Kläre like the warm evening breeze. She let go of the young man and turned to his wife, and the two women embraced with wordless mourning, gratitude, and love for what had gone before and what each had found to live for.

"God bless you both in all your life yet to come," Kläre said, releasing Hannah. "There is no measure for the joy and peace you've brought to me today."

Ansel moved to Kläre's side and put an arm around her. "Amen," he intoned quietly.

Epilogue: The Last Garden
July 1996

She died in July, a month of great occasions in the Ente family: birthdays, marriages, and now death. Ansel made her grave in the cemetery across the drive into a small shrine. He tended her garden behind the house, both for order and for the time to remember her, and while it grew, he found laughter in its measured beauty beside the towering church of Baumstadt. The gardens of her influence remained everywhere—in Ansel's eyes when his thoughts turned comfortably to her, in every piece of furniture placed exactly as when she presided over each room. The sea-foam greens, the gold brocade, the rose velvets, the Bauhaus paints on bedroom furniture were all gentle on the senses and a perfect setting for the memory of her tailored suits and red-gold cloud of hair. As she'd grown older, Kläre's sight had left her—but the blinder she became, the larger the magnification of her scrutiny into the hearts and minds of those who sought her company. Love sown and reaped grew on.

Ansel strode purposefully out of the Baumstadt Post Office and across the cobbled village square. He had completed the last of his errands, and now, in the long light of the northern German late afternoon, he walked past the new grocery and turned into the lane with St. Michael's at his back. He felt the gravity of the massive church bearing down on him, the spire seeming to cast a directed beam at the letter in his breast pocket. Yet he smiled, nodded, or spoke to the neighbors and parishioners as they passed, stopping to admire a new baby or hear of an illness.

In just a few minutes, he left the bustle of the village center and entered the cemetery. As the early evening cool took its first breezy pass over the perfectly tended rows, he walked directly to the lovely plot near the far corner and stood, head bent, hands clasped behind his back, before Kläre's grave. Love for Kläre enshrined every detail of the small plot. Bronze letters mounted on the craggy headstone provided the simplest details: Kläre Kohler, 1895–1994. A low, box-trimmed border of privet defined the plot on three sides. Fragrant juniper, rosy begonia, a miniature azalea, and splashes of blue veronica were artfully placed among the stepping-stones. It was a marvel—a bonsai landscape.

Alone in the little cemetery, eyes closed, Ansel prayed for a solution to the problem that had intruded into his quiet life through the letter in his pocket. Here he stood, before the God to whom he had devoted his life, and also before the grave of the woman whose love had blessed his heart and spirit. There must be an answer. Ansel withdrew the letter and read it once again.

Dear Father Beckmann,

As you may already be aware, our committee has elected to create a Stolperstein to honor the memory of Jakob Kohler, husband of the late Kläre Kohler. Arrangements have been made to install the stone in front of their former residence at 14 Virschow Strasse, Hörde.

We wish to similarly honor the memory of Frau Kohler's bravery and suffering during the National Socialists' years. Perhaps at her gravesite, or in the town of her long residence after the war, there will be a possibility to accomplish this. Your name was provided to us through the archive at Dortmund, as a resource. Your assistance in this effort would be greatly appreciated. At your convenience, please contact our offices at the address below.

Ansel had indeed learned of the Stolperstein, the "stumbling stone" project of an artist in Cologne. The memorializing of Nazi victims with the setting of paving stones in front of their former residences was an extraordinary undertaking. Ansel had confirmed the information sent to him regarding Jakob Kohler. Kläre would have wanted Jakob honored in that way; Ansel knew it without question. But Kläre herself? Throughout the nearly fifty years of Ansel's life with her—after Jakob, after the war—she had expressly chosen to keep her Jewish background a secret from all but a few of their best friends, and no one here in Baumstadt knew.

Ansel raised his eyes, drew one last, scented breath, and walked across the lane to the rectory. At seventy-two—balding but still vigorous—he bent his tall frame slightly forward as if ready to address an unseen congregation. His face remained fair and unlined.

He entered the house and passed quietly across the marble floor, silently scrutinizing one of the six Chagall lithographs arranged around the foyer. He washed his hands in the tiny washroom and, at precisely 6:00 p.m., entered the sitting room, its tasteful repose a tribute to the woman who had spent fifty years at its command.

The mullioned windows let the golden evening light into the cozy space. The warm scent of polished walnut rose from the antique furnishings. The tick of a mantel clock measured the tranquility of the room.

Ansel closed the window blinds, poured a crystal glass of whiskey, and watched the television news. At 7:00 p.m. he sat at the dining table, set with china and silver—Kläre's china and silver—for one. As he closed his eyes to say grace, what rose within him instead was a vision of Kläre, alive and sitting across from him, presiding over the evening supper of white asparagus rolled in *schinken* served with a good potato salad.

The ethereal Kläre asked in her high, musical voice, regarding him with failing eyes through thick lenses, "How goes the Sunday sermon?"

He heard himself answer with a clear essence of the sermon he'd struggled with. The dreamy imagining continued.

"At the butcher today, I saw the young Schmidt girl who cleans the church," Kläre said.

"Hmm." Ansel waited.

"She asked if our families were related . . . yours and mine. Can you imagine? What do you suppose she wishes to know about us?"

The amused, knowing look on Kläre's face cut to Ansel's heart. There it was—the intimacy, the love, and the delighted humor that Kläre had inspired during all their life together, and which he missed so much.

Abruptly, Ansel ceased his imagining. Kläre lay peacefully in the cemetery across the lane. Ansel accepted his own sin in knowingly burying a Jew in the cemetery of his church. It wasn't the first time that doctrine had been bent to accommodate human need in Ansel's life. He hoped it wouldn't be the last. He had no regrets. He would remain Kläre's memory keeper, and it would not be a burden.

Acknowledgments

The enduring inspiration of the family members upon whom *Even in Darkness* is based acted as a powerful guide and taskmaster in its writing. Love and devotion as redemption for pain and suffering come into our lives in unexpected ways; more so as we become better able to give and receive them. This very Christian notion has as its Jewish soul mate that the good we create on earth lives on in the people we touch; not only our children, but all those in whom our spirits have found a home.

For this story, my special thanks and dedication go to my great aunt Klare, my grandfather Ernest, and their sisters, Frieda and Trude, all of blessed memory and the family of origin for so much of this tale. Further appreciation goes to my grandmother Edith, her cousin and friends Lily, and Mercedes, my parents, Walter and Margaret, and my sisters and brother, all of whom recognized the power of these stories. I especially thank Achim, a living character still, whose remarkable memories and insights were invaluable to my writing. My sisterhood of friends and co-artists: Margaret Singer, Joan Mandel Eisenberg, Mary Higgins, Simone Yehuda, and especially my writing group, Patty Hoffmann, Kathy York, and Claudia Whitsitt, have my eternal thanks for their hours of listening, careful reading, and generative ideas. Further thanks go to early readers Elizabeth Jordan, Steve Carpman, Kathe Langberg, Sarah Nemon, Lynne Tobin, Pamela Grath, Maya Slobin, Dan I. Slobin, and Rabbi David J. Fine.

To my cousins still in Europe, and for the research assistance of the

Leo Baeck Institute in New York, Yad Vashem in Jerusalem, The United States Holocaust Memorial Museums in Washington D.C. and the Holocaust Memorial Center in Detroit, Michigan, The Central Archive for Research on the History of Jews in Germany, The University of Michigan Libraries, Dr. Werner Himmelman, Natan and Hannah at Kibbutz Yechiam, and Anat Bratman-Elhalel at Ghetto Fighters' House in Israel, I am deeply grateful. To Elizabeth Kostova goes my gratitude for her early encouragement, inspiration and direction of this project. Many, many thanks go to Brooke Warner, Krissa Lagos, Cait Levin, Katie Caruana and all the design and production staff at She Writes Press, and the She Writes community of writers, for their support and guidance.

About the Author

© Mark Bennington of Mark Bennington Headshots

Every story needs a narrator, and Barbara Stark-Nemon stepped up early in life. She learned storytelling, and a fascination with the magic of language from her grandfather, an attorney who escaped Germany in 1938 and wove unforgettable tales of his former life. An undergraduate degree in English literature and Art History from the University of Michigan led Barbara to a teaching career in English and then a Masters in Speech-language Pathology. Everywhere, there were stories. Working in schools, universities and hospitals as a therapist, Barbara specialized in child language disorder and deafness. She learned much about the impact of different languages on the forms of narratives, and the need to be heard and seen that we all share. She writes, gardens, cycles, swims and enjoys her family in Ann Arbor and Northport, Michigan. *Even in Darkness* is her first novel.

Selected Titles from She Writes Press

She Writes Press is an independent publishing company
founded to serve women writers everywhere.
Visit us at www.shewritespress.com.

The Sweetness by Sande Boritz Berger
$16.95, 978-1-63152-907-8
A compelling and powerful story of two girls—cousins living on separate continents—whose strikingly different lives are forever changed when the Nazis invade Vilna, Lithuania.

All the Light There Was by Nancy Kricorian
$16.95, 978-1-63152-905-4
A lyrical, finely wrought tale of loyalty, love, and the many faces of resistance, told from the perspective of an Armenian girl living in Paris during the Nazi occupation of the 1940s.

Shanghai Love by Layne Wong
$16.95, 978-1-938314-18-6
The enthralling story of an unlikely romance between a Chinese herbalist and a Jewish refugee in Shanghai during World War II.

A Cup of Redemption by Carole Bumpus
$16.95, 978-1-938314-90-2
Three women, each with their own secrets and shames, seek to make peace with their pasts and carve out new identities for themselves.

The Belief in Angels by J. Dylan Yates
$16.95, 978-1-938314-64-3
From the Majdonek death camp to a volatile hippie household on the East Coast, this narrative of tragedy, survival, and hope spans more than fifty years, from the 1920s to the 1970s.

Benediction for a Black Swan by Mimi Zollars
$14.95, 978-1-63152-950-4
A lush, provocative collection of poems about childhood, children, marriage, divorce, alcoholism, and the sensual world.